Life,
and Death,
and Giants

Also by
Ron Rindo

Breathing Lake Superior

Stories

Love in an Expanding Universe
Secrets Men Keep
Suburban Metaphysics and Other Stories

Life,
and Death,
and Giants

Ron Rindo

ST. MARTIN'S PRESS
NEW YORK

First published in the United States by St. Martin's Press, an imprint of St. Martin's Publishing Group

EU Representative: Macmillan Publishers Ireland Ltd, 1st Floor, The Liffey Trust Centre, 117–126 Sheriff Street Upper, Dublin 1, DO1 YC43

www.stmartins.com

Designed by Devan Norman

The Library of Congress Cataloging-in-Publication Data is available upon request.

ISBN 978-1-250-37533-9 (hardcover)
ISBN 978-1-250-37534-6 (ebook)

Our books may be purchased in bulk for specialty retail/wholesale, literacy, corporate/premium, educational, and subscription box use. Please contact MacmillanSpecialMarkets@macmillan.com.

First Edition: 2025

10 9 8 7 6 5 4 3 2 1

For Jenna

Life, and Death, and Giants—
Such as These—are still—
Minor—Apparatus—Hopper of the Mill—
Beetle at the Candle—
Or a Fife's Fame—
Maintain—by Accident that they proclaim—

—Emily Dickinson

Prologue

Founded in 1851, the town of Lakota, Wisconsin, is today little more than a rural crossroads where County Roads JJ and Y meet like modestly crossed legs, with the Mecan River passing beneath the knees. The river flows across the whole of Waushara County, winding its way through woodlots, farm fields, and tangled swampland of willow, dogwood, and boggy prairie. In the Winnebago language, *waushara* means "good land," but some believe the Winnebago were trolling the white settlers who took it from them, since the soils of the county are among the least fertile in the state. After a hard rain, stone arrowheads still rise from sandy farm fields and backyard gardens, reminders that the past doesn't always stay buried.

In the 1870s, during a surge of nationalist fervor initiated by western Indian wars, some locals wanted to rename the town Custer. That motion was soundly defeated when an old conjurer with one eye and raven hair rose to say the land would be cursed if they renamed it for someone who'd had his ass handed to him by a mob of screaming savages. When that one-eyed woman later died, two nuns going through her cabin discovered she was Lakota Sioux. They found a moldy crucifix wedged in her chamber pot and a daguerreotype of Sitting Bull under the feed sack of thistledown and milkweed fluff she'd used for a pillow.

By the turn of the century, a prosperous town had appeared, rows of houses with level front porches, a one-room school, a dry goods store, a bank, a saloon. Much of the money came from virgin pine, clear-cut and transported by rail to Chicago. When the trees were gone, the money left with them, and most of those who stayed scratched out a living on farms. Then the Dust Bowl came, ten years of drought sandwiched around the Great Depression. People ate their cattle and chickens, then their horses, then their dogs. Slowly, then all at once, Lakota went under. Most of the houses burned when lightning set fire to the marsh. In time, any structures spared by that fire succumbed to water, the emperor of rot and decay, leaving only stacked stone foundations, crumbling and overgrown by vines and brambles.

Today the only buildings at the Lakota crossroads are a rustic tavern called Shaken, Not Stirred, popular with the locals, and behind it, across a sandy field brightened by oxeye daisies in summer, a small Quonset hut set back in the woods, like a giant, silver grub, where the National Guard stays during training exercises. From the tavern's gravel parking lot, someone with a decent arm could throw a rock and skip it across the stone bridge on County JJ, which is so narrow only one car can cross it at a time. On occasion, someone petitions the county board of supervisors to widen the bridge to two lanes. In response, the town chair simply asks everyone present to raise a hand if they have ever encountered a car coming from the other direction. No hands ever go up.

Many of the locals still live on modest holdings their families have farmed for over a century, passing poverty down through the generations, along with a stubborn independent streak, alcoholism, a facility with shotguns and deer rifles, and an eagerness to skirt the law when necessary. Those who left for the promise of steady factory wages in the cities often sold their land to Amish farmers moving in from Pennsylvania or Ohio, where the price of an acre was five to ten times higher.

So, if you were a stranger passing over that one-lane stone bridge anytime in the past thirty or forty years, Lakota probably wouldn't have impressed you. Certainly, the Amish seemed to be doing all right. Their white homes and barns dot the landscape like drifts of snow. But you also would have seen a lot of houses so long buffeted by western winds they tilted east like drunks on a bender; dilapidated trailers with barking dogs out front, carving dusty circles with their chains; acres of stunted field corn and yellowed soybeans; old cars cancerous with rust; and boarded-up meth shacks, their former owners serving sentences at the maximum-security prison in Boscobel. Why, you might have wondered, would anyone choose to live *here*?

Sometimes, it isn't where you're going, but rather what you're running from that determines where you find yourself. For people like that, Lakota felt like a refuge, because above all, the locals treasured anonymity, the rare luxury of being left alone. And because they'd been judged harshly all their lives, they made it their business to not judge one another, and to grant anyone who came to town the one freedom Americans typically refused to honor: the freedom to fail without punishment or censure.

Dr. Thomas Kennedy was one of those people.

An introvert who preferred the company of animals to human beings, Doc Kennedy had moved his veterinary practice from Milwaukee to Lakota at the age of forty-seven following the horrifying death of his wife, Angela. Though the accident had ultimately been ruled a suicide, Thomas had been investigated, urged to hire a lawyer, his picture plastered across newspapers and the local television news. In-laws and friends stopped speaking to him. Longtime customers canceled their appointments. Coworkers whispered behind his back. Traumatized and desperate, Thomas quit his job and fled. Months later, at the urging of a grief counselor, he took up trout fishing, something he'd enjoyed as a younger man. And one afternoon, while fishing for brown trout on the Mecan River, he'd happened upon a single-story log home with attached office space for sale on County Road JJ, just a couple miles upstream from the stone bridge in Lakota. A month later, he closed on the house; by early July, he was living there.

What he envisioned initially was semiretirement, a small, one-man veterinary operation, morning hours only. By coincidence, the area did not enjoy the services of a large-animal vet. Few wanted to work with cows and horses anymore, preferring the safety, regular hours, and greater remuneration of a companion-animal practice. So Thomas's dream of semiretirement faded, and his schedule filled. He put thirty-five thousand miles on his truck his first year and learned the names of every farmer in a sixty-mile radius of his home. The area also supported that large community of Amish and their Anabaptist counterparts, the Mennonites, who lived austere lives and took the biblical admonition to hold dominion over their animals seriously. Though comfortably agnostic himself, Thomas found these deeply religious people pleasant, humble company. They never proselytized or, for that matter, spoke any more than necessary. In fact, their taciturnity often rivaled his own. He discovered that an exchange of smiles or frowns could communicate more than a five-minute conversation with their more gregarious English neighbors, as the Amish called them.

Most of Thomas's customers expected to be extended interest-free credit or could afford to pay him only in garden produce, fresh eggs, or butchered animals. He got used to accepting a half dozen frozen fryers in exchange for treating mastitis in a heifer, a quarter of beef for delivering twin calves and repairing the prolapsed uterus of a valuable Angus cow. And he felt fortunate. Lakota had proven the ideal place to escape the notoriety that dogged him: invisible to the outside world; too poor to attract the grubby grasp of commerce; oblivious to the frenetic, digital doom of hashtags and viral videos; and dismissive of the unquenchable American thirst for fame and fortune.

It would not long remain so. And the irony was not lost on Thomas that he would be the reason Lakota's sleepy anonymity faded, why it would become, in fact, one of the most famous places in the world.

It began one morning in late September, just over two years after Thomas had arrived in town. He'd just returned home from Mel and Birdy's ranch out near Oxford, where he'd been summoned at three in the morning to perform an emergency fetotomy on an Arabian dam. The women had cried, distressed to see their colt extracted in pieces from its beautiful mother, but Thomas had assured them the colt was already dead and if he did not remove it, the dam would die as well. Now he sat at home and tipped his face up to the sun. His backyard glowed beneath a shower of yellow maple leaves that fluttered to earth in waves as the wind swelled. His arms, his knees, and his lower back still ached from the morning's work, and he planned to spend a few more minutes in the sunshine before retiring indoors for a nap.

He heard Jasper Fisher's pickup before he saw it, the pinging of gravel spun up into wheel wells, the dusky growl of a muffler riven by holes. Thomas sighed and got to his feet.

Jasper threw open the door, his bony face a mask of fear. Dirt-poor, seventeen years old, the boy grazed a handful of sickly dairy goats on a ten-acre farmstead of thistle and stunted jack pine with his mother, Rachel. His grease-stained jeans and sweatshirt had gone ragged with holes. Hard years had worn ironic smiles through the toes of his dry leather boots.

"You could have just called me, son," Thomas said. "I'd have come to you." He walked stiffly toward the truck as Jasper untied one corner of the sun-bleached canvas tarp he'd thrown over the bed of the pickup.

"You got to help us!" Jasper said.

"What's the problem?" Thomas slid a thumb beneath the tarp, but Jasper grabbed his wrist.

"Not here." Jasper's muscular hands were crisscrossed with scars. "Behind the house," Jasper said. "Please!"

Thomas sighed. "Okay, sure."

The boy pulled the truck around back of Thomas's home, where they could not be seen from the road. He removed the tarp.

Unconscious and nearly unrecognizable, Rachel Fisher's ghastly, swollen body reclined in the bed of the pickup on a bloodied quilt spread across a mound of wheat straw. A soiled pink blanket had been draped over her body, though she was so big it barely covered her. Her face was thick and dappled, her belly bloated like a road-killed deer in the heat of summer, her feet purple balloons.

"Oh my God," Thomas said. "Did she drown?"

"No, sir!" Jasper said. "She's having a baby. Four or five babies, she thinks. I tried to give her whiskey for the pain."

"How long has she been laboring?"

"Two days. Maybe three. She stopped screaming this morning."

"I'll call an ambulance." Thomas reached for his phone.

Jasper shook his head. "No, sir!" he said. "Mama forbid that. She don't believe in it."

"This isn't about belief, Jasper."

Jasper kicked the ground. "Sure is. 'God's will be done,' she told me. I give her my word."

"She needs a doctor."

"That's why I brung her here. Those babies are still moving."

"Jasper, I can't help her."

"Yes, you can."

"I can't."

Jasper opened the door of his truck. "I'll take her home, then."

"Jasper, wait!" Thomas stuffed his phone into his pocket. "Your mother's in serious trouble, you understand? Toxins are pouring through her body. She's probably had a stroke, maybe more than one. She needs to go to the emergency room. We can drive her there ourselves."

Jasper shook his head. "Never."

Thomas shouted, "I can't save her!"

"Save the babies then," Jasper said. "God's waiting for her. She told me that. No man will have her honest, but God will take her hand. The babies, you can save them if you want to. I know you can. I seen you do it."

"Those were animals!" Thomas said. "I'm not a medical doctor. How many times do I have to say it?"

"You can do whatever you want to do," Jasper said.

Thomas exhaled. He yanked open the tailgate, crawled up into the bloodied hay. Gently, he placed his palms on Rachel's stomach. A baby's knee or elbow swiped across his hand. Rachel's thighs were wormed by stretch marks, her vulva swollen and bloodied. He probed the birth canal with his fingertips. Nothing. Rachel's stomach jerked, her uterus contracting, and a bright rivulet of blood ribboned down her abdomen. Thomas folded the blanket up over Rachel's swollen breasts and winced. Her belly, a delta of translucent stretch marks, had grown so large the skin had split open. Someone had attempted to close the bleeding wound with duct tape.

"My God, this poor woman has suffered. Why didn't you call a doctor?"

"She forbid me, I told you," Jasper said. His lips quivered.

"Did you tape her like this?"

"No, sir," he said.

Rachel's abdomen hardened again. Thomas shook his head. He'd always steered clear of poor decisions by planning ahead, by refusing to act impulsively; his wife had often complained that he didn't have a spontaneous bone in his body. He'd counter by saying people in a hurry make terrible mistakes, that careful planning is a virtue, not a fault. But what choice did he have now? He'd pulled hundreds of lambs and calves into the world. He sent Jasper into the house for his medical bag.

He doused the surgical fields with iodine, then filled a syringe with lidocaine and made multiple injections around the perineum, adding injections across the muscle a few inches below Rachel's swollen navel, though performing a Cesarean seemed out of the question. Infection would be unavoidable.

As he considered what might be necessary to deliver multiple infants, Thomas fell back on his veterinary training. Dystocia in lambs and goats was not uncommon. When a lamb presented inappropriately, front legs out but head twisted back, for example, the remedy was to push the legs carefully and gently back into the birth canal. Then, reaching a hand inside the ewe, by feel, one could pull the head forward, pinning the snout to the front legs, enabling the proper presentation.

In the case of triplets, the tinier lambs might complicate the process by descending into the birth canal together, and the legs of two or, rarely, three different animals might show themselves. In such cases, one had to go inside the ewe and sort the lambs, untangling their legs. One of his veterinary school professors compared this to tying a shoelace with one hand while the shoe was tightly wedged inside a wet sock. One had to be certain the limbs belonged to the same body, or the lambs could be injured or killed by the delivery.

Thomas lubricated and inserted his right hand until his fingertips felt the crown of an infant's head. When he touched it, he noticed a pointed swelling in Rachel's abdomen just beneath her sternum. A whole foot? Another head? Thomas rose higher on his knees. He stretched his left arm over Rachel's belly and placed his hand on the spot where he'd seen the movement; then, with the tips of the fingers on his right hand, he applied gentle pressure against the baby's head, as if seeking to return the infant to the womb.

To his surprise, as he pushed with his right hand, a powerful kick struck his left, and the skin along the abdomen stayed distended. When Thomas pushed with his left hand, the pressure on his right remained and grew, and the crown of the infant's head moved a bit farther into the birth canal. Thomas smiled. He repeated the process, just to be certain. Once again, a kick and steady pressure on the left hand.

"All right, then," he said. He recalled the masterful work of an elderly veterinarian he'd met during his residency who could palpate the abdomen of a full-term sheep or goat and within a minute announce how many lambs she carried. Though he could not be certain, Thomas felt energized by his discovery: This was not a case of multiple births at all. Rachel Fisher carried just one fetus, one improbably, impossibly large baby.

"Jasper!" he shouted. "Get up here. I'm going to need your help." Jasper leaped into the truck bed, and it creaked with the extra weight. "Get behind your mother, wrap your arms around her, and hold on."

Thomas fingered a scalpel. Rachel's perineum had already torn, but this baby would need far more room. He extended the tear another inch in a slight curve, like the arc of a crescent moon, then set the scalpel aside, dug into his medical kit, and found a lambing snare. Working counterclockwise, he carefully threaded the snare around the baby's head. He continued to work the snare deeper, hoping to hook it over one shoulder, beneath an armpit. He worked a long time at this, pausing with each contraction, but he abandoned the prospect as impossible.

Instead, Thomas threaded the snare tightly around the upper third of the infant's head, above the ears and across the forehead, just above the eyebrows. This was a risk, but he had no forceps and could see no other option. He attached wooden handles to the other end of the snare and took a deep breath.

"Okay, Jasper, I'm going to apply a steady draw. Lean back and hold tight, son. It's going to feel like I'm trying to pull your mother out of the truck." Jasper tugged his mother toward him and buried his chin in her hair. "All right, Rachel," Thomas said. "Be strong, love. Let's get your baby out into the sunshine."

A contraction came. Thomas pulled. The next contraction came, and Thomas pulled again. Inch by inch, over the next twenty minutes, as his arms quivered and both of his biceps began to cramp, Thomas carefully coaxed the huge head of the infant down the birth canal. When it finally crowned, he let out a deep breath.

"Almost there," he said. "You're doing great, Rachel." Finally, after several more contractions, and with Thomas pulling with all the strength he had left, the infant's large head emerged, face up, eyes squinted closed against the bright sunshine. Thomas removed the lambing snare, which had left a bright red, swollen ring around the child's head. A halo of bruises would follow, but there would be no permanent damage; the snare had done its work. Thomas cradled the infant's head, waiting for the next contraction. When it came, he pressed on Rachel's belly with one hand and tugged on the infant with the other. In time, one shoulder came free, then the other, and the infant's huge body slid into the fallen world.

"It's a boy," Thomas said. "Jasper, you have a brother." He put the squirming baby on his mother's chest, and then clamped and cut the cord. He dipped the stub in a cup of iodine, and the child came to life. He lifted his head and raised his shoulders. He opened his mouth, bayed like a young coyote.

"That's the boy," Thomas said, smiling. "Let everyone know you're here."

From the woods just beyond Thomas's yard, a red fox barked, and squirrels began chattering. A half mile down the road, farm dogs howled; cattle lowed in their sunny pastures. With the help of Thomas's gentle coaxing, the boy rooted until he found a nipple, swollen and dripping colostrum, and he suckled contentedly.

When the infant finished eating and fell asleep, Thomas wiped him down, swaddled him in a clean cotton dish towel, measured him, and weighed him. The boy weighed eighteen pounds. He was twenty-seven inches long.

Eighteen pounds! Thomas tapped the scale and squinted at the dial to be certain that was true. It was.

As the child grew and flourished, the story of Gabriel Fisher's birth would be retold again and again until the truth had mostly disappeared. Many believed his mother had passed away with the infant still sealed inside her womb, and Gabriel had gently cut his way free with the blade of his thumbnail. Others swore that Gabriel's gestation had been fifteen months long, that through sheer force of will, Rachel Fisher had delayed her delivery in an effort to get the boy's father—who remained unknown—to admit paternity. Still others claimed with zealous certainty that when Gabriel emerged from Rachel's body, he was already thirty-six inches tall, and, like a newborn fawn, stood up and walked an hour after birth.

These exaggerations were understandable, given what the boy would one day become.

But on that bright September afternoon, Gabriel Fisher was born minutes before his mother drew her final breath, pulled into the world by a soft-spoken veterinarian haunted by his past who only wanted to live a quiet life someplace the modern world had left behind.

Part One

1

Hannah Fisher

My Rachel was an easy birth, the easiest. Her brother Caleb, no. All nine months I carried him, I felt too sick to eat. Some days I managed only a few spoons of warm oats and honey. In my final month, the fire shooting down my legs was so intense I could not sleep. When my waters broke, Caleb gave me pain I didn't know a woman could bear, a thirty-hour labor through one sleepless night into the next, each contraction exquisite agony. In my feeble efforts to endure it, I thought of Jacob Hutter and Dirk Willems, Amish martyrs who had been burned at the stake; I pictured our dear Lord on the cross, nails through His hands and feet, my own pain so meager compared to theirs! In the frightened, tear-stained faces of the women at my bedside—my mother; my closest friend, Abiah; my sister, Meg—I could see I might die and take Caleb with me. I was but a girl of eighteen, married to Josiah, my Godly husband, for less than one year.

I prayed to endure the Lord's affliction, that special suffering He reserves for His own, and I should have opened my arms to death, overjoyed to join my Savior in His kingdom. But I did not. I sobbed like a child, spilling tears for the babies I would never hold, for my loving husband, whom I as yet barely knew, and most ashamedly, for my comfortable home, my gardens, my beautiful herd of goats—all earthly things of no consequence, the vanity of vanities. I believe that is why God sent me back into this world. My faith had not been large enough.

As I felt the shadow of death cover me like a heavy blanket, the Lord saw fit to contract my womb so powerfully, I felt my body cleave in half, as if His mighty sword had opened me. My sister, Meg, who had been on the floor on her knees, sprang up on the bed and burrowed between my legs like a badger.

When I awoke to find Caleb on my chest, his soft infant skin pressed to mine, the rope of life still connecting us, I cried tears of thanks. But my joy was short-lived. Soon my beautiful boy's hands and lips, and then his body, went blue. He would not suckle. Listless, he opened his mouth to cry but made no sound. Abiah sent for an English midwife, but my lovely firstborn perished in my arms before she arrived. My grief proved nearly unshakable. It would be a year before I consented to begin again in our marriage bed.

Rachel decided early on she'd make up for all Caleb had put me through. All nine months she floated blissfully inside me, soft and gentle as a bubble. I had no morning sickness, no shooting pains down my legs. And when it came time for her to join us in the world, she announced her intentions in the morning, after I'd had a full night's rest, her waters spilling warm on my feet.

An hour later I'd barely begun my lying in, with Meg and Abiah at my bedside, when I felt this powerful, beautiful heat, as if I'd spread my legs immodestly wide before the summer sun. Meg squealed in surprise. I had not even begun to push, and Rachel's head emerged, the crown a swirl of dark hair, her bright eyes open. With the next contraction, Meg turned Rachel's shoulders slightly so, and my daughter slid free of my body, the easiest birth God has ever given to a mother and child. That night I was able to take a walk outside. I carried Rachel with me, naked in my arms next to my warm skin but for a shoulder wrap of Shetland wool. I walked along the fencerow and watched the sunset spill itself pink and orange along the horizon, and I cried with happiness. I had a beautiful daughter to love, another woman in the house to be a woman with.

But the Lord does not often give without taking away. He understands our weakness. When our desires are granted, our gratitude wanes, and we almost immediately turn to wanting more. Just months after Rachel's birth, our Lord sent Josiah a terrible sickness, no appetite, fever, fatigue. He took to bed when his throat began to swell like a bullfrog's. Beneath the covers, his manly parts grew to the size of oranges. His bloodied urine stained the bedsheets. He suffered so. How fervently I prayed for his recovery. Mumps, my mother said. A bad case, but he won't die. Josiah was in bed for a week. It took another week to regain his strength, but a hidden injury remained. Though we wanted many more children, and yearned for them, Josiah's infection rendered us infertile. I cried many hours over this, but always tried to be contented with the two beautiful children the Lord had provided me, though He took one to be with Him in heaven.

Even as a young girl, Rachel drew the gaze of boys and men. A mother sees such things, the subtle shift in their hungry eyes. Their hands remain busy at their work, but their eyes—those of Godly men, too—wander. Her brown hair curled in soft ringlets when a baby and by age twelve cascaded down her back. Such beauty. Even in a plain blue dress to the ankles, with her hair tucked under her kapp, Rachel radiated loveliness. Her eyes, the gentle curve of her jawline, the pink fruit of her lips, these could not be concealed. Every time I looked upon her, my heart swelled with a terrible pride.

It was not until much later that I realized the gravity of my mistake. God had not sent my beautiful daughter so easily into this world to give my life greater joy. He sent her to test my love for Him, to give me new opportunity to resist the pleasures of this world. It is when we are at the heights of earthly delight—sensual pleasure, pride, vanity—that we find ourselves furthest from heaven.

I grew up with three older brothers, Thomas, Abel, and John, and one sister, Margaret, whom we called Meg. Three years older than me, Meg was far more beautiful. Everywhere I grew plain, my thin lips, my boyish body, she swelled and bloomed. My wispy hair, dry as the browned silks of ripened field corn, fell barely past my shoulders and could be hidden easily beneath my kapp. Meg's hair grew in thick, golden curls, like ropes, and by the time she reached the age of twelve, it would take Mother a long time to secure the bulk of it beneath Meg's kapp, and even then, it radiated beyond the edges like the rays in a child's drawing of the sun.

When Meg turned thirteen, an English boy made her the gift of a large, ivory-colored comb, and at night she would comb her hair over and over, running her fingers through it proudly. One spring afternoon, the worst of my childhood, Meg began combing her hair while Mother read to us after lunch from the Bible. We were kneeling on the floor near the hearth of the woodstove, and Mother and Father sat in chairs on either side. I still remember the words that stopped inside Mother's mouth: "Beareth all things, believeth all things, hopeth all things, endureth all things," when Father leaped from his chair and lifted Meg by the head, his strong right hand wrapped in her hair. Meg dropped her comb and screamed, kicking her legs and clutching at her head with both hands as Father dragged her toward the door.

Father had cautioned Meg many times against her vanity. It is one of Satan's most devious tricks, how easily he can plant it in our hearts with just a glance at our reflection in a window. Once Meg had gotten lipstick from an English girl and colored her lips in secret. She'd removed it but missed a speck. When Father noticed, he grabbed her chin and rubbed her lip clean, roughly, with his thumb, causing her mouth to bleed. Another time Meg had arranged her hair on top of her head, with pins and such, like a glamorous English movie star. Fortunately, that time Mother had corrected her. But to reach for her comb during Bible reading! Father could not abide it.

This was late April, shearing season. Father pulled Meg, barefoot, out the kitchen door and across the gravel driveway into the barn, where the shearing stanchion remained inside one of the large, empty horse stalls. The ewes rumbled in their lambing jugs as they heard Father enter, thinking they might be getting a treat, but soon went silent. Her feet cut and bleeding, Meg knelt in the straw and pleaded with Father to forgive her, promised to melt the comb in a fire. Father dragged Meg to the stanchion and ordered her to lie across it, her beautiful hair hanging like willow branches over her face. With quivering hands, and loud, angry breaths, Father yanked the hand shear from where it hung on a nail driven into the wall. He oiled the steel blades until they dripped. Meg sobbed but remained still. The rest of us watched in horror, heads bowed. Father pushed down on one of Meg's shoulders, and then the other, as he sheared the long hair from her head. It fell in tangled ropes into the straw below, mixing with snippets of wool and pellets of manure.

Meg kept the comb, though she never used it again in Father's presence. When her hair grew back, almost as if in rebuke to Father, its curls were tighter and even more beautiful. In the sunlight, its golden sheen made it appear as if lit from within. Meg remained wary of Father thereafter, seldom spoke to him unless spoken to first. At her earliest opportunity, at age seventeen, she married an Amish man with family land in Pennsylvania. After she moved away, Meg returned home only four times, twice to attend to the birth of my children, once for Mother's funeral, and a final time when Father's body was laid to rest.

The summer I turned eleven, Father sold off our sheep and dairy goats and converted our barn into a sawmill, Absalom Yoder's Custom Hardwoods. For some time afterward, with almost no income as the business became established, we often relied upon the generosity of our people, and the ingenuity of our mother, to keep us fed and clothed. We ate a lot of soup, weak broth, sometimes nothing more than boiled farro and a little salt, the only spice Father allowed in our kitchen. Too much sweetness on the tongue, he said, distracts from the true sweetness of the Lord. In the winter, with candles too expensive and oil for lamps in short supply, we went to bed early, Meg and I together in one bed, doubling our blankets and piling raw fleeces over them to stay warm.

As is our way, we children helped to run the new business. It was noisy, messy, dangerous work, not nearly as pleasant as tending crop fields outside in the sunshine or caring for young animals, though I grew to love the scent of freshly cut wood. Because I was small, I was spared the most physical labor. I spent my days carrying scraps to the slab pile; sopping up spilled diesel fuel; sweeping the endless sawdust into waist-deep piles, with wads of merino wool jammed in my ears to muffle the fierce whine of the saw blade.

Mother begged Father to allow me and Meg to help with the housework instead, arguing that mill work was best suited to the boys. Father partially relented, granting the respite only to Meg. He said I worked harder, and took better direction, than Abel, Thomas, or John, and for these reasons he thought of me as a fourth son, rather than a daughter. I believe he meant this to be a compliment. It hurt me deeply, though I pretended to be flattered.

A tireless worker, Father toiled in the mill ten or twelve hours every day. Sometimes, in the throes of insomnia, he would work through the night as well. Quick to anger, he demanded a similar commitment to work from his family, and he let us know when we'd fallen short. Meg and my brothers feared him, as Mother did, I know, much of the time. Once, in a rage, he'd broken Abel's arm by yanking him from the table when Abel had refused to eat boiled brussels sprouts, bounty of the Lord's earth. Still, as the youngest, and shy, I was spared his Vesuvian rages. Sometimes if I were alone with him over lunch, he would give me the treat from his own lunch—an apple, sometimes a cookie Mother had made—winking at me as I savored it, as long as I did so quickly. "Don't dawdle, Hannah. The Lord didn't rest until the seventh day, and Genesis says nothing about a lunch break."

After a difficult year, Father's business grew and thrived. He custom cut hickory, hard maple, red and white oak, black walnut, and cherry, and he sold to furniture and cabinetmakers throughout the Midwest. His hardened steel, rough-cut sawblade was three feet across with over one hundred triangular teeth sharpened and oiled daily with Father's obsessive precision. Belt-driven by a rebuilt Cummins diesel engine mounted to the floor, that blade spun so fast it looked almost invisible, but it could slide through hard maple like a straight razor cutting flesh. "Don't get too close, Hannah," he once said to me. "That blade will slice through your skinny little neck so fast you will be looking back at your body while your head rolls across the floor."

Though quarrelsome, Father could also be exceedingly generous. In fact, I believed him to be the most pious and generous man I knew. One summer I asked for a baseball glove, but Mother refused to buy it. She said baseball was a boys' game. But a few days later, when I arrived in the mill for work, I found a new baseball glove hanging on the nail where I kept my dust apron. Excitedly, I tried it on. Father winked at me, said, "Hang that back up now, Hannah. You can't push a broom with that contraption on your hand." I know of many Amish families and young widows suffering from poverty, illness, or some other affliction and short of firewood who woke up one frigid winter morning to discover two free cords of slab wood had been delivered secretly in the night, cut and stacked and already seasoned, ready for burning. I know this because I sometimes accompanied Father on these midnight missions, helping to stack the wood, my fingers numb, breath clouds of vapor. On the way home, he'd put the reins in my hands, let me lead the horses, while he tipped his head back and looked at the stars.

When I was seventeen, I fell in love with Josiah, a poor local boy, who worked in a cabinet shop for a man who often purchased wood from my father. With no land of his own, upon our engagement, Josiah accepted my parents' offer to deed us forty acres of land along the river, contiguous to their own, and with help from Father, Josiah's brothers, and friends, Josiah built our house. It is a modest home, strongly built, with a root cellar beneath the kitchen. After a year we raised our own barn, and I began to keep milk goats, as my family once did, while Josiah started his own carpentry business. Like most of our people, we have no electricity or family telephone, though Josiah keeps a cell phone for business, as many do. Josiah's work is contracted nearly a year in advance, and he keeps a calendar in our desk drawer with his schedule posted. Josiah is skillful and responsible, charges a fair price, keeps his word, and does high-quality work. It is surprising that these qualities are so rare in the English world, where the rule seems to be to charge as much as you can for something as cheaply made as possible, though it is impertinent of me to say so. Before I met Dr. Kennedy, I often wondered why anyone would willingly choose to live in a world so rife with corruption and false promises, where everything worshipped is transitory. My mother used to say we Amish have much that is beautiful about America without accepting her ugliness. I don't know if that is true.

For years, after Sunday services, Josiah and I hosted a family gathering for restful fellowship and an early dinner. By this time, Meg, Abel, and John had moved away, but my oldest brother, Thomas, lived the next church district over, and he would come with his wife and five children. My mother and father always joined us as well, wandering across the lawn from their home next door. Though he worked tirelessly the other six days of the week, Sundays my father took seriously the Lord's admonition to rest. The scent of frying chickens, roasting potatoes, and baking fruit pies would linger in the air as we all talked and laughed and sang. Those were beautiful days! When it got too noisy in the house, Father would take Rachel and his other grandchildren outside, where they'd play freeze tag or hide and seek. Sometimes Father would pitch a baseball and cheer every time one of the children hit it with a broomstick into the pasture, scattering my goats. On the hottest days, Father would lead them down to the river, where he'd sit high on the bank in the sunshine, slide his suspenders down over his shoulders for comfort, and relax. The little boys would roll their pants over their knees, and Rachel and the other girls would bunch their dresses up around their thighs to wade barefoot in the cold, rushing water.

If he'd had a difficult week, Father would lie back in the sun, his straw hat tipped over his face, rest both hands on his chest, and fall asleep. An hour or so later, when we rang the dinner bell, the children would wake him and fight over who got to lead him by the hand back to the house. Because Rachel had been working in the mill every week, sweeping sawdust, carrying slab wood, as I had as a young girl, he'd often choose her, prompting the other children to complain of favoritism. So, he began holding his hands high, offering them to the first child who could recite a chosen Bible verse. Once, I was with them when he asked someone to name the fruits of the spirit. Rachel immediately recited the list, from Galatians: love, joy, peace, patience, kindness, goodness, faithfulness, gentleness, and self-control. This earned her a kiss on the head and Father's large, calloused hand in hers as we all walked back to the house.

Throughout her young life, Rachel's faith grew so profound it sometimes shamed me. Of course, faith comes easily to a child, so ready to believe all things. God's miracles seem no more incredible to a young girl than a chick pecking its way from an egg, or a newborn goat steaming in the frosty pasture. Still, it persisted, and by age fourteen, she confessed herself ready to devote her life to God, to join the church as a full, communing member. I felt proud but uneasy. For us, giving your life to God is an irrevocable decision. Adult baptism following the freedom of *Rumspringa* is a commitment made with eyes open. My mother said you must sample the sweets so you'll never wonder what you might be missing, but you return for true nourishment.

Rachel sensed our hesitation. My heart aches to remember it. As parents, we sometimes must think for our children when their inexperience puts their judgement into doubt. Wait, we said. Please, Rachel. We are so pleased you love God, and we do not doubt the earnestness of your intentions. But in a year or two, when you are a woman, your eyes might see differently. Divine love is weakened by regret, which can grow into spite, or worse. You have not seen enough of the world to know what your commitment means.

My dear girl obeyed. I could see the crushing disappointment in her eyes, but Rachel did not beg. She honored us, accepted our decision, as always. At age sixteen, she was baptized into our church, her beautiful face beaming with the love of Christ in her heart.

When Rachel was nine years old, my dear mother passed away. She had a bleeding incident that left her unable to speak, her right arm and leg paralyzed. She lingered for several days. My father was so aggrieved by her passing he could barely speak of it, and he never remarried. After her funeral, with Josiah's help, he brought her cedar clothing chest to our home. They carried it upstairs and left me with it.

Inside was the dress she wore on her wedden's day, not much different than those she wore every day (though of course much smaller, she being a larger woman at death than when first married, as are we all); envelopes of our baby teeth, some of them still stained with dried blood, and snippets of our baby hair; yarn she'd spun years earlier from her Shetland ewes; a muslin dish towel her mother had given to her with a verse from Hebrews stitched onto it, "Now faith is the substance of things hoped for, the evidence of things not seen." All these things I had seen and remembered. But on the bottom in one corner, hidden beneath the balls of yarn, and wrapped and tied inside a kapp, was a book. The covers had been removed, its pages frayed and dirty from use, sanctified by garden soil and cooking grease from my dear mother's fingers. It was a collection of poems, cryptic, oddly written, by a woman named Emily Dickinson. One early page featured a photograph of her, dressed in black—Amish? I wondered, at first—staring directly out with large, dark eyes, her small hands folded modestly. With her dark hair and pale skin, and her thin, angular face, she looked a bit like my own mother did as a young woman. I read a few of the shorter poems, stopping at those pages most soiled by my mother's more frequent interest. At that time, their meanings puzzled me. I could not dwell on them—I could hear Josiah speaking to my father just downstairs. I tied the book back into my mother's kapp and returned it to the place she'd reserved for it in the bottom of her chest.

Many nights, long after Rachel had gone to sleep, and only when Josiah was kept away by a job too distant to return home at night, I would open Mother's chest and find the book. Sometimes my fingers would tremble as I lit the candle. I would breathe deeply, my heart quivering, the candle's light fluttering with my breaths. As I read those beautiful poems, my mind would come alive.

Miss Dickinson wrote so often of God, I told myself this reading was akin to devotions, solitary prayers, in a way, at eventide. Remarkably, I recognized myself inside those pages. In a life devoted to goodness, devoted to God, there can still be yearning. A quiet mouth, a devoted heart, does not mean a quiet mind. Sometimes while reading, I found myself crying, overwhelmed by the depth and breadth of Miss Dickinson's daring, by the baring of her soul.

We are taught all our lives that Satan has no better deceiver than those self-deceived. But to me, it did not feel like deception. I would pay dearly for that mistake.

2

Billy Walton

Amish have been living around Lakota for as long as I can remember. Back in the day, we all went to school together, and everyone got along. Sure, they were different. They all dressed the same, and sometimes you could hear them talking to one another in that old, guttural German they spoke among themselves. But they liked to play games at recess and hated school as much as we did. That all changed in the early '70s with the Yoder decision, a Supreme Court ruling that said Wisconsin Amish kids could not be forced to attend public schools until age sixteen, like the rest of us. After that, Amish kids started going to their own schools and quit after the eighth grade. Damn, but I was envious.

As a kid, Josiah Fisher was a friend of mine. He could hit a baseball a country mile. Sometimes he hit the dang thing so far it landed in the cornfield, and we'd spend the rest of recess searching for it. If you'd met his old man then, you'd see right away where Josiah's strength came from. I once saw Pop Fisher pick up a telephone pole, hoist it to his shoulder, and walk with it like he was carrying a baseball bat.

We used to talk about what a great high school baseball team we were going to have someday. No one could hit my curveball, not even Josiah, and we had a couple boys bigger than Josiah who could hit a fastball almost as far as he could. But Josiah's father pulled him out of school after the eighth grade, and the rest of us, well, we never amounted to much on the baseball field, or anywhere else, for that matter.

All my life, my pop ran a tavern, Crossroads Tap, in lovely downtown Lakota, and I own that establishment now, though I renamed it Shaken, Not Stirred. We lived above the bar, and I still do. Pop drank up his profits, but Mom did some bookkeeping for a few local farmers, and we got by. He wasn't one of those drunks who came home at two in the morning and put his fist through the wall. Drinking made him happier. Give him a few beers and a half dozen shots of Jack Daniel's and he'd stick his dick into a lightbulb socket just to get a laugh. On school nights, Mom unplugged the jukebox at ten o'clock, but on weekends she'd let me stay in the bar drinking fountain sodas until midnight. I started putting beer in my soda cup around the age of twelve. Pop was too busy to notice, and if I went back to drinking soda at around eleven, by midnight I could make it up the stairs without stumbling, so no one would be the wiser.

I was an alcoholic before I graduated from high school, and I spent my twenties and thirties so far under the influence there are huge swaths I don't remember. I drank my way through two marriages, had two kids I never quite figured out how to care for, and wrecked three cars. I had a heart attack at forty-five that nearly sent me to the worm party. Got a scar running up the middle of my chest that looks like the zipper on a sleeping bag. I'm in AA now, even host meetings at the bar sometimes. A couple of my fellow drinkers refuse to come when I host, say it's like attending a meeting for sex addicts at a whorehouse. I tell them to grow some balls. If you're not drinking, you're not drinking.

I don't get a lot of Amish coming in. Pop always said it was his bad luck to own a tavern surrounded by the only group of Germans in the world who did not get stinking drunk every weekend, though sometimes a few of their young men will stop in for a beer. On occasion, some of the locals get a little stupid when Amish come in. Usually it's beer-brave idiots who'd get their heads handed to them if the Amish boys chose to fight. They ignore the insults, finish their beers, and head out the door. One time, though, the drunk jerk who was giving them grief went out to find a still-warm pile of horse shit on the seat of his Ford F-150. I guess the Amish sometimes respond with the weapons they have available.

One time years ago, my old man got into it with an Amish guy, Absalom Yoder. When Josiah married Absalom's youngest daughter, Hannah, that old buzzard became Josiah's father-in-law. Old Yoder, he was a sly son of a gun, all piety and charity on the outside. He was known for delivering wagonloads of slab firewood from his mill (scrap wood, largely worthless, I'll add) to those in need, to widows and orphans and so forth, and he made these deliveries in the dark of night, because Amish believe good deeds must be done in secret. But on the inside, Yoder was vicious as a cockfighting rooster. If Mother Theresa herself were walking across the road and Absalom was coming in his buggy, he'd run her down if she got in his way.

How he and Pop got into it came about by accident. A half dozen kegs rolled off Pop's flatbed as he passed Absalom's buggy on County Y. One of those kegs rolled into Absalom's horse and shattered a front leg, and he had to put the animal down. Dad offered fair compensation, but Absalom refused it. Bastard got a lawyer and sued for damages. Amish are forbidden from suing in court, but somehow, he did it. Pop said that horse must have shit gold bullion for what Absalom claimed it was worth. Had to take out a second mortgage on the business to pay the judgement, and he never spoke Absalom Yoder's name aloud thereafter. Referred to him only as That Amish Son of a Bitch.

Josiah's daughter, Rachel, came into my place just the one time, and I wish she hadn't. I'd seen her often growing up, beautiful girl, a real looker. Sometimes I'd pass her on the side of the road as she and her mother walked their flock of goats from one pasture to another, or I'd see her at the farm stand at the end of their driveway, where they sold goat milk, goat cheese, and summer vegetables. Rachel had an angelic face and her daddy's dark eyes—I could see Josiah in her, no question. I heard she had a wicked volleyball spike, that even in a dress she could jump like a kangaroo.

When she came in, I didn't recognize her at first, because she wasn't dressed in Amish clothing. She was with a boy I'd never seen before. He came in trailing behind her in blue jeans and a black T-shirt with that Rolling Stones tongue and lips logo on his chest. Rachel had her beautiful hair down, and she wore a sleeveless white blouse with a chain around her neck, a big silver cross hanging from it, and a skirt down to the ankles—nothing revealing, mind you, but I saw her arms for the first time, and they were thin and beautiful, like the rest of her. She and the boy sat across from one another in a booth underneath the mount of a forty-three-inch musky Pop caught in the Chippewa Flowage back in 1974. They didn't really talk, seemed like strangers, if you want to know the truth. When I wandered over to ask for birthdays, I learned Rachel was sixteen and the boy was seventeen. They didn't protest when I told them I couldn't serve them alcohol, but they were welcome to unlimited refills of soda, on me. I felt a little responsible for Rachel's well-being, given that I was friends with her father, or at least had been at one time, so I kept an eye on them, just the same.

They didn't talk, didn't dance. At one point, Rachel got up and wandered around. She seemed to want everyone to notice she was there, which surprised me, because she'd always seemed shy to me. Pop collected wildlife prints, ducks landing in a marsh at sunrise, a pheasant flying over a cornfield, that sort of thing, and she looked at all of those pictures and went back by the pool table to make small talk with a couple guys waiting their turn. No one pawed at her, but I could see their eyes running down her body like syrup when she turned her back. It was like a lamb had wandered into a wolf den to ask directions home. I kept looking at that little pup she came in with, wondering when he'd get his ass out of that booth to be at his lady's side, but he was watching the Yankees pound the White Sox on TV, didn't even seem interested in her.

It wasn't like Rachel was lying on her back on my bar letting strangers suck shots of Wild Turkey from her belly button. But something seemed off, made me uneasy. When Rachel and that boy finally left my place, she smiled and waved as they went out the door, and I nodded and smiled back. I felt good thinking of that boy driving her home to Josiah's place, where maybe Rachel's mother or Josiah himself was waiting up for her at the kitchen table.

When I heard, six or seven months later, that Rachel had gotten herself knocked up, thrown out of her parents' house, and banished from her community, I felt sick about it. The door would open, and two or three young men would wander in wearing sweaty ball caps, shirts and jeans dirty from a day of pouring concrete or making hay. I'd draw their beers and look into their grimy faces, hoping I'd recognize that boy who'd been with Rachel. Because if that kid had had the balls to show his face in my place again, I would have taken him by the scruff of the neck and demanded he support the kid he'd planted inside of Rachel. It was the least he could do after ruining that girl's life. But I never saw him again.

The Widow Charlotte took Rachel into her home. Charlotte lived directly across from Josiah and Hannah's place, their forty acres separated from Charlotte's ten by the river—it runs wide but shallow there—an overgrown hedgerow and a rusted-out fence line on Charlotte's side. From the high land right before the acreage dropped toward the river valley, I'm sure people at Josiah's could see Charlotte's barn and the back of her house, and vice versa. Maybe Charlotte and Rachel used to converse from time to time across the river. I don't know.

Pushing seventy, long widowed, Charlotte never had a daughter of her own. A tree-hugger and bra-burner type, she went to county board meetings and raised holy hell from time to time. Guessing if she'd lived three hundred years earlier, Charlotte might have been burned as a witch. She hung her wet laundry on lines outside to dry, even in the winter, and if you happened by while she was out there, you might notice her puffing on a pipe. Said the smoke kept her lungs warm. If she had trouble sleeping, she'd come to my place for a night-cap, a shot of Rumple Minze with a Budweiser chaser she chugged like water. She never cut her grass, never weeded her flower gardens, and let barn cats breed like rats in her dusty haymow.

Word got around that she'd taken in the Amish girl who had gotten herself knocked up by a ghost, and I felt ashamed I had not treated the Widow Charlotte with greater kindness over the years. I heard the whispers, the rude comments, men calling her a dyke under their breath, never mind she raised two boys on her own after her husband died young and never complained about it. I served her drinks and took her money, but I could have asked after her health and her children. Right up until she died and even afterward, when she willed all she owned to Rachel Fisher, the Widow Charlotte—who proudly professed her atheism to anyone who dared to evangelize in her presence, including the Jehovah's Witnesses who sometimes tried to save the lost souls drinking in my tavern—seemed to me the most righteous and kindly of neighbors.

3

Hannah Fisher

As a young girl, I once burned my fingers on a muffin tin that had just come from the oven. My fingertips swelled like tight little balloons, and Mother lowered my hand into a crock of cold spring water. She said, I'm sorry for your pain, Hannah, but such afflictions are the Lord's reminder to us. They help us to imagine our bodies tortured by eternal fire and brimstone, with the devil and the damned our only companions. Hell is an agony beyond human comprehension.

No doubt. No doubt. But there are other forms of incomprehensible pain.

When Rachel told me she was with child, unmarried, seventeen years old, I did not believe her. How can this be? I asked her. You have just been baptized, taken into the bosom of the Lord and our church. You cried holy tears, my love. Surely you're mistaken? Surely you have only dreamed it?

Every night I cried and prayed. I listened. I watched. I nearly convinced myself she'd only been dreaming, and then one morning, I heard Rachel retching. Months passed. Her breasts swelled, her belly grew. Soon all would see and know. When she refused to name the father, I believed she would change her mind in time. Josiah spoke to her many times about it. But she remained steadfast. She met with our minister and our deacon. She met with our bishop. All were gentle with her, acknowledging our fallen nature is certain but not beyond redemption. She need only confess her sin and name the fellow transgressor, and she could be forgiven.

When she would not, church members began to talk openly of excommunication, of *meidung*, what the English call shunning. I begged Rachel then. Please, Rachel. You are my only child! What must I do to convince you? Tell me. She smiled and hugged me, her swollen womb, like a melon, between us.

Among our people, *meidung* is a last resort, practiced rarely, far less than most English believe. It is a gentle practice to bring sinners back into the fold following minor transgressions. Say a man falls behind and works in his fields on the Sabbath. Once, twice, this happens, he'd be spoken to. If it continues, the minister will visit the house to see if others might help during the week so he can return to church on Sundays. If he still refuses, *meidung* enters the discussion, but he will still be given encouragement. Only when all else fails will church members vote to shun such a fellow. Moreover, in our district, at least, the vote must be unanimous. Every baptized member of the church present must vote for *meidung*, and if we do, it means only that we cannot eat or worship with the sinner. He is not welcome at table or in worship until he repents of his sin and asks to return. We can still speak to him and work with him. He is not an outcast. Normally, this small reminder of the importance of community is enough to bring the sinner home. If he returns, we will welcome him as the father welcomed his prodigal son. With open arms.

But in rare cases in which the sin is serious, cases where the sinner is defiant, self-assured, proud, a more profound shunning, *streng meidung*, is the remedy. It requires absolute social and spiritual isolation. The sinner is unwelcome at all community events; no one can eat with him, or trade with him, or even speak to him.

One of our ministers, Amos Miller, and Eli Lapp, the bishop, came to our house and met privately with Rachel. In her eighth month, for one week, Eli came every afternoon. Rachel would not be moved. A vote on *meidung* was scheduled for the Sunday before Easter. I could not bring myself to go. I would not. Josiah urged me to reconsider, but I refused him. I'd cried myself dry of tears. Where will she go? I asked Josiah. How will she live? How did this happen?

When he arrived home, in the early afternoon, he looked as if he'd been crying too. "*Streng meidung,*" he said, softly.

By then, Mrs. Charlotte Chesterfield had heard of Rachel's predicament and invited her to move into her home just across the river. Crying all the while, I helped Rachel pack her things. Josiah and I helped load the belongings into Mrs. Chesterfield's truck, in which she sat, frowning, staring straight ahead, in the cab. She was not one of our people, but I thanked her, and I thanked the Lord for her generosity. At least Rachel would be near and cared for. In the summer, when the trees were in full leaf, we could hear Mrs. Chesterfield's hungry sheep baaing when she went out to feed them. In the winter, the trees bare, I could stand at my sink after dinner, boiled water poured steaming over the dirty dishes, and look out the window and see the brightly lit windows of Mrs. Chesterfield's house. If I watched long enough, sometimes even until the water went cold, I might eventually see someone pass across one of those windows.

Rachel gave birth to a healthy baby boy, and she named the child Jasper. I learned of this days afterward from Abiah. Mrs. Chesterfield had gone into Maddie Hershberger's bakery to buy bread and shared the news. It hurt deeply to learn so many knew of Jasper's birth before I did, but at least I knew my daughter and her son were well. So many nights afterward, my mind churning, I could not sleep. I would lie still as I have always done, listening for the music of marsh peepers, the whip-poor-will, the night thrush. Normally, these songs bring me peace. They are a sign to me that the Lord has not left us alone in so much darkness. But when cold weather came, when November snows brightened the dormant grass, the nights grew silent but for the rare hooting of a horned owl or the wail of coyotes. Night after night as I lay awake, I would think of the most comforting Bible verses I knew, but my tears would wash away all, and I would be left repeating Job over and over in my mind: "When shall I arise, and the night be ended? For I have had my fill of tossing until dawn."

Of course, I knew: no Bible verse, no song or stillness, could mute the warring in my own soul, the Tempter calling, calling me to the kitchen window, where I might stare at Mrs. Chesterfield's home for an hour, or more. At that time, she heated her home with wood, as so many country people did, and I would pray to see the smoke rising from her chimney, so I could believe Rachel and her infant son were warm and comfortable. I told myself I only needed a drink of water from the pitcher beside the sink, and I would pour a small glass and drink, allow myself a peek out the window. We can trick ourselves into believing such small capitulations do not count, that we are not yielding to the Tempter but merely satisfying our human curiosity. Then, soon, we fall deeper.

In late November, a cold front dropped temperatures far below zero, the earth a sphere of ice. We kept our goats in the barn with propane heaters. I had to break up the ice on their water troughs every few hours, and each morning I had to dump the solid block of ice that had formed overnight to refill them.

That night, a light snow began, tiny spherules like bits of stone ticking against the window glass. At one in the morning I rose from bed, the bitter cold in the air palpable, even inside our house, heated by a single propane heater in the upstairs hall and a woodstove downstairs. I wrapped my arms across my breasts and went down to the kitchen. A low half-moon illuminated the landscape, and through a curtain of lightly falling snow I stared at Mrs. Chesterfield's house, at the single, glowing window on the southern corner. I saw a flash of movement. My heart leaped up! Then another flash in the opposite direction. My Rachel was up walking Jasper on her shoulder, back and forth, perhaps bouncing him slightly, as countless generations of women have done, to lull their infants to sleep. Back and forth she went, back and forth. I found myself swaying in the window, as if I, too, held a baby in my arms.

As I watched them, the yearning in my heart boiled over, and

I yielded. I pulled the feather bed from the cedar closet. My dear mother had filled it with goose and duck feathers she'd plucked from fowl she herself had butchered. I pulled on Josiah's snow boots and my coat, hat, and gloves, and with the feather bed over my shoulders, I grabbed a kitchen chair and clomped out into the snow.

The cold hit my face like iron, but it did not deter me. Through the snow I hobbled, dragging the chair behind me, casting a long shadow in the moonlight. On a slight rise, just before our land tips down toward the river, I set the chair down in the snow and sat down. I wrapped the feather bed over my shoulders and down along my lap. I could now see Rachel quite easily, perhaps eighty yards away. She was walking Jasper, shifting him from arm to arm, his red face twisted, shedding baby tears.

Large, feathery flakes of snow stuck to my hat and slowly coated the feather bed. I took a deep breath of icy air. Softly, I began to sing, "*Schloof, Bobbeli, Schloof,*" "Sleep, Baby, Sleep," a lullaby I'd sung to Rachel so many times. My own voice startled me. It had never sounded so pure. I sang that lullaby again and again, the song visible in the white clouds of my warm breath, until I could no longer feel my fingers, until my toes went numb, until, at last, the lone lighted window in Mrs. Chesterfield's house went dark.

For the first few years of Jasper's life, that is how it was, my sleeplessness now a boon to me. In my nocturnal wandering in the warmer seasons, I joined the community of night peepers and fireflies, raccoons, opossum, and white-tailed deer. In time these creatures knew me nearly as one of their own and would barely glance my way as they passed through, the deer belly-deep in timothy and clover. Each time I left the bed, Josiah slept or pretended to sleep, his silence a gift to me, and when I returned, an hour or more later, smelling like the outdoors, even if he awoke, he did not inquire. Fortunately, he worked hard and slept soundly.

Each year, on Jasper's birthday, Bishop Lapp would go to the house to ask if Rachel felt prepared to confess and return, and each year she politely denied him.

The fall after Jasper turned five, he started in the English school. Each morning, a yellow bus stopped and picked him up for kindergarten. Early April the following year, Mrs. Chesterfield died, and for a few days we wondered what would become of Rachel then. Josiah and I were at Maddie's bakery when we heard the news, that in her last will and testament, Mrs. Chesterfield noted she'd had a falling-out with her grown sons, who now lived in California, and she generously transferred ownership of her home and barn and all her land to my Rachel, not even her flesh and blood. This gift felt like a rebuke to me, her own mother, who had given her nothing. Even though *streng meidung* was our church's righteous sentence, and the Lord's will, I still felt the shame of it. Josiah said we could not be certain if Mrs. Chesterfield's gift were the work of the Lord or the devil, given Mrs. Chesterfield's atheism, but we never spoke of it afterward, thankful our daughter and her son had a home and barn to call their own.

One month later, I was outside on a warm, moonlit night following a rainstorm, near two in the morning. By then I'd simply been leaving an old milking stool out in the field, so I no longer needed to carry a chair with me. I sat down and breathed deeply of the delicious night air, which smelled of fresh rain, honeysuckle, and lilacs. All around me trilled crickets and other insects of the darkness. The trees had begun to leaf out, but I could still see Rachel's barn and the chimney of her house across the way. Between breaths, I heard the creak of a door opening on unoiled hinges, and I listened and stared intently toward the sound. I saw a flash of white, like a moth passing through candlelight, and I held my breath to listen: footsteps. Rachel wore a white blouse, her long hair down and gathered behind her. She paused to inspect her garden. She knelt there a moment, pulled at a few weeds, stood, and rubbed her hands together. As she grew closer, I could hear her voice, humming. An English hymn, "Amazing Grace." She kept walking to me, toward the hedgerow of overgrown honeysuckle, plum, and buckthorn, the trees further tangled by unruly wild-grape vines that spread in every direction. My heart pounding, I stood, my hands folded before my mouth as if in prayer.

Rachel walked along the hedgerow until she reached a narrow opening, a deer trail that led down to the river. I'd seen many deer use that pathway, after which they'd splash through the river and hike up the small hill, leap our fence, and wander into the pasture to graze. Rachel squeezed through the opening. At the edge of the river, which ran fast and high after the rain, Rachel stopped and looked up, her beautiful face lit from above by the moon behind my shoulders.

"Good evening, Mother," she said.

"Rachel!" I wanted to say so much more, so much! Ecstatic tears flooded my eyes, and I stood mute.

"Me and Jasper are well," Rachel said, seeming to know my questions before I asked. "God has provided all we need, and more. I drive a car now. I've taken a job in town during the day, when Jasper is in school."

"My dear Rachel," I said. "I love you. I have missed you so."

Rachel looked up the hill behind me, and I heard footsteps swishing through the field, growing louder, more purposeful than the cautious gait of a deer. I didn't need to look. I knew who it was.

I felt Josiah's hands on my shoulders, his chin on my head, his warm breath in my hair. We stood this way for some time, the insects and running river the only sound beyond our own breathing. Then, gently, Josiah turned me away from the river and led me slowly back toward the house, one heavy arm draped across my shoulders.

"Daddy," Rachel called out, softly. I could feel the catch in Josiah's breath, the pain in it, the warring in his own soul, but he did not break stride or turn to respond.

When we reached the porch, he took my hands in his. Josiah is my husband. As the Lord is the head of the church, he is the head of my body. I bowed my head to him, but my shoulders shook with sobbing, and I covered my face.

Josiah pulled my hands away, gently lifted my chin with his fingers. "What will you have me do, Hannah? It is *streng meidung*, you know this."

I sniffled and nodded. "But she is my only child!"

Josiah nodded. "And mine."

"And a daughter. It is not the same."

Josiah sat down on the top of the porch steps. "I'm not always asleep when you leave the bed," he said. I nodded. Married couples keep many small secrets silently, and for years, this had been one of ours. Josiah ran a hand through his beard and then rested it on one knee.

"Please, Josiah. Please."

Maybe if we'd been stronger, if we'd have acknowledged the vanity of earthly things, if we'd confirmed our trust in the Lord, all of what happened thereafter, including Rachel's suffering and death, might never have come.

"Hannah, no one can know," he said. He tipped his head toward my father's house, just across the yard. "No one can see. You must be more careful."

Happy tears filled my eyes. I crooked an arm behind his neck and pulled him to me. I kissed him hard on the lips, kissed him as a confident young woman might kiss her new husband on their wedden's night.

It was not a full life by any means, stealing a half hour with my daughter every few days, in the darkness of night or early morning, in the heat of summers and the cold of winters. Some nights, if Josiah was away and the river running low, Rachel would kick off her shoes and wade across to me, with Jasper on her shoulders, and my heart would sing as I held my beautiful grandson on my lap. Rachel and I would visit until Jasper grew tired or became too noisy, and then we'd hug, and she'd take him back across the river home.

Those were golden hours, lived in moonlight and under starlight. We were discreet, and when Jasper grew older, we were even more careful. Rachel would wait until he was sound asleep before making a visit. They were never enough, these stolen moments. Like small sips of cool water when thirsty, they only increased my desire to drain the cup.

The years passed. Jasper grew into a young man and I into a woman of middle age.

Then one warm March morning, in the gray light of early dawn, a few birds singing, Rachel and I stood on our respective banks of the river, and she told me she was once again with child.

What does a mother say at such times? I know that in the English world, among secular people, such a pregnancy does not bring shame. It is not even frowned upon. Rachel, I said. Why? Why? My heart must have opened and bled into my body, it ached so.

Rachel told me not to worry, that she knew the Lord was with her. How? I asked. How can you know this?

She smiled at me. Please, Mother. Let's speak of it no more. I wanted you to know so you wouldn't be surprised. I did not seek it, but it is what the Lord has given me to bear. I will carry this child with love.

Her womb grew fast. In five months, she looked ready to give birth. I'm so big, Rachel said, cradling her belly in her arms. Perhaps it's triplets! Lord, I prayed, do not let it be so. Please be with her. Carry her when her burden grows too great. Rachel gained so much weight she grew unrecognizable, wore long, billowing robes, went barefoot when no shoes would fit her swollen feet. The ninth month came, and six days running, she did not leave the house. I yearned for news. I sat in the pasture for hours watching, waiting. I begged Josiah to take me to her house in the buggy after dark.

I never saw Rachel alive again.

I know my grief must be a mere sliver of what Mary felt as she watched the Romans crucify her dear son, his flesh laid open by scourging, the sharp thorns pinned to the bone of his skull, spikes driven through hands and feet. Our Lord suffered unspeakable tortures, and his mother's suffering, well, we cannot imagine it. Yet when I think of Rachel's final hours, when I consider the agony she endured birthing Gabriel, my mind sometimes goes black. Were it not for the spirit of God and the strength of His grace, I might die of heartbreak. I am Rachel's mother. I should have been at her side.

To compound my loss, Rachel was denied an Amish burial. Josiah agreed to take me to the funeral, though he stayed in the buggy when I went inside. Jasper built his mother a plain pine box, the wood still

turpentine scented, unfinished, as is proper, and the box—covered—
rested on a table in a small, dark carpeted room nearly devoid of people.
Jasper was there, shoulder to shoulder beside the undertaker, wearing
an English suit and tie. It hurt to consider Rachel's body tended for
burial by a stranger, but in my calmer moments I reminded myself that
once the soul ascends to heaven, the body is a Godless shell anyway, a
husk of no consequence.

I stood alone. Rows of chairs had been arranged, nearly all of them
empty. One man sat near the casket on one side, in the second row:
the tavern owner, Mr. Walton. He'd been polite enough to remove
his baseball cap, which rested on the chair beside him. He'd been a
friend of Josiah's when they were schoolboys, and they were still on
friendly terms. The man on the other side, two rows back, looked
uncomfortable, like a farmer wearing his stiff, best clothes. When he
turned his head, I recognized him: Dr. Kennedy, the veterinarian.

The service was brief and forgettable. Afterward, Josiah did not ask
for details. He just raised the leather reins and let them fall, and we
began the slow trot home, the rhythmic clopping against blacktop a familiar comfort. Normally, Josiah and I talk or sing hymns when we're
riding in the buggy, but we remained silent. Halfway home, Josiah began
crying, and I put a hand on his knee. Then he said, "Weeping may linger
for a night, but joy comes in the morning," but he fell into weeping again
even before he finished speaking, so his words carried no confidence.

I confess that I had secretly hoped to see the child, this boy, Gabriel, everyone was speaking of. I'd heard he was delivered by the animal doctor with steel cables or a pulley of some kind, the way you'd
pull a calf from a cow. It was said he weighed twenty-five pounds and
was born with a thick head of black hair down to his shoulders, and
silvery eyes the color of a weathered zinc roof. Such a child cannot
exist, I thought to myself, a child of my own blood! I yearned to know
the truth, to hold him in my arms, but Josiah said it could well be like
cradling the devil.

No, I said. No. I whispered, "Josiah, you are mistaken."

4

Thomas Kennedy

A few days after Rachel's funeral, Thomas Kennedy drove out to check on how Jasper was managing. A recent rain had put down the dust on Jasper's driveway, and the chicory that grew between the wheel ruts plinked against the undercarriage of his truck as Thomas approached the barn. He found Jasper inside, the doors open to the sun. The barn smelled pleasantly of lanolin, manure, and hay.

Jasper nodded toward an apple crate propped against a weathered post that rose into the darkness above the beams, like the mast of a sailing ship. Pigeons cooed in the eaves, and an orange cat curled lazily beside the crate. Gabriel slept on his back, wrapped in a buffalo plaid flannel shirt, Jasper's Renk Seed baseball cap propped against his forehead to block the sun. One bare foot dangled over the edge of the crate just above the head of the sleeping cat.

"I keep him with me when I'm doing chores," Jasper said. "He's no more trouble than a bottle-fed lamb."

Thomas smiled. "Is he eating all right?"

"He weren't at first." Jasper shrugged. "Couple of Miss Charlotte's friends come by with baby formula and glass bottles, showed me how to boil them in a pot. They left a big bag of diapers. I ain't used no diapers as yet. Baby lambs get by fine without them. He didn't take to the formula. I gave it a taste, and I didn't like it neither."

"He has to eat, son."

"Oh, he's eating," Jasper said. He motioned for Thomas to follow him to a stall where a beautiful, white Saanen doe lay chewing her cud, waving at flies with large, almost translucent ears. Her swollen udder was the size of a basketball. She wore no ear tag, though Thomas could see the hole where it had been removed.

"Couple days after Gabriel come, I found this lady grazing in the yard, her sack so full she was dripping milk."

"That's a beautiful animal," Thomas said. He ran a hand over the doe's bony head. Hannah and Josiah Fisher raised Saanens, Alpines, and a few Toggenburgs. They had the most productive herd in the area, and the Saanen doe in Jasper's barn looked to be the best of the lot.

"I milk her morning and night, keep pitchers full in the refrigerator. Gabriel sucks it down so fast he barely stops for breath. The ladies didn't believe he'd take to it."

"Goat's milk has lots of good fats in it. Does Gabriel keep you up nights?"

Jasper shrugged. "I never been one to sleep much. I miss my mom. That part's harder than having a brother to care for."

"I'm so sorry," Thomas said.

The orange cat lurched and startled awake. From inside the crate two tiny fists floated like planets into the dust motes drifting across the broad beam of sunlight. The baby cried out, a sound like the mewing of a hungry kitten. Jasper lifted Gabriel from the crate and handed him to Thomas.

"He's wearing Mama's shirt," Jasper said. "He took to crying one night and wouldn't stop, but soon as I wrapped that shirt around him, he went right to sleep. I'll fetch his bottle."

Shading the baby's eyes from the sun, Thomas carried him outside and walked out to the vegetable garden that grew along the hill.

His left arm quivered under the weight of the boy, and he shifted the cooing child to one shoulder. A dozen tomato plants remained tied to stakes with baling twine along the north side of the garden, the few remaining tomatoes soft and rotting. Beside them, stretching toward the south, hills of winter squash and pumpkins grew, overrun by chickweed, crabgrass, and creeping charlie. Beyond the garden, Thomas came to an old fence line, a series of cedar posts now splintered and weathered gray, some nearly hollow, with pieces of rusted barbed wire sagging between them. Across the river, he could see the Fishers' bright white barn and house, and closer still, just over the tree line, their pasture, filled with grazing and dozing goats. He counted thirty-nine— twenty-seven white Saanens, the others mottled in white, brown, and black.

Jasper came from the house bearing a bottle of warm goat's milk, and Thomas returned to the yard and sat down, his back pressed up against the barn. He propped the baby's head inside the crook of his left elbow and lowered the bottle. As soon as the nipple touched his lips, the baby engulfed it all the way to the plastic cap and began suckling noisily. Thomas smiled down at him.

At first, Thomas concocted reasons to alter his route to ensure he'd pass Jasper's farm on the way home from work every few days, but eventually he ended the pretense of being in the neighborhood and simply asked if he'd be welcome to stop by on occasion to hold the baby and give him a bottle. Jasper gratefully agreed. Each Friday thereafter, Thomas stopped at Shaken, Not Stirred to purchase two orders of the Friday Fish Plate: three filets of perch fried in beer batter, French fries, coleslaw, and two slices of buttered rye bread. He and Jasper would eat, sometimes outside in the barn, sometimes inside, while Thomas held Gabriel. And each week, Gabriel seemed substantially larger than he'd been the week before. Thomas had never raised children of his own, so had no measure by which to judge this growth. He tried not to overreact. Gabriel's birth weight was eighteen pounds, after all. Still, in December, he suggested that

Jasper take Gabriel to the free clinic in Oxford to let a doctor look him over. The boy had not yet had a full medical examination. Jasper had already refused to have his brother immunized against childhood diseases since Jasper himself had never been vaccinated, but Thomas didn't think Jasper would mind a well-baby check. When asked about this possibility, Jasper politely declined.

"No sense going to the doctor if there ain't nothing wrong with you," he said. "I have never been to a doctor once in my life, and I'm strong as a mule."

Gabriel kept drinking goat's milk, and then moved on to finely ground garden vegetables and bananas. Then fish and potatoes in all manner of being cooked, baked, mashed, and fried, then lamb and beef. He crawled at four months, stood at five, and by eight months had taught himself to walk by holding on to a small doeling in the barn, leaning a hip into her like a sailor on shore leave being escorted back to his ship.

In September, on Gabriel's first birthday, Thomas ordered a cake and brought it to Jasper's house. Gabriel devoured two huge pieces, squeezing the frosting between his fingers. Afterward, they went out to the barn, where he could play with the baby animals. Jasper had erected a baby swing along one of the beams. Above the seat of the swing, Thomas looped a piece of rope around the beam and hung his scale on it, then briefly attached Gabriel's swing, with the toddler inside, to the scale. At age one, Gabriel Fisher weighed thirty-four pounds and stood forty-one inches tall.

It was not only Gabriel's unusual size that dazzled Thomas, but also his unusual way with animals. As a three-year-old boy, Gabriel would often sit on a milking stool beside Jasper's chicken coop with a piece of bread hidden behind his back. He'd wait, watching the chickens scratch in the yard until his favorite hen, a barred rock named Betsy, eased her way close to his feet, and then he'd reveal the bread with a flourish. The other hens would race toward him, but Betsy would immediately hop on his lap and peck at the bread until she'd eaten it all. Afterward, Gabriel would cuddle her while he napped in the afternoon sunshine, and she'd turn her beak into the hollow under his armpit and fall asleep. Sometimes, the other hens would inspect them, and two or even three others would hop, fluttering, onto Gabriel's knees to roost. A year later, when Gabriel learned to ride a small bicycle, Betsy perched on the handlebars, her feathers rustling in the wind as the boy coasted down the driveway with his gangly legs spread for balance, like the outriggers of a canoe.

Wild or domesticated, it didn't matter, Thomas noticed, animals seemed soothed by Gabriel's presence. Skittish barn kittens ran to him and purred as he gripped them tenderly, their legs and tails dangling from his pudgy hands. The most nervous sheep allowed him to lie with them as they rested, chewing their grass-scented cuds, Gabriel's unkempt curls tangled in their lustrous wool. If he cupped a few golden kernels of cracked corn in his palm, pigeons would flutter down from the silo and perch on his fingers to eat it.

Seeing Gabriel's love of animals reminded Thomas of his own childhood. As a boy he'd carried bird eggs home in his upturned baseball cap, hoping to coax them into hatching by placing them under his bed near the heat register. He brought home many wild animals as well: baby squirrels, a baby opossum, once a young screech owl with a broken wing. He'd had some success domesticating the opossum, named Virginia Woolf. (His mother was an English professor, so she inevitably christened his pets with literary names.) Virginia might have stayed forever, so fond did she become of hot dogs, bologna, and leftovers from Thomas's supper plate. Even after a bath, Virginia was never a beauty—an angora rat, Thomas's father called her. When she grew too large, and her poop started stinking up the basement, his parents decided it was time for Virginia to go back into the wild. Thomas cried when he let her go, watching her waddle away through the leaf litter, her scaly pink tail trailing her like a long hair ribbon, his sadness tempered by her obvious joy in being at liberty.

Ophelia the owl never recovered from her broken wing but lived two years in an ornate, gilded cage propped on the antique Victrola in the corner of the den. To one side of the cage a large window faced west, and through it the falling sun would pour in the late afternoons. To the other side were the bookcases that held his mother's library: one case filled top to bottom with Library of America volumes; another, her Complete Novels of Jane Austen; others, works of English and American literature, continental writers, women poets. Sometimes, when suffering from insomnia, which she struggled with most of her life, Thomas's mother would come downstairs at two or three in the morning. She'd turn on the wall sconce above the overstuffed leather reading chair beside the Victrola, and she would read aloud to the owl in a soft whisper.

The summer Gabriel turned five, Thomas asked Jasper to allow the boy to accompany him on weekend veterinary calls, and Jasper readily consented. Thomas had come to treasure the energetic child's company, and while it was certainly true that he wanted to spend more time with Gabriel, he also believed Jasper needed more time to himself. Jasper had earnestly attended to his responsibilities raising Gabriel with a selflessness rare even in older men. He never missed a feeding or a milking; the water founts in the barn and chicken coop never ran dry; Gabriel didn't lack for clean, well-mended clothing or decent shoes, the latter of which he outgrew every few months. Thomas helped when he could, bringing groceries with each visit, taking Gabriel for new shoes and clothes, always careful to avoid offending Jasper's pride.

As Gabriel accompanied Thomas on those veterinary calls, even people in communities far beyond Lakota got to meet the boy. Few asked how old he was, though Thomas could tell when Gabriel's voice and behavior did not square with their internal assessment of his age. They'd look at him, puzzled, and scratch their heads. If they said, "It's sure nice you've got a grandson to assist you," Thomas would say, "Thank you, he's like a grandson to me, it's true." If they asked outright who the boy was, he would tell them: This is Rachel Fisher's son, Gabriel. Amish farmers and many non-Amish who lived near Lakota knew of Rachel Fisher and her terrible death birthing the child, but unless they asked, they rarely believed Gabriel could be that child, given his size.

Eventually, and particularly once summer baseball season arrived, and Gabriel began hitting home runs in T-ball that often flew so far off the field we couldn't find the ball, word got around that Rachel Fisher's orphan son was assisting the veterinarian on his calls, and that he was the biggest five-year-old anyone had ever seen.

5

Billy Walton

As Gabriel grew, speculation about his paternity grew as well. The first time around, when Rachel had Jasper, we figured she was raped by the young punk who brought her into my place, but there was no knowing for sure. Gabriel's birth set everyone's tongues wagging again. The boy's size led most people to focus their attention on the two largest men everyone knew. The first was Zack Foster, who drove a milk truck for Sunrise Dairy. Zack knew every dairy farmer in the tricounty area, and at six foot four and over 360 pounds, he was one of the most imposing men in town, and by far the most famous. The pride of Westfield, Wisconsin, in his prime, Zack had played offensive guard for two years at Western Michigan before blowing out his knee against Ball State. He dropped out of school, married a local girl, and started driving the milk truck.

Though no longer an athletic legend, Zack still had a Paul Bunyan—esque quality about him. One summer day a year ago, I watched him chug three ice-cold mugs of Budweiser in under two minutes, belch, lay a ten-spot on the bar, and head back out to his truck to finish his route. Not only was Zack large, but the timing seemed right, too. About a year before Gabriel's birth, Zack's wife ran off with the UPS man (yes, it happens; she shopped a lot online, resulting some weeks in almost daily deliveries). But Zack Foster, available, about the same age, and still good-enough-looking, despite his girth, to attract a woman of Rachel's beauty, had an alibi. Drunk one night at my place, and aware of the rumors, he declared that as much as he would have enjoyed a trip down Rachel Fisher's drawers, he'd never even spoken to the woman. Besides, even if he'd made the trip, he could not finish the job because he'd had a vasectomy at age twenty-six. He shot blanks, he said, and would gladly produce a photocopy of his medical records to shut everybody the hell up. That ended our speculation.

The other local contender for Gabriel's paternity, based solely upon his size, was Oliver Edwards, a turkey farmer who lived with his elderly mother in a double-wide at the end of County Y. Close to being a hermit, Oliver kept a rusted steel cable strung across posts on each side of his gravel driveway and was seen only occasionally in town, driving a 1950s-era Ford pickup. Oliver's mother rarely left their trailer but sometimes could be spotted out in her housecoat with a small dog, tending flower beds of colorful zinnias that bordered both sides of the driveway in summer. No one really believed Oliver could have been the father of Gabriel Fisher. He could barely look you in the eye let alone talk to you. Few people had even heard him speak. But he was the tallest man in the county—at least for the time being—and that kept the speculation alive in the minds of some.

A few people half-heartedly suggested the new veterinarian might be Gabriel's biological father, but no one really believed that. Human nature being what it is, some folks resented the fact that an outsider had become so important in Jasper and Gabriel's life, and they tried to bring him down a notch by suggesting he'd forced himself on Rachel during one of his visits to her farm. Doc Kennedy did spend some time at Jasper's place both before and after Rachel died, but there's no way that guy would force himself on a woman. I've spent my adult life around people, looking into their eyes when they have the truth serum of alcohol in their systems and when they don't, and while I have seen sadness in the eyes of Doc Kennedy, I have also seen kindness and care, a father's love for both Jasper and Gabriel, yes, but in name only.

I wasn't much of a father to my own kids. I regret that now, though I'm not going to cry in my beer about it. When I finally dried out enough to get some visitation, it felt more like an invasion by two surly strangers every other weekend. They watched TV and played a lot of video games, and then Sunday night I drove them home, to two different homes as they came from two different ex-wives. To be truthful, when the kids finally told me they just wanted to live with their mothers, I felt relieved. Pull the Band-Aid off fast and be done with it, I guess is how I felt, though these days they live so far away I never see them at all. Get a five-minute phone call on Christmas, and that's about it.

Maybe to make up for that, maybe not, I don't know, I sponsor T-ball and Little League baseball teams every summer. Billy's Bombers, we call ourselves, and I comanage with my buddy, Charlie Mayfield. It's a hell of a lot of fun, and it gets me out of the tavern and into the sunshine. I was a decent ballplayer as a kid, and I don't think I'll ever get the game out of my system.

Every spring we hold Little League and T-ball sign-up day at Mecan Springs County Park, and one fine, sunny Saturday it was Doc Kennedy himself who showed up hand in hand with Gabriel Fisher, the April before the boy started kindergarten. I was at a table taking checks, and when they got to the front, I didn't recognize the boy at first, because of course he'd grown. "Little League or T-ball?" I asked, expecting the former, given the boy's size. He stood just a few inches shorter than Doc Kennedy. "T-ball," Doc said. I looked up and realized I was looking at Gabriel and not some twelve-or thirteen-year-old.

"How tall is Gabriel now?" I asked, quietly.

"Five foot six," Doc Kennedy answered.

"Yes." I searched my pile of Billy's Bombers T-shirts for a kid's XXXL, but the largest I had was XL. I gave him the XL but promised we'd have a larger shirt made (Gabriel ended up in a men's small). I would also have to customize a tee, raising it two feet. Though at first the T-ball league allowed Gabriel to use an aluminum bat appropriate for someone his size, he hit the ball so hard in his second at bat—a line drive that broke the arm of the little boy playing first base—that he was restricted to T-ball bats thereafter. A T-ball bat looked like a hammer handle in his large hands. Even so, whenever Gabriel batted, coaches from the opposing team instructed all their infielders to join their brethren in the outfield to avoid possible injury.

That first summer, Gabriel hit .820 for Billy's Bombers championship T-ball team, including thirty-two home runs, three of which went so far into the thicket of hedgerow beyond the field that the balls were never recovered. But that was nothing compared to what was to come.

6

Hannah Fisher

In time, my affliction taught me this: in slow, almost imperceptible increments, as winter darkness gradually gives way to spring, debilitating grief passes. How this happens, I cannot say.

Though long in my troubles, I did not face them alone. Josiah carried me with his love. Abiah visited often. Meg wrote to me every week, her beautiful letters guiding me to scripture and to hope. But most wondrously, my own mother came back to me in an unexpected way. Though she'd been with the Lord for many years, she'd left that book of poems. This poet, Miss Dickinson, probably did not have any children. She did not write of any, in the event. But she felt grief and loneliness, and the pleasures and pain of a contemplative soul. She knew God, too, but in a quarrelsome way. She seemed above all a wanderer, mapping the soul's wilderness for those who might arrive later, lost and in despair.

Turning the soiled, dog-eared pages of that book was like feeling my mother's rough hands in mine. Those pages contained grease and dirt from her dear fingers, of course, but even more meaningfully, notes, messages, as I liked to think of them, written in the margins, in Mother's neat, tiny script. The ink had dried brown on the paper, and her German spelling took liberties, but even the tiniest letters were legible.

Down the right margin beside the poem, "After great pain, a formal feeling comes," for example, Mother had written: *prellungen vergilbten, kalte kuche, Herz in dünnem Eis eingefroren, Christus sei mit mir.* By which I believe she meant, "yellowed bruises, cold kitchen, heart squeezed by skim ice, Christ be with me." Beneath another, short Dickinson verse, "I lived on dread," Mother wrote, simply, *hilflos, gehorsam, verdammt*: "helpless, obedient, damned."

But she found joy in the hidden book, too. She dated her note beneath one poem, two months before my birth:

"Hope" is the thing with feathers—That perches in the soul—And sings the tune without the words—And never stops at all—
And sweetest—in the Gale—is heard—And sore must be the storm—
That could abash the little Bird
That kept so many warm—

January, 1963. Hannah Treten—Gott, der in meiner Seele singt: "Hannah kicking—God is singing in my soul."

For a time, we hoped that Jasper might come to church services, bringing Gabriel with him, but we understood from others he had vowed never to speak to us or be in our company. We were blood relations, and yet we had joined in Rachel's *streng meidung*. If the Lord's ways are difficult for believers to understand, they are well-nigh impossible to grasp for souls trapped in atheism. Though I understood his reasons, it pained me Jasper would not consent to be in my company, and it hurt even more to have Gabriel beyond reach of my arms.

When warm spring winds blew from the south, we heard Gabriel's bright laughter blowing across the river, rising with the crowing of roosters and the bleating of sheep. Like all young children, he had such energy! I could see him gamboling about like a goat kid, often with a stick in his hand, running with the lambs and chickens. As a toddler, he often ran naked, the bright, uninterrupted white of his skin glowing in the sunshine. His hair grew long and curly, a floppy mop, like the crest of a Polish hen.

Years passed, and he grew fast. In his fifth summer, he stood nearly as tall as Jasper.

That summer, a strange car came up the drive. Mr. Walton, the barkeep, came calling. As many know, we do not seek the company of English people. Second Corinthians is our guide in this matter: "Come out from among them and be ye separate, saith the Lord." Yet we do not rudely reject visitors to our home. We invited him in. He took off his baseball cap, hung it on our coat-tree, and sat down in the kitchen. I offered him pie, wild blueberry. He looked like so many English men his age: skinny legs, a belly round as a chamber pot, a thin patch of graying hair above his ears. Like most English, he wore bright-colored running shoes, blue and yellow, with white laces, though he probably had not run anywhere in decades. He had a pack of cigarettes in the front pocket of his shirt, and he smelled like tobacco.

In time, as he and Josiah reminisced about their schoolboy days, it did not seem quite so strange. He ate his pie, drank some water, and then sat back in his chair.

"That was delicious," he said, sliding his plate a couple inches from the edge of the table. "Thank you." He turned toward Josiah. "Josiah," he said. "You have to see the boy play."

Josiah raised his hand to keep Mr. Walton from saying more. "I've heard."

"What have you heard?"

"He's got a beautiful swing, natural power."

"What boy?" I asked. I didn't know, as yet, they were speaking of Gabriel. That such things matter to men—who can lift the heaviest barn beam, who can run the fastest, who can hit a baseball the farthest—I've long known. It is among the mysterious passions of men I have never understood. We play volleyball and sometimes other games of skill at community gatherings, but for fun, to laugh and enjoy fellowship. It is difficult to live with humility while trying your best to defeat someone.

"Josiah, hear me out," Mr. Walton said. "Gabriel's not even five years old, and he's hitting a baseball two hundred feet. *Two hundred feet!* Off a tee! My next best player, on a good day, hits eighty, maybe ninety. The home-run snow fence is one hundred feet out. When Gabriel makes good contact, the ball is still going up when it clears."

"Gabriel's big for his age," Josiah said, though I could see the subtle quiver of his lips as he worked to contain a prideful smile.

Mr. Walton nodded. "Kid's a monster, that's true. But I've never seen his level of hand-eye coordination even in high school ball players. And bat speed! He's an athletic freak, Josiah."

Josiah stood up from his chair, bringing the conversation to a close. "I'm glad you're coaching Gabriel," he said. "I'm pleased he's doing well."

Mr. Walton pulled a piece of paper from his back pocket, unfolded it. "Here's our schedule for the rest of the summer. T-ball games are on the Lions Club fields over in Neshkoro, just a few miles from here. Come see Gabriel play. I mean it. Kid's amazing."

"We'll consider it."

Josiah put the schedule in the kitchen drawer and never asked me if I wanted to see Gabriel play. I suppose he didn't believe I would be interested. I should have asked him to take me. It is not good for husbands and wives to carry too many unspoken thoughts. They have no shape or weight, and yet over time, they can grow into something solid, something unseen that stands between you.

In early August, Josiah had to be away. He was putting a new porch on an English house in Wild Rose, and he wanted to finish in three days, so they were sleeping on site.

As it happened, Gabriel had a game scheduled while Josiah was away, so I arranged for Abiah to come for me in her buggy. We ate an early dinner and left for Neshkoro on a Friday afternoon at five o'clock. Abiah could handle a horse and buggy. She was sturdy, with broad shoulders, muscular hands, and a loud, boisterous laugh. Many Amish women have strong hands from kneading bread dough every week, but Abiah also milked cows and tended her family's draft horses. Every spring she turned the soil in her vegetable garden behind a horse-drawn plow she guided herself.

We visited during the journey, talked and laughed together as if starved for conversation. The buggy wheels rumbled along the pavement amid the steady, rhythmic clopping of Abiah's horse, Lily. Because she lived near Maddie Hershberger's bakery, where gossip changed hands along with baked goods, Abiah often knew other people's business and liked to share it in the right company. It would probably surprise the English to know we Amish gossip as much as any other people, though we probably feel more guilty about it afterward.

We arrived at the baseball field a few minutes after the game started. Gabriel's team, sponsored by Mr. Walton's tavern, was called Billy's Bombers. They wore red shirts with their last names and the logo of Mr. Walton's bar—a tall, slightly tipped martini glass—on their backs, and "Billy's Bombers" spelled out on the front. It was not difficult to find Gabriel on the field. He looked like an ostrich who had wandered into a flock of sparrows.

Abiah and I watched from the parking lot in the buggy. She spread a few flakes of hay and a handful of oats in front of Lily to keep her contented. Many English sat in the bleachers watching, shading their eyes from the falling sun, but I did not see Jasper. I saw Mr. Walton, and I heard his booming voice, too. Some of the English turned around to stare at us. I can't know for certain, but it may have been the first time they had seen Amish women at an English baseball game. They might have thought we'd gotten ourselves lost and were looking for directions.

"What is the purpose here?" Abiah asked me.

"I'm not sure," I said. "I think the goal is to hit the ball as far as possible."

Abiah frowned. "A puzzling game."

"It appears so."

When it was Gabriel's turn to bat, Mr. Walton came onto the field to place a plastic waste can under the tee, which raised the ball up higher, though not quite to Gabriel's waist. While Mr. Walton did this, all the children on the other team—even the ones sitting on the ground not paying attention—ran out into the grass to line up along a distant fence made of narrow, red lath wood. They stood with their backs along this fence. Some of them put their baseball gloves on top of their heads. Others crouched and covered their heads with their hands.

"Gabriel is a fine-looking boy," Abiah said. "He has Rachel's curly hair."

I could see Rachel in his face, too, his cheekbones, the gentle curve of his chin. I stared at him, enthralled.

"And so tall!" Abiah said, elbowing me in the shoulder.

When Gabriel struck the ball, it left the tee and rose into the sun so quickly I lost sight of it. The children scattered, screaming, but the ball passed thirty or forty feet above their heads. Gabriel, meanwhile, ran in a perfect square around the sandy part of the field, touching each of the white pads before arriving back at the tee, where all the children on his team, most of whom stood only slightly taller than his belly button, waited to jump on him. Gabriel greeted this jumping with a broad smile, and when he smiled, I could see my Rachel so clearly in his face I had to swallow my tears.

Josiah did not return home until late Saturday night, tired and dirty, sawdust clinging to his hair and shirt. I boiled water for him, and he washed up and went to bed. I considered telling him about Gabriel's baseball game, but I didn't, and thereafter, though it troubled me, I decided not to bring it up. Perhaps I feared his chastisement. At Sunday gathering, I pulled Abiah aside and whispered that I wished to keep our trip between us. She smiled and pretended to button her lip closed.

I spoke to Gabriel for the first time the following spring, when he was six years old. It was a cool April morning, the pastures and gardens muddy from snowmelt and rain. Canadian geese had been passing north for several weeks by then, resting in melt ponds for the night, the bright alto of their voices a joyful song day and night. Seven of my does had lambed earlier in the month, including my lovely Alpine, Magdalene, who birthed twins on April ninth with no assistance. She was *cou blanc*, white head and shoulders with charcoal hindquarters, and large for an Alpine, nearly as big as Rebecca and Delilah, my queenly Saanens, who slept like snow drifts on the highest mounds in the pasture.

Magdalene was the most contented goat I'd ever owned. She never rushed for feed when I came with oats as the others did. She waited, sidling up beside me when the others had eaten and run off, rewarded for her patience with her own oats and a surprise from my apron pocket, a cube of sugar. She'd been born prematurely during a blizzard and nearly died. I took her into the house, started her on warm sugar water, then bottle-fed her every two hours. She slept on a rug near the woodstove until she could walk, and I swept up her droppings, tiny as morning glory seeds.

On April twenty-fifth, when they were less than three weeks old, one of Magdalene's kids died. I found her on her side in the early morning, stiff and dusted with frost. Magdalene licked her body, nudged her with her nose. Her other kid looked frail, too, and seemed unable to suckle. When I reached under Magdalene to start the milk, I discovered her udder hot and swollen on both sides, oozing corruption. Mastitis, I suspected. I felt terrible for missing the early signs, weakening lambs, a mother hesitant to nurse.

I isolated her in a sunny stall in the barn and treated the infection earnestly. Five times a day I applied warm compresses, and I massaged her udder with sweet peppermint oil morning and evening. But she did not improve. I began to bottle-feed her surviving kid. In two days, Magdalene grew too weak to stand, her breathing labored. Josiah saw me fretting. He knew she was my favorite doe. In his kindness, he called the English animal doctor.

When Dr. Kennedy arrived, Gabriel was with him.

"Hello, Mrs. Fisher," Dr. Kennedy said. "Gabriel is my assistant. He helps me out on Saturdays and during the summers. I hope you don't mind that I brought him along."

Gabriel smiled at me, his eyes squinting nearly closed. Girls often favor their fathers and boys their mothers, I know this. Gabriel's dark eyes, the sprinkle of freckles across his nose, even the way he stood with one hip jutted to the side, reminded me so much of Rachel, I found myself unable to speak.

"I'm so sorry," Dr. Kennedy said. "This was insensitive of me. I can come back alone this afternoon."

"No," I said, finding my voice. "No, of course not. I'm rude to be staring."

Dr. Kennedy nodded and smiled. He'd tended to my animals on two prior occasions, but I'd never noticed his kind face, his gentle eyes. The backs of his hands were mottled brown by long exposure to the sun. I led them to Magdalene's stall. Gabriel handed the satchel to the doctor and knelt before Magdalene with a leg on each side of her neck. He put his forehead gently against hers and rubbed his dirty hands along her face, over and over, and she allowed this, though all her life she'd feared strangers.

"Are you feeling bad, girl?" Gabriel said, his voice high and sweet. My heart shifted in my chest; it was as if Rachel herself had been speaking.

By this time, the corruption from Magdalene's udder was thick and bloodied. Dr. Kennedy palpated her. "How long has she been this way?" he asked.

"Three days."

He gently squeezed each side of Magdalene's udder, and she kicked her rear leg in the straw. The doctor sat back on his heels and sighed, frowning.

"If this were a severe case of mastitis, we could cup her teats with an infusion of antibiotics, and I could inject her, and she might recover," he said. "But Mrs. Fisher, I'm sorry. I'll have to do a lab test to confirm it, but I've seen enough cases to know that your doe has what is called 'hard bag,' or CAE, caprine arthritic encephalitis. It's fancy words for a terrible viral infection, this one untreatable, I'm afraid."

"You can't help her?"

"I can't cure her, no," he answered. "It's contagious, too. You don't want to expose the rest of your herd. You'll want to isolate her surviving kid." He ran a hand gently over Magdalene's hip bone, where the hair had been warmed by the sun. "I'm so sorry. She's a beautiful animal."

"Bottle-fed," I told him. "The first weeks of life she lived in my kitchen."

Dr. Kennedy smiled. "She's had the best of care since birth, then," he said.

"I missed this infection," I said. I fought tears, ashamed.

"Don't blame yourself," he said. "It wouldn't have made a difference. She's resting in sunshine on clean bedding. Anyone can see this goat is loved and well-tended."

"You're kind."

He stood up and removed the blue rubber gloves, turning each inside out as he peeled it from his hand, then sealing them inside a clear plastic bag.

"She will die," I said.

He nodded. "I can inject her with barbiturates to spare her further suffering. I could leave the syringe with you, if you'd like. I can see she is important to you."

"What will happen?"

"She'll fall asleep and stop breathing. It's painless."

"Yes," I said. "If you can show me how."

The doctor filled a syringe with the medicine, the needle covered by a plastic cap, and showed me the place along Magdalene's hock where I should give the injection. "Practice on an orange or apple if you'd like. A single, quick motion." He demonstrated this. "The needle is sharp, but goat skin is tough, so be firm. When the needle is all the way in, slowly depress the plunger until it's empty, and then remove it."

I put the syringe in my apron pocket and walked Gabriel and the doctor to his truck. Sunlight shone on Gabriel's hair, and when the wind blew through it, it moved like a thick field of alfalfa in purple bloom. I asked Dr. Kennedy what we owed him, but he said he would not charge anything to euthanize a goat. I thanked him for his kindness and wished him God's blessing.

Gabriel put the doctor's satchel inside the truck, then came to me. He stood looking into my face. Though not quite six years old, he stood two or three inches taller than I did. "I'm sad your goat is sick," he said in his girl's voice, and then before I could say anything in return, he closed the distance between us and embraced me. He put his long arms around my shoulders, pulled me gently to him. I smelled the sweet boy-sweat along his neck, the scent of barn animals, lanolin, and hay along the shoulders of his sweatshirt. I put my hands on the small of his back, felt the gentle, rolling necklace of his spine under my fingers. He released me and stepped back.

"Thank you, Gabriel," I said.

I went into the barn, pulled the syringe from my pocket, and did as Dr. Kennedy had instructed me. I sat in the straw with Magdalene until her breathing stopped. I spent the next hour digging in one corner of the muddy pasture nearest the river. The mud stuck to my shovel like pudding on a spoon, and I was covered in it by the time I finished. In a sled, I pulled Magdalene out of the barn. A light rain began falling as I covered her. I would miss her dearly, but I thought only of Gabriel, the smell of his body, the song of his voice, the feel of his long arms around me. His grandmother.

7

Billy Walton

When we traveled to tournaments, rival coaches demanded proof of Gabriel's age, so I began carrying a photocopy of Gabriel's birth certificate. I kept it folded up in a plastic bag in the glove box of my car. They'd look down at the birth certificate, then at Gabriel, then at the certificate again before shaking their heads and wandering off.

Gabriel moved up to the minor league division at age six, though most of the players in that division were between seven and eleven. Nonetheless, he continued to dominate. By age seven he was deemed too dangerous to opposing players to continue playing in that division. He was just shy of six feet tall then, with size fourteen feet. I had trouble finding baseball cleats that fit him. But, of course, he was just a kid, too, and he cried when he skinned his knee just like other children his age.

The incident that got Gabriel banned from the minor league division occurred in our seventh game of the season. In his first at bat, Gabriel hit a blistering drive down the third base line that was caught for an out by the third baseman, a talented eight-year-old named Johnny Polkowski, who also happened to be the coach's son. The ball jumped off Gabriel's bat with such explosive force and reached the third baseman—sixty feet away—so quickly, most people were astonished Johnny had been able to see the ball at all, not to mention catch it. The crisp snap of the baseball popping leather sounded like a clap of thunder, and Johnny dropped his glove and started screaming.

His left hand looked like someone had placed it on an anvil and struck it with a hammer. A shard of bone had torn through the skin, and blood surged through the wound. Johnny's father wrapped the hand in a roll of toilet tissue that immediately went red and pulpy, and his mother drove him to the emergency room. Gabriel's line drive had broken four bones in Johnny's glove hand. Poor kid needed three hours of surgery, a metal plate, and five screws.

While coaches were tending to Johnny on the field, parents from the other team mutinied, demanding that Gabriel be banned from play. Two loudmouths led the charge, and they worked the other parents into a lather, some of them even pointing at Gabriel, who sat on our bench in tears. Kid was seven years old, and crazed parents in the stands behind home plate were calling him the Antichrist. It took all my self-control, not to mention the strength in Charlie Mayfield's arms, to keep me from blowing my top and running up into the stands to shut them up.

Coach Polkowski approached the backstop and raised his arms, calmly insisting that Gabriel had a right to play. He pointed out that Gabriel was the youngest player on the field, clearly still a small boy emotionally despite his size and power. He'd seen the boy's birth certificate with his own eyes. Baseball could be a dangerous sport; everyone knew this. Little League Baseball had established strict guidelines regarding age requirements, the distance from the pitcher's mound to home plate, and the distance between base paths to ensure safety for players in all age ranges. None of those rules were being violated. "So let's play ball," he said.

But then the loudest father stood up again. He had a full beard and a beer belly larger than mine. "I don't give a rat's ass about the rules," he shouted. "That kid is too fucking big to play baseball against our boys."

The chorus began again: "He's going to kill somebody."

"How do we know that birth certificate isn't forged?"

One by one, mothers and fathers came down onto the field, took their children by the shoulders, and walked them beyond the foul lines toward plastic coolers full of soda and Popsicles that awaited the end of the game.

Dave Polkowski met me and Charlie at home plate. "Looks like we're going to forfeit, Coach," he said.

I shook my head. "The kid's seven years old, goddammit. He and his brother are poor as the dirt under your fingernails. This is all Gabriel's got, you understand? I'm not going to let a bunch of whiny pricks ruin it for him. I'll sue their asses."

Charlie put a hand on my elbow. "Billy, come on," he said. "You're not suing anybody."

"What about putting him in major league?" Dave asked. "My oldest boy is twelve and I coach that team, too. Gabriel's already better than any hitter that I've got."

"Some shavers in major throw seventy or seventy-five," I said. "They ain't supposed to but some of them can throw a nasty hook already, too. I don't want the kid to lose his confidence. Besides, it's too late for me to put together a team."

"He can play for me."

"His brother can't get him to the games. I pick him up now and drop him back off, but I run a business, so I can't just take off in the afternoons to be a taxi service, either."

"Come on, Billy," Charlie said. "You know this is what he needs. Let him go." He looked at Dave. "I'm retired," he said. "I can get him to the games and practices."

Maybe I was being selfish wanting to keep Gabriel to myself. I'd been playing or coaching baseball for forty-five years, yet it was like I'd been looking at stick-figure finger paintings all my life, and suddenly I was standing in front of a Michelangelo. Of course I wanted to keep the boy close. I let him go, but it wasn't easy.

When I dropped Gabriel off at Jasper's farm that night, I walked Gabriel inside. Jasper sat at the kitchen table in the dark, a half dozen empty beer cans splayed in a half circle around his plate. He'd been drinking more often in my tavern in the evenings, too. Young guy like that, twenty-five, twenty-six years old, works hard all day, a few beers at night isn't going to kill him.

Gabriel turned on the lights, and Jasper squinted at us in the brightness. I explained what happened, told him Gabriel needed to play in a higher league. He asked for a cigarette, and I lit one for him. "Jasper," I said, "your brother is gifted. Even though he'll be the youngest player on the field, he'll be bigger than most other players, and far more skilled."

Jasper belched when I finished talking. He looked at Gabriel.

"That what you want to do, Gabe?" he asked. "Play baseball with the big boys?"

Gabriel nodded.

Jasper clapped his hands slowly, once, twice. He was drunk. "Doc tells me you can talk to the animals, too," Jasper said, slowly. "Gabe Fisher, the wonder boy."

"Jasper, knock it off," I said.

"Long as he gets his chores done around here, he can play whatever he wants."

Jasper took a deep drag on his cigarette and blew the smoke up in the air. It swirled under the light over the table and disappeared. "Gabriel," he said, "take a flashlight and go water them sheep. Check for eggs in the coop, too."

"Okay," Gabriel said. He grabbed a flashlight from a drawer and ran outside, still wearing his baseball cleats.

"I had a visitor today," Jasper said. "A man from the county, a tax assessor. You know what he said? I'm behind on my taxes. Said he'd put me on a payment plan. If I don't pay, at some point the sheriff will come out here and put a lock on the door, and they'll put the place up for auction."

"Jasper, I'm sorry," I said.

"Don't quite know how I'll be able to do it." Jasper forced a laugh. "I'm already paying installments on the electric bill."

"Everything seems worse at night," I said. "In the morning things won't seem so bad. I've been down in that hole a couple of times. You just get a shovel and, little by little, dig your way back out."

"Been digging my whole life," Jasper said.

"So maybe you take a part-time job in town to make ends meet. It's not the end of the world."

"No, guess not," he said. He stubbed the cigarette out in the center of his dinner plate, an old piece of cream-colored china with several chips around the rim.

Gabriel came in with a basket of brown eggs and began rinsing them clean in the kitchen sink. I wished them both well and left for home.

Couple weeks later I saw Jasper in my place again, throwing darts, drinking tap beers one after the other. He came in around ten, probably after he'd put Gabriel to bed. He had sawdust in his hair along the sides of his greasy ball cap and sawdust on the shoulders of his soiled sweatshirt. He thanked me for watching out for Gabriel and apologized for his behavior that night; said a drunken man is rarely good company. I told him no worries, I'd been drunk often enough to know that was true. He also told me he'd taken my advice and gotten a job off the farm. Where? I inquired. Just across the river, he said. Absalom's sawmill.

"Your grandfather's place," I said.

"That's right," Jasper said.

I wondered about the wisdom of this choice. Just about anyone who knew old Yoder would tell you the same thing: If you looked up "mean, low-down son of a bitch" in the dictionary, you'd find his picture there.

"Absalom makes some beautiful lumber," I said, trying to be generous, for Jasper's sake.

Jasper shrugged. "He's an asshole, but he pays in cash," he said. "You know what he calls me? RB. It's always RB this, RB that. I finally asked him, what is it you're calling me? He said, 'RB? Son, that's short for Rachel's Bastard.'"

My anger, always quick to boil, rose up over the pot. "Don't let that prick get you down," I said. "Anybody will tell you, compared to Absalom Yoder, a cow's flappy asshole smells like honey."

Jasper laughed. "Hadn't heard that one," he said. "It don't bother me none. My mom was one of the most perfect people God ever made, and if the name he wants to call me puts me and her together, I'm good with that."

I got to see Gabriel Fisher's first game playing for the Coloma Cardinals in the boys major league division. They were playing in Neshkoro against the Lakota Ducks, our local major league team. On the mound for Lakota that night was a twelve-year-old pitcher named Dominic Quartullo, a heavily muscled kid who threw hard. He'd already received a couple letters from college scouts, and his older brother, Damon, pitched for Florida State on a scholarship. Dominic had a seventy-five-mile-per-hour fastball and was averaging sixteen strikeouts and four wild pitches per game. He was just wild enough to leave you thinking he might plink you in the face, your worst nightmare as a hitter.

Gabriel struck out his first at bat. He seemed shy, understandably even a bit fearful, at the plate. Dominic whistled the first pitch high and inside, right under Gabriel's chin, and he had the boy backing up with every pitch thereafter and struck him out looking. Between innings, I got up behind Gabriel's bench and whispered him over. I told Gabriel to choke up on the damn bat to increase his bat speed, keep his left foot in the freaking bucket, anticipate the fastball, and send it screaming straight back at the pitcher's smug mug. He giggled at my final rhyme, but he got the point.

Next at bat, Gabriel took the first pitch, high and tight, ball one. The second pitch was in the dirt but called a strike, because the umpire had glaucoma and cataracts. "Strike for a mouse, maybe!" I yelled from the stands, but Charlie hushed me before I could say more. The third pitch, though—that third pitch! Dominic reared back and threw a fastball with everything he had on it. That ball came spinning in toward the plate like a meteor, just above knee high, outside half of the plate. As Dominic let it go, Gabriel shifted his left heel slightly toward the mound the way he does when he's about to turn on a pitch, beginning that weight transfer from right to left that gives a hitter his power. He'd choked up so a couple inches of the bat showed under his left hand, and I'm guessing that gave him maybe 20 percent more bat speed, and the kid already had the fastest swing I'd ever seen, short of major league hitters.

Gabriel turned into that pitch, and when he made contact, it even sounded different. It's physics, of course, but music, too. Because of the velocity of the pitch and the speed of Gabriel's bat, the ball was only against the aluminum for a fraction of a second. The time could be measured in the thousandths of a second, and only an ear tuned to the music of calfskin stretched over wound string colliding with an aluminum bat might notice the difference. I stood up immediately. When I heard that sound, I knew the ball was about to go farther than it had ever gone on this baseball field. Everyone else stood up, too. Gabriel's first home run in the boys 9–12 league was still eighty or ninety feet high when it cleared the two-hundred-foot home-run fence. It flew beyond the first two rows of cars in the parking lot and came down on the hood of a Jeep Cherokee in the last row, leaving a shallow crater there and setting off the car alarm in the Lexus parked beside it. Gabriel circled the bases, and people in the stands applauded and stared, mouths open, at what they'd just witnessed. I wiped tears from my eyes, lest anyone see me and think I was going soft.

By the end of that summer, Coach Polkowski didn't have to carry Gabriel's birth certificate with him anymore, because everyone in the six-or seven-county area knew who Gabriel was and what he could do with a baseball bat. Most of the parking lots were full an hour before the games, and some of those people had driven a couple of hours just to see a seven-year-old kid play baseball. I didn't have to, but I would have driven all night to see him take just one at bat. Gabriel hit fifty home runs that year, as a seven-year-old against twelve-year-old pitching. It's still the record and always will be.

8

Thomas Kennedy

On a cold, overcast October morning, rain pelted his truck as Thomas drove west across Wisconsin's sand counties, headed for the southbound interstate, with Gabriel Fisher beside him. Now nine years old, the boy was reading Jack London's *Call of the Wild*, but sometimes he looked up from his book to watch raindrops trace their crooked paths along his window or stared out the windshield through the metronomic wave of the wipers.

At age nine, Gabriel stood six feet four inches tall, with size 16 feet, and attended fifth-grade classes at the local middle school. Older boys had begun teasing him, calling him the Jolly Green Giant or Bigfoot. Thomas told him the biggest bullies were the most insecure boys in the school, and to ignore them. Jasper, on the other hand, had encouraged Gabriel to stand up for himself. "You're a big kid, Gabriel—pop them a good one in the mouth!" he said. "Loosen a few teeth and they'll leave you alone." When pressed by Gabriel for his view of Jasper's advice, Thomas waffled. "Well, it's probably not what I would do," he said, "but if that time comes, protect your chin, and swing for the fences."

Gabriel loved animals and he liked to read, so Thomas took it upon himself to supplement the boy's schoolwork with books that had captivated him as a boy. His mother's entire library, including all of Thomas's childhood books, was stored in sixteen moldering boxes stacked in his basement. Rummaging through the damp boxes, he'd found *The Yearling*, *White Fang*, *Black Beauty*, *The Wind in the Willows*, *Where the Red Fern Grows*, and many others he thought Gabriel would enjoy. He set these aside on a shelf in his living room and passed them along to Gabriel when the boy grew old enough to read them.

Thomas had taken no veterinary appointments that Saturday so he could drive to Milwaukee to visit his mother, and Jasper had agreed to allow Gabriel to keep him company. It had been five months since he'd seen his mother, who lived in the memory care wing of a nursing home in Shorewood, and if the weather cleared, he hoped to take Gabriel to the zoo afterward.

Dorothy Kennedy had been a lioness in life, a vibrant, intelligent woman, chairperson of the English department at the University of Wisconsin's Milwaukee campus, onetime president of the League of Women Voters of Wisconsin, a season ticket holder to both the Milwaukee Symphony and the Milwaukee Bucks. She'd published monographs on Emily Dickinson's poetry, on Margaret Fuller, on Willa Cather. She'd been interviewed multiple times on public television. To see her reduced to someone who could no longer read or write, who could not even identify the current president of the United States, was almost too painful for Thomas to endure.

The rain had softened to a steady drizzle by the time they arrived at the nursing home, with blue sky beginning to show through breaks in the clouds. Dorothy was sleeping when they entered her room, the television tuned to a game show that Thomas promptly turned off. Her eyeglasses and a glass of ice water rested on the wheeled table beside the bed. Three desiccated houseplants in red pots rested on the windowsill in the sun. His mother's thinning white hair looked like a tuft of dandelion fluff. Always a small woman—five foot four in high heels, she used to say—she had shrunk further in old age, a skeleton of a woman under a yellowed cotton sheet. Thomas gently took her hand, and she awoke.

"Good morning, Mother," Thomas said.

She squinted her eyes at him and pulled her hand away. "You forgot again, didn't you?" she said.

Thomas nodded. "I'm sorry. What is it I've forgotten?"

Her chin dropped in exasperation. "How should I remember?" Gabriel chuckled, and Dorothy noticed him. "Who are you?" she asked.

"I'm Gabriel," he said.

She looked up at Thomas and squinted. She looked at both of them in turn, swinging her head from side to side, working her mouth as if she were chewing something.

"You must be half giraffe, you're so tall," she said to Gabriel. He smiled and nodded.

"And who are you?" she asked Thomas.

He told her. She continued pursing and unpursing her lips, perhaps trying to wed Thomas's face to a memory buried too deeply to be unearthed. Gabriel leaned over the bed farther, his face just a few feet from Dorothy's.

"Is this my grandson?"

"This is Gabriel—" Thomas began.

Dorothy's mouth opened wide, and she raised her wrinkled, age-spotted hands above the sheets. Gabriel slid his body along the railing and leaned his head closer so that she could touch him. Dorothy put one hand on each side of his face. Tears welled in her eyes.

They carried on a conversation that made little sense, though Thomas didn't mind. Dorothy had seemed incapable of speaking more than a word or two on previous visits, so hearing her talking pleased him. Gabriel turned out to be masterful at making nonsense conversation.

"That grass needs mowing, but of course you can't cut it if you can't find it," she said, nodding. "Invisible grass, isn't that something? Animals can see it, so they can eat it, but we can't."

"What color do you think it is?" Gabriel asked her.

"Well. The cat has told me it's blue," she said. "But cats lie, brother. Don't they ever."

"So, it might not be blue?"

"Might be pink, might be purple. Depends on the color of the rain."

Dorothy closed her eyes and dozed for a while, her legs jerking in brief spasms under the bedsheet. When she opened her eyes again, she looked frightened, or sad, or confused. Gabriel spoke to her gently, picking up the lost thread of conversation.

"Looks like you're growing something," Gabriel said, pointing to the plants on the windowsill. She looked over at the red pots.

"Those are tomatoes," she said. "One of them is a watermelon. Just started from seed."

"I like watermelon," Gabriel said.

She nodded. "They're not ripe yet. But they will be. I must weed them every day. You would not believe the weeds. And smart! You go to pick them, and they get up and walk away. And then you turn your back, they sneak back in again."

"It's sneakweed," Gabriel said, smiling.

"I used to know the Latin name for it, but I've forgotten." She looked as if she might cry. "I used to know a lot more things."

A nurse came into the room with a plastic tray of food: a small dish of tomato soup, a grilled cheese sandwich cut diagonally into two triangles, a carton of milk, and a chocolate chip cookie. "Lunchtime, Dorothy," she said, her voice bright and enthusiastic. The nurse wore blue jeans and a bright nursing blouse covered in vibrantly colored tropical birds.

"Lunch?" Dorothy said. "I haven't had breakfast."

"You did, honey," the nurse said. She glanced at the whiteboard on the wall. "You had pancakes and bacon for breakfast."

"I don't remember that," Dorothy said.

"Well, Mom, we're going to leave you to it," Thomas said, seizing on the opportunity to leave. He knew they often changed his mother's diaper after lunch, and he wanted to miss that somber moment. He leaned over the bed and kissed her on the forehead. Gabriel did the same. While Gabriel kissed her, she hooked a hand over one of his shoulders, and held him to the bed a few seconds longer.

"This boy!" she said to no one in particular. Her eyes welled with tears. "This boy is going to save the world."

When Thomas was young, he begged his mother to take him to the zoo as often as possible, sometimes weekly in the summer when she wasn't teaching. On zoo days, his mother would wake early and make him waffles for breakfast, and while he ate, she'd pack a picnic basket with their lunches—peanut butter and jelly sandwiches and fruit, usually apples or bananas, which they'd share with the horde of chipmunks that terrorized the picnic area. His mother would also bring along a book and a large, silver thermos bottle into which she'd pour a mixture of fresh lemonade and vodka.

Once inside, his mother would take up residence at a table in the shade along the artificial river that reflected the elegant, pink bodies of the flamingos who freely roamed the grounds. She would kiss him once on the forehead, bid him farewell, and open her book, her thermos of hard lemonade at her elbow. Thomas would wander off, his mind alight with the prospect of all the beautiful animals he was about to see.

He loved the regal emperor penguins who lived inside a refrigerated enclosure with a glassed-in pool of cold water. He'd press his face to the cold glass as they glided inches from his nose, their bodies and nostrils trailing streams of silvery bubbles. The smaller penguins, the Humboldts, lived in an outdoor enclosure surrounded by a glass-walled moat. Thomas didn't spend too much time with them because their waste reeked. His mother could make him collapse in hiccupping laughter with her disquisitions on Humboldt penguin shit, which she said "squirts out of a penguin's butt like ground-up anchovies sprayed from a garden hose."

If it was a cool day, he returned again and again to the moist, bright heat of the aviary, where hundreds of spectacularly colored birds lived freely in a soaring habitat of rocks and tropical foliage, with a small stream fed by artificial waterfalls flowing along the floor. He also enjoyed the reptiles and bats in their dark, heated habitats, and the fish of

Lake Wisconsin, a room-sized aquarium filled with native fish, including muskies and giant channel catfish, the strange gar with its straw-like mouth, and the odd, prehistoric-looking lake sturgeon.

But Thomas spent most of his time in the primate house. It contained the great apes, and the star of the building—indeed, the greatest attraction of the zoo, and always the most crowded of the exhibits—was a giant, male silverback gorilla named Samson, who at his peak weighed over 650 pounds. In those days, zoos were not attuned to an animal's social and environmental needs, so Samson lived alone in a large, pale-blue-tiled enclosure with a glass wall made up of ten large panes, two inches thick, separating him from zoo visitors. Two old tires hung from thick ropes tied up into the ceiling, and fire hoses also dangled in large loops at various points in the enclosure. In the center was a large, square, silver scale, with the weight—if Samson chose to climb upon it, as he often did, particularly at feeding time, three o'clock each afternoon—displayed for everyone to see. Usually sedate, his eyes like tiny seeds sunken in his massive, silvery head, he'd peel orange quarters with his great black fingers, sliding the slices between his lips past two-inch incisors into his mouth.

But he could be cantankerous, too. He would suddenly pound his chest like a cartoon ape—the percussive, hollow thumping sounded like a horse's shod hooves on blacktop—and charge the glass, slapping it with huge, open palms, causing everyone to jump in alarm. Samson died after thirty years in captivity, and though Thomas didn't go to the zoo nearly as often when he grew older, he always found himself drawn to the primate house, even though Samson no longer lived there.

Thomas parked the car, and he and Gabriel crossed the parking lot together, headed for the main entrance.

"Your mom always took you, never your dad?" Gabriel asked. He'd taken Thomas's hand, as he often did when they walked together.

"My dad didn't have summers off like my mom did. He had to work."

"What was his job?"

"He was a foreman at Miller. Where they made beer."

"Did he get free beer there?"

"Yes, he did, in fact."

"Jasper would like that," Gabriel said, and laughed. "Did your dad want to take you to the zoo, but didn't have the time?"

"Something like that," Thomas answered.

Thomas paid for their tickets and stuffed a colorful map into his shirt pocket so they could eventually find their way back to the main entrance. The afternoon passed too quickly. They spent nearly an hour in the aviary, laughing and pointing at the tropical birds, some of whom had feet far too large for their bodies, like Gabriel himself. The male lions were roaring in the Africa exhibit, their rib cages inflating and deflating like bellows, and the polar bears were out in the water swimming, playing with a silver quarter barrel, tossing it about as if it weighed no more than a volleyball.

By early evening, they were exhausted. Thomas bought pizza and sodas at the snack bar, and they ate their dinners quietly, comparing their favorite animals of the day in categories Gabriel selected: favorite bird, favorite reptile, favorite mammal.

"Is this how you decided you wanted to be an animal doctor, coming here?" Gabriel asked, as they slowly walked toward the exit.

Thomas nodded. "Sometimes I'd see one of the zoo workers in the cage feeding or grooming one of the animals, and I would wish that were me."

"Me too," Gabriel said.

Thomas thought back to those golden afternoons, the exhausted feeling that crept over him when he slouched down in the seat of his mother's car, his eyes closed, as she drove him home. Thomas never felt lonely at the zoo. So much of his life he'd felt isolated, the only child of a distant father and a loving, intellectually gifted mother. For Christmas every year, their brightly decorated tree bloomed with colorful gifts for him. While those gifts were thoughtful and generous, they focused on keeping him occupied alone: books, always; a microscope; a telescope; a remote-controlled plane; a metal detector; a crystal radio. Never, in all the years he could remember, did he open a gift that required him to be in his parents' company—no board games such as Monopoly or Clue; no cribbage or backgammon; nothing whose implicit purpose was not to give him something else to do by himself. He had vowed he'd be different as a father, more engaged with his children, but he and Angela were never able to have any.

Gabriel fell asleep shortly after they'd left Milwaukee, the lights along the freeway flashing steadily across his face. An hour out of the city, Thomas turned the radio on softly, and tuned it to a classical station. His mother played classical music whenever she drove in the car, and she played it on the stereo at home, too. Thomas's father preferred country music—Johnny Cash, Conway Twitty, Loretta Lynn, Tammy Wynette—which his mother dismissed as hillbilly yodeling. So Thomas grew up hearing both: Vivaldi, Bach, and Brahms in the library while his mother read; Johnny Cash and Tammy Wynette in the garage on a greasy radio while his father changed the brake shoes or did a tune-up on one of their cars.

The public radio station was celebrating the birthday of Franz Liszt. Thomas recognized Hungarian Rhapsody No. 2 as soon as he found the station. For solo piano, the piece opened slowly and simply, with deep, dramatic, melancholy chords, then grew brisker, lighter, a blistering pace few pianists in the world could play. Then, near the end, the music rose and fell in powerful waves like great swells of stormy ocean.

His mother had introduced this Liszt piece to him in an unusual way. She saw him lurking in the hall, and she called him into the library. He couldn't have been older than nine or ten. "This is Hungarian Rhapsody No. 2 by Franz Liszt, the most famous of his rhapsodies. He published it in 1851, the same year Melville published *Moby-Dick*. While he surely didn't intend it, this music could be the soundtrack to that novel. Listen, Thomas. It's beautiful." His mother pulled him up on her lap, and he listened, though not intently, happy to be invited into her sanctum, enjoying the feel of her arms wrapped around him from behind, the smell of her hair. She played Liszt's Hungarian rhapsodies so often she wore out the record.

A light rain had again begun to fall, and he turned on the intermittent wipers, annoyed by their occasional squeaking. A few deer, bright and ghostly in his lights, crossed the road, and Thomas slowed down.

It was nearly ten o'clock when Thomas turned into Jasper's driveway. He was surprised to find the house dark, lit only by the automatic, dusk-to-dawn yard light mounted on a boom from the peak of the barn.

"We're home," Thomas said, as the boy stretched and smiled. "It's raining."

The boy ran into the house, turned on the lights in the porch and kitchen. Thomas followed close behind him. Gabriel pointed at the kitchen table, where Jasper had constructed a pyramid of empty Budweiser cans, thirteen in all: six on the bottom, then four, then two, then one.

"Your brother is becoming quite an artist," Thomas said, nodding. "I've got to use your bathroom, Gabriel." The white toilet bowl and sink had both been stained orange by iron in the well water. He noticed an empty beer can on the floor under the sink. He worried about Jasper's drinking but tried not to betray any concern to Gabriel. When he left the bathroom, he snuck down the hall and pushed open Jasper's bedroom door. He approached the bed and waited until his eyes adjusted to the darkness. Rain hammered the roof and blew against the windows. Jasper's blankets and pillow were on the floor, the bed empty.

He returned to the kitchen, where Gabriel stood at the sink, drinking a glass of water. "I'm not sure where your brother is," Thomas said.

"He's not asleep?"

"No. Maybe he went for a walk and got himself caught out in the rain."

Gabriel laughed. "He won't be happy. I better go get eggs." He opened the drawer where they kept the flashlight.

"Can't the eggs wait till morning?"

"Jasper will be mad if the raccoons get any." Gabriel slipped into his mud boots and opened the door, clutching the egg basket in one hand.

"Run fast and maybe the raindrops will miss you!" Thomas said. He followed Gabriel outside but stopped on the covered porch, his back against the house. Rain overflowed the gutters along the width of the roof, a thin waterfall that Gabriel splashed through. His flashlight beam bounced along the puddles as he crossed the expanse of driveway and disappeared into the barn.

Through the din of the rain, Thomas heard something that sounded like a far off bird call, the throaty warble of a sandhill crane in the distance, perhaps, or the hungry cry of an adolescent horned owl. He took a step away from the house toward the barn, still protected from the rain by the porch roof, and turned his head to listen more carefully. It wasn't a bird call. It was Gabriel. Screaming.

"Gabriel!" Thomas splashed through puddles, his shoes filling with water, the cold rain soaking through his shirt and pants.

Inside the barn, Gabriel had dropped the flashlight and backed up against the wall, where he stood, mouth open, screaming. Thomas picked up the flashlight. Gabriel's eyes were pinched closed.

"Shhh, Gabriel," Thomas said. He pulled the boy to him. "What's the matter?"

Gabriel raised an arm, pointed a finger.

Thomas turned, and as the flashlight beam spread its yellow light into the darkness, it cut across Jasper's body hanging from a barn beam, a thick, greasy rope tight around his neck.

"Don't look, son," Thomas said. "Put your head down. Keep your eyes closed. I've got you. I've got you."

9

Hannah Fisher

I'd been dreaming when the knocking began. I was rocking a newborn by the woodstove, my breast warm and perspiring where I clutched the child, and each time I rocked, the warped floorboards creaked four times under my feet. It is a mystery, isn't it, the way the Lord keeps the door slightly ajar between our dream life and the wonders of His creation? When I opened my eyes, I found myself in bed beside Josiah, our bedroom dark as tar. Outside, rain hissed like gravel thrown against the windows. The percussive knocking came again, four rapid beats. Downstairs, someone was at the door. I lit a lamp and woke Josiah. It wasn't yet midnight.

"Who would be out so late on such a night?" Josiah said, as he hooked suspenders over the shoulders of his nightshirt.

In the flickering light, I pulled on my robe and kapp.

As we descended the stairs, the knocking grew louder.

Josiah opened the door and held up the lamp. Gabriel and Dr. Kennedy squinted in the rain, no Weatherproofs or umbrellas. The doctor held a large, black plastic bag, like a sack, over one shoulder. Gabriel carried a bright blue pack on his back. Josiah welcomed them into our home.

"What's wrong?" I asked. "What's happened?"

"Hannah, wait," Josiah said, frustrated by my impatience. "They need towels and blankets. The boy is shivering."

Gabriel and the doctor removed their muddy boots. Josiah lit another lamp in the kitchen, and I carried the bedroom lamp to the back hall. I pulled towels and blankets from the linen closet. They dried their hair and faces while I helped Gabriel out of his shirt and spread a quilt over his bare shoulders, a Jacob's Ladder pattern Meg had given us as a wedding gift.

Gabriel wiped tears from his eyes and shivered. I handed Dr. Kennedy a Shetland wool blanket. He thanked me and wrapped himself in it. I carried their wet socks and dripping shirts to the sink, wrung them out as best I could, and hung them on a line over the woodstove to dry. We moved into the living room and sat down.

Dr. Kennedy took a deep breath and sighed. "I'm so sorry for coming so late. I'm afraid I have terrible news."

As the news of Jasper's sinful death closed around my heart, the caustic sting of guilt and shame filled my mouth. I was of no comfort to him in life, and it made his loss so much more painful to me. My tears spilled freely, and I fled to the kitchen to hide my grief from Gabriel. Josiah lit a fire in the woodstove, and our house warmed, the scent of woodsmoke and the muffled snap of burning oak a calming balm against our sadness. Gabriel stayed close to the doctor, who occasionally put a hand on the boy's leg to comfort him. Eventually, Gabriel placed his head on one of the sofa pillows, rolled to his side, and fell asleep. Dr. Kennedy tucked the quilt over his shoulders and opened it to cover his bare feet. Even when folded, bent at the elbow and knee, the boy barely fit on the sofa.

I boiled water and made tea with dried peppermint, lemon balm, and the ground, dried hips from wild roses. We drank the tea and ate soda bread with wheat berries and sunflower seeds, warmed on a grate over the woodstove, and spread with wild raspberry jam. Dr. Kennedy complimented the rich flavor of the tea and the warm bread. He shared tender stories about Jasper, told us what a selfless and loving young man he'd been, how he had devoted his life to Gabriel's happiness. When Josiah asked if Jasper had in any way expressed desire for salvation, the doctor said he didn't know. When he thought of Jasper, he said, he was reminded of Benjamin Franklin's statement that the best way to serve God was to serve one's fellow man.

"Jasper was never baptized," Josiah said.

"He might have been," I said, louder than I'd intended. "Rachel might have had him baptized in an English church."

Josiah shook his head. "I doubt that."

"I haven't been baptized either," Dr. Kennedy said. I sensed he shared this admission to bring peace between Josiah and me. "My mother was a proud atheist. She believed religion was an invention to give men dominion over their wives." He smiled. "She lives in a nursing home now. She has dementia, so she's in memory care. She has a cross hanging on the wall in her room."

"Maybe your mother is not in the grip of atheism any longer," Josiah said.

"Maybe not," the doctor said. "I don't know who put it there."

Josiah seemed as comfortable with the doctor as he would have been with Amish men. The transformation intrigued me. Not since my schoolgirl days had I been so long in the company of someone English, and never in the intimacy of my own home. When you have been taught all your life that being too long in the company of nonbelievers is to find your feet on a path that could lead to damnation, you tread carefully. And yet for two hours, as Josiah and I made conversation with this gentle man speaking so lovingly of Jasper, with Rachel's dear son asleep on his knee, I felt only comforted, only peace. As I watched him, though, something began to trouble me. I looked upon him as I had not looked upon a man other than Josiah for many years. It was nothing untoward, really, just a simple wish to talk with him, to be in his company. Since my marriage, I'd never felt any desire to visit with any man other than Josiah, so this caused me some consternation. Later, I even spoke of it to Abiah, and we wondered without resolution whether Satan had somehow had a hand in it, or not. Abiah said the Tempter knows to strike when we are weakened by grief, pain, or lust, but she believed me too strong to be tempted.

Amish insistence on separation does not grow out of any belief in our own superiority. It is, in fact, the contrary, an acknowledgment of our fallibility. The English world is full of comforts and pleasure— music and movies and technology and beautiful clothing, something new and exciting to experience every day. God has made that world so alluring we must constantly shield ourselves from its beckoning light, reminding ourselves always that it is of no consequence. Mortal life is transitory, as brief as a spark that jumps from an open fire; it is eternal life we seek, and that cannot be found on a television or inside a computer. We are not ignorant; we know what these things are. We choose to be without them, to turn away from the temptations they bring.

Immersed in our conversation, Josiah, Dr. Kennedy, and I never noticed the storm had ended. Outside, a calm, gray glow shone in the east as the earth turned toward morning.

"The bus picks Gabriel up in the morning at six thirty-five at the end of Jasper's driveway," the doctor said. "I'm sure they'll adjust the route to stop here instead. I can call them to arrange it. The bus drops him home about four o'clock." He rubbed a hand gently over Gabriel's hair. "I would like to keep seeing the boy, if that's all right. He helps me on calls Friday afternoons and Saturdays. I will employ him full-time when he's older, if he's interested."

"It's clear you care for him," Josiah said.

"You have been so dear to Gabriel," I said. "We wouldn't wish to take that away." As an unbaptized child, Gabriel had never been sub-ject to *meidung*. We could raise him as our own, though his previous, English life would complicate that, as we'd soon discover.

When the doctor stood to leave, Gabriel awoke. He stood up and wrapped his arms around Dr. Kennedy from behind.

"Don't go," Gabriel said.

Dr. Kennedy turned to face the boy, put a hand on each shoulder, and looked up into his face. "I'm just heading home to sleep. You will help me as you always have. But instead of coming to your brother's house to get you, I'll come here."

"You'll have a room of your own here," I said. "Upstairs. It was once your mother's room. Some of her things are still in the closet. I can show them to you."

Gabriel relented, allowing Dr. Kennedy to put on his boots and depart. Josiah loaned him a dry shirt, and I told him I'd launder his clothes, which had not yet fully dried, and return them in time.

I took a lamp and walked the boy upstairs. Josiah followed with the plastic bag of Gabriel's clothing. Gabriel had to duck his head to clear the stairwell ceiling. I led him into Rachel's small room and set the lamp on the table beside her bed. We'd painted the walls a simple, pale white, and the oak floor had not been stained but only varnished to protect the wood. The headboard of Rachel's bed was a smooth slice of a cottonwood tree, across the grain, varnished to a subtle golden hue, its many rings arcing like a rainbow. Josiah helped me put sheets on the mattress, and then he said good night to Gabriel and left us. I added blankets and a pillow to the bed, and then folded and stacked Gabriel's clothes on the table. I could put them in the dresser in the morning.

"Do you have pajamas or a nightshirt you want to wear?"

Gabriel shook his head. "I sleep in a T-shirt and underwear, except when it's hot in the summer."

"That's fine." I found a clean T-shirt and handed it to him. He pulled it over his head, then I turned my back as he took off his pants, kicked them aside, and climbed into bed. "Is the power out because of the storm?" he asked.

I smiled. "No," I said. "We don't have electricity. We use these lamps instead."

He turned his head to look into the glass globe where the tongue of wick burned. The flame, like a prairie fire in a bottle, bathed his beautiful face in golden light.

"How does your TV work then?"

"We don't have a television." He weighed this revelation briefly but offered no reaction. He seemed entranced by the flame. "When your mother was your age," I said, "she used to go outside in the summer and catch fireflies in a mason jar, and when she put the jar on that table, those fireflies would light up this whole room."

Gabriel smiled. "Can I try that?"

"Of course."

He kicked his legs against the sheet and blanket until they became untucked from the bottom of the mattress. Two bright white feet and a few inches of skinny legs poked out over the end of the bed. "My stomach feels jumpy."

I smiled. "It's normal to feel frightened when you're someplace new. Do you want me to sit with you until you fall asleep?"

"Maybe," he said. "Where do you sleep?"

"Across the hall." I pointed out the door. "I'll fetch a chair." I retrieved the chair and set it beside the bed where I could rest one arm on the mattress near Gabriel's pillow. "Do you like music?" I asked. "I could sing to you."

He slid back down under the blankets, yawned, rested his head on the pillow. "You can sing if you want. I'm pretty tired."

I nodded. "You close your eyes." I removed my kapp and blew out the lamp. Gabriel rolled to his side, facing away from me, his knees pulled up toward his chest, so he fit on the bed. Softly, in a voice just above a whisper, I sang *"Schloof, Bobbeli, Schloof,"* in Old German:

> *Schloof, Bobbeli, schloof!*
> *Der Daadi hiet die Schoof.*
> *Die Mammi schittelt en Baemelein,*
> *Es fallt d'rfun en dramelein.*
> *Und kummt net heem bis Marriye frieh.*
> *Schloof, Bobbeli, schloof!*

Sleep, baby, sleep; your father tends the sheep; your mother shakes the dreamland tree, and from it fall sweet dreams for thee. Sleep, baby, sleep! I sang through all the verses I could remember, and then

I sat quietly until Gabriel's breathing slowed. As I left his room, I glanced out the window to see that God was about to give me the gift of a beautiful sunrise. Along the barely closed eye of the horizon, a thin strip of orange and pink glowed, shining through the east window at the foot of Gabriel's bed like the glory of creation day.

10

Thomas Kennedy

That winter was the coldest Thomas Kennedy could remember; for twenty consecutive days in December and early January the temperature did not rise to zero. At night, the mercury fell to negative twenty-five with windchills in the minus fifties. Normally, Thomas enjoyed taking evening walks in the winter season. The stars seemed especially bright against that black coldness, and he liked the feel of the crisp air against his face, the squeak of snow beneath his boots. But in those temperatures, his hands grew numb in minutes, and the cold felt like an assault, pushing through layers of wool and the thickest down parka.

Across the county, the brutal cold made itself known in other ways. Water pipes froze, and car batteries went dead. Frost heaves closed sections of county highways. Forced-air furnaces couldn't keep up, running without interruption for days at a time. The boiler at the local high school failed one morning, and the children were sent home for the rest of the week while it was repaired. Then the following week, when windchills reached seventy below, the school buses broke down so often, all local schools were canceled for four days.

On New Year's morning, someone found Duke Smithson frozen in deep snow along the county road, sitting with his back against a pine tree, a HAPPY NEW YEAR! button still pinned to the lapel of his sport coat. He and his wife, Estelle, had been to the New Year's Eve party at the Knights of Columbus hall. He'd taken Estelle home after midnight, then returned to the party, where he'd had too much to drink and departed again around two thirty in the morning. When his truck broke down three miles from home, he decided to walk the rest of the way wearing dress shoes, no coat, and no gloves. The temperature was twenty-seven degrees below zero. Duke made it about two hundred yards before the cold overwhelmed him. When a truck driver happened upon his body after sunrise, Duke Smithson was coated in frost, his frozen flesh as white and shiny as marble.

Thomas did not know Duke well. They'd spoken once on the telephone when Estelle's pet dog had gotten tangled up with a skunk. She had bathed the dog in tomato sauce, a folk remedy she'd remembered from childhood. The treatment dyed the bathtub and the dog a vibrant red, and the animal now smelled like skunk Bolognese. Thomas laughed and prescribed a warm-water scrubbing with a blend of hydrogen peroxide, baking soda, and dishwashing soap.

Provided they had fresh air and water, goats and sheep thrived in the winter, with deep snow more problematic than cold. Goats grew a thick layer of cashmere that insulated them from even the worst windchills, and with their feet folded beneath them, healthy sheep could sleep comfortably outdoors even when temperatures reached thirty below. Animals knew enough to conserve their energy and would not venture into deep snow; they spent the days and nights lying still, eating, chewing cud, and they loved afternoon sunshine, not unlike most human beings in those latitudes.

Professionally, Thomas enjoyed the decreased winter workload. It was the calm before the storm of spring births and warm weather diseases. He could catch up on paperwork and reading, attend to delayed dental and doctor appointments, his yearly eye exam, schedule maintenance he'd deferred on his truck. A sluggish torpor settled over him that winter. In the spring and summer, he awoke at five in the morning, but by late January he was taking his breakfast at nine or even ten o'clock, sleepily stirring a couple teaspoons of brown sugar into a steaming bowl of oatmeal. He tied flies or read until well after midnight, often by candlelight, books on the Civil War or the American Revolution, biographies of notable figures, Jefferson, Franklin, Adams—old-man books, his wife had called them, when he'd discovered an interest in American history.

Sometimes he'd spend an hour going through boxes of his mother's books in the basement, seeking something new and interesting to read, and occasionally he'd begin one of the monographs that she herself had written. Twice he'd started—and then abandoned—her study of Emily Dickinson, *A Species Stands Beyond*, which sought to reach an understanding of Dickinson's faith within what his mother called "her enthusiasm for the sciences, including botany, astronomy, and geology, and her often transcendental vision of nature." Such language baffled him. He'd begin reading with the best of intentions, but inevitably his mind would wander, and he'd discover he'd passed three or four pages without any memory of what he'd read.

Biographies held his interest. A biography told the story of a life, birth to death, the good and bad, highs and lows. Franklin, for example, was born with nothing, yet taught himself to speak six languages; invented bifocals, the lightning rod, the Franklin stove (among other things); lent his wisdom to the Constitutional Convention; and helped revise the Declaration of Independence. How little he'd done in his life, Thomas sometimes thought, when confronted with the extraordinary accomplishments of others.

Most young boys dream of doing great things, but somewhere in middle age they look back and realize they haven't, and they won't, that they'll leave no substantial legacy at all. Even if he'd had children, in another two generations no one would remember he'd been alive or that he'd spent his flicker of time on earth healing animals, delivering calves, foals, lambs, and kids, trout fishing, reading, shaving, sleeping—the repetitions of an unremarkable life. Modest though it was, and lonely at times, he had few complaints. He had a calling, a

a favorite restaurant, celebrating both their tenth wedding anniversary and the purchase of a crib and changing table, which Thomas had put together the previous afternoon in a spare bedroom they'd turned into the nursery. Throughout the day, from time to time, Thomas had noticed Angela holding her stomach, feeling for the baby's kicking, her brow knit in worry. Thomas reminded her that their obstetrician said infants often felt a mother's movement like the rocking of a cradle and slept during her most active periods. Thomas assured her she'd feel the baby move in time, and that she need not worry.

That evening at the restaurant, Angela's face went pale. She dropped her napkin into a still-full bowl of soup and stood up from the table. What's wrong? Thomas asked. When she stood, she pulled the back of her skirt around to the side, and Thomas saw it at the same moment she did, a splotch of blood, bright crimson against the pale green cotton.

They drove directly to the hospital emergency room, Angela sobbing, her hands pressed into the bloody crotch of her skirt. Samuel was stillborn just after midnight, a tiny baby boy, perfectly formed, who would fit in the palm of your hand.

Thomas and Angela gave up after that, unable to face the prospect of another miscarriage. The loss also opened a cleft in the rock of their marriage that years of patient waiting would not heal. By slow degrees, outside of their own awareness, at least initially, the loss of Samuel pushed them apart. During moments of discord—often a disagreement about something small, whether to travel to visit Angela's parents during the July Fourth holiday, for example—Angela would remind him that he had told her she had nothing to worry about. You never listen to me, she said. I told you I could not feel him moving, and you ignored me. Thomas reminded her of the ER physician's clear directive that even if they'd come in sooner, nothing could have been done. It was a terribly painful tragedy, but no one was to blame. Thomas had merely been trying to comfort her, doing what they both knew she expected him to do. Was he wrong in his assurances? Yes, of course. But he had not *caused* the loss of their baby.

In time their silences became a thick layer of separation, like a hypoxic zone in a lake or ocean where nothing could thrive. Angela grew impatient and quick-tempered, Thomas withdrawn, emotionally isolated, disconnected. On some days, it seemed that they were incapable of having a polite conversation about anything. One evening, she excoriated him for coming home late from work without texting her, and he said he found her sudden interest in when he arrived home calculated and cruel. He did not recognize the woman screaming in the kitchen, and he did not recognize himself.

"We don't have to be cruel to one another just because something terrible has happened to us," he said.

"Don't tell me how I should or should not behave," Angela said.

Thomas nodded, said that wasn't his intention at all. "May I at least ask you to be kinder, as I will try to be? You can choose kindness. I am hoping you do."

If their armistice had put an end to open warfare, it did not result in greater intimacy, or anything close to what they'd had before their losses. Five and then ten years passed. Thomas poured himself into his work, took calls he might not have taken years earlier. Angela became the head of their local library, read voraciously, volunteered at the local animal shelter. They made a good living together, remodeled the kitchen, invited friends over for dinner.

But from time to time, Angela turned on him, often in the presence of company, pointing almost gleefully to his flaws and failures, moments when he had not measured up to her unspoken expectations. If he remembered twenty things but forgot one, she recalled the moment his memory failed him. Once, for example, they'd taken an extended vacation to wine country in Northern California, where they'd enjoyed themselves, but what she'd recall later was the night they couldn't be seated at a marvelous restaurant in Santa Rosa because Thomas had neglected to make reservations.

Thomas understood her long depression bled into all of this, and he remained patient, hopeful that she might again be the vibrant, loving, generous woman he'd known, even though Angela often mistook his patience for weakness, or passivity. Over the years, their relationship accommodated itself to this dynamic. Thomas spoke less, offered less of himself, grew self-protective, less joyful. Once he had let himself be soft and vulnerable, open to Angela in ways he'd never been open to anyone, but after Samuel's death he needed armor, closed himself off in preemptive defense.

Tens of thousands, perhaps hundreds of thousands, of marriages functioned this way, he told himself. He'd just never envisioned his own would become one of them.

11

Billy Walton

By late April, the local kids start riding bikes through melting snow to the ball diamonds with their fathers' snow shovels strapped across the handlebars. They shovel off the base paths, spray-paint a couple baseballs orange, and play, with old shingles or pieces of barn board stomped into the snow or mud for bases. I was one of those boys back in the day, and every April when meltwater starts dripping off the rooftops, I can't wait to hear the ping of aluminum bats striking baseballs in the crisp spring air.

I'd heard rumors of Gabriel in Amish clothing, and I lost sleep wondering if Josiah would allow the boy to play baseball when Little League started up again. Spring and summer are a busy time for farm families, I understand that. I knew Gabriel might be needed to help out. But Gabriel wasn't just any Amish boy, and he wasn't just any baseball player. When the weather warmed and the snow started melting, I drove out to Josiah's place.

We made small talk for ten minutes—the weather, the late spring, Duke Smithson's frozen demise. Josiah said the winter had given us over eighty inches of snow. Over two dozen new kids had been born to Hannah's flock of goats. She was considering expanding her flock now that she had Gabriel to help with the milking.

I made my pitch. I laid it on as thick as mashed potatoes. I said I'd bet my life there weren't two or three boys in the world who could hit a baseball as far at age ten as Gabriel Fisher could. What if Roberto Clemente's mama or Babe Ruth's daddy had kept them away from the ball diamond as boys? What if the pop of the Earl of Sandwich had told little Earl to stop playing with his food? Prodigious talent, I said, must be allowed to blossom.

Josiah smiled. Maybe, he said, the Lord has other plans for Gabriel.

Understand, I respect religious people. I do. The Amish, I think, have some things figured out. Yet—and it may be a shortcoming in my own intelligence, no doubt one of many—I have a hard time believing people who claim to have inside information on the Lord's plans for anything. How, I wonder, are such plans communicated? By some heavenly Morse code only the faithful can decipher? I've been to hundreds of AA meetings, and I've heard dozens of previously drunken sots exclaim that they'd accepted Jesus Christ as their Lord and Savior and understood that only He (always the capital *H*) had the power to defeat their alcoholism, yada yada yada. And those holiest of rollers were often the very guys who ended up falling off the wagon. For a lot of them, that trip back into the bottle ended at the cemetery. So, whenever I hear anyone say the Lord has communicated some plan or purpose to them, my little bullshit antennae start to wiggle, and the skeptic in me grows belligerent.

"And what might the Lord's plans be for Gabriel?" I asked.

"Hard to say," Josiah answered. I waited for more, but Josiah just shrugged.

I admit I lost my temper. "If the Lord's plan is to have the boy shoveling animal shit and plowing fields for the rest of his life, then your Lord has no eye for talent."

Josiah's eyes narrowed, but he remained quiet.

"Look, I'm not trying to insult you, Josiah. Farming is important, meaningful work. I know that. But if there is a God, he sent Gabriel here to play professional baseball! Bonds has seven hundred and sixty-two dingers, maybe Gabriel hits eight hundred, even a thousand, in his career. He'll be a first-ballot selection to Cooperstown, a million-aire many times over. Please don't take that away from him."

Josiah put his hardened, calloused fingers on my arm. "I can see you care for Gabriel," he said. "But even if what you say is true, baseball is just a boys' game. Grown men are paid well for playing, but that doesn't change the fact that it's a game. We play volleyball at our gatherings. Gabriel's good at that, too. He's good at a lot of things. Animals love him, and he cares for them with uncommon understanding. At the rate he's growing, he's going to be bigger than two normal men and stronger than any three. God has given him many gifts. How can we be sure of His intentions so soon, when the boy is only ten years old?"

At that point the back door slammed, and Hannah and Gabriel entered the mudroom, Hannah first in her kapp and cape, which hung over her shoulders and down beyond her knees. She spun to the side as she removed the cape and hung it on a hook along the wall. Gabriel followed closely behind her. When they entered the kitchen, my breath caught in my throat. Gabriel had grown over the winter. He had to be at least six six or six seven, his arms spider-long in his white Amish shirt, which was smeared with mud and blood across the front.

"Light a lamp, Gabriel," Hannah said. The light had fallen since I'd arrived. A match flared, and the wick of an oil lamp on the kitchen island glowed orange and spread its light throughout the room.

"We have company," Josiah said.

"Mr. Walton, hello," Hannah said.

"Coach!" Gabriel said, striding toward me excitedly. I stood up and extended my hand, but he walked through it and embraced me. Leaning back with his arms tight around my back, he lifted my feet a couple inches from the floor and set me back down.

"Hey, slugger," I said. He had mud smeared across his face and in his hair. "Great to see you! How the heck you been?"

"Lydia just had triplets! Three little rams. Grandma said Lydia was a bottle-fed runt last spring, and she almost died. And now she has three kids! I want to name them SpongeBob, Patrick, and Squidward."

"Sure! From SpongeBob SquarePants," I said, chuckling.

"I told you!" Gabriel said, smiling at Hannah. "They're on TV."

"We'll see," Hannah said. She kissed Gabriel on the shoulder. "Go wash yourself for supper now. I can heat water if you'd like."

"No," Gabriel said. "Cold is fine."

I said my goodbyes and drove back to the bar. Gabriel seemed happy, and given all the boy had been through, I should have been thrilled for him. I'd had a little talent myself back in the day, and I'd wasted it. But compared to the thought of Gabriel as a young man with a manure shovel in his hands instead of a baseball bat, my own regrets weren't worth the spit on a postage stamp.

Later that night my brooding got so bad, I called Charlie to share the news. I said, Charlie, it looks like Gabriel Fisher won't be playing baseball anymore, can you believe it? He said, Billy, what the Christ, it's eleven thirty at night and you're waking me up to tell me that? I thought somebody died! I said it was like a death, at least for me.

Charlie coughed on the other end of the line. I'm hanging up now, he said. My advice to you, Billy, is get a grip.

It wasn't easy, but Charlie was right. I had to let it go.

The next few summers rolled by. I fielded a Little League team, but the magic of it was gone for me. We won a few games every year, lost the rest, but the kids had fun, and it got me outside on sunny days, so I was grateful for that. The parents and kids all seemed to appreciate it, both my sponsorship of the team and the coaching that Charlie and I did. But there was no thrill in it for me anymore, and I decided I'd continue to sponsor a team but Charlie could manage on his own.

Fortunately, the local high school football team had started showing some signs of life, and that gave me something else to look forward to. For decades, our local team had been awful. We went whole seasons without winning a game and burned through something like ten head coaches in twenty years. Then, by some act of providence, we hired a real coach, with legitimate credentials and experience. His name was Trey Beathard, and he came from East Texas, where they play high school football games in front of thirty thousand people. He'd won a conference title with Texas Methodist and for a time he'd been considered for openings at major programs such as Auburn and Tennessee. But he'd abruptly resigned from Texas Methodist and disappeared, reappearing here a year or so later to coach the Fighting Hornets. How that came to be, no one really knew. Sometimes it's best not to ask. I started going to the games again. Nothing quite like Friday nights under the lights, a nip in the air, the marching band playing in the student section. I even took out an advertisement in their program: "Shaken, Not Stirred. Stop by for a nightcap after the game!"

Miracles don't happen overnight. Coach Beathard's first two seasons, we had just nineteen boys out for the team. We were competitive in a few games, but we lost every one. But then fate intervened. Some of the best high school athletes in our area came from Texas or farther south, the sons and daughters of Mexican migrant laborers who'd driven up in the spring to plant and pick cucumbers for one of the local pickle farms, or to work at one of the factory dairies milking cows. Sometimes, instead of heading back to Texas for the winter, those families stay in Wisconsin, and their kids enroll in school.

Coach Beathard's third season, the Fighting Hornets won two games. That first win lit up the town. You would have thought we'd won the Super Bowl. Someone in town set off fireworks to rival those the Lions Club sponsored on the Fourth of July. The Lopez brothers, Jesus and Julio, were stars that year. Julio played quarterback and Jesus split end, and for two kids who grew up kicking a soccer ball along the Rio Grande (no one was about to ask on which side) they sure took quickly to American football. Julio could spin it forty yards on a string, and Jesus could fly. As he streaked down the sidelines, you could hear his mama shouting from the bleachers, "*Corre rapido! Corre, corre!*" Every time Jesus or Julio scored a touchdown, the Waushara High School marching band would break into a raucous version of "La Bamba," and people in the stands would clap and stomp their cold feet, and all the young and old people who knew Spanish would sing along.

We had twenty-seven players on the team Coach Beathard's third year, and seven of them had to play both ways, which tired them out, especially the big farm boys who played on the line. By the fourth quarter, some of those kids could barely get up off the ground at the end of the play, or you'd see them on their hands and knees, puking through their face masks. In the off-season, Coach Beathard put them on a weight lifting and conditioning program, and that alone would have made a difference. But that spring a new kid arrived in the district, adopted from Africa by a missionary family at one of those raise-your-arms and speak-in-tongues Bible churches that convened in an old, out-of-business grocery store. His name was Chinua Ngobo, and he was from Burkina Faso, a country none of us had ever heard of, and the rumor was he had raced Jesus Lopez in gym class in the two-hundred-meter dash and beat him by fifteen meters.

That fall, Coach Beathard had Chinua in a Fighting Hornets uniform, wearing number 40. The first time I saw him carry the ball, I said to myself, Lord Jesus, it's the Second Coming of Gale Sayers, the Kansas Comet. Send him on a sweep right, and he'd be at the edge before his pulling guards had taken their first two steps. This meant he had no blockers out in front of him, but it often didn't matter. He'd plant that right heel in the ground and explode north, and it must have been like trying to tackle a cheetah. If you ever saw Herschel Walker play at Georgia, or Bo Jackson at Auburn, you know what it looks like when someone that big and strong can also run that fast. Mother Mary, it was something to see.

Problem was, our linemen couldn't get out ahead of him, and if we tried to run off-tackle, we weren't talented enough to blow a hole through the defensive line with any consistency. We had Dom Perignon at running back, champagne at quarterback and split end, and swamp water everywhere else. Even so, we won six games that year, lost two, and advanced to the first round of the state playoffs, where we lost, 42–20, to the eventual champions.

I increased the size of my advertisement in the football program to a quarter page, complete with a photograph of my place. I joined the booster club and became president. Coach Beathard started coming by after the games just to visit and thank us for our support. He always refused my offer of a cold one but accepted congratulations from my patrons on the latest win. A good high school football team can pull a whole town together, and happy football fans like to celebrate at an establishment like mine after a big win. I made enough cash to put a new roof on my place and remodel the inside. Added a couple electronic dart boards, graded and regraveled the parking lot, and put a seventy-two-inch, high-definition flat-screen up on the wall for Packer games. Didn't seem that life could get much better, but as anyone who has lived at all knows well: life can surprise you.

12

Hannah Fisher

May the Lord forgive me, but the first six years after Gabriel came to live with Josiah and me were the happiest of my life. Gabriel embraced our simple ways and opened his heart to the Lord with the zeal and bright hope of a child. In his innocence, he gave us a glimpse of what life might have been like in an unfallen world, the Creator's early light, the sunshine of Genesis, pouring down upon our uplifted faces.

When Gabriel came to us, we allowed him to finish his term at the English school. Each morning, I stood with him at the end of the driveway until the bus stopped, the children's faces like little moons in each window, the caution lights pulsing red. I'd watch Gabriel climb the stairs and duck his head as he moved through the aisle to find a seat before the bus rumbled away. Josiah did not approve. It had been decades since English law released us from mandatory school attendance, and no other Amish in our district sent their children to an English school. It made me uneasy, too. But the boy had suffered so much. How many changes must he endure at once? Give him time, I said. We must be patient, let the Lord's will be done.

That spring the problem resolved itself. Two of Gabriel's new Amish friends, Amos Stolzfus and Aaron Yoder, lived nearby and attended Amish grammar school taught by Esther Hershberger, the mother of

Maddie, who ran the bakery. Gabriel asked if he might attend Amish school with them. Though we would like to think religious principles led to this request, I'm certain he simply wanted to be with his friends.

By January, on his own, Gabriel had begun to dress in plain clothing. No doubt he felt out of place among us in the colorful T-shirts and bright sporting shoes Jasper had purchased for him. He owned the biggest straw hat of anyone in our church district, and the largest pair of leather boots. He joined us at Sunday meetings and proved to have a beautiful singing voice. He loved *Das Loblied*, as I did, and I often heard him singing it alone, though he did not yet understand the meaning, while watering the goats or weeding the vegetable garden.

In the beginning, no one in our district knew how to approach Gabriel. Adults were wary, as if the boy somehow carried the sins of his mother and brother inside him. Because Gabriel towered over them, Amish children initially feared him, though it wasn't long before the younger ones stood in line waiting for rides high on his shoulders, laughing as he cantered across the grass, each child gripping his hair like the reins of a horse.

Older Amish boys challenged Gabriel to feats of strength, something that continued for many years. Gabriel enjoyed these requests (he often told me of them at prayer time, just before bed); he was a boy, after all, and loved to test his strength, as boys do. When Gabriel was eleven, Amos snuck Gabriel and several other boys into his father's barn and dared Gabriel to lift Ahab, the family's prized Corriedale ram. Corriedales can weigh three hundred pounds, with heavy, full-curled horns on massive heads, and Ahab was the largest of the flock. Gabriel calmed and then crouched beside the animal, reached his arms under, and stood upright while the other boys cheered. At age twelve, on a dare, Gabriel hopped into the pasture with a carrot in his pocket and lifted all four feet of Bishop Eli Lapp's year-old Belgian colt off the ground; Mr. Lapp witnessed this from a window in his barn and upbraided the boys for trespassing. Gabriel felt terrible, but afterward Eli privately complimented his strength and care for the animal.

As I've said, for our people, humility is a daily practice. But for Gabriel, physically, even though he dressed as we did, it was not possible to blend in. A giraffe cannot hide in a herd of pygmy goats. At our volleyball games, Gabriel could stand in the front row and block every shot that came over the net from the other side, often without even jumping.

Josiah wondered if Gabriel diminished himself with such displays and brought shame to us as well. How, he asked, can the boy not swell with pride when he does what no one else can do?

"He is a boy playing with his friends, Josiah," I said.

"He makes a spectacle of himself."

"People stare at him everywhere he goes, yes?" I countered. "How can they not? Some English stare at you and me, too. Do we make spectacles of ourselves?"

"It's not the same."

"What will you have him do?" I asked. "Pretend to be short? Pretend to be clumsy? Josiah, you build beautiful things. Last month you finished a fine chest of drawers. Do you stop making such things if the people who buy them pronounce them beautiful and compliment your skillful work?"

"You are willfully misunderstanding me."

"I am trying to understand. But you must try, also. It is one thing to resist the allure of pride. It is another to deny the gifts of God because your grandfather ordains it."

"I have ordered no such thing. I wish you could hear yourself, Hannah! Sometimes I no longer recognize you."

This hurt me. How could it not? For over thirty years of marriage, our Godly union has strengthened us, sustained us through every affliction. It is only when life is good and rich with meaning that we have struggled. When we are not leaning into one another in support during our shared sorrow, we often find ourselves tipped apart. I have asked so many times in my heart: Is happiness against God's will? Though suffering brings us closer to Him, must we suspect every smile, every moment of joy, to be the secret work of Satan?

The matter of Gabriel's work with Dr. Kennedy also caused tension between Josiah and me. In the beginning, we agreed that Gabriel could continue accompanying the doctor on Saturday calls throughout the year, and these occurred more frequently in the summer. Josiah didn't want this, but for the boy's sake, he allowed it. Gabriel loved working with animals, and he was always so happy to see Dr. Kennedy, a joy obviously mutual when you saw them together. Dr. Kennedy would contact Josiah by telephone to inform him of when he would arrive for Gabriel, and the two of them would drive off in the doctor's truck, usually in the early morning. Dr. Kennedy would return Gabriel to us when their work was done. For two years after Jasper's death, this continued without interruption.

But when Gabriel turned twelve, Josiah began to express misgivings about these frequent trips into the English world. In the first place, he said, Gabriel was needed on our farm and in his shop. We were getting older, and he was young and strong; he could do more work in a day than we could do together in three. Beyond that, he argued, we had become too permissive. We had bent the dictates of our faith into knots to accommodate Gabriel, allowing him continuous exposure to atheism and temptation. Furthermore, our bishop and deacon had expressed their own concerns about the arrangement. If we did not act, in time they would.

I stood as firm as my conscience would allow. Gabriel loved Dr. Kennedy, and it was obvious to everyone that the doctor loved Gabriel as well. It would be cruel and heartless to separate them. Josiah agreed that Dr. Kennedy was as honest and caring as a man without God in his heart could be. My quarrel, Josiah told me, was not with him but with our church.

"Dr. Kennedy is like a grandfather to the boy!" I protested, my tears coming.

"He has a grandfather already," Josiah said.

"Josiah, I will not consent."

"We have no choice, Hannah. You know this."

I did know it, and when my mind quieted, I understood. But there was a way to honor our faith and allow Gabriel's fellowship with the doctor to continue. I proposed that we extend a dinner invitation to Dr. Kennedy on the first Friday of every month. This would not conflict with the bishop's wishes to move Gabriel more deeply into the protective security and anonymity of our people, yet it would give Gabriel at least some contact with his loving friend. Josiah objected gently at first, but he understood on this point I would not be moved.

In the beginning, these dinners were awkward. Josiah and I are quiet people, and Dr. Kennedy measured his words carefully. Without Gabriel at the table, we might not have spoken much at all. He was the bridge that brought us together, and in time Dr. Kennedy became a welcomed guest and a friend not only to Gabriel, but to me as well.

We knew when Gabriel came to us that he was not a normal-sized child. Like many people, at first we thought he'd simply bloomed early. Some boys do. Josiah began borrowing his father's straight razor to shave when he was thirteen, but today his beard is no longer or thicker than that of any other man his age. Similarly, though indelicate to speak of it, my sister's bosoms began to swell at eleven, pressing against the placket of her dress, whereas mine did not grow until I was fourteen (and though stunted thereafter, proved as useful in their purpose as God intended, swelling to provide an endless supply of milk for Rachel). Like most people, we believed Gabriel's growth would soon slow and stop. But that did not happen. He kept growing, beyond anyone's reckoning. He grew as if descended from the biblical Anakim of Canaan, the race of giants.

The day Gabriel turned ten, and each birthday thereafter, he stood erect with his back to the wall in the kitchen, where it opened to the hall that led out the back door. He leaned against the irregular ladder rungs of marks I'd made each year as Rachel grew taller. (When Rachel died, Josiah wanted to paint over these marks, but I denied him.) I balanced on a chair and drew a thick line along the top of Gabriel's head with a graphite pencil and then extended Josiah's tape measure from the floor up to that mark. At age ten, Gabriel stood six feet six inches tall, already seven inches taller than Josiah as a grown man. The day he turned twelve, he stood six feet eleven inches and weighed 255 pounds.

Josiah made many changes to our home to accommodate Gabriel's size. Most days, it seemed like the only flaw in Gabriel's mastery of the physical world was his inability to correctly gauge the reach of his body as he moved through it. The boy constantly bumped his head— against the head jamb of the doorways to the barn, the house, and his bedroom; against the milking stand as he sat milking goats. Josiah remedied this as best he could. He cut out the wall above the front and back doors and replaced them with doors eight feet high. He did the same with the door to Gabriel's bedroom. He raised the bedroom ceiling to nine feet, and he removed the framing and sheetrock above the staircase, leaving it open to the second floor, so that Gabriel could climb the stairs without crouching. Josiah extended the frame of Gabriel's bed to ten feet and customized a mattress by adding a half mattress to the end of a full one, bending the springs beneath the ticking to connect them. I sewed new sheets, a wool blanket, and a goose-down comforter to fit the new bed.

I sewed all of Gabriel's clothing, and the cobbler, Abram Glick, made pigskin work gloves to fit his large hands and leather boots to accommodate his giant feet. Gabriel wore a size 19 boot as a twelve-year-old, and he went up a size about every six months. To reduce costs, Abram made Gabriel's boots two sizes larger than they needed to be, and he included soft, padded leather stoppers that could be pushed into the toes at half-size thicknesses. As Gabriel's feet grew, we could remove these stoppers one at a time, so that a pair of boots might last a year and a half or even two years before they needed replacing.

The summer before Gabriel turned seventeen, he stood over eight feet tall, weighed 388 pounds, and could cross the pasture carrying a one-hundred-pound yearling ewe under each arm, their legs thrashing as if running in air. I watched him through the kitchen window one morning, tears in my eyes as he and Josiah separated the elderly, dry ewes from the younger ewes and kids, for culling. The previous evening, I'd sorrowfully wandered the pasture marking the old and frail by placing a cross of blue grease pencil on their foreheads before hugging each of them goodbye. Several animals were so arthritic they could barely get to their feet. God has ordained a season for every purpose under heaven. Yet, I could not bear to participate in the culling. I did not want my beautiful goats to see my face as they died.

In his way, Gabriel handled our elderly animals with touching gentleness. He lifted them so easily, the strength in his arms so certain, I believe they felt comforted and secure. I don't know what he whispered in their ears as he clutched them to his body, but sometimes they did not even move as Josiah drew the sharpened blade across their throats. Like the waters of their birth, their warm blood steamed as it spilled into the tub. When they went limp, Gabriel carried them as sweetly as newborn lambs into the shed for butchering.

Paradise is not of this earth, and time cannot be frozen in its most hopeful and happy moments. I knew *Rumspringa* was coming, that the allure of English life Gabriel had already tasted when young might draw him back. Already that spring, his best friends, Amos Stolzfus and Aaron Yoder, had wandered into the wilderness. Amos had purchased an old truck and learned to drive, and he and Aaron had been seen for months in the company of English girls, smoking cigarettes and drinking beer. They'd grown lazy at home and loud abroad. One night, Amos returned home at three thirty in the morning, his English clothes reeking of marijuana. Locked out of the house, he'd broken a window to get in, and his mother, Anna, had confronted him. She tearfully whispered the news to me at Sunday gathering.

Though it is God's greatest gift to be a mother, it can be unbearably painful. For an Amish mother, other than mourning a child's death, perhaps no more painful time exists than *Rumspringa*. Children and grandchildren are set loose in a world rife with danger and temptation, and we must wait, silently and patiently, to see if they will return to us. I do not question the wisdom of *Rumspringa*. It has served our people for hundreds of years. Regret is endemic to human life. The only way to defeat it is to open the door to temptation, to allow anything, having faith that our children will recognize the emptiness of transitory pleasure and the uselessness of earthly things, and return to the fold. Nearly all do.

I listened to Anna's sorrowful story with a tiny, terrible beating of joy in my own heart. Gabriel had not joined Aaron and Amos in their worldly recklessness. I could not stop this swell of selfish comfort and righteousness, hidden from men but not from God. It was the beginning of my undoing, because the summer just before Gabriel turned seventeen, the English world came for him, too.

It was a warm Saturday afternoon. Gabriel and Josiah were away, and I was alone in the garden, weeding my tomatoes. A black pickup truck arrived, and a tall, English stranger wearing a ball cap stepped down from the truck. He slowly crossed the yard and approached, limping slightly, taking care to keep his feet between the rows of tomato bushes. I raised my muddy hands at him, and he stopped six feet from me. He removed his hat and nodded, squinting in the sunlight. His bulbous nose was marked by tiny veins, like little red worms, and the joints of his fingers were swollen and gnarled like knots. On his feet he wore garish cowboy boots the color of indigo buntings, pointed at the toe, with shiny silver buckles along each side.

"Afternoon, ma'am," the man said, his voice soft and strangely accented.

"My husband's not at home," I said.

He nodded. "I'll speak with you, if I may," he said, "if that's all right." Though his eyes and voice seemed kind, even gentle, they betrayed persistence. JC Beathard was the football coach at Waushara High School. He had come to ask if Gabriel might be interested in playing football for him in the fall.

If I could have reversed time, I would have done so that day. What began with a simple question on that bright afternoon would grow the way a single drop of rain becomes a flood. In time, almost a hundred men just like Mr. Beathard would knock on our humble door, suntanned, cologne-scented, fast-talking men in bright, shiny clothes, all promising the same thing, all wanting the same thing: the chance to pull Gabriel so deeply into the English world he might never find his way out again.

Part Two

13

Trey Beathard

Folks in Texas grow up thinking it snows twelve months of the year in Wisconsin and people up there put cheese in everything, including their morning coffee. I had no desire to discover if those things were true. Seriously, it's the last place I ever expected to find myself, not to mention jobless, homeless, divorced, bankrupted in spirit and every other way. But Mama always said if you're smart you take any port in a storm (and she laughed every time she said it because she's from Galveston), so when Daddy's exiled sister, my Aunt Birdy, threw me a lifeline from Oxford, a one-stoplight town in central Wisconsin, the nowhere in the middle of nowhere, I tied it around my waist and let her pull me in.

When I was a kid, Aunt Birdy smoked cigars and wore her hair in a throwback crew cut like Johnny Unitas. She lived in Fort Worth with Melinda, her "lady friend," as people said back then. Mel was from a wealthy family that raised thoroughbred racehorses. My kin called her Godiva, because we suspected she rode bareback in the altogether, with bluebells in her hair. Sometime in the late 1970s, around the age of twenty-two, Aunt Birdy and Melinda got themselves arrested in Dallas for public indecency. Apparently, they had kissed at a candlelit table in the restaurant where they'd gone to celebrate an anniversary.

Because Melinda's parents had connections at the Tarrant County courthouse, Mel and Birdy paid a heavy fine but avoided jail time. They left Texas and fled north. I don't think they expected to find someplace where lesbian lovers could kiss publicly without raising eyebrows, at least not then, but what they found was a repossessed horse farm on a hundred eighty acres that they bought from the bank with some of Mel's trust fund money in a place where people were nice and left you alone. Everybody drank a lot of beer and brandy, too, which probably made them nicer. Even their Amish neighbors were kind to them. Mel and Birdy settled in and built a happy life together. But their bitterness toward the Lone Star state never left them. In the dining room of their farmhouse is a framed map of the United States, six feet across and four feet high, with the state of Texas removed, the empty space painted to blend in with the tranquil blue waters of the Gulf of Mexico.

Looking back, I can see now the seeds of my self-destruction were being sown in my boyhood. I had a compulsive personality, though when you're a boy people spin that positively. They told me I was determined, a striver, or—my favorite—a winner. Some kinds of addiction, such as an addiction to work, can produce positive benefits for a long time before taking you down. An addiction to sex, to gambling, to drugs or alcohol—I've sampled them all—sends you to the bottom faster. Whether you're at a craps table in Vegas or coked up at a Bourbon Street hotel on a Saturday night with a couple of escorts who know their way around a man's body, you feel invincible. On Sunday mornings, you're wracked with guilt and shame. It's a seesaw between heaven and hell, and you can't figure out how to get off.

All my life, though, one healthy obsession formed me, and that was the game of football. In the thick Piney Woods region of East Texas, where the hot summer wind carries the scent of turpentine, by the time most boys learn to talk they know the Trinity is not the Father, Son, and Holy Ghost but God, Oil, and Football, in that order, except on game day, when God has to give way to the gridiron. Lone Star folks are proud that everything's bigger in Texas: the horns of the cattle and the prairie they graze, the megachurches, the East Texas Oil Field, and all those beautiful high school football stadiums lit up like galaxies on Friday nights. Ask a southerner to name somebody famous from East Texas, and they might say Janis Joplin or Don Henley. Ask any Texan the same question, and you'll hear the names of some of the best football players ever to lace up cleats: the "Tyler Rose," Earl Campbell; Dandy Don Meredith; Bubba Smith; Mel Farr; Adrian Peterson. Ask them to name the greatest coach in the history of East Texas football, and they won't hesitate: Josiah Crocket Beathard II. I'm certain there are other coaches more deserving of that veneration, but I don't come to that observation without prejudice. JC Beathard II was my daddy. I worshipped him the first half of my life, detested him the rest.

I played for Coach Beathard for four years at Magnolia High in Beaumont, and we won the Level 3A state championship my senior year. We should have won it my junior year as well, but I blew out my knee in the first half of the quarterfinals against East Bernard. Their running back, Alphonso Cartwright, weighed 235 pounds and ran the one-hundred-meter dash in 10.7 seconds. We couldn't stop him. I cried like a baby all second half, kept trying to walk off my injury to get back on the field, Daddy screaming at me to stop being a pussy and get in there, but it was like my lower leg wasn't connected to my upper leg at all, just sort of hanging by a single thread at the knee, the whole joint burning like a blowtorch. I had surgery and rehabbed like a maniac. Senior year I was a captain and an all-state linebacker, and we won it all.

My daddy used to say that football is a violent game, but violence under control is what makes it beautiful, the channeling of animal aggression in eleven young men united for a common purpose. He said winning isn't free, that you pay ahead in installments of pain, sweat, and blood. Daddy had the words "Never Quit" painted above every football locker, on the floor of the locker room, even on the walls of the shower. At home, he painted those words on the ceiling above my bed, so they were the last thing I saw at night and the first thing I saw when I opened my eyes in the morning.

JC Beathard II compiled a record of 387 wins against just 46 losses in his career at Magnolia, including seven 3A state championships. He could have coached at the college level, but he turned down every opportunity that presented itself. Mama said he loved what he did so much, he didn't want to change. He also had no desire to work the eighty hours a week necessary to be a successful college football coach. I thought that made him weak, and I vowed one day I'd eclipse the legendary JC Beathard II by becoming the head coach at a major university.

Coming out of high school, I didn't have many scholarship offers. The University of Texas only offered me walk-on status, and that hurt. I'd dreamed of being a Longhorn all my life, of playing on the same field where Earl Campbell won the Heisman. College scouts all told me the same thing: at six foot three inches and 230 pounds, I was big enough; I could bench 225 pounds eighteen times, so I was strong enough. But when it came to wheels, you had to be a Ferrari to play major college ball, and I was more like a bus. Never a speedster to begin with, after my knee injury I could never run the forty-yard dash any faster than 5.4 seconds. My vertical was only twenty inches. A scout from Texas Tech said, Son, on a field of jackrabbits, you'd be an armadillo wallowing in the mud.

No major college would sign me, but I accepted a partial ride to Stephen F. Austin State University, the jewel in the crown of East Texas football. Every kid in Beaumont revered the Lumberjacks, and the whole state of Texas stopped whatever they were doing each fall when Stephen F. Austin played its fierce rival, Sam Houston State University, in the Battle of the Piney Woods. I rode the pine most of my college career. At that level, the speed and strength of the athletes exposed my weaknesses.

When my playing days were over, Coach offered me a graduate assistantship to join the Stephen F. Austin staff, and it took fifteen years and position-coaching changes at eight different universities before I finally got the call. I'd finished my second year as the defensive coordinator at Montana State. My family loved it there. We lived on a little trout stream with a view of the mountains, and it was beautiful, though I was seldom home to enjoy it. I had a wife and a twelve-year-old daughter by then, and they were tired of living out of suitcases.

I took the call at my office in Bozeman, and even before I telephoned my wife, I called my daddy. I told him I'd just accepted the offer to become head football coach at Texas Methodist University, which had not enjoyed a winning season for something like fifteen years. He said, Son, I hope you know what you're doing, because that is one of the sorriest-ass excuses for a football program in the entire US of A.

I worked one-hundred-hour weeks for four years, traveled tens of thousands of miles recruiting, and in our fourth season we went 8–3 and won the conference championship, thumping Louisiana Tech in the title game 30–13. I don't think I slept at all during the final three weeks of the season, and around Thanksgiving, my life started coming apart.

I'd been drinking a lot for years, taking ephedrine or sniffing coke for the energy, oxy to help me sleep. I had the numbers of my favorite escorts in cities where I recruited saved under men's names in my phone—Coach Angelo was Angel, in New Orleans, for example. I'd built a skyscraper of lies with no truth at the base. I'm sure Gail suspected something. I was putting whiskey in my coffee in the morning, and sometimes my bookie would call, and she'd overhear me talking to him. I'd fallen over a hundred K in the hole. What finally stopped the merry-go-round was a single, stupid mistake. At sixteen, our daughter, Ruth Anne, had her wisdom teeth pulled, and I picked up her prescription for painkillers at the pharmacy. Oxycodone was weak water compared to the OxyContin I could get from the training room. But I pulled over before I got home and took five of Ruth Anne's pills. An hour later I took three more, and soon after I found myself writhing with seizures on the kitchen floor. While I was in the ambulance on the way to the hospital, my wife started calling some of the numbers in the contacts on my phone. The jig was up.

By the end of January, Gail had full custody of Ruth Anne—who wasn't speaking to me, anyway. I had no job, no bank account, and no place to live. My new AA sponsor let me crash on his sofa a few nights, but he had six cats and I was allergic, so that wasn't going to work. Repulsed by my behavior, and shamed that I shared his name, Daddy wouldn't take me in. Mama cried and cried, begging him to reconsider. I was their only child, Christian mercy demanded it, and so forth, but he wouldn't budge. The court allowed me to keep my clothes, some personal items, and a ten-year-old Ford F-150 with 178,000 miles on it. When Aunt Birdy called from Wisconsin, I filled my truck with gas and drove north. It was some forty years after Birdy and Melinda had made the same journey. I hit a snowstorm in Illinois. Driving through those squalls reminded me of Saturday mornings as a boy, when Mama used to hang the bedsheets on the line, and I'd go stand in them, the cotton flapping like loose sails in the wind. I'd close my eyes and pretend I was on a ship sailing out of the port at Galveston, sunshine on my face, seagulls hovering in our wake.

I reached Oxford around five o'clock in the afternoon. The sun had already set, and the snow shone blue in the light of the rising moon. Driving along Cottonville Road, I flanked one of Birdy and Mel's pastures the final quarter mile, a large expanse of drifted snow surrounded by barbed wire, with a herd of beautiful horses gathered around two large, round bales of hay fifteen yards from the rear of the barn. The two-story farmhouse was white, with a red barn behind it, and a concrete silo standing beside that. Farther in the distance stood a much larger, more modern-looking building, perhaps a quarter mile long, where the horses were stabled. Birdy and Melinda had placed a lone electric candle in each of the house's upstairs windows. Perhaps the candles remained from the Christmas season, or maybe they were lit for me. Either way, it looked like the picture you might see on a calendar for the month of December, beautiful, warm, and welcoming, nothing like the chaos roiling inside my head.

Birdy and Mel took me in like a son, offering no advice or judgement other than my hands felt soft and I looked exhausted after driving all night and all day. They moved me into the guest bedroom on the second floor, which overlooked the east pasture. "You can see the sunrise from that window every morning if you get up early enough," Birdy said. A queen-size brass bed stood in the middle of the room, and paintings of a tall, dark-skinned woman with bushy, black eyebrows, surrounded by monkeys, covered the walls. Downstairs, the rooms were decorated with Birdy's oil paintings—horses, cranes, birds of all kinds. Over the fireplace was a portrait of Mel, close to life-sized, reclined in a field of daisies, a chickadee perched on her shoulder.

"I'm making pasta with artichokes and capers," Aunt Birdy said to me. "You like pasta, don't you?"

"Yes," I said. "Thank you."

She nodded once. "Well, you go upstairs and do whatever it is you need to do. We'll eat around seven. We usually eat at eight, but we knew you'd be tired. You need anything, and I mean anything at all, you just ask."

"I will."

"Oh." She grabbed my arm gently, then released it. "This is the last I'll speak of it, but my brother is an asshole, turning you away, and that's putting it as kindly as I can. I just thought that needed saying."

"Thank you," I said. "To be fair, I've made a mess of my life."

"Well"—Birdy shrugged—"who hasn't at one time or other?"

For the next six months, I rarely left the farm other than to attend weekly AA meetings in the basement of the Oxford Presbyterian Church. Though I had no obligations, I struggled every day. I had to learn to sleep again, which wasn't as easy as it might seem. I'd so seldom slept without any pharmacological assistance that my body needed to figure out how to do that. A guilty conscience also does not make for restful slumber. I'd gone from living at a hundred miles an hour with my hair on fire to walking, slowly, surrounded by nothing but trees and grass, horses and a few chickens, the smell of manure and fresh hay. That is as peaceful as it sounds, but such peace allowed no distraction from my shame. Like a race car driver suddenly forced to cross the country at twenty-five miles an hour, I had to learn an almost maddening level of patience, and I had far too much time to dwell on the terrible things I'd done.

I wanted to help on the farm, but it was surprising just how little I could actually do. I didn't know how to cook, I knew nothing about gardening, and I was afraid of horses. I knew everything there was to know about one thing: football. Birdy taught me to cook, Mel taught me about horses, and they both showed me how to plant a vegetable garden. They bought me my own set of knives for Christmas at the end of the year, and by then I could cook just about everything in their worn copy of Julia Child's *Mastering the Art of French Cooking*, proudly offering an all-day-simmered coq au vin for Christmas dinner.

I'd never intended to stay long, but I had rarely felt so at home in a place, and Birdy and Mel really wanted me to stay. We made an odd family, but I guess most families are odd in their own way. We planted a garden that next spring, and it was that summer, my second in Oxford, that Mel came home from grocery shopping and found me out in the barn, where I was helping the farrier shoe a horse. By this time, I'd taken a job as an evening cashier at the local gas station, but Mel handed me the local newspaper, turned to the classifieds, with one advertisement circled in blue pen. Waushara High School was seeking a new football coach.

I called that afternoon, interviewed with the principal and athletic director the following morning. That night they called and offered me the job.

Throughout my years of college coaching, I'd traveled the richest veins of college football talent in the country. I'd seen premier five-star high school athletes on the field, elite prospects who starred in college and signed multimillion-dollar contracts with the NFL. So it seems ridiculous, beyond belief, really, to admit that the two greatest athletes I have ever seen, Gabriel Fisher and Chinua Ngobo, showed up at the same time in a godforsaken little burg of scrub oak and jack pine in the middle of nowhere, Wisconsin.

First time I ever laid eyes on Chin was the opening day of practice my third year at the helm. We'd had a little success the previous season with Julio Lopez at the trigger and his brother, Jesus, at wide receiver, and we'd made some gains in the weight room over the summer on the offensive and defensive lines. I thought a reasonable goal would be to win a couple more games than the year before.

Then Chin showed up. He'd been adopted from Burkina Faso the previous winter by a local minister and his wife. They'd planned to home-school him until they realized he spoke no English. They enrolled him at the high school in January, and he found the climate so frigid he wore his winter parka and gloves all day, even inside the building.

Shy, soft-spoken, sixteen years old, he didn't know the first thing about American football. He'd grown up playing soccer at the orphanage in Ouagadougou. At our first practice, he showed up in street clothes and refused to wear his helmet or his mouth guard. Through some pantomime and fuzzy translation from my right guard, Johnny Baker, who'd had two years of high school French, I learned that the helmet hurt Chinua's head, and that he felt like he couldn't breathe wearing his mouth guard. I told him, Son, the helmet must fit like a glove or you'll get concussed, and that mouth guard is going to keep your teeth from getting knocked out. The rules require you to wear both of 'em, so you best get used to it. He smiled and nodded but didn't understand a word I said. He'd picked up a bit of English by then but no football English, and I knew no French, which he spoke fluently, or Mossi, his African language, which he used when he needed to cuss.

Fortunately, running is a universal language, and that first practice, we were only testing. I let Chinua skip the helmet and mouth guard for the day. Our first test was the forty-yard dash. Coach Spaulding, one of my assistants, was at the start on the fifty-yard line. My other assistant, Coach Lain, a hippie-dippie middle school art teacher and former soccer coach, who coached my kickers, stood on the ten with me, recording the times as I read them off the stopwatch. We had thirty-one kids out, and they sorted themselves, with the linemen going first, then the rest. Like the previous year, Jesus ran last, or in this case, next to last. He ran 4.55, which for a sophomore high schooler in cleats and a helmet on long grass, is damn quick. Jesus was a long strider, too, stronger in the hundred meters than the forty, no question. Chinua watched all of this from a seated position about ten yards behind Coach Spaulding. He sat cross-legged, his back and body erect, like Buddha.

When Coach Spaulding called Chinua up to the line, the boy removed his shirt, a button-down blue oxford, tossing it in the grass beside him. He also pulled off his shoes and socks, and then his pants. Fortunately, he was wearing boxers, and he kept them on. I made a mental note to myself to get the boy some cleats and practice clothes. I raised a hand to signal I was ready. Chinua crouched at the line, and Coach told him to go any time.

I started my watch on his first movement, and he exploded like he'd been shot out of a gun. I could tell the kid had speed. He had that effortless glide you see in boys who'd been running fast all their lives. Kids like that, I say they run happy. It's like the body's way of expressing joy. His hamstrings were as thick and curved as quarter moons, like those of all great sprinters, and I could see every muscle rippling under the skin of his powerful thighs, shiny and black as eggplants. Kid was beautiful, a kinetic work of art. I stopped the watch when he hit the ten and he blew on past me and stopped somewhere in the end zone, turned around, and smiled. I looked down at my watch and blinked: 4.23. Coach Spaulding showed up at my elbow.

"Holy Christ," he said, out of breath. I held the watch out and he looked at it, slack-jawed. "You start late? That watch on the fritz?"

"That's accurate," I said.

"Holy Christ," Coach Spaulding said again. "That kid's fast as a bullet."

Chinua also had a forty-two-inch vertical jump, and he bench-pressed 225 pounds six times, though I'm certain the kid had never seen the inside of a weight room in his life before that morning. Unfortunately, his football IQ was zero, and I struggled to teach him the game. We went through two weeks of two-a-days in summer camp and the first couple weeks of the season, and Chinua had still not learned the offense. He went the wrong way at least half the time, and even when he went the correct direction, he never knew if he was supposed to get the ball or pass block or head to the flat as the safety valve. We had the best high school athlete in the country on our sideline, but I couldn't figure out how to get him on the field for more than a few plays a game.

We kept it close but lost our first two games to teams who'd made the playoffs the previous season. Desperate, I offered the high school French teacher, Mademoiselle Mouglalis, a hundred dollars and a home-cooked French dinner on Saturday night, my famous-in-my-own-mind coq au vin, if she'd translate my playbook into French for Chinua. Merryn wouldn't accept the money, but she loved French food, and she agreed. She even came to practice to clarify things for Chinua. By Friday night, the kid had it figured out. I gave Merryn Mouglalis a sideline pass and appointed her special assistant to the head coach.

I started Chin at halfback on offense, and we blew the doors off. Chin carried the ball sixteen times for two hundred eighty yards and four touchdowns, Julio was fourteen of sixteen passing for another couple hundred, and we won that game 56–10. We went on to run the table that season and finished six and two. Then we lost a heartbreaker in the first round of the state playoffs. But I felt okay about things. We had our three best linemen coming back the next year. Chinua was a junior, so he'd be back for another year. He already had a box full of letters. There was some interest in Julio and Jesus as well. I hoped another year in the weight room and having Chinua for the full season would get us to the next level of the state playoffs, maybe even further. But we weren't quite there yet. We had lightning but not the thunderclap. We could outrun you, but we could not outstrong you. That was about to change.

But for a chance encounter, it never would have happened at all. Sometime in June, I'd been invited to speak at the summer fundraiser of our Fighting Hornets booster club. The club president, Billy Walton, hosted the barbecue at his bar in Lakota. He had a couple half-barrel barbecue pits going in the parking lot and was charging twenty bucks for a quarter chicken, baked potato, and all the beer you could drink, and he was donating the beer. Fifteen bucks a ticket went into the booster club treasury. You don't have to ask a Texan twice to eat some barbecue, and like me, Billy was on the wagon, so I knew I'd face no pressure to have a beer.

I shook some hands, talked a bit about our plans for the upcoming season, answered a few questions, ate some barbecue, and headed off in my truck. I had a few errands to run, then picked up some groceries, and visited Alycia Lopez, Jesus and Julio's mother, at the Shoprite. I also stopped and bought a couple of swim floats. My French dinner with Merryn Mouglalis had gone well, and we had plans to picnic and swim at the quarry the next afternoon.

The sun was just starting to set when I started home to Mel and Birdy's place. A few miles out of Lakota I passed some Amish boys far off in a distant alfalfa field. The crop had been cut, dried, and baled, and they were loading a wagon drawn by a pair of brown draft horses, stacking the hay ten or fifteen bales high, beyond the railings that circled the flatbed. They seemed to be making a game of it, seeing how high they could go. A boy maybe twelve years old was on the wagon leading the team, and there were two others doing the loading, both in black pants, white shirts, and suspenders, straw hats on their heads. One of them seemed to be down on his knees.

It was a beautiful scene. In the setting sun, the horses glistened with sweat, and when the breeze blew toward me, I could hear the wagon squeaking as it rolled along, and sometimes I heard the boys' laughter. What I saw next brought my foot to the brake pedal. The boy who was standing bent over, and when he stood up again, a bale of hay flew off the ground into the air, flipped over once, then twice, as it rose several feet above the top of the hay stacked in the wagon, and came down and nestled there. The other boys clapped their hands. As they began to walk forward together, I realized that the other boy in the field wasn't kneeling at all: the larger one was that much taller, so tall that his smaller companion's head reached, at best, to just above his waist.

Perhaps this was a trick of the eye? The boys were a hundred fifty or two hundred yards distant. I put the window down and watched as the wagon rolled forward to another bale. The taller boy bent over again. As he stood, in a single motion, he launched that bale into the air, only this time he got the angle wrong. The bale spun, rotating slowly, completely over the wagon, coming back to earth on the other side, snapping the twine holding it together and exploding into pieces. More laughter followed. That boy was throwing bales of hay twenty-five or thirty feet into the air.

When I got home, I took Aunt Birdy's bathroom scale out into the barn, set it on the floor, and weighed myself: two hundred thirty pounds. I lifted a bale of hay, rolled it up to one shoulder, and got on the scale again. Two hundred seventy-four pounds. The bale weighed forty-four pounds. I tried another bale: forty-five pounds. A third: forty. I took a bale outside to the back of the barn where someone long ago had nailed a basketball hoop, now rusted and missing a net, to the siding ten feet above the ground. I'm long past prime but still fairly strong. I warmed up a bit, and then I gripped both strands of twine in my right hand. I grunted as I released the bale, and I succeeded in getting it over-head. It would have cleared seven feet. Maybe eight. I tried a second time and got the same result. That huge Amish kid could have topped that from his knees.

Back at the house, Mel and Birdy were on the porch drinking cranberry wine and playing cribbage by candlelight.

"Everything okay?" Mel asked.

"I saw the strangest thing today. Some Amish kids were loading a hay wagon, and one of those kids looked like he was walking on stilts. Kid had to be over seven feet tall. And he wasn't some skinny flagpole, either. He was throwing forty-pound bales thirty feet into the air. With one arm."

Mel and Aunt Birdy laughed. "That must be Gabriel," Birdy said.

"You know him?"

Birdy nodded. "Gabriel Fisher. Sweet boy. Haven't seen him for years, though. He used to work for Doc Kennedy. Our horses loved that boy. He was big for his age. Could look a horse in the eye when he was just eight years old."

"You know where he lives?"

"Somewhere near Lakota, I imagine," Mel said. "We see Amish buggies pass when we're swimming in the Mecan."

"Do you think he'd play football for me?"

Mel shrugged but Birdy shook her head. "Trey, he's Amish," she said. "Don't get your hopes up."

Gabriel's grandparents were not receptive to my proposal, but it was that time in an Amish boy's life when he could try on parts of the outside world, see if they fit, so to speak, so they left the decision to him. I stopped by every week or so, didn't make a nuisance of myself, but wanted the boy and his grandparents to get to know me. I know Gabriel didn't want to disappoint them. For most of the summer, it didn't look like he would play. But on the last Friday of August when we hit the field for our first game of that magical season, Gabriel Fisher was with us, wearing a custom-made, size 12½ Riddell helmet that cost $1,500 (bought and paid for by the Fighting Hornets booster fund) and size 27 cleats custom-made by an Amish cobbler. The boy was over eight feet tall and heavier than the total weight available on our scale, which went up to three hundred and fifty. He was most likely four hundred pounds in pads, and most of that was muscle.

Gabriel Fisher didn't just alter our expectations for success that season; anyone who saw him play knows this is no exaggeration: he did things on the field no one will ever see again.

14

Billy Walton

I'd just unlocked the front door at Shaken and started tapping a barrel of Bud when Charlie came through the door. It was late morning, third week of August, hot as the hinges of Hades and dry as the devil's martini. Charlie flopped in wearing his bedroom slippers, dirty dungarees, and a black-and-yellow-striped Fighting Hornets baseball cap. Even before sitting down, he dropped the news, like Little Boy falling out of the Enola Gay.

"I swear to you," Charlie said. "Gabriel is sixteen years old and big as a Kodiak bear, and he's playing football for Coach Beathard."

"I don't believe it."

"I didn't either. The kid just disappeared, and now here he is, blocking out the sun. People are driving in from all over just to get a look at him."

I had to smile, remembering Josiah's insistence that God had a different plan for Gabriel. Who knows, maybe he was right. Or else we just got lucky. Either way, Fighting Hornets fans had won the lottery, because fate had brought together a coaching genius from Texas, a blue-chip quarterback and a wide receiver from Mexico, a five-star running back from Africa, and an Amish kid eight feet tall and strong as a Brahman bull.

Coach Beathard always said you had to play the best if you wanted to be the best, but all summer I'd worried he'd overscheduled our nonconference opener. St. Mary's won the private school conference title the year before, and they had a quarterback returning who had committed to Western Michigan, and a state sprint champion at wide-out who was a verbal commit to Notre Dame. But it was an opener none of us will ever forget.

We got to the stadium just after the teams had taken the field, and Gabriel was out there in a yellow number 77 Fighting Hornets uniform, a black helmet about the size of a bushel basket on his head. On both sides of the field, the stands were already full. News trucks from the networks that broadcast out of Green Bay were parked behind the bleachers, the big, gray flowers of their satellite dishes pointed northeast. It was a beautiful night for football, no wind, the smoky odor of burgers and brats rising from the concession stand. The student band was belting out movie tunes, the *Star Wars* theme, *Pirates of the Caribbean*, "Tequila."

When the players stood up and began doing jumping jacks, Gabriel looked like a Dutch windmill. The St. Mary's players kept turning around to look at him, and their coaches kept yelling at them to pay attention. I'm guessing it was like King Louis gazing at the guillotine as the mob jeered during the French Revolution. Those St. Mary's players were contemplating their end.

Charlie and I toddled up the bleachers and put our ass pads down near the other old birds ten rows up at the fifty-yard line, an area roped off for booster club members and elderly. From the chatter around us, I came to understand that Gabriel was not actually attending school. Coach Beathard had recruited him under a state law allowing homeschooled children to play sports at the public school in their home district if they chose to do so. Apparently, this wasn't all that uncommon.

Our Fighting Hornets won the coin toss, Jesus Lopez took the opening kick up the middle out to the forty-five-yard line, and our offense trotted onto the field. When the huddle broke, Gabriel took his position at right tackle, the proper place for him, in my view, since Julio was left-handed, and Gabriel could protect his blind side. If anyone held the slightest doubt that Gabriel Fisher could move well enough at his size to play football, those worries were erased on that first play from scrimmage. At the snap, Julio pivoted and handed the ball to Chin for a belly run off right tackle. We must have run it a thousand times the previous season. It gives linemen decent angles and the fullback a full run at the defensive end. Gabriel was supposed to block down, meaning his assignment was to push the defensive tackle lined up inside him farther inside; the right guard would block the strong side backer, the fullback would kick out the defensive end, and Chinua would run through the hole they created. But at the snap, Gabriel took a quick hop to his right, hooked the defensive end, pushed the defensive end into the defensive tackle, and then drove them into both St. Mary's linebackers, plowing all four players eight or ten yards across the field. Our guard and center doubled the noseguard, and the fullback had no one to block until he reached the secondary. I don't think a St. Mary's player came within five yards of Chinua as he blew through the hole and ran untouched fifty-five yards to the end zone. It was one of the most beautiful things I've ever seen.

We won that opener 73–0. We scored every time we had the football, and Coach Beathard started kicking field goals on second down in the third quarter to keep the score from getting out of hand. On defense, Gabriel alternated between noseguard and defensive tackle, and he could not be blocked, not by one player or even three or four. On one play when he lined up at nose, he ran over the center and had a lineman hanging on each leg as he roared into the backfield, but it was like a couple of remoras fluttering along the flanks of a great white shark. He sacked the St. Mary's quarterback before he'd even had the chance to turn around.

By my count, Gabriel finished the game with twenty-nine tackles, seventeen for a loss, and eleven quarterback sacks. His performance on offense was even more dominant. He rarely blocked fewer than three of St. Mary's defensive players, and Chinua's uniform looked as clean at the end of the game as it did on the opening play. Chin's final stats were garish: twenty-one carries for four hundred and eighty-five yards and eight touchdowns, all in the first half.

One win piled upon another that magical season. Charlie and I had to show up earlier and earlier to get a seat at home games, and with the stands filled to capacity, spectators lined the fence that encircled the field three or four deep. To make additional room in the stadium, the student band was moved down onto the track, and a set of rented aluminum bleachers was erected beyond each end zone. Television news trucks started arriving regularly from out of state, and by the third game, we started seeing college scouts in the bleachers as well. They weren't just there to watch Gabriel, of course. Chinua Ngobo had already received scholarship offers from LSU, Alabama, Oklahoma, Michigan, and Wisconsin. Julio Lopez had drawn similar levels of interest from Ball State, Illinois State, and Fresno State. But if you looked at the scouts or coaches during the game, you could see the player they couldn't stop looking at was Gabriel. Once, against Endeavor, he was lined up in the gap between their guard and tackle, both senior all-conference players weighing over 290 pounds apiece. At the snap, they double-teamed Gabriel, seeking to drive him off the line of scrimmage, but he fired an open hand into each of their chests and lifted both of those players off the ground. He tossed the tackle left and the guard right, splitting the double-team and sacking the quarterback.

The program listed Gabriel at eight feet, four hundred pounds, but we knew that weight was just an estimate. The height seemed to be ballpark as well. A student standing on a step ladder had traced Gabriel's silhouette against the side of the two-story concession stand with a Sharpie, and from the graduated table beside him he looked to be eight feet four inches tall. His shoulder pads, custom ordered, were four feet across. Charlie heard that Gabriel did eleven reps on the bench press with 550 pounds on the bar. Coach Beathard could not get a max for him because the school owned only 550 pounds of free weights.

By the sixth game of the season, we were still undefeated and unscored upon. We'd beaten our first five opponents by a combined score of 297–0. In game six we were at home against the Eastlake Spartans, the undefeated defending state champions. Eastlake had won the conference title seven of the last eight seasons and regularly advanced deep into the state playoffs, winning the title the previous season. The day before the game, Chinua sprained his ankle dunking basketballs in gym class, and even with so much tape on the ankle it looked like a walking cast, he wasn't going to be able to play. He limped terribly and took off his pads before kickoff. We still had Jesus and Julio, and of course we still had Gabriel anchoring our offensive and defensive lines, but playing without Chin would handicap us significantly.

Jesus fumbled the opening kickoff at our own twenty, and Eastlake recovered. On first down they hit their wideout on a quick slant across the middle. Julio, who also played safety on defense, slipped trying to make the tackle, and the kid sprinted into the end zone. On offense we couldn't move the ball, and their stud took our punt back to the house but missed the extra point, putting us into a 13–0 hole.

We spread things out with three receivers and a tight end, but Eastlake seemed ready for it. They double-teamed Jesus and Carl Witte, our top two pass-catching threats, and neither could get open consistently. Coach Beathard moved Jesus around, using him in the slot and at tailback. We ran Jesus behind Gabriel eight plays in a row, reaching the end zone on the last one, cutting the deficit to 13–7 by halftime.

In the second half, they made some adjustments and shut down our run game, too. If Jesus was in the backfield, they moved their smaller, quicker linebackers and safeties up to the line of scrimmage on Gabriel's side, rotating their defensive linemen away from him. Gabriel was huge and strong, but their safeties were small and quick, and they could often run around him, neutralizing his effectiveness. Even so, we traded touchdowns in the third quarter. Both teams traded punts through most of the fourth quarter, and we entered the final minute and twenty seconds of the game down 20–14, with the ball on our own thirty-yard line, one time-out remaining.

A light rain started falling. Everyone was on their feet. Eastlake's fans were making noise.

On first down, Julio dropped back to pass and overthrew Jesus, who was well-covered on a skinny post. On second down, he hit Carl Witte in the flat for a gain of two. We hustled back to the line of scrimmage without a huddle and snapped it on third down. Using Gabriel as a decoy, we lined up with Jesus in the slot behind him. Jesus sprinted into motion as Julio took the snap, and he handed the ball to his brother going full speed on a jet sweep to the left. It was a masterful call. Eastlake had overloaded our right side, and nothing but open field awaited Jesus once he cleared the line of scrimmage. Unfortunately, that didn't happen. Their defensive end just got a hand, maybe only a finger, on the foot of Jesus, tripping him up on our thirty-three, leaving us facing a fourth down and seven. Coach Beathard called our final time-out and brought the whole offense to the sideline. Thirty-seven seconds remained on the clock.

"Jesus Christ," Charlie said, "my heart can't take this."

"It don't look good," I said.

Charlie covered his eyes with his hands. "I can't watch. Tell me what happens."

The time-out ended, and our offense came back on the field and huddled up. When the huddle broke, Gabriel Fisher did not jog up to his usual position on the offensive line. Tucker Hunt, a sophomore, took Gabriel's place at right tackle. Gabriel lined up in the backfield behind our fullback, seven yards deep in the I-formation, hands on his knees.

"For the love of God, Charlie," I said. "He's got Gabriel at tailback!"

At the snap, Julio pivoted and handed the ball up to Gabriel, who followed the fullback to the right. He looked a little tentative, a little slow, at first. Tucker Hunt blocked down on the defensive tackle, not a perfect block but he got in the way; our fullback, Jason Kosharek, fired out of his stance and drove his helmet into the nuts of the defensive end, opening a gap just wide enough for Gabriel to squeeze through. Eastlake's all-state linebacker, Jeff Riesberg, who had made at least a dozen solo tackles by that point, met Gabriel in the hole, and we could hear the collision through the screeching of three thousand hysterical Eastlake fans. The laws of physics took over. Gabriel Fisher did not even slow down. The star Eastlake linebacker bounced off Gabriel's legs as if the boy were made of rubber. Eastlake's free safety and weak side linebacker arrived as Gabriel reached first-down yardage, but that didn't slow him down, either. The free safely leaped onto his back, and Gabriel carried him down the field, his long legs gobbling yardage, the tiny football hidden behind both of his arms, clutched to his chest, all the way into the end zone.

Popcorn, soda, nachos, cans of beer, you name it, flew into the air across the stadium as we roared in celebration. Charlie lost one of his slippers jumping in the bleachers, and I screamed so loud I lost my voice. We made the extra point and sent Eastlake home with their first loss, 21–20. When the final seconds ticked off the clock, our younger fans mobbed the field, and a half dozen of our players tried and failed to lift Gabriel up onto their shoulders to carry him into the locker room. Gabriel moved slowly, waist-deep in that churning sea of happiness, accepting pats on the ass and on the back, smiling and nodding as well-wishers took pictures of him with their phones, and when he cleared the crowd, he ran slowly with his teammates into the school.

It struck me then, as I watched him disappear, that he'd probably been the only player on the field without a single member of his family present to see him play.

15

Hannah Fisher

By October, Josiah and I were barely speaking. He wanted to blame me but knew that wasn't fair or right. It was unfair to blame Gabriel, too, but sometimes he did. It was no one's fault. Still, we argued. Josiah felt more deeply the disapproving gestures of our people, the stares, the shaking heads, the whispers. Everyone's lives had been disrupted by Gabriel's decision, ours most of all. Every night I cried and prayed, struggling to discover some respite from our predicament, torn between my love for Gabriel, who had never seemed happier, and my fervent desire to keep our feet on the path of meekness and righteousness.

Gabriel had been playing football only a short time when the cars started coming. They drove by at all hours, fifteen or twenty at a time, sometimes an endless parade. I'd be out hanging laundry or turning over manure in the garden, and cars would be stopped along the shoulder of the road, the people inside, often young people but not always, holding up the screens of their telephones, taking pictures, shouting Gabriel's name. People from the English television stations stopped as well. The bold ones came up the driveway and knocked on our door with their cameras running, wanting to speak to Gabriel. If Gabriel happened to be outside working, they went straight to him.

People of all ages ran to him, asked him to sign his name on pieces of paper, on footballs, even on their bodies.

Living next door, my elderly father, Absalom, also experienced this unwanted traffic and attention, and he did not abide it. He hobbled outside, waving his cane at anyone who pulled into his driveway or parked along the road with their car tires on the grass. Adults and older people apologized and moved on, but some of the younger ones laughed at him, which only increased his fury. When one car of young men refused to leave, my father turned his cane around and swung the curved end into one of the headlights. The glass shattered. I believe those young men would have hurt him if Josiah had not overheard the commotion. Josiah gave them forty dollars to buy a new headlight and politely asked them to leave.

Each morning as Josiah dressed for the day's work, I could feel the tension in his noisy breaths. Because Gabriel attended football practice every afternoon, he was only able to help Josiah for half the day. By two thirty, Gabriel would come inside to clean up and change clothes. He would pull on his Amish pants—no English pants would fit him, they were not near long enough, his inseam fifty-six inches—and a brightly colored English T-shirt, size XXXL, which fit snugly, showing every muscle in his shoulders and upper arms. He left his suspenders hanging over the chair in his bedroom, his woven hat on the bed. Then he would come downstairs and sit with me for a bit. Just before three, one of Gabriel's football coaches, or perhaps one of his friends, would pull up the driveway in a pickup truck and sound the horn. Gabriel could not fit inside an English car, and he enjoyed riding in the bed of a pickup, his back up against the cab. Gabriel would kiss me gently on the cheek, would say, "Bye, Grandma," before ducking through the door and bounding down the steps. On practice days, Gabriel returned home by six thirty, and I held supper for him. Josiah insisted on eating earlier, so I fed him at six. It was easier to have them at the table at different times. Some days I ate with Josiah. Others, I waited for Gabriel. I know Josiah loved Gabriel in his own way, a man's love, a grandfather's love, which carried certain obligations. Perhaps that love could not be unconditional, as a mother's or grandmother's love surely must be.

Fridays—game days—were the most difficult. Gabriel was often distracted, and Josiah's patience, stretched throughout the week, often snapped. Sometimes they would argue, and Josiah would send him into the house, saying he preferred to work alone. Someone would pick up Gabriel at four thirty or five o'clock, just as they would on practice days. But on Fridays he did not come home until midnight, or later. To celebrate after winning, he would go to the home of one of his English friends, and they would play video games and talk deep into the night. Sometimes there was drinking. Well before he arrived home, other cars would drive past our house, flashing their lights, beeping their horns, shouting and laughing. On occasion, the young people spilled from their cars into our yard, and in the morning, we'd find our maple tree filled with hanging ribbons of white paper bunting, as if it were wearing a long, pale wig.

"What is the meaning of this?" Josiah asked Gabriel, the first time it happened.

"We've been TP'd," he said, smiling. "That's toilet paper. It's a prank."

"It's a waste and a terrible mess," Josiah said.

"The rain will bring it down in time," I said, seeking to make peace.

Friday nights when we went to bed, Josiah put cotton balls in his ears so that he could sleep, but I would lie awake, listening. There was so much life and energy in those voices. Often, I could hear them singing a song through their open car windows, over and over, a kind of march. I heard Gabriel humming it one morning and asked him about it. He said it was the school's fight song.

"It sounds dangerous," I said.

He smiled and kissed me on the forehead. "We wear helmets and lots of padding," he said. "It's like armor. It keeps us safe."

"You enjoy it, then? This game?"

"I love it."

"And you're kind and humble when you play?"

"I try to be."

I smiled. "Then there may be but little harm in it."

Gabriel smiled. "A lot of college coaches come to the games. They all want to talk to me. They've been sending letters to the high school, and my coach gives them to me."

"What kind of letters?"

He went upstairs to his room and came down carrying one of the large, lower drawers from his dresser. It was filled to the top with mail, a snowdrift of white envelopes. Mr. Beathard had warned me. I knew those letters would soon be followed by knocks on our door, and I tried to hide my sorrow.

"Coach says I can play anywhere I want. I could go to college for free on a football scholarship."

"Is that what you want to do?"

"Maybe," he said. He shrugged as he shuffled through the envelopes. "I met the coach from Alabama last week. Coach says he's the best there is."

"He came all that way just to see you play?"

"Yes, me and Chin—Chinua, our running back. Chin doesn't want to play football in college. When he graduates, he wants to go back to Africa to find his brother and his sister."

"That does sound much more important."

"I don't have any brothers or sisters."

"No," I said. "But you have cousins, aunts and uncles. Josiah and me."

Gabriel hugged me. With one long, heavy arm, he squeezed me against his giant body, my face pressed to the muscular ripples of his stomach. "I know. You and Grandpa have done everything for me." Tears came to my eyes. I suspected then that he would be leaving us. I drew blood from my lip, biting it so that the pain might distract me from the terrible ache rising in my heart. But it brought only more tears, and Gabriel held me to him as I sniffled, his strength steady against my distress.

In October, coaches started knocking. A plague of locusts, Josiah called them. When possible, Mr. Beathard, Gabriel's high school coach, arranged to be there to help answer questions. I tried to be kind, to simply listen to what all these men had to say, with Gabriel seated beside me. Sometimes, two or three came in a night; on Saturdays, four or five came, waiting their turn in cars idling outside. In the beginning, Josiah stayed to listen, but after a few visits he said he'd heard enough, that Gabriel could do whatever he wanted, but he didn't feel the need to be a part of it.

In truth, what each coach had to say was much the same. All professed to have Gabriel's best interests at heart, said he would grow and thrive as a human being, a student, and an athlete at their institutions. Mindful of who they were talking to, a few of them enthusiastically reported that Gabriel would grow as a Christian at their institution as well, though I suspect some of them had never uttered a single prayer to the Lord in their lifetimes. Of course, I am only guessing and being unkind. Coaches with winning teams bragged about winning. Coaches from losing teams told Gabriel he'd make them winners, that he would be a huge part of returning their programs to former glory. More than a few said Gabriel would transform the game, that no lineman had ever won the Heisman Trophy for being the best player in college football, but Gabriel would be the first, they were certain of it. Many of the coaches had syrupy accents like Coach Beathard's. Some did not. All of them wore a uniform, as we Amish did, but theirs were more colorful, usually windproof jackets in their school's bright colors and a baseball cap that matched.

In the end, Gabriel narrowed his choice down to three schools, Alabama, Georgia, and Wisconsin. Coach Beathard told him with that list, he couldn't make a wrong choice, though of course I hoped he'd stay in Wisconsin so that I might still see him from time to time. In November, Gabriel's team traveled to Madison to play for the high school state championship, and afterward, Gabriel accepted a scholarship to play football in that same stadium for the Wisconsin Badgers.

He would live with us just another eight months before leaving for a life in the English world. I tried to fill every day of those final eight months with all the love I had. I baked something every week, cooked Gabriel's favorite meals, enjoyed his company in the late spring as he turned over my garden with a shovel Henry Stolzfus had made for him by welding together two large coal shovels and attaching an ash handle as thick as my wrist and seven feet long. Gabriel could turn over a bushel-basket-sized chunk of earth with each shovelful.

Because Gabriel had not yet been baptized, he could still come back to us whenever he desired. His decision to play football during his *Rumspringa* challenged our church district with something new to consider, and our bishop understood we needed to await Gabriel's decision with Godly patience. Even Josiah had relaxed now that he knew Gabriel would be leaving soon for Madison. He regretted the many times he lost his temper with the boy, and in many ways, they got along better than ever. The attention of the English world, at least through those eight months, diminished somewhat, though never completely. Someone told me that Gabriel was the tallest living man on earth, and this alone attracted attention. Strange cars and trucks continued to drive by, day and night, but most respected our desire for separation and peace.

Of course, each day that passed brought me closer to the day I would have to say goodbye. Many, many nights, I awoke and could not return to sleep, saddened as I was by Gabriel's imminent departure.

16

Trey Beathard

There's probably some rule that says boys all turn into their fathers in spite of themselves, because when I became a football coach, I started repeating the same tired old clichés Daddy used. The fact is, human beings avoid pain, and it hurts to do the common things it takes to train your body to do uncommon things (yes, that's one of Daddy's). Sit-ups hurt. Push-ups and reps on the bench press hurt. I had to motivate young men to drive themselves through that pain, to develop and expand their God-given gifts through hard work and repetition. For whatever reason, painting "Hard work beats talent when talent doesn't work hard" on the wall of the weight room helps to do that. I discovered there was some truth to those clichés after all, at least until Gabriel Fisher came along.

Gabriel violated every sports cliché ever spoken. He never lifted a weight or ran so much as a mile to get himself in shape. He never did two hundred push-ups a day all summer long to make himself stronger, and yet across the line of scrimmage from boys who did those things, Gabriel dominated. He was not just a man among boys, to use another cliché. He was the state of Texas stomping on Rhode Island. He was a whale in a school of dolphins. Granted, the boy had spent his life outdoors on a farm, tossing bales of hay and straw, working in his grandfather's cabinet shop, turning over his grandmother's garden by hand with a shovel as big as the bucket on a backhoe. Even so, his body had developed unmatched—heck, *unimagined*—strength and dexterity. I've seen a lot of great athletes, huge young men who could run fast and jump high, the top tenth of one percent of the most physically gifted and developed human beings on the planet, but nothing I'd encountered had prepared me for Gabriel Fisher.

Even though he weighed over four hundred pounds, Gabriel ran the forty-yard dash in 4.9 seconds, and his vertical jump was thirty-six inches. I doubt many low-post players in the NBA can jump thirty-six inches. With minimal effort, the boy could stand flat-footed beneath the basketball hoop, jump up and grab hold of the *top* of the backboard with both hands. The first time he did that was the last time, too, because after he dropped back down to the gym floor, we noticed that hoop was now several inches lower than ten feet: the pipes holding the rim and backboard to the wall had bent under Gabriel's body weight.

We didn't get a bench, squat, or deadlift max on Gabriel because the school didn't own enough free weights. I'm guessing he could have deadlifted a thousand pounds. We've got a blocking sled our offensive line trains on that's made of steel and welded angle iron; it's ten or twelve feet wide and must weigh three or four hundred pounds. After practice if rain is in the forecast, I'll have the boys push it over under the eaves of our equipment shed to keep it from rusting. Usually takes four boys to slide it over there. Gabriel, he just picked it up in the middle like the pole a tightrope walker might carry, walked it into place, and set it down.

Once we'd done the testing and I'd seen Gabriel through those first couple of practices, I knew what would be coming, and I tried to prepare him for it. I had brought it on by asking him to play, so I felt responsible. Few people had seen Gabriel in public since he was in the third grade, so when he suddenly appeared on our football team, all eight feet plus of him—I mean, the kid had to crouch through doorways and duck inside any house with normal eight-foot ceilings—it's understandable that he would get some attention. That attention grew quickly. After a week, everyone in Wisconsin knew his name. In two weeks, YouTube videos and social media posts had sent Gabe Fisher around the world.

I took him home from practice the night before our third game and explained this to his grandparents. Scouts from twenty-one different teams would be coming to the game. More would be coming thereafter. A lot of people would want to talk to Gabriel, and most of them would want to talk to Josiah and Hannah as well. Gabriel's grandparents were lovely, quiet people, and they made it clear their preference was to be left alone. At their request, I arranged to have all communication run through my office or the athletic director's office at the high school. I told Josiah and Hannah that as custodial caregivers of a minor child, they would have to be involved in the process to some degree, but I would do all I could to keep that to a minimum.

I knew things might get crazy, but no one could have predicted the feeding frenzy that was to come. We had to hire a student worker to sort the mail. Gabriel got over a hundred pieces of mail a day. The phones never stopped ringing. The circus called, offering a job. So did the Worldwide Wrestling Federation. Though Gabriel had never touched a basketball, dozens of basketball programs contacted my office, too. A Chinese shoe company sent a contract offering Gabriel a hundred thousand dollars to advertise its shoes; they sent a large, rectangular box and asked Gabriel to airmail the imprint of his size 32 foot so that they could make a set of football cleats for him. Radio stations from every continent on earth except Antarctica called to seek interviews, and every week five or six times that number of television stations requested interviews. The fourth week of the season, *Sports Illustrated* did a cover story. ESPN sent a crew to every game. Morning television shows from all three major networks invited Gabriel to visit their studios for interviews. Agents and public relations professionals somehow got my cell number and started calling at all hours, offering their services. Everybody wanted to get their fingers into the pie.

Inevitably, journalists also uncovered the tale of my sordid past.

I was embarrassed and ashamed, but the community didn't turn on me. Billy Walton gave a television interview from his bar, painted in Fighting Hornets black and yellow, and his defense of me proved so artfully vulgar that it went viral on social media and was picked up by *SportsCenter* (though one had to read lips because the audio was punctuated by so many bleeps).

The Monday before every game, our athletic director was besieged by far more requests for media credentials than could be accommodated. The local police in every community where we played had to bring in officers from other towns to handle traffic and crowd control. But on the field, we won every game and looked invincible, and once we defeated Eastlake with Chin out injured—Gabriel's touchdown run as time expired had been watched over three million times on YouTube—we had clear sailing into the playoffs, with hopes of winning the state championship.

We roared through the playoffs unscored upon. The size of the crowds, the media, the quality of play on the field, all of it felt like Texas, at least on our sideline. Twenty-four thousand people saw the playoff semifinals against Port Huron, ten thousand of them sitting on blankets in the grass, watching the simulcast on a giant screen, like an outdoor movie theatre, right next to the stadium. Because the simulcast was on a two-second delay, you could hear the crowd yelling behind you, and then you could hear the crowd yelling over on the simulcast. The band's halftime performance sounded as if they were performing in the echo chamber of the Grand Canyon. We won the semifinal 49–0.

Eastlake made it to the championship. I figured they would. Other than us, regardless of division, they were the next best team in the state. Three of their kids had accepted D1 scholarships, and they had several others who went on to play in college at lower levels. The night of the game, that Saturday before Thanksgiving, over fifty thousand people showed up at Camp Randall in a lightly falling snow to see the game.

Eastlake was ready for us, too. They did exactly what I would have done. To neutralize the effect of Gabriel's blocking on the offensive line, they opened the game on defense without defensive linemen, opting for speed over size. This can sometimes be effective. Show me a fight between a weasel the size of a hot dog and a groundhog fifteen times its weight, and my money will be on the weasel every time. But that's in the animal kingdom. On the football field, that formula is not nearly as reliable.

Whenever Eastlake pulled its defensive linemen, putting four smaller linebackers on the line of scrimmage, backed by three other linebackers and four defensive backs, I instructed Julio to audible. At his call, Gabriel shifted from offensive tackle into the backfield, Julio moved up to Gabriel's tackle spot, and Chin sprinted out wide as a receiver. At the snap, Gabriel got the ball, always the same play, a wedge, directly up the middle. The wedge is the simplest play in football, caveman stuff. At the snap, the offensive linemen all step to the inside and forward, their shoulder pads touching, roughly twelve hundred pounds of pad and muscle joined into a single, united force. Gabriel could get in behind that and then pick and choose a hole, bouncing it to the outside, or he could simply power forward. By this time Eastlake knew they had to tackle Gabriel by grabbing his legs, and it usually took at least three, and often four, defenders to bring him down, but never before he'd gained at least ten or twelve yards. It wasn't the prettiest football I've ever seen, but after four or five plays in a row—I mean, exactly the same play, Gabriel Center Wedge, we called it—with us gaining ten or twelve or even fifteen yards at a crack, Eastlake would send its defensive line back on the field, Gabriel would return to right tackle, and we'd go back to Chinua, or Julio would sling it to Jesus. Pick your poison.

By halftime we held a 35–0 lead. I started playing freshmen and sophomores at the start of the third quarter. Sat Gabriel and Chin down at the start of the fourth quarter. We defeated Eastlake 61–13. At the end of that game, a half dozen Division 1 coaches texted me offering me the defensive coordinator job at their university if I brought Gabriel along with me on scholarship. I will keep the names of those desperate programs to myself. At one time, I might have found those offers tempting, but I had found a new, sober life, a beautiful woman who loved my French cooking, and a state championship in the last place I ever expected myself to be. I wasn't going anywhere, and neither was Gabriel. He committed to the University of Wisconsin a few hours after the championship game, signing his letter of intent right in the coach's living room. Gabriel was going to join the illustrious string of offensive linemen who had given the Badgers a reputation as the most successful power-rushing team in the nation.

17

Thomas Kennedy

Life around Lakota got a lot quieter when Gabriel Fisher went off to college, his celebrity trailing him like the tail of a comet. Like a garish, colorful balloon, the community had swelled almost to the breaking point with all the attention, and now it had shriveled back to near invisibility. The buzz and bright lights of television news vans and the steady stream of cars and SUVs with out-of-state plates disappeared, replaced by a few familiar pickup trucks, the clopping of horses' hooves, and the clatter of Amish buggies along the backroads. Though he missed Gabriel terribly, Thomas welcomed the peace.

When one of the town supervisors floated a proposal to erect a sign on the county line celebrating Lakota as the home of Gabriel Fisher ("Welcome to Lakota, Birthplace of Gabriel Fisher!"), the move was soundly defeated, four votes to one. Though everyone was fond of Gabriel and proud of the town's affiliation with him, a sober caution carried the day. "He's just a kid," Supervisor Nelson noted, clarifying the chief objection. "Let's allow him to grow up and live a little before we collar him with that kind of attention." Of course, it was difficult to imagine Gabriel getting any more attention than he'd already generated.

The state championship trophy was propped in the Fighting Hornets' trophy case. Billy Walton commissioned a large-scale facsimile of the trophy and mounted it on the roof of his bar. Though he continued to serve as the president of the Fighting Hornets booster club, inside Shaken, Not Stirred he signaled a shift in his allegiances. He closed for a week and had the interior walls painted cardinal red and white, Badger colors, and he posted the Badgers' football schedule on every wall of the place.

That fall, Coach Beathard and Merryn Mouglalis got married on the fifty-yard line during bye week, the weekend before homecoming. The marching band played "The Yellow Rose of Texas" and "La Vie En Rose" at the wedding, and the students in Family and Consumer Sciences made a huge chocolate sheet cake in the shape of a football to eat at the reception. Football fans were thrilled with the coupling, since it meant the flashy Texan would continue to coach the Fighting Hornets, but some wished Merryn and Trey had waited until the season was over to attend to the formalities. Weddings, they noted, could be scheduled anytime; football season came but once a year.

Gabriel Fisher went down to Madison and the traveling circus of media attention went with him. He became the largest human being ever to enroll at the University of Wisconsin, and it was certain he'd become the most dominant lineman ever to play college football. While his exploits on the field would become legendary, it was his life off the field that caused him the most anxiety initially. Every night, he would sit down at a laptop computer the university had provided him and write to Thomas, who read the emails after supper and responded before going to bed. Everything overwhelmed Gabriel in the beginning: the size of the campus, the number and variety of students from all over the world, the content of his classes, even the adjustment of having a roommate. Often Gabriel said he was so overwhelmed he felt like coming home. Thomas urged him to be patient, that all new shoes are stiff in the beginning but become soft and comfortable in time.

Football, at least, was familiar, though that, too, carried its difficulties. The complexity of the playbook and the size of the other players surprised him, but the coaches seemed more amused than angry when he made a mistake on the practice field. He always remembered what Coach Beathard had told him: "Son, football isn't complicated. If you forget your assignment, just hit the first guy you see. When he falls down, hit the next guy, and the next guy, and so on, like dropping dominoes." So even when he was in error on his blocking assignment at left tackle, Gabriel typically took out two and sometimes three players, often at least one of whom was a returning, all-conference starter. He began summer practices on the scout team, but it wasn't long before Gabriel joined the starting offensive line. This happened in part because the scout team offense scrimmaged against the first team defense, and with Gabriel on the field, the scout team overpowered one of the finest defensive lines in the country. Wisconsin's coaches also feared Gabriel might injure one of their starting players.

Gabriel emailed Thomas two or three times a day in those initial weeks of summer practice, though the emails decreased when the other students flooded campus for the start of the fall semester. Thomas urged him to write regular letters to Josiah and Hannah, too, and Gabriel assured him that he would. Students swarmed him at freshman orientation activities, and he could not walk across campus or down State Street without a stream of gawkers close behind him. He had to stand in the back or sit on the floor in each of his classes on the first day because his body would not fit in the desks or chairs provided. While he assured his professors he was quite comfortable sitting on the floor, all of them arranged to have larger, armless chairs or benches delivered to their classrooms for Gabriel's use, though these were also too small. It would have been akin to asking a normal-sized person to sit on a chair ten inches above the floor. Gabriel used these chairs for a couple days to be polite, but then returned to the floor. All but one of his classes met in spacious lecture pits with high, vaulted ceilings. The discussion section of his Introduction to Psychology course met in a regular classroom, and Gabriel was so accustomed to crouching in rooms with eight-foot ceilings that he felt more comfortable there.

Gabriel's roommate in the athletes dorm was an offensive lineman from Nebraska named Colt Bender, a talkative country boy who shaved his head, chewed tobacco, and wore cowboy boots like Coach Beathard. Badger linemen benefited from both larger rooms and larger beds in the dormitory (as well as a limitless supply of protein and carbohydrates in the athletes cafeteria). While Gabriel's lower legs and feet still hung over the end of his eight-foot, double-wide dorm bed, it was as comfortable as the custom bed his grandfather had made him at home. Colt was six foot seven, three hundred pounds, with blue tattoos of barbed wire encircling his throat and each of his massive biceps, and Gabriel loved walking places with him because it made him feel slightly less conspicuous. Unlike Gabriel, Colt was an extrovert who enjoyed line dancing, drinking, and going to house parties, and he dragged Gabriel along whenever Gabriel could not think of an excuse quickly enough to beg off. At one such party, Gabriel had his first taste of Jell-O shots, sweet, rubbery concoctions served in ice-cube trays. Colt brought him a tray, and Gabriel ate a dozen and heard a slight ringing in his ears; he ate another dozen and felt a pleasant heat, like sunshine or a tropical artesian spring, warming the inside of his head. Students at these parties took a lot of selfies with Gabriel, and in time pictures of him were spread across hundreds of Facebook pages and Instagram feeds, on his knees with smiling students from China, India, or Japan clinging to his arms, or standing outside beside Colt, each of them in a muscle-man pose with a scantily clad college girl sitting on each shoulder holding up red plastic party cups.

At one of these early house parties, Gabriel wrote to Thomas, a girl named Isabella introduced herself and asked him to dance. She wore blue jeans, sandals, and a bright yellow T-shirt, and she had several colorful beaded necklaces around her neck and smaller bracelets on both wrists. Her black hair reached almost to her waist. She couldn't have been much more than five feet tall, but she grabbed Gabriel's hand and tugged him to the center of the dance floor. He watched as she closed her eyes and swayed her body to the music. He ducked his head and moved his feet slowly, trying not to stomp on anyone. She shouted over the music, told him to just do what she did, and he tried to mirror her, swinging his hips from side to side, raising his elbows like the wings of a chicken on the run. But when she lifted her arms and waved her hands over her head, he accidentally punched through two of the ceiling tiles, which fell from their frames down to the floor in a shower of dust. Isabella laughed and hugged him, took him by the hand, and pulled him outside into the quiet. They walked across campus together, sat down in the dewy grass by the freshman dorms along the lakeshore, and started talking, and it was like nothing Gabriel had ever done. He had rarely even spoken to a girl his own age, and never so intimately. He didn't want it to end.

Isabella's mother was from Mexico, and her father came from California. She'd been born in San Diego, taken to Nogales for a few years, then raised on a carrot and celery farm in California's Central Valley, where her father maintained the equipment and irrigation system. Thereafter, she hated celery. She was an elementary education major and a women's studies minor, and she wanted to be a teacher. She'd never been to a football game. She listened intently when he spoke about his Amish grandparents and the farm where they lived without electricity or running water. She grabbed his arm and nearly cried when he told the story of his mother dying while giving birth to him, and she did cry when he revealed that the brother who raised him hanged himself. He didn't know who his father was, and no one wanted to talk about it. He missed his grandmother and Thomas, but he also missed being around animals, particularly his grandmother's herd of milk goats. He told Isabella about his work with Thomas and his hopes of becoming a veterinarian someday.

They talked deep into the early morning, beyond the flow of students staggering back to their dormitories at two thirty. Bats fluttered over Lake Mendota, and sometimes they could hear a barred owl hooting down along the path that skirted the lakeshore through the woods. Neither of them wanted the sun to rise, but Isabella had an eight o'clock class and Gabriel had to be in the weight room at the Bennett Center to lift with other football players at six. Isabella

hopping to a buzzy, wild song that reverberated around the stadium at the end of the third quarter. Gabriel tried to say hello to the Pueblo State players across the line of scrimmage, but they just stared. One of them called him a freak and told him to shut the fuck up. Gabriel gave up trying to establish a rapport and drove him ten yards off the line of scrimmage every running play, then stoned him cold and pancaked him on passing attempts. It took Gabriel a few snaps to grow accustomed to the stronger players and the faster pace, but he enjoyed such an overwhelming advantage in size and strength that even when he made a mistake or got off-balance, he was still dominant.

After the game, sports reporters swarmed his locker, most of them asking different versions of the same general question: how did he feel about his performance? Gabriel gave them the same answer each time: he felt fine. It went okay. He had fun. He enjoyed it. Near the end, someone asked him if his height and weight in the program were accurate. Gabriel smiled and said he didn't know, what did the program say? Eight feet five inches, the reporter answered. Four hundred ninety pounds. Gabriel nodded, give or take, he said.

In the end, Gabriel told Thomas, he felt disappointed by only one thing that afternoon. Pueblo State's mascot was a peregrine falcon, and at one point, as the players were warming up before the game, someone let the raptor out of its cage. It circled the stadium twice and then returned to its gloved keeper, who fed it a bit of raw chicken. Gabriel wanted to talk to the keeper and perhaps ask him to hold the falcon. He'd never seen one up close. As they stretched beside one another on the field, he asked Colt if he thought it would be okay to walk over and see the bird. Colt shook his head. Fish, don't be stupid! he said. Get your game face on, man. C'mon! We're not out here bird-watching! Gabriel waited until after the game, but by the time he got out of the locker room, both the falcon and the keeper were gone.

18

Billy Walton

That fall, my place was hopping every weekend, and I thought about adding on or remodeling. Charlie wanted me to put in a karaoke machine. I told him I was running a sports bar and did not want to listen to drunk people singing country songs off-key all night. I had the inside painted Badger red and white, and while those painters were working, something came to me, an inspiration, if you will: the idea for Billy's Badger Bus. I'd buy an old school bus, paint it red, wire a stuffed badger to the hood, install a bar in the back, and run a fan bus from my place to Madison for home Badger games. For the price of a Badger ticket plus seventy-five dollars, which included the bus ride, all-you-could-drink beer on tap, and two rail drinks, one each way, fans could ride to Madison, see the game, and ride back to their cars in my parking lot. All forty seats sold out before every game that first season. To give myself a better margin, I raised my price to a hundred dollars the second season, but it didn't matter. That year, I sold out of every seat even before the season started.

Gabriel's sophomore season, Coach had him playing both ways, left tackle on offense and nose tackle on defense, and he'd been selected to every preseason All-American team in the country. He was also a Heisman favorite. Gabriel could have played anywhere on the defensive line, but the coaches had him at nose tackle, where he could be most disruptive. With his speed, Gabriel had enough range to stuff any running play between the tackles, and on passing plays being over center gave him a straight shot to the quarterback. He looked like he'd put on another forty or fifty pounds of muscle over the summer, because he wasn't just dominant, he was unstoppable. On offense, he effortlessly pancaked All-American defensive ends when he had a single assignment, and on combination blocks, say when he had to chip the end and move on to the linebacker, he flattened both players. Defensively, he was an even bigger weapon. He was like a tank in the middle of the field with a race car engine under the hood. He split every double team, overpowered every triple team, tossed three-hundred-pound linemen around like bowling pins. Every time Gabriel ran onto the field when the Badgers were on defense, the marching band played the ominous cello music from *Jaws*. Gabriel was our great white shark, and opposing players were chum.

The Badgers were cruising that season, undefeated heading into the Ohio State game. The Buckeyes were coming to Camp Randall with just a single loss, and of course, as always, they were loaded for bear, had the best stable of athletes in the Big Ten, certainly the most five-star recruits. But Bucky had Gabriel Fisher, the only freaking ten-star recruit in the land, and we were yelling our lungs out when the Badgers took the field, feeling like we had OSU's number for the first time in a long while.

It was a sunny day in late October, not a cloud in the damn sky, one of those bright, perfect fall days when the red and orange leaves of hard maples shined like neon, and the punch of the kettle drums and booming of the brass instruments in the marching band echoed as if amplified. Christ, it was paradise. How could a day like that, a day with such promise, go so damn wrong? Well, there's no explaining it, right? Even the memory of it makes me sick to my stomach.

The Badger offense was clicking early, grinding out huge chunks of yardage running behind Gabriel on the left side, and they took a 17–0 lead. Offensively, Ohio State could not get anything going. Gabriel blew up every running play. They could move the ball through the air, but only on quick, short throws when they sprinted their quarterback out to one side, which eliminated half the field. Even so, the Badgers adjusted and kept them out of the end zone, and we led at halftime 20–3.

Things got a little chippy in the third quarter. By throwing quick slants to the wideouts and hitting the tight ends short in the seams, Ohio State took the second-half kickoff and marched down the field to the Badger ten. But then Gabriel stuffed a running play on first down, and on a second down sprint out he took an angle through the guard and tackle and sacked the quarterback for a seven-yard loss. On that play, Gabriel drove the tackle on top of the quarterback, and after falling under eight hundred pounds of human bone and muscle, the quarterback did not get up right away. The tackle took offense and tried to reach up and put a finger through Gabriel's face mask, but one of our defensive tackles, Colt Bender, stepped between them and stiff-armed the OSU tackle in the chest. Gabriel just walked back to the huddle, but on the next play, that tackle and Colt ended up in a scrum on the field. Penalty flags flew. Ohio State was penalized fifteen yards for unsportsmanlike conduct and had to kick a field goal to cut the Badger lead to 20–6.

Wisconsin went up 27–6 on the next possession, and it seemed over by then. Ohio State could not consistently stop us, and we were moving the ball at will. The third quarter ended, "Jump Around" was blasting out of the speakers, and Camp Randall was hopping, eighty thousand people in Badger red bouncing up and down like pogo sticks.

Ohio State had the ball to start the fourth quarter, and they tried to sprint out their quarterback to throw the quick slants, but the Badgers had it figured out. He went left on first down, and Gabriel knifed through for a sack. On second down, the quarterback sprinted out right with the same result. On third down, well, that's when everything went to hell. To this day you can go on any online sports discussion board and the debate is still raging. Whether it was dirty and intentional or not in the end really doesn't matter. On that third down, the Ohio State quarterback took two steps to his left as if he were going to sprint left, and Gabriel moved to his right, running over OSU's center to begin trying to cut off the quarterback. But the quarterback handed the ball to the tailback on a counter back to the right, and as Gabriel pivoted to turn and follow the play, his right leg planted like a tree, with those size 32 cleats sticking into the Camp Randall turf like roots, Ohio State's left guard, tackle, and tight end, three players with a cumulative weight of over one thousand pounds, exploded together into Gabriel's right thigh and knee, and he went down like a giant redwood. The tailback slashed through the hole and gained twenty yards before our safety knocked him out of bounds, but then the stadium went quiet. Gabriel stayed down.

Linemen wear those black plastic braces on both knees, the top part mounted around the thigh and the bottom around the upper calf. The braces are hinged in the center so the knee can bend as it is supposed to, but the braces are designed to prevent the knee from bending backward or to the side. Beside Gabriel on the turf, pieces of his knee brace were scattered like branches broken off a tree. Wisconsin's trainers ran onto the field, but before they reached Gabriel, anyone could clearly see from the angle of his lower leg that the injury was serious. The replay, shown only once on the Jumbotron, in slow motion, confirmed it: with the force and weight of those three heavy linemen, Gabriel's knee had bent backward, straight back, like a flamingo's, shattering the brace. No way the knee bends that way without tearing something inside, and it looked as if his kneecap, which was about the size of a saucer, had dislocated as well, had spun around to the inside.

Because my eyes aren't so good, I had my binoculars with me. I kept my eyes on Gabriel and the trainers that surrounded him. The first inkling we had that something wasn't right came a few minutes later, when Ohio State's trainers ran onto the field. By this time, the ambulance had driven out, and the paramedics had unloaded a wheeled gurney. They laid the backboard down beside Gabriel, but it looked woefully too small, like trying to put a whole side of beef on a bread board. Frankly, there's no way he would have fit on the gurney either, and a couple guys sitting behind us wondered how he would possibly fit inside the back of the ambulance. Someone removed the remains of the broken knee brace, cut Gabriel's uniform pants up the side, and rolled down his sock. Several more people and several Badger players, including Colt Bender, gathered around him. Colt knelt by Gabriel's head, removed his helmet, and locked one of Gabriel's giant hands in his. Gabriel looked as if he might be crying.

Another five or ten minutes passed. Ohio State's players began to mingle with Wisconsin's players, and soon both teams were together at midfield, down on one knee. I kept trying to get a clean look at Gabriel's face, and when I did finally see him again, he looked as white as a bleached bedsheet. His eyes were closed, and he was no longer moving. Colt still had him by the hand. Tears were streaming down Colt's face.

Grown men were running on and off the field, some of them shouting into walkie-talkies, others talking on their phones.

"Jesus Christ," I said to Charlie, sitting next to me. "Something ain't right. Something ain't right."

Over the intercom came an announcement: we were asked to evacuate the stadium in a fast but orderly manner. We could remain in the bowels of Camp Randall, but not anywhere near the open seats. A helicopter had been summoned from University Hospital, and for everyone's safety, officials wanted fans out of the stadium when the chopper landed. It took about twenty minutes to get everybody out. Some people didn't leave, but most did. Security guards ousted the rest. It was so quiet, it felt like we were all going home from a funeral. A lot of people were crying. As we filed out, the paramedics put their empty backboard and gurney into the ambulance and moved it off the field. A police officer or security guard arranged orange plastic cones in a large circle around the fifty-yard line. All the players except Gabriel and Colt, who would not abandon him, left to go into their respective locker rooms. Soon, even from beneath the concrete infrastructure of the stadium, we could hear the *whump, whump, whump* of an approaching helicopter. I don't know how they got Gabriel inside that Flight for Life, but they did, and that chopper lifted straight up and roared away. By the time I made my way back up the tunnel so that I could see the field, the helicopter was just a speck in the distance, and Colt Bender was on his knees alone, holding Gabriel's giant helmet against his chest.

The Badgers ended up winning the game, 27–20, but no one really cared. People scrolled through the news feeds on their phones as the bus traveled back to Lakota. The mood stayed somber. No one was drinking. Gradually, bits and pieces of news began to leak out, but no firm details other than that Gabriel was undergoing emergency surgery.

When we got back to Lakota, people got in their cars and went home. I waited for the ten o'clock news, and Charlie stayed up with me. We talked about Gabriel when he was a boy, remembering how that string bean used to hit a baseball so far people learned to park their cars far from the field, wishing now in our hearts he had continued playing that far safer game. No more details came out on the news, so Charlie finished his beer and went home, too.

The next day, around noon, officials held a news conference at University Hospital, broadcast on live television. I'd just opened and had no customers, but I had every television in the place tuned in. Coach Beathard was there with his wife; the surgeons were there; some of the players. Coach looked exhausted; black half-moons hung thick under his eyes, and his wife looked as if she'd been crying. The lead surgeon went to the podium and started speaking. Gabriel Fisher, he said, had suffered catastrophic injuries to his right leg. (No shit, I thought.) I grabbed a pen and recorded what I could on a bar napkin to share later with Charlie. The injuries included a knee dislocation and ligament tears, severe tibial plateau fractures, a supracondylar femur fracture, and, most seriously, a complete tear of the popliteal artery, which remained asymptomatic for several hours. Sounded bad, but even while I was scribbling all that down I thought at that point the kid would be all right.

Blunt trauma to the knee, the surgeon explained, can often include hidden vascular occlusion, or rupture. In everyday language, that means an unseen vein or artery can rip open on the inside, and that's what happened to Gabriel. Even after emergency room physicians had stabilized him, introducing morphine to reduce the pain and shock, Gabriel's blood pressure remained low, and other vital signs continued to deteriorate. Surgical intervention and reconstruction on blunt-trauma knee injuries is rarely undertaken so soon, but in this instance, physicians suspected vascular occlusion or arterial rupture and opted for emergency surgery. That decision had saved Gabriel's life.

Gabriel was recovering in intensive care; his vital signs were good. However, the surgeon added, a shredded artery, bone fragmentation, and substantial necrosis of tissue and tendons prevented limb reconstruction. Irreversible ischemia had occurred. In other words, he said, much of Gabriel's lower right leg had been deprived of blood for too long.

Gabriel Fisher's right leg had been amputated above the knee.

By that point, everyone near the podium was in tears. My legs buckled, and if not for the fact I could brace myself against the bar, I think I would have fallen down. All the swallowing I did could not stop my own tears from dripping down my face. Jesus Christ, I thought, they butchered him. They cut off the kid's leg! It was just a knee injury, for Christ's sake. How in the hell is he supposed to play football on one leg?

The surgeon took a deep breath and seemed to rally some enthusiasm, the worst of the news now behind him. He noted that advances— incredible advances, he said, his words—in prosthetic technology would enable Gabriel to walk again and to live a normal life. He paused and smiled. Well, he said, I mean as normal a life as a young man eight feet five inches tall can possibly live.

19

Hannah Fisher

Each morning since my baptism at age seventeen I have awakened from the soft death of sleep, and my first thought, always, has been: Lord, Thy will be done. I do not say it for my own credit. It has not been easy. Though my life has been gilded by blessings, the Lord in his wisdom and love has seen fit to nurture my faith by affliction. Intimately knowing my heart and my unbounded love for children and grandchildren, He has spared me physical agony, choosing instead to send it in full measure upon my progeny: Caleb; my dear daughter, Rachel; and then both of her sons, Jasper and Gabriel.

It is folly to question the dealings of the Lord, through whose grace we walk and breathe and flourish. In the face of His wisdom and holy power we are but motes of dust. Thus, we strive, if imperfectly, to live in constant readiness for eternal life to come. I know these things. I repeat them in my head every eventide, as I watch my goats fold their legs beneath them and drop to the earth to sleep.

Yet the day Josiah and I learned of Gabriel's maiming, something new opened in me, a tiny wound as fine as a needle's point. It distracted and would not leave me, raising a terrible fog of sorrow and anger that clouded my mind. I sought solace in the scriptures. I opened first to the Psalms, those beautiful songs of hope and love I have read a thousand times. "The Lord also will be a refuge for the oppressed, a refuge in times of trouble. . . . The Lord is my light and my salvation; whom shall I fear? The Lord is the strength of my life, of whom shall I be afraid?" I read in Lamentations, "For the Lord will not cast off forever: But though he cause grief, yet will he have compassion according to the multitude of his mercies." Finally, desperate, I turned to Deuteronomy: "And the Lord, He is the one who goes before you. He will be with you. He will not leave you nor forsake you; do not fear nor be dismayed." But I felt terribly dismayed. I found no comfort in these words. None. They scurried like black ants across the page, and the more I tried to still them, the faster they ran.

When I was a girl, my mother used to tell me, if your mind is troubled, Hannah, move your body; do some physical work and pray, and it will calm you. I busied my hands in the garden. With my spade, I began turning over manure and old straw to decompose through the coming winter. As I worked, I tried to pray, but this provided no comfort or fruitful distraction. Instead of abating, my anger and confusion swelled. Provoked, and in tears, I fell to my knees in the cold dirt, my prayers dissolving into blasphemy: When I say, Thy will be done, Lord, I mean to me. To *me*! Split *my* body with the birth of a colossal child. Tighten the murderous noose around *my* throat. Tear off *my* limb. Though sweat poured down my face, my body shivered as if from cold.

A woman of true and abiding faith would have said, take them, Lord, they are yours. Take Caleb, though newly born. Take Rachel; take Jasper; take mighty Gabriel piece by piece if that is Your will. But my anger was at a high boil and would not be cooled. I took up my shovel again. Down one row and then another, I dug. My arms and back burned with the labor. I worked through hunger and thirst. Blisters split and oozed on my hands, my blood sticking like glue to the handle of my spade. Darkness fell and cold with it. Steam poured from my mouth. Up at the house, lamplight danced in the windows. Josiah called to me through the kitchen screen, but I shook my head. "I will finish my work," I said, my voice hoarse. Mud clung in clumps to the bottoms of my shoes. The hem of my dress hung heavy with dirt and dew. At eleven o'clock, beneath a sliver of moon, Josiah slowly walked out to me. He put a loving arm over my aching shoulders, wrapped the other hand around my shovel.

"Hannah, please," he said, "you can finish in the morning." I opened my cramped, bloody hands, let the shovel drop.

Inside, Josiah had boiled water and filled a bath, scented with lavender goat milk soap. He helped me remove my shoes. "Gabriel will be okay," he said from his knees, almost in a whisper. "We don't know that," I said, aloud. He put his hands along my face, kissed my muddy forehead. "We do, Hannah," he said. Then he left the room and closed the door. Steam rose from the bathwater. I did not deserve such kindness or comforts. My arms were so weary, I could barely remove my dress and underthings. I pulled off my sweaty kapp, let it fall to the floor. As I lowered myself into the tub and reclined, the steaming water flowed up my body, over my legs, my bottom, my breasts and shoulders.

I drew my hands underwater, and the blistered pain across my palms and fingers stung like a swarm of bees.

Though exhausted, and with my dear husband snoring beside me, I could not find my way to sleep. In the past, I would quietly go downstairs, light a lamp, and curl up in a chair with the Lord's word, my certain navigation. Soon, comforted, I would find myself drifting off. But that was not my intention. I slid from beneath the warm covers, the floor cold on my feet, and in the slightest of moonlight, felt my way along the wall toward the door. As I passed my mother's cedar trunk, I bent over and put my hands on it. Of course, this was no accident. While reclining in the warm bath, I had begun thinking about the book. I had never read from it with Josiah present. Always, I'd waited until he was out of town, but I was desperate. The brass latch glowed where moonlight touched it, and my swollen, oozing fingers slid toward the shining metal. I lifted the latch and swung open the lid.

Downstairs, I added oak to the embers still aglow in the woodstove. They caught fire, and the flames began to lick and crackle. I lit a single tallow candle, wrapped myself in a wool blanket, removed Mother's kapp, and opened *Poems of Emily Dickinson*. Against my leg, I also kept my Bible. I planned to open it quickly if I heard Josiah coming down the stairs. So troubled was my mind that I had consciously prepared this deception for my Godly husband.

The poems were cryptic, as I'd remembered, and yet even the tiniest verses opened whole worlds to wander in. I favored those that included notes or passages underlined in my mother's shaky hand. In these notes she was many times not the person I'd known and loved. She was larger, less meek, less certain of things, willing to consider ideas that would have led our bishop and ministers to cast the book into the fire. But I craved every page she'd written upon. It was as if she were there beside me, whispering in my ear. Perhaps this was key to what I'd sought and found in the book that night, I don't know. But it changed me. It did.

One poem Mother had circled with a series of tiny stars, and it moved me close to her, made me feel as if I were not alone in that darkness, since it invoked the long nights of insomnia I knew so well:

> *Will there really be a Morning?*
> *Is there such a thing as Day?*
> *Could I see it from the mountains*
> *If I were tall as they?*
> *Has it feet like Water lilies?*
> *Has it feathers like a Bird?*
> *Is it brought from famous countries*
> *Of which I have never heard?*
> *Oh some Scholar! Oh some Sailor!*
> *Oh some Wise Men from the skies!*
> *Please to tell a little Pilgrim*
> *Where the place called "Morning" lies!*

Beside another poem, number 1205, Mother had written a note: "Sinful," she wrote, "but I feel it true." With thick pencil marks, she had

also underscored the last two lines. On another day, when less brave
or less troubled, this might have caused me to turn the page without
reading it. But now I tipped the book closer to the candle's light so that
I might see each word more clearly.

Immortal is an ample word
When what we need is by
But when it leaves us for a time
'Tis a necessity.

Of Heaven above the firmest proof
We fundamental know
Except for its marauding Hand
It had been Heaven below.

Dear Mother! I thought. When did you read this? Like me, were you
wandering in darkness, sneaking illumination, the comfort of some hidden light? What were you feeling? What did you need? I read the poem
again and again, trying to grasp its meaning. The gift of the first section
was its certainty: assurances of immortality are especially necessary at
times of our greatest need. Of course. It is the theme of the twenty-third
Psalm, and many other verses. But the final four lines, and in particular,
those Mother had underlined, challenged me. They wrenched my mind
into contortions, then cut me in two. Were it not for Heaven's "marauding Hand," earthly life itself would be heaven enough. The promise
of immortality is a gift, yes, but also, to put it most mildly, a burden.

I took a deep breath and looked up from the book, astonished. Exalted, somehow. Around the room, as far as the candlelight reached,
I saw familiar things: the kitchen table and chairs, the rocking chair
where so many nights I'd nursed Rachel, the brown sofa across from
the woodstove where Josiah and I have often sat together to read or
to talk. Through the soot-stained glass door of the stove, I watched
the wavering of orange flames. I did not feel damned. I did not even
feel troubled.

What did I feel? Perhaps I can explain it this way: A dog runs through a fallow field in the sunshine, nose to the ground, sniffing, bringing the world into his brain the way a dog does, through his nose. Then he scents a pheasant, or thinks he does. He concentrates and moves more carefully now, with more purpose, snuffling along, retracing his steps, venturing out farther, through thick underbrush and thorns that pull against his ears and cut into his feet, and then just as he feels he is mistaken, that his nose has tricked him, the scent grows stronger: there before him, crouched and still in the orchard grass, is the pheasant. With one final leap, the dog pounces, and the pheasant explodes into flight and flaps away.

Sometimes we feel we are on the scent of hidden things, but we doubt ourselves. Sometimes it's because we believe we must be mistaken. Other times, it's because we fear we might be right and we don't want to be, or can't be, because of who we are or where we live. But then something comes along to reveal that what we have scented with our innermost soul simply *is*, and our fear subsides. This revelation was my mother's legacy, a book of poems she'd hidden, like a pheasant in the orchard grass.

I read many more poems, and as I did, I grew tired, until I finally fell asleep.

When I awoke, the book of poems remained, covered, on my lap. I opened my eyes to blinding sunshine, the smell of bacon frying on the stove, and the sound of Josiah humming. I could feel heat radiating from the fully stoked stove. My neck and bent knees ached from sleeping in the chair. Josiah saw me stirring under my covers and smiled. At some point, he'd thrown a second blanket over me and tucked it in around my shoulders. The tallow candle in the mason jar had burned itself out.

"Good morning, Hannah," Josiah said.

"What time is it?"

He looked at the kitchen clock. He must have wound it, because I'd forgotten to do it the night before. "Time for breakfast," he said.

I sat up and looked at the time myself. Ten o'clock! "Josiah! Why didn't you wake me?"

"You need to ask?" He turned one strip of bacon, then the others.

I swung my feet to the floor and then arranged the blankets so that they hung down over my shoulders and past my thighs. With one hand, I carefully held the book of poems to my chest to keep it hidden. As I stood up, my Bible fell to the floor. Josiah moved as if to fetch it for me, but I retrieved it with my other hand and placed it on the chair.

"I'll dress and be down in a few minutes. Thank you for making breakfast."

He smiled. "Before you go, I have news. Someone from the hospital telephoned this morning. Gabriel is coming home."

"When?" I felt unworthy of this gift and yet warmed by a surge of joy.

"They didn't say."

I shuffled to the stairs and began to climb, my mind already swelling with happiness and anticipation.

"Hannah," Josiah said. I stopped. He hurried from the kitchen and crossed the room. He lifted my mother's kapp from the floor and handed it to me. "Your kapp," he said.

"Thank you." When I got upstairs, I discovered I'd left Mother's trunk open in the night, and Josiah had not closed it. I tied the book of poems into her kapp, returned it to the bottom, then closed the lid.

In the weeks before Gabriel's arrival, we received a visit from a social worker, a tall, young Black woman named Danielle, to prepare us for his return. She had once been a rower on the crew team at Gabriel's university, and now she worked for a hospital in Madison. Danielle spoke fast and was often interrupted by incoming calls on her telephone, but she seemed kind and caring, particularly whenever she talked about Gabriel.

For the time being, Danielle explained, it would be best if he could live on one level at home. No stairs. No steep hills or uneven surfaces.

And no rugs. She pointed to the woven rag rugs in the entry and on the floor in the kitchen. Gabriel was getting better using his crutches, but stairs and uneven surfaces remained dangerous. In a short time, he would be fitted with an artificial limb, and in several months, after learning to use and care for it, he could begin to return to a nearly normal life. He would eventually obtain other prostheses as well, as needed for whatever activities interested him. I must have looked skeptical, because Danielle smiled. Prosthetics are not what they used to be, she said. So many limbs, hundreds, even thousands, of arms and legs, had been lost in recent wars in Iraq and Afghanistan, that medical engineers had been able to perfect new, highly functional, lightweight prostheses: fingers that could grasp; knees and elbows that could flex, feet with multipositional ankles that automatically adjusted to any surface with the help of microprocessors, which enabled the wearer to run, dance, even swim.

"Swim?" Josiah said "With a fake leg? It must be made of wood, then. Maybe ash?"

She smiled. "You would think so, wouldn't you? No, new prostheses are made of polymers, lightweight carbon fiber, and metal alloys. Many of them have computers inside that run on batteries." In many ways, she said, technology is the easy part. The physical challenge of adapting to the prosthesis is usually easier than adjusting psychologically. In her experience, this has been particularly true for athletes, young men like Gabriel, accustomed to doing things with their bodies most nonathletes could only dream about.

From the driveway to the house, Josiah built a wide, sturdy ramp that switched back upon itself twice before ending in a small porch, six foot square, at the door. With the help of neighbors, he carried Gabriel's bed and dresser downstairs. We arranged them in one corner of the living room near a large, sunny window that faced the river, overlooking the main pasture. This would give him abundant natural light during the day, and he could also look out and see the animals. For the other two walls, I sewed pockets into large curtains and strung them at right angles to one another along ropes Josiah tacked to the ceiling. Gabriel could close these for privacy. The bathtub was already downstairs in the same room as my washtubs and wringer, just off the kitchen. Our privy was out the back door. It shared one wall with the house, and on that wall, Josiah had installed a large window of privacy glass that could be opened in winter to allow some heat from the kitchen stove to enter.

Gabriel arrived home in early December. A light snow was falling as two men rolled his large wheeled chair up Josiah's ramp. Gabriel looked so much larger than I'd remembered him. The muscles in his arms and neck, and across his chest, had thickened. He wore a beard and mustache, untrimmed and bushy, like the wool of merino sheep. Flakes of snow stuck to his beard and long hair, which reached to his shoulders. Even seated in the chair, he was taller than the men pushing him. When they grew closer, I could see the stump of Gabriel's maimed leg protruding forward from the chair like the bowsprit of a ship. Though he brought his elbows together and turned sideways to narrow his shoulders, his upper arms brushed each side of the doorframe as he rolled across the threshold, and the chair itself squeezed through with barely an inch to spare on each side. For the first time in his young life, I thought, sadly, Gabriel did not have to crouch or duck coming through that door.

One of the paramedics rolled Gabriel's chair to the center of the room while the other went back outside. He returned with Gabriel's crutches, which were taller than me, and a large suitcase that held his clothes and shoes. The men wished Gabriel well and departed.

"Dear Gabriel," I said, wrapping his head in my arms. His hair smelled of brightly scented shampoo. I felt his large hand centered on my back.

"Grandma," he said, his voice rumbling deep into my shoulder. "I'm so sorry."

"Oh, honey," I said, through tears. "Oh, honey."

Gabriel cried like a child, his tears darkening the shoulder of my dress, and I comforted him until he quieted.

"Would you like a glass of water?" I asked Gabriel. "Perhaps some pie? I've baked your favorite, cherry."

"Just the water, please," he said.

I went to the kitchen and pumped cold water up from the well, filling a tall glass for him. Before I returned, Gabriel had pulled the blanket from his lap. He wore a bright red sweatshirt, but he leaned forward and removed that as well, leaving him in only a white T-shirt and bright red sweatpants. His single foot, as long as a sheet cake pan, rested on a large tray connected to the bottom of his wheeled chair. On his maimed leg, the pants had been cut off and cinched tightly, the way you might tie a link of sausage. As I approached and he reached for the water, his muscular arm cut across the bar of sunlight and bloomed in an array of bright colors. From his wrist all the way to where his T-shirt stretched tightly across his shoulder, Gabriel's skin glowed in bright reds and greens and blues. At the top, I could see a large, red *W*, and beneath that, vines and flowers, and strange letters unrecognizable to me.

"Gabriel," I said, pointing. "What is this?"

He lifted his elbow so that I could see. "Tattoos," he said. "When you have them down your arm like this, it's called a sleeve." He passed the glass of water into the other hand and lifted the elbow of the other arm as well. It, too, was painted in colors. "This," Gabriel pointed to a large symbol near his elbow, drawn in black, "is the Japanese symbol for warrior. All the defensive linemen got that one on the same day, a week before summer practice started this year."

"These are permanent?"

"They are," he said.

"Such adornment, Gabriel," I said. "It seems so showy. So prideful." As a girl, I had memorized sections of my grandmother's copy of *Rules of a Godly Life*. In the chapter on works, the book spoke plainly: Practice modesty in the wearing of clothes and have nothing to do with pomp and luxury in raiment.

Gabriel nodded. "I guess they are a little showy. I sort of had to get them, to be a good teammate. But I like them okay now." He raised the massive stub of his maimed leg, adjusted himself in the chair, and let the leg drop.

"Well," I said, "at least they can be covered by long sleeves."

"That's true, they can." Gabriel nodded. "I can cover them if you want. You should see my friend Colton's. His tattoos curl up the sides of his neck and look like barbed wire wrapped around his throat, with bright red ink at the barbs so it looks like blood. Sometimes the refs stop the game to make sure he's not bleeding, it looks so real."

I smiled. "You've been away a long time. You've seen a lot."

"I plan to go back if I can," Gabriel said. "I had to take medical leave, but I didn't lose my scholarship. I dropped microbiology. I was failing that anyway. They said I could finish my other courses online, but I told them I can't do that where I'll be living." He smiled. A loud noise came from behind Gabriel, an English song of some kind, the sound of musical instruments and people screaming. He leaned forward, pulled a cell phone from his back pocket, ran his finger across the screen, which stopped the music, and put the phone to his ear.

"Hey, Colton." He paused. "Yeah, I made it home okay. They dropped me off today. Come and visit, I'll show you around." Gabriel paused again. He looked over at me and smiled. I could just make out the deep voice of his friend on the other end. "Yeah," Gabriel said, "they did the scans and everything, and they're building my bionic leg right now. Just a temp, but it should be done soon. First thing I'm going to do is kick your butt with it." He laughed, but then he grew serious. "They told me I'm done. It stinks. I hate it. I can still bench, at least, do upper body stuff. Maybe I'll do some powerlifting or something when I get back, I don't know. I've got to learn to walk first." He paused and listened for a while, then he laughed. "Okay, then, you better get going to that lit class or you're going to flunk it again. Got to read the stuff. That's the secret. Later, man."

Gabriel tapped the phone with his finger and put it face down on his lap. "That was Colton, my roommate." He took his empty water glass off the floor and handed it to me. "Thank you, Grandma."

Sadness trickled down into my stomach. Naïvely, I'd been expecting a different kind of reunion. The boy who left our house was not the young man who returned to us. "I thought this game, this football business, was safe, Gabriel," I said. "You told me so. I remember."

"I thought so, too. This"—he slapped his leg—"was just a freakish thing. They came at me from the side, and I didn't see them coming, or I would have kept them off me with my hands." He raised one hand and held it to the right side of his head about a foot from his ear. "I don't know when it started, but sometimes I can't see over here. Peripheral vision. I can see fine straight ahead, but sometimes I can't see to the side unless I turn my head."

"Like blinders on a horse," Josiah said.

"Exactly," Gabriel said. "Exactly like that. That's how they got me."

"Maybe you need glasses."

"I don't think so. I see fine straight ahead. I'm sure it'll go away now that I'm not knocking my head against other people." He shook his head and sighed. "Every morning I wake up and look down, hoping my leg will be there, thinking maybe it was just a bad dream. I really wanted to play in the NFL. I was going to surprise you guys with a big, new house, and I wanted to give you enough money so you didn't have to work anymore. Planned to get Dr. Kennedy a new truck, too, one of those new Ford Lariats that cost fifty grand, got USB ports all over, hands-free cell service, voice-activated GPS with a screen the size of a small television. Now that's never going to happen."

"It's generous of you to think of us," I said, "but we have all we need."

Gabriel glanced around the house, at his bed, at the chair Josiah had made for him, then up at the curtains bunched against the walls that could be drawn closed. He picked up his phone. "I don't suppose you installed electricity here while I've been away?"

Josiah smiled. "Of course not."

Gabriel smiled back. "How about internet service with a router so I can use my laptop?"

Josiah laughed but didn't say anything.

"Nothing's changed here, Gabriel," I said. "Life here is no different than when you left for school."

He nodded. "I understand. I really love you guys, and I love it here. I do. But life's a little different for me now, and I might need some things I didn't need before."

"For generations, Gabriel, we have had all we needed."

Gabriel sighed. "Before I left, I would have totally agreed with you. But"—he held up his phone—"this has to be charged every couple of days. And eventually my new leg will have rechargeable batteries inside it, too. Seven million people follow me on Twitter, or at least they used to. I know it's stupid and shallow, but I kind of like it."

"The glory that comes from man is false glory," Josiah said.

"Josiah, please," I said. "Gabriel, we'll figure something out."

"My girlfriend won't be happy if I don't call her every night."

"You have a girlfriend?"

He smiled. "Bella."

"Well, we'll make it work, somehow," I said. "Won't we, Josiah."

"You can use the generator in the shop to charge your phone," Josiah said. "We can take you to town in the buggy when you want to use your computer."

Gabriel sighed. "Thank you."

Gabriel received many visitors in those initial days in our home. Dr. Kennedy came the first morning, and they spent several hours talking about the animals he'd been treating. It warmed my heart to hear Gabriel laughing with him. Josiah and I had not seen the doctor for some time, and I was grateful for his calm, loving presence. Other neighbors and friends visited as well. Coach Beathard and his new wife came by, and they talked a long time. Mr. Walton stopped off with a case of root beer. Friends from Gabriel's college football team came, too, huge, muscular young men, including the one with the barbed wire tattooed around his neck. They stayed well past dark and seemed most interested in watching Josiah light the oil lamps, and two of them insisted on drawing their own cold drinking water from the hand pump in the kitchen.

Gabriel's girlfriend visited, too, a lovely young woman named Isabella, tattooed like Gabriel along the arm and wrist, a small, bright blue butterfly on one side of her neck. She spent an hour sitting on Gabriel's lap, one arm around his shoulders. Josiah could not abide it and left the house, but I tried to be gracious and understanding, knowing the English courted differently than we did, their young women far less modest. She loved our home and helped me prepare lunch, and then afterward she came with me to the barn as I fed our goats. She wanted to learn everything, she said, about our beautiful way of life.

For nearly two weeks, I felt encouraged and even hopeful. Josiah shoveled a wide, smooth path through the snow from the house to the barn, and Gabriel went out every morning and afternoon with a pillowcase to gather eggs for me and to sit with the animals while his telephone charged. They were as entranced by him as they'd ever been. One afternoon I found him asleep in the hay, with a Saanen ewe asleep beside him, her chin across his thigh, and her yearling kid on his lap. Gabriel's broad hand stretched across the kid's back. Even chickens who were frightened of me would, with some quiet coaxing, fly up to perch on Gabriel's shoulder to take kernels of cracked corn from his fingers. Greasy barn cats accustomed to fleeing the kick of Josiah's angry boot purred and slept in Gabriel's arms.

But in the end, what I wanted for Gabriel I could not provide. He'd eaten the magic fruit of English life, and though its sweetness offered little nourishment, its flavor proved addictive, because he could no longer live without it. Gabriel grew agitated by the slow pace of winter life on our farm, the short days and dreadfully long, dark nights. Inside the house, he kept reaching for invisible light switches, gently complained about the cold water, the stink of the privy, the uneven cycles of heat put out by the woodstove, even though Josiah began to set an alarm to refresh the fire in the early morning. Sometimes Gabriel's telephone battery went dead, and with it his patience and sweetness.

He and Josiah resumed their arguments, and it was clear to me that our love and goodwill were not enough.

I did not realize until far too late that when Gabriel lived among our people as one of us, the greatest gift we offered him was invisibility. Here, in all ways that mattered, he was no bigger than anyone else. When he ventured into the English world, he began to see himself as the English did. That new person needed many things we could not provide, and though it broke my heart to do so, I did what I did out of love for Gabriel. I asked Josiah to telephone the one English person I trusted, who loved the boy nearly as much as I did, to ask if he would take Gabriel in.

20

Thomas Kennedy

Though he'd recently visited Gabriel at the Fishers' home, Thomas was freshly taken aback by the boy's size as he ducked through the doorway and hobbled inside behind Josiah and Hannah. Most of the time Thomas had spent with Gabriel had been outdoors, where his size had been at least partially mitigated by open sky, large trees, and livestock, or in the Fishers' home, which had been remodeled, ceilings and doorways extended, to make Gabriel's life easier. Inside Thomas's home, everything now seemed reduced in scale beside the boy, his doorway fit for a hobbit, his sofa suited to a doll's house. Hannah bent over and pulled off Gabriel's single snow boot, a leather upper sewn to the tread from an old tire, that Abram Glick had fashioned for him several winters earlier. Though it was just two degrees outside, Gabriel wore no coat, hat, or gloves. Black sweatpants covered one leg, with the other side cut off and tied at the end of his stump with a shoestring, and his brightly colored, muscular arms bulged from a gray T-shirt cut off at the shoulders.

Josiah had delivered Gabriel's long bed and a custom-made chair earlier that morning. The seat of the chair was three feet wide and forty inches from the floor, as high as Thomas's hip. Constructed of white oak milled in Absalom's sawmill, the back of the chair reached six feet high. It looked like a throne, impressively huge but simple in design, with no frills or decoration. Josiah had also fashioned a large, wooden tray that fit across the arms of the chair so that Gabriel could eat his meals there and type on his computer.

"It's really hot in here," Gabriel said, craning his neck to look around the room. "But it sure smells good." Thomas's cats crouched nervously under Gabriel's bed.

"I've got chickens in the oven, and the thermostat's turned up," Thomas said. "I'll turn it down."

"No," Gabriel said. "I'll be fine." He tugged once on his T-shirt, the muscles in his forearms rippling.

"You all hungry?" Thomas asked. He had driven into town the previous afternoon to purchase six bags of groceries. He had three rotisserie chickens and a large tin of mashed potatoes warming in the oven.

"We ate lunch before we left," Hannah said. "But thank you so much."

"We'll let you get settled," Josiah said. He shook Gabriel's hand. "The Lord bless and keep you," he said.

Gabriel nodded. "Thank you, Grandpa."

Hannah wrapped her arms around Gabriel's head and pressed her lips into his hair. He encircled her waist with one arm and pulled her closer. She whispered something Thomas couldn't hear.

Finally, Hannah stood and rubbed her hands gently along Gabriel's bearded face. "I love you, Gabriel," she said, tears shining on her cheeks.

"I love you, too, Grandma," Gabriel said. "Visit anytime. Gideon knows the way."

"Of course," Thomas said. "Come day or night. You're always welcome."

Josiah and Hannah departed, and Thomas checked on his chickens. They needed a few more minutes, but the mashed potatoes steamed, the butter a golden, bubbling pool, when he lifted the foil. He pulled out the potatoes, put them on the stovetop, and covered the pan with a towel. When he looked up, Woolly Bugger had already draped herself across Gabriel's lap and was contentedly kneading his sweatpants with her front claws, and Mickey Finn had leaped from the floor to his right shoulder, where she sat surveying the room and occasionally licking his ear. "Didn't take them long to warm to you." Thomas pointed to the oven. "I'm going to eat lunch in a couple minutes, and I'd hate to eat alone."

Gabriel smiled. "Oh, you don't have to twist my arm. I'll eat again," he said. "That chicken smells awesome."

For the first few days, there was an awkwardness between Thomas and Gabriel that seemed to come partly from the newness of the situation and partly from each man's desire to be accommodating to the other. Because the ceilings in the A-frame portion of the main house rose fifteen feet above the floor, Josiah and Thomas had set up Gabriel's bed in that room, on the south end between the windows. Once inside the house, Gabriel never had to duck when he moved around, at least until he had to use the bathroom. And with his pillows propped against the wall, Gabriel could lie in bed and see the television and the kitchen. When Thomas asked if Gabriel would prefer to move to a bedroom instead, for more privacy, despite the lower ceilings, which were at least a half foot shorter than he was, Gabriel said he would move if Thomas wished it. "I'm asking what you would prefer," Thomas said.

"I'll do whatever works best for you," Gabriel responded.

Thomas sighed. "I think you'll be more comfortable out here."

"So do I."

Similarly, Gabriel always ate everything Thomas prepared for his meals. If he made three scrambled eggs and a half pound of bacon for Gabriel's breakfast, Gabriel ate it all. If he made six eggs and the same amount of bacon, Gabriel would eat that, too. One chicken for dinner, Gabriel ate it. Two chickens, he ate both. And yet, each time Thomas asked if he'd cooked enough food, Gabriel always said yes, the meal was perfect, thank you.

"Gabriel," Thomas said, finally, "you must tell me the truth. If I'm not making enough food, I'll make more. If I'm making too much and you're eating it all just to please me, I'll make less."

Gabriel nodded. "I don't eat as much as I did when I was playing football. After practice I was always starving."

"Well, how about this," Thomas said. "I'll make a good portion for a man your size, and if you're still hungry and you need more, you just tell me. Fair enough?"

"Good deal," Gabriel said. "Thank you."

Though Gabriel protested it wasn't necessary, that he would be content to ride in the bed of Thomas's pickup on errands and to medical appointments in Madison, Thomas traded in his truck for a one-ton Chevrolet pickup with a crew cab—a back seat with a second set of doors—then paid to have the rear seat removed and the front seat on the passenger side moved to the rear and down on the floor. Even with this accommodation, it remained a bit of a squeeze for Gabriel to fold himself inside, but with the seat all the way back, and his knees bent, he had adequate leg room, and, if he slid down slightly, his head just brushed against the ceiling.

In the mornings before breakfast, and again in the evenings an hour or so after dinner, Gabriel exercised: push-ups, sit-ups, single-leg squats, triceps lifts with his hands behind his back on the seat of his chair. He stretched as well, naming the yoga poses for Thomas as he watched: down dog, cobra, pigeon, tree. Twice each week, a therapist came to work with him; Gabriel quickly mastered his crutches, moving easily through every task the therapist assigned him. She inspected his wound, which was healing nicely, and complimented him on his care, promising that his training prosthesis was nearly ready and that she would call when it was finished.

On some weekends, Gabriel received visitors, often his college roommate, Colton, and several other students who drove up together from Madison. They were boisterous and energetic young people, and they took Thomas at his word when he told them to eat whatever they could find in the kitchen; they emptied the cupboards and the refrigerator, even polishing off the onions and the celery. His grocery bill swelled to $200 a week, but he didn't mind. It warmed him to be caring for another human being again, someone he dearly loved. When the friendly cashier at the grocery store said he must be feeding a dozen children, he came in so often, Thomas smiled and nodded.

Isabella continued to visit, too, and sometimes when Thomas awoke in the morning, she was still there, sleeping beside Gabriel.

Coach Beathard and his wife stopped by; Charlie Mayfield tearfully reminisced about Gabriel's days as a Little League slugger, rattling off memories of Gabriel's longest home runs, the windshields he'd shattered and car alarms he'd set off in parking lots. Every Friday evening, Billy Walton brought Styrofoam take-out boxes of his "world-famous" fish fry, free of charge, and he kept Gabriel supplied with endless bottles of root beer. Billy walked with a limp now, arthritis having taken a toll on his hips, but the pain didn't diminish his energy or his loquaciousness. He repeated the same stories, embellished others, recalling football games he'd seen in Madison: the big win against Michigan in which Gabriel recorded forty-one tackles and eleven sacks; Gabriel's first start at offensive tackle in Camp Randall against Fresno State, when he blocked down on a jet sweep and collapsed the entire defensive line like a row of dominoes, hooking two linebackers with his right arm, to boot, a play rebroadcast on SportsCenter, in slow motion, several dozen times since then.

"Christ, you got a raw deal, kid," Billy said. "It's like somebody yanked off Nolan Ryan's arm. Or busted up one of Secretariat's legs. If I could give you one of my legs, I would. Course it's all flab, looks like melting wax. The hip's shot, and in the mornings my knee is stiffer than a porn star's weenie." He got up and slapped Gabriel on the shoulder. "Got to run, my new bartender's probably stealing me blind. She's a beauty, but beautiful women are expensive. Remember that."

"I will," Gabriel said, laughing. "Thanks for stopping by."

"You bet, kid."

Hannah came to visit every other day in the beginning, sometimes with Josiah, but often alone. If Thomas was home at the time, he'd go outside to feed Gideon a carrot or a few alfalfa cubes, maybe shovel the sidewalk a bit or clean the snow from around his mailbox by the road, stalling to give Hannah some time alone with her grandson. Gabriel taught her to play a card game he'd learned at school, called Nerts. They played at Gabriel's table, with Hannah standing across from him. They laughed and shouted together, slapping their hands on the piles of cards that grew between them, and Gabriel kept score on a small sheet of paper. Sometimes they just sat and talked quietly. Hannah told him which of her goats had been bred that fall, anticipating the three dozen or so births coming in April; the jobs Josiah had taken on; written news from her sister in Pennsylvania or from her many nieces and nephews.

In the evenings, Thomas and Gabriel turned on the television, usually tuned to a college or professional basketball game. With the sound muted, they talked, sometimes late into the night. Gabriel's enthusiasm for returning to college seemed to wane the longer he was away. Though Thomas encouraged Gabriel to continue his studies, he told him he had only one life, and he should spend it as he pleased.

"Honestly," Gabriel said, "lately I've been thinking maybe I could just work for you full-time, once I'm on my feet again."

"You can, and I'd love that, you know I would," Thomas said. "But I don't want you to sell yourself short. Don't decide now. You're young. You have time."

One evening, Gabriel asked Thomas to tell him about his mother.

"Rachel," Thomas said. "I knew her, but not very well. I spent perhaps six or seven hours with her over a span of two years. She or Jasper would call when one of their goats was ill."

"Did she ever say anything about my father?"

"No." Thomas shook his head. "There was a lot of talk, you know, people trying to guess, that sort of thing, but no one ever knew, other than your mother, obviously. Don't hold that against her. She was an amazing woman. That I can say for certain."

"Tell me everything you can remember."

"It isn't much. As you've probably heard from others, she was beautiful, but she was even more beautiful on the inside. Being around her always felt peaceful."

"Jasper said she liked to sing."

"She did." Thomas nodded. "Amish hymns, usually. I could never understand the words, but it sounded lovely."

"Great-grandfather Absalom said she was a harlot and a temptress. The whore of Babylon, he called her. And he said God took my leg because I was abhorrent in His sight."

Thomas sighed. "Absalom lives in a different time. And in a different place, a hateful place where self-righteous old men live by rules that give them power. You and I don't live in that forsaken place, and Rachel didn't either."

"I know she died having me, but did she at least get to hold me?"

Thomas shook his head. "No. I'm sorry. She fed you before she passed, but she wasn't conscious. It took every last bit of strength, every ounce of her life, to get you into this world."

In mid-January, Thomas took Gabriel to Madison to be fitted with his temporary artificial leg. Because his residual limb, or RL, the terms therapists used instead of the more figuratively descriptive and disturbing "stump," would continue to change in shape and size over many months, the permanent prosthesis—or prostheses, since Gabriel, like many amputees, would acquire different legs for different activities—could not be fitted until the limb had finished healing, approximately six months after amputation. Thomas was shocked at the overtly mechanical look of the temporary leg. It looked robotic, something out of science fiction. Constructed of unpainted metal and white plastic, with interior cables and joints exposed, it was, the therapist said, the most technologically sophisticated leg available that was not wired into the human nervous system.

The therapist, a bright young woman named Molly, with curly brown hair and a cheerful smile, first taught Gabriel to pull a compression sock over his residual limb. The liner in the socket of his temporary leg contained silicone, which was durable and comfortable, she said, but suitable only for light activity, such as learning to walk. Molly explained that his more permanent leg would come with a polyurethane liner more suited to high activity levels and larger, heavier clients.

"Am I one of your larger clients?" Gabriel asked, playfully.

"Oh, no," Molly said. "I've had many other patients," she looked down at his chart, "who were eight feet seven inches tall and weighed five hundred and forty pounds. Nothing special about you, buddy."

Gabriel laughed out loud, and Thomas smiled. Eight feet seven inches. Twenty years old, and Gabriel was still growing.

In the center of the room were two parallel beams set about three feet apart and roughly waist-high for Gabriel. Molly asked Gabriel to sit down on a large box near the end of these beams, then she asked him to stand beside them on his crutches while she adjusted their width and height. She told him they'd replaced the normal bars with customized four-by-six beams to support Gabriel's weight.

With Gabriel seated again, Molly tightened a thick leather harness around his waist and over his shoulders, then tethered the harness to a strap that rose into a steel track above his head along the ceiling, ten feet above the floor. When Gabriel stood and prepared to move between the beams, Molly tightened the strap. The winch clicked as the strap tightened, and Molly said Gabriel could move confidently because the strap had originally been made to tow cars.

"I could swing on it like Tarzan?"

"Well, let's not test it quite that much. How does it feel? Your RL snug inside the socket?"

"Feels weird," Gabriel said. "Feels like when your leg falls asleep while you're sitting down, and when you stand up to walk, there's nothing there."

"No proprioception—no sense of your foot or leg in space. Totally normal. You'll get used to that. You ready to walk?"

"Let's go."

"Okay, you're going to lead with the RL, okay? Look down to see how it follows your cue. When you lift your thigh, it will engage the prosthetic knee and raise the heel. Then you lift the toe, and the leg will stride forward. We can adjust the length of the stride to match your other leg. Pay attention to how you shift your body weight for each stride. The RL is going to cue to that as well. Small steps, hands on the beams, stiff arms. I'll keep the winch tight. You're at roughly twenty percent of your body weight to start."

"Like walking on the moon."

"Exactly."

It took several minutes for Gabriel to traverse the eight or ten feet to the end of the track, and to Thomas it did not look easy or comfortable. Gabriel smiled at him when he reached the end, and Thomas smiled back.

"Way to go!" Molly said. "Amazing job. How did that feel?"

"Very weird," Gabriel said. "But way better than crutches."

"You bet. You'll be dancing in no time."

By late March, with the snow mostly gone and skeins of geese flowing northward overhead, Gabriel was walking a mile a day, usually with Woolly Bugger striding along at his side like a pet dog. It was a quarter mile from Thomas's mailbox to the intersection at County Q, and Gabriel walked from the mailbox to Q and back each morning and again each afternoon. He cut a box elder tree as thick as his wrist from the hedgerow behind Thomas's garage and peeled the bark from it, and in the beginning, he carried this walking stick for security. The muscles in his RL had atrophied, the thigh considerably smaller than that of his left leg, and sometimes the leg tired and became unsteady on the way back. In two weeks, the RL had grown stronger, and Gabriel began leaving the walking stick at home.

He began walking longer routes through the countryside; when Woolly Bugger grew tired and began sitting in protest at the extra distance, Gabriel picked her up and put her on his shoulders. Because locals drove these back roads, there were frequent car horns and waving arms out open windows as drivers passed him. In April, Thomas formally hired Gabriel to be his veterinary assistant. He set up a bank account for him at the Farmers and Merchants Bank, and he drew up a contract paying Gabriel eighteen dollars an hour for office work and calls during regular hours, and twenty-five dollars an hour when the calls came overnight between seven P.M. and seven A.M.

In the first two weeks, they made three separate trips to Oxford to deliver Arabian foals for Birdy and Mel, two beautiful fillies and a healthy young colt, and Gabriel maintained his balance and moved so effortlessly through the stalls, someone unaware might never have guessed he was wearing a prosthesis. After completing their work, they stayed for dinner, a French feast cooked by Coach Beathard and his wife, Merryn, who announced they were expecting a child at the end of the summer. Later in April, Gabriel and Thomas made several trips to Hannah and Josiah's place to assist with the birth of forty-two goat kids, including two sets of triplets.

In early June, Billy Walton threw an outdoor party at Shaken, Not Stirred. It was the evening after Gabriel got fitted with his permanent prosthesis, and the whole community turned out to celebrate with him. Though Gabriel was not quite twenty-one years old, Billy bent the rules a bit, winking at Gabriel as he handed the young man a bottle of root beer. Gabriel took a drink and winced as he swallowed. Billy put his mouth to Gabriel's ear. "That's a double brandy and seven, Gabriel. I hope you like it. I know you college boys move on from root beer sooner or later."

It wasn't long afterward, though, that Thomas noticed a restlessness in Gabriel, a preoccupation or dreaminess that turned him inward. He grew quiet, sometimes impatient. On veterinary calls, Gabriel rode silently in the truck with his earbuds in, listening to music, and while they were working, Thomas sometimes had to repeat himself when he asked Gabriel to do something. That morning, he'd asked Gabriel to hold the neck of an exhausted ewe while he pulled two stillborn lambs from her body. Gabriel just stared at him until Thomas repeated himself. The ewe bellowed in pain as Thomas completed his work, and Gabriel barely comforted her. Afterward, when Thomas asked Gabriel to prepare a bolus of antibiotics and numbing agent to be placed in her womb, Gabriel wandered from the lambing jug and didn't return.

At home, Gabriel grew impatient when Woolly Bugger or Mickey Finn meowed loudly for their dinner, and every evening, instead of watching television and talking with Thomas, Gabriel went outside for a long walk, often returning after Thomas had gone to sleep.

Near the end of an almost silent dinner, Thomas finally asked. "Gabriel, what's going on?"

Gabriel shrugged but remained silent.

"Is something bothering you?"

Gabriel sighed. "I don't know what's wrong," he said. "I've always loved it here, loved being with you and the animals, and I still do, but it's like some invisible part of me is missing, or something."

"You miss your friends. Bella, too. You've got some money saved. You can get your own place if you want. I'll help you with that."

"It's not that. Or it's more than that, really. I miss playing football, the challenge of it, all the people screaming in the stands, being with my guys, lifting weights, getting stronger. I miss all of that so much."

"That's understandable."

"I feel like a failure."

"Now, that's ridiculous."

"Is it?" Gabriel asked. "I mean, look at me. I'm this huge guy, right, who can pick up a car or dunk a basketball without jumping. I feel like I should be using that, somehow. And I was, and I loved that so much. Like, look at you, you're super smart and you have steady hands. You can diagnose a disease and perform surgery on an animal, healing it. What if instead of doing that you were just, I don't know, building little ships inside bottles, or something? Wouldn't you feel that somehow your gift, this thing you've been given, was being wasted, at least a bit?"

"Well," Thomas said, "you have a gift with animals, too, Gabriel. Far greater than mine. They are relaxed and at peace under your touch. People are drawn to you, too. Yes, you're eight feet tall and stronger than any three normal-sized men. But that should not be a burden to you. Maybe you should go back to college. Your scholarship is still good. Okay, you can't play football anymore, but you can go back to Madison, enroll in classes again."

"I don't want to go back, not if I can't play."

"Then what is it that you want?"

"I don't know," Gabriel said.

Weeks passed, and Gabriel's mood did not brighten, though he seemed more attentive to the needs of the animals they tended. Then one afternoon, Gabriel took a phone call. He raised the phone to Thomas, who was suturing the leg of a horse that had become tangled in a loose coil of barbed wire. Thomas nodded and Gabriel went out into the pasture to talk.

Thomas figured it was Bella. She and Gabriel talked every day, usually two or three times. She still visited some weekends, slept with Gabriel in his bed, went for long walks with him. Thomas believed at some point after graduation, she and Gabriel would move in together, perhaps somewhere nearby.

Thomas could have been imagining it, but after that phone call, Gabriel seemed both more agitated but also, somehow, more energetic than he'd been in a while. A week went by, with more telephone calls coming at odd times during the day and night. Sometimes when Thomas left his bed to use the bathroom, he'd hear Gabriel talking on the phone at two or three in the morning.

Again, Gabriel grew more distant, preoccupied. He lost the thread of conversations, sometimes seemed so deeply lost in thought he was no longer conscious of the world around him.

"Gabriel," Thomas asked, finally. "What's happened? Is something wrong?"

Gabriel shook his head. "No. I'm sorry. I've got a lot on my mind."

Thomas waited for a minute, but Gabriel didn't elaborate. "You care to share what that is? You've been on your phone a lot. You and Bella having trouble?"

"No," he said. "It's not that." He smiled and shook his head. "You know how it is, sometimes, when you really want something, and then it looks like you can get it, and suddenly you're not sure you want it anymore?"

"Maybe in the abstract. I don't know. What's going on?"

"Someone's been calling me. I don't know how he got my number, I think from someone in Madison. At first, I thought it was some kind of prank. But he kept calling. He emailed some information, and I checked it all out. It's legit. I've been offered a contract. A job."

"What kind of job?"

"You have to promise not to laugh."

"Gabriel, why would I laugh?"

Gabriel pulled out his phone and scrolled to a website. Thomas heard crowd noise, people cheering and clapping. Gabriel held the screen up. Two huge, shirtless, bloodied men, one Black and barefoot, the other wearing a bright red leotard with a Union Jack emblazoned across the front, were mauling one another while a small crowd screamed.

"Professional wrestling?"

"That's right. It's not football, but it looks like something I could do, something I could be good at. The guy calling me is the CEO, a British guy, and the company is based in Hong Kong. He's offered me a six-month contract for one hundred thousand dollars. To train me. And then I'd sign another contract after that, depending on how the training goes."

"And you'd have to go to Hong Kong for this training?"

"No." Gabriel shook his head. "London."

"London! What about your leg?"

"My leg won't matter," Gabriel said. "The guy says we'll have one made just for the ring. He wants it to be part of the act, actually. I know I can do what these guys are doing, and I'm twice their size. Edward— that's the guy I've been talking to, Mr. Edward Wainright—says I'll be famous. Says he'll make me a millionaire."

"And this is something you want to do?"

"Yes," Gabriel said. "I think it is."

21

Hannah Fisher

So Gabriel boarded an airplane, the first person in my line or Josiah's to do so, to fly clear to the other side of the world. In the months before his departure, I spent as much time as I could with him. We took many long walks together. People driving by honked their horns, and Gabriel always waved and smiled. Amish friends stopped their buggies and wished us well. Even domestic animals stopped to stare as he passed. Pastured cattle or goats wandered to the fence lines bordering the road and poked their heads through the wire to be closer to him. When his passport came in the mail, he proudly showed it to me, a little blue booklet with his picture glued in the front. I had never seen one before.

I knew nothing of this English business, this professional wrestling. I was curious, of course, but unwilling to grant it legitimacy by showing interest or asking questions. From Gabriel's descriptions, it sounded garish and immodest. When he tried to show me video of a wrestling match on his telephone, I would not look. I turned my head and closed my eyes. Please, Grandma, he implored me. I said, Gabriel, I am not ashamed of you or disappointed by your choice, I just do not want to share in it.

I was devastated to be losing him. After his injury, when I learned he would return home to us, I selfishly prayed that Gabriel would welcome our humble life with open arms, that he would stay and choose baptism and all that might follow: a lovely wife, a life of honest labor beside Josiah, and, God willing, many children, my great-grandchildren. I hoped he would see the loss of his leg as a summons from the Lord offering him passage through the narrow gate, for, as the Lord said, "the gate is wide, and the road is easy that leads to destruction."

But Gabriel was a young man, proud and strong, his massive body a match for his earthly ambitions. Even as a young boy, he always loved tests of his strength.

"The world is a huge place, Grandma," Gabriel said. "I want to see as much of it as I can. You understand, don't you?"

The Lord's earthly paradise is beautiful, there is no denying that. Even the small piece of it I know, the only piece of it I will ever know, often overwhelms with its beauty and bounty. Gabriel had already seen more of it, much more, and it had planted a need in him. I remembered something my mother used to tell me. "Hannah," she'd say, "you cannot put a pumpkin back into its seed." Certain things, in other words, cannot be undone. Most often, she reminded me of this when a boy began to show interest, especially if it were an English boy, but also an Amish boy from a family of questionable virtue. Most sadly, she would sometimes say this after my father had done something cruel or mean-spirited, belittled her or denigrated her cooking or cleanliness in front of us children.

Only after many years of marriage to Josiah could I understand how unhappy Mother must have been. Josiah is not perfect; he would be the first to admit this. I am also a deeply flawed wife, impatient, argumentative, prideful, even deceptive, at times, as I have already shown. He is often intemperate with me, and just as often, I have taken shameful pleasure in pointing Josiah to mistakes he has made. Yet his love is as certain and regular as the air I breathe, and each night as we end the Lord's day together, I give thanks for such a husband, who always takes my hand in his beneath the covers as we fall asleep.

I sighed and smiled at Gabriel. "Do I understand your desire? Yes,

I do. I was a young woman once. You want to spread your arms wide like a net and gather in everything the eye touches. Every young person has such dreams."

"And is my dream such a bad thing?"

"Not that long ago, I might have said yes. Now I'm not so sure. It's just that the closer you get to worldly things, the further from God you may find yourself. If you get too far away, you may not find your way back."

Though I did feel at least some Godly spirit in my desire to keep Gabriel at home, I understood my beseeching was dishonest. I did worry about Gabriel's eternal life, but my earthly life also motivated me. When I see Maddie Hershberger at the bakery, dusted with flour working beside her daughters and three beautiful granddaughters, or my dear friend, Abiah, who has seven children and nineteen grandchildren, all of whom live in our church district, I feel pangs of uncharitable envy. It is God's will that Josiah was smitten just weeks after Rachel's birth, and though we remained active in our marriage bed for many years afterward, I bore no more children. I am thankful for all God has provided me. I am. But it is not the life I had imagined.

In the week before Gabriel's departure, each evening I sat alone, often deep into the dark, early morning, with my embroidery. I had not taken it up for many years, my crooked fingers sore, my eyesight clouded. By lamplight, on a large dish towel, I embroidered the final paragraph of *Regeln eines Gottseligen Lebens* (*Rules of a Godly Life*). My grandmother gave me her copy of this book, worn and crumbling, printed in 1793, the very copy her grandmother had passed on to her. With the binding gone, the crumbling pages were held together by string wrapped about them in both directions. Perhaps one day I will pass it along to my grandchild, but in the meantime, I made this towel for my dear Gabriel, to go with him into the English world, to remind him of what is genuine and right and good:

"Finally, in your conduct be friendly toward everyone and a burden to none. Toward God, live a holy life; toward yourself, be moderate; toward your fellow men, be fair; in life, be modest; in your manner, courteous; in admonition, friendly; in forgiveness, willing; in your promises, true; in your speech, wise; and out of a pure heart gladly share of the bounties you receive."

I embroidered animals around the edges, goats of many colors, and chickens, horses, a few sheep. I wove about them long, green vines and leaves, and in among them some bright orange pumpkins. With black thread, in the middle, I embroidered our buggy, raised in the center to accommodate Gabriel's height. All were imperfect, of course. I am no artist. I folded it into a small box and left it with him when I said goodbye, told him not to open it until he was in the airplane somewhere above the Lord's mighty oceans.

I did not think this small token would serve to blanket Gabriel from the torments and temptations of the English world. But I hoped it would remind him of the goodness that lived in his heart and of the Lord's protective grace. For Darius sealed Daniel in the lion's den with only the clothes on his back, and in the morning, Daniel emerged without a scratch.

Part Three

22

Billy Walton

Seems like after Gabriel left for London, life went crooked for a while. That winter Brenda, my first ex-wife, hit an icy patch down in Carbondale and rolled her car. She wasn't wearing a seat belt, and she flew through the windshield like she was shot from a cannon. We hadn't spoken for thirty years, but her death shook me up. Regret came home to roost like a big old buzzard perched in my chest, picking at the bones.

In January, Oliver Edwards's mother, Inez, finally passed at 103, her mind gone at least twenty-five years before that. Ollie keeps her cremains in a coffee can on the kitchen counter. One trusts he won't wake up groggy one morning and accidentally brew a hot cup of Inez to drink with his toast. Later that month, Charlie's wife received a diagnosis of metastatic breast cancer. It's in her bones, in her head. Even with drugs to slow down the plague, they gave her six months, likely less. She asked Charlie to take her to the Caribbean. He's afraid to fly, and he's tighter than a driven nail, but I said, Charlie, stick a crowbar in your wallet and take her down there. Slam a few vodka martinis at O'Hare if you must and get on the damn plane. They went to Aruba in March and had a great time, said it felt like the honeymoon they'd never had.

"Carol held my hand the whole flight home," Charlie said.

"Listen to you, Romeo."

"She had her head against the window, and she said, 'Chas, why didn't we do this years ago?' I said we'd pick another island and go again in the fall."

Carol passed in June. At the funeral, her casket was closed, and the large, framed photograph on top pictured her with Charlie on Eagle Beach in Aruba. The sun was shining on their faces, they were holding mai tais garnished with pineapple, and the water behind them looked too blue to be true.

I haven't escaped, either. Started pissing blood awhile back. Thought maybe it was just on account of my nuts dangling six inches lower than they once did. They get bopped around some when I'm walking. I let it go for about a year, and when I had it checked out, my PSA was through the roof. Doc wanted to do a biopsy, but I said, I'm seventy-three years old, let's just let it ride. You said yourself it's likely slow growing. I could drop of a heart attack in a year or get hit by lightning tomorrow, and I'd just as soon not have a needle shoved up my ass and then go through surgery and all the rest only to die of something else. He said it's not what he'd do, but it was my funeral, so I could pick the music.

In spring, Doc Kennedy stopped by more often on his way through town, and he kept us apprised of the progress of Gabriel's new career. The boy had been lifting weights and getting stronger, and he was also learning the throws and holds and falls one needed to put on a good show in the ring. Gabriel told Doc Kennedy it was more ballet than boxing, only instead of ninety-pound ballerinas you had three- and four-hundred-pound men on stage pretending they were trying to kill each other.

Gabriel had his first exhibition matches in March, and by April he was already developing a following. He started out wrestling in school gymnasiums, clubs, that sort of thing, with the plan to move on to smaller arenas in Europe. In early May, Doc Kennedy came by for a fish fry, and when he pulled out his wallet to pay, he also gave me a slip of paper. On it, he'd written the address of a YouTube link Gabriel had sent him. "I thought you might want to watch this," Doc said. "It's a match Gabriel had a couple weeks ago, in Amsterdam."

We had maybe twenty people in the place. I opened my laptop and plugged it into the big-screen TV, clicked on the link, and came out from behind the bar so I could watch it myself. The videographer needed a tripod, because the camera jumped around so much at first it was like he was filming from a boat on rough water. But when the focus came in and steadied, it fell on Gabriel standing in one corner of the ring, his arms raised like he was Moses about to part the Red Sea, with a couple thousand screaming people behind him in the dark.

Gabriel Fisher was now called Anakim, the Amish Giant, and the kid looked like Hercules. Muscle on muscle, must have weighed six hundred pounds.

He'd bleached his long hair and beard a bright blond. His chest, which looked as wide as a rowboat, was covered in tattoos. He wore Amish pants and suspenders, his body slick and his hair and beard dripping sweat. By normal standards, the other wrestler was a big guy, kind of fat, the flesh on his arms and shoulders bulging, but he stood two feet shorter than Gabriel and probably weighed 250 pounds less. Near the end of the match, he backed into one corner and seemed to beg for mercy as the crowd roared. Gabriel lowered one shoulder into the man's chest, then bent over and, in a single motion, lifted the man in his arms, balancing him across the front of his body at shoulder level, and turned toward the center of the ring.

Cell phones flashed throughout the arena as the crowd chanted "An-a-kim! An-a-kim! An-a-kim!" in a rising crescendo. Gabriel wandered to the center of the ring and then, with a grimace, lifted the other wrestler completely overhead, ten or eleven feet above the mat. Gabriel circled the ring this way, the tree trunks of his arms extended, the other wrestler pretending to try to free himself. The crowd began chanting something that sounded like *"Hemel! Hemel! Hemel!"* over and over. And then after about ten seconds the chanting changed again. As Gabriel returned to one corner of the ring, the crowd began shouting a single word, in unison, "Hell! Hell! Hell!" Gabriel opened his mouth, flexed his one good knee, and threw the wrestler halfway across the ring, where he bounced once on the canvas like a discarded doll, rolled to his back, and was still. Gabriel walked over and placed a giant black boot on the man's chest. He crossed his arms proudly, and the referee dropped and slapped the mat three times. The video went black.

Everyone in my place erupted. They begged me to replay the match. I played it a third time, too. And then after I closed for the night, I sat at the bar and watched it again. I read the comments, too. Most were in Dutch, which I obviously couldn't understand. But a few were in English, and from them I figured out that the sequence at the end of the match was called "From Heaven to Hell." Gabriel lifted his vanquished opponent overhead, into "heaven," and then, when the crowd called for it, cast him down into "hell." Crazy.

I could not take my eyes off him. He was nothing like the skinny beanpole who tripped over his own big feet running to first base. He was a giant, yes. He'd been a giant for a long time. But now his extraordinary strength was on full display. He was about to become one of the living wonders of the world.

By early summer, Gabriel was wrestling in larger arenas and auditoriums across Europe and Asia. Me and Charlie started following him on Twitter. While it was obvious that he had millions of admirers, with Gabriel's fame came a degree of unwelcome attention, too. Charlie showed me one thread that had spun out along the hashtag #AnakimsShlong, where people speculated about the size of Gabriel's penis, or posted photographs with that hashtag, pictures that included the Washington Monument, the Leaning Tower of Pisa, and the Great Pyramid of Giza. A man in Hong Kong offered $250,000 for a picture of Gabriel's actual penis. Life's rich online pageant.

"And get this," Charlie said. "There's a porn company offering Gabriel a million dollars to have sex on camera with a porn star of his choice."

"Jesus, Charlie, what's this world coming to?"

"Aw, it was headed to hell in a handbasket long before this, Billy," he said. "The internet just sped up the ride, is all."

In time, there was video of Anakim wrestling somewhere new almost every week. It was ridiculously entertaining, and I loved to see the kid doing so well for himself. He defeated ten wrestlers in a Royal Rumble in London, beat the European tag team champions on his own in a match in Lisbon, and met the world champion, a scary-looking ox called the Sheik, in a cage match in Rio de Janeiro. That match Anakim won by disqualification when the Sheik's bodyguards climbed over the cage to assist him. Anakim bloodied all four men, incapacitating three of them, but when Anakim's back was turned, the Sheik pulled a large, black asp, five feet long, from a wriggling cloth bag and got it to bite Anakim's leg. Anakim collapsed, the crowd went into hysterics, and the referee disqualified the Sheik, enabling him to keep his world title, since apparently the championship belt cannot be lost by disqualification. Comments beneath the video debated the likelihood of the snake actually being an asp. Anakim's defenders argued vigorously that his massive size and blood volume enabled him to survive the bite of a venomous serpent that would easily kill all other men on earth, but I believed the carefully worded explanation of a herpetologist from the Universidade de São Paulo, who explained that after examining the video, he'd determined that the snake was a nonpoisonous black rat snake, common throughout North America.

In July, we learned that Gabriel would be making his American wrestling debut in August at the Sizzling Summer Slam in Chicago. Charlie wanted to drive down for it, but I hate big city traffic, and besides, I could stream it on pay-per-view and charge a cover, probably make enough to put in a new furnace and air conditioning unit, which my place needed pretty badly. The International Alliance of Professional Wrestling was running advertising on ESPN. They were holding a full card at the United Center, with Gabriel wrestling for the world championship in the final match of the evening. All those international matches had primed the pump, as it were, to build momentum and a following, so that when Anakim finally came to the United States, the largest market in the world, at the end of the summer, he would be the biggest thing since the Beatles. Hell, Charlie said, when Anakim returns, it will make the Beatles seem like a sugar cube tossed into a vat of coffee. He wasn't far off.

23

Thomas Kennedy

Thomas visited with Hannah and Josiah less frequently after Gabriel left town, but he still joined them for dinner from time to time, and in quieter moments when Josiah was away washing his hands, or tending to an outdoor chore, Hannah would whisper questions: Where was Gabriel living now? Was he happy? Did he have a girlfriend? Whatever happened to Bella? Thomas told Hannah what he could. Gabriel and Isabella had broken up a week before he'd left for London. It had been quite a scene, a conversation that went on for hours, with Bella crying, running out, and slamming the door, then returning. She'd graduated that May, and it seemed as if the plan had been for them to move in together, but after the breakup, she returned home to California. Gabriel said he felt bad about the split, that he loved Bella, but he could not pass up the opportunity that awaited him. He shared an apartment in London's West End with another wrestler, though he traveled so much for matches, he was hardly ever there.

Thomas offered to bring his laptop with him so Hannah could see a match for herself, but she declined. She was curious, though. Sometimes Thomas narrated highlights for her. In one recent match, Gabriel had thrown five of the six wrestlers he'd faced out of the ring when he was struck in the back by a folding chair wielded by the referee, who had been "secretly" paid by Gabriel's opponents to help defeat him. When he staggered into the ropes after this blow, his wrestling prosthesis—the fake leg that had been customized for his work in the ring—fell off.

Reduced to one good leg, his stump wrapped in its padded leather-and-Velcro sock, Gabriel found himself in danger of being pinned, as planned, but near enough to his leg that he could reach it. He reached for it. Improvising, his final opponent, a muscular bad guy with flowing black tresses called Pretty Boy Cloyd, pretended to hold him just a fingertip away from the leg. Each time Gabriel reached for it, Pretty Boy dragged him away. As the drama neared its peak, and Gabriel seemed certain to lose by being pinned, he made one last effort, this time seizing his prosthesis, which was nearly five feet long. To the delight of the crowd, he swung his leg into the crooked referee, who flew over the ropes out of the ring. Then he turned to face Pretty Boy.

Pretty Boy dropped to his knees, pretending to beg for his life, and as the audience roared, Gabriel gripped the leg by its ankle in both hands, raised it over his shoulder, and swung it like a baseball bat into Pretty Boy's side. Pretty Boy ricocheted across the ring. Gabriel stalked him, hopping on one leg, swinging the other leg overhead like the blade of a fan, then clobbered Pretty Boy over the head. Pretty Boy went down, and Gabriel flopped on top of the now prostrate and bleeding wrestler, rolled him to his back, and smiled as the audience chanted one, two, three seconds for the pin.

"That sounds horrifying," Hannah said.

"Well," Thomas said. "It's not high art. Wrestlers are entertainers. The most popular ones are paid well, and Gabriel is very, very popular."

Thomas did not tell Hannah certain other things anyone familiar with the internet could easily discover. Gabriel was sometimes photographed in the company of beautiful, often barely clad young women. He'd been arrested for possession of marijuana at the airport in Seoul, and he'd been surreptitiously filmed in a hotel hallway in São Paulo carrying a nude, dark-haired young woman in his arms. He also did not share that Gabriel's wrestling name was Anakim, the Amish Giant, and that his "costume" was, in essence, the plain clothing of Hannah's people in Lakota. Gabriel even wore a straw hat as he walked into the ring.

He'd already told Hannah about Gabriel's upcoming championship match in Chicago. Gabriel had sent Thomas a pair of tickets and backstage passes. On several occasions, Thomas had considered asking Hannah if she'd like to go see it with him, but he always lost his nerve. Then during one evening visit after they'd finished dinner, Josiah informed Thomas that he would be gone for a week in August, roughly from the twenty-first until the twenty-sixth. He'd gotten a contract to renovate and expand a kitchen in a home near Wisconsin Dells. He'd arranged to stay with Amish friends in nearby Delton while doing the work. As always, when Josiah traveled, Hannah would stay and run the farm. The dates coincided with Gabriel's championship match in Chicago, so when Josiah left the house to walk a plate of food over to Absalom's house, Thomas finally gathered the courage. He and Hannah were at the sink, where he was helping her with the dishes. He asked if she wanted to go with him to see Gabriel in Chicago. He planned to stop in Milwaukee on the way down, as well, to visit his mother.

Hannah continued washing the plain white plate in her hand, scrubbing it deliberately as she always did, first in a circle around the edge, then in gradually decreasing circles toward the center of the plate before rinsing and setting it in the drainer for Thomas to dry. In the beginning, he found it odd that she wouldn't simply pass the plates to him. He stood beside her with a dish towel, his hands otherwise empty. But then one evening he sat and finished his coffee while Josiah dried the dishes, and he noticed that Hannah passed each plate, each glass, each piece of silverware directly into her husband's waiting hands. Thomas understood, then, that setting the washed dishes in the drying rack was a simple, elegant precaution: it prevented her hands from ever even accidentally touching his.

Hannah lifted a second plate from the stack and repeated the cycle, looking down into her dishwater as if embarrassed, or as if she hoped to discover some secret lurking there. Though Thomas had grown used to the longer pauses in conversation that occurred during Amish dinners, this silence made him uncomfortable. The longer it went on, the more certain he became that he'd violated some unspoken understanding in their friendship.

"I'm so sorry," he said. "I shouldn't have asked you that. I apologize."

She turned her head to smile at him, the orange light from the setting sun filtered through the kitchen window against her face. "No," she said. "I'll go with you." She nodded. "I'd love to. We'll have the day."

She rinsed the plate and began to reach toward the drying rack, but then she stopped herself. She turned the plate to its side and held it out to Thomas. It hovered there like the moon between them. He gently took the plate from her hand, dried it, and added it to the stack. The next plate she washed went, again, into the rack.

We'll have the day.

As he struggled to fall asleep that night, Thomas thought about those four words. He thought they bespoke an unintended intimacy. The day would be theirs alone. They might be twelve hours, perhaps longer, in one another's company. He had not been alone that long with a woman, with any woman, even chastely, since Angela died. With some disappointment, he realized that Hannah might have meant something more, too, that their time alone together would be circumscribed to *only* that day. It would happen once. Its beginning would also contain its end. Nonetheless, he could think of almost nothing else in the days to come.

24

Trey Beathard

Gabriel Fisher
AKA Anakim, the Amish Giant
217 Montagu Square
London W1H 2LF
UK

Dear Gabriel,

Please forgive this old-fashioned paper letter. Thomas and I spent a pleasant afternoon on the river fly-fishing the other day—he caught more trout than I did, but we both enjoyed the company. We got to talking about you and your life as a wrestler, and he was kind enough to pass along your London address. When I got home that night, I couldn't sleep. Something was bothering me, and I knew what it was, so I came downstairs to put pen to paper.

I want to make sure I say the right things in the right way. I hope I don't flatter myself to say that as a coach, I'm perhaps the next best thing to a father. I'm writing to impart some fatherly advice without the anger and judgmental harshness that usually accompanies it, at least in my own experiences as a son.

Gabriel, you were the finest football player anyone's ever seen, and there will be no one better to come along in my lifetime, of that I'm certain. Though injuries, even career-ending ones, are part of the game I love, the tragedy of your situation, the loss of your leg, has haunted me. I nearly quit coaching after your injury. I still consider giving it up every spring now, particularly since Merryn and I welcomed our beautiful daughter, Caroline, into our lives, but when August rolls around and I smell freshly cut grass and drive by the ball field, and I see those goal posts standing on each end, my love of the game overpowers any impulse I had to step away. I'd never have guessed I could find love and such happiness coaching high school football in a place like this. I still freeze my Texas nuts off in the winter, but the beautiful spring, summer, and fall make it worth it.

I'm so glad you have found an outlet for your incredible physical talent. I had my doubts in the beginning. But you look amazing, so huge and so strong. Some of the things you do in the ring defy human strength and physics. At his tavern, Billy often shows videos of your matches that fans have uploaded on YouTube, and I know folks in Lakota are proud to share in your success. I certainly am proud of you. You are (obviously!) the biggest thing to ever happen here, or I guess anywhere, for that matter. While I wish it had come on the football field in a sport with a long and distinguished history, I am thrilled for you and for your success.

That said, I'm writing today with some words of caution. Please understand that they grow from the respect I have for you and your family, and from hard experience. Fame and fortune have come your way, and with them will be opportunities that could lead to decisions you will regret. I made many of those regretful decisions in my life, so I feel a responsibility to warn you of what may come, though of course it is your life to live as you see fit. You may or may not know that before I became your football coach, I lost everything I cared about in my life. I had no one to blame for that but myself. Your grandmother's religion will tell you the love of money is the root of all evil. I know that money is also a ticket to paradise. But that can go bad quickly. Drugs and women, in particular, were my undoing, though gambling played a role as well. You have even more reasons to be wary. Anyone with money and fame will attract charlatans and leeches as certain as moths fly to porch lights after dark.

Gabriel, I've read some things about you online. I've seen pictures and video. Unlike my own mistakes, which I managed to keep secret for some time, nearly everything you do will wind up on the internet. I understand that a beautiful woman or two in combination with a bottle of wine, a joint, or a few lines of coke makes for a night of overwhelming pleasure. I've been there. Many young men have. I didn't know it when I was in the grip of addiction, but each time I succumbed to those illicit temptations, I lost a bit more dignity, a bit more pride, another piece of myself that I couldn't get back. I had to lose everything before I found myself again, but pieces of me will always be missing. Even after putting my life back together, with the help of Aunt Birdy and Mel, and even after Merryn and I married and brought a child into the world, I am still not whole, and may never be.

Gabriel Fisher, you will see far more of the world than everyone living here in Lakota, put together, will ever see, and you will make more money than you've ever dreamed of making. Live a little, of course. You're not a monk. Order the biggest steak and the best bottle of wine. Buy the Lamborghini (but make sure you can fit inside of it first!). The world is your oyster, and its pearls are in your hands. But live wisely. Choose wisely. Love wisely.

And never quit.

Love,
Coach Beathard

25

Thomas Kennedy

On the appointed morning of their departure for Chicago, Thomas arrived at Hannah's home just after sunrise, as they'd agreed. In the distance, her white goats reclined on the hillside, and he could hear roosters crowing from somewhere behind the barn. Songbirds were also singing, the lovely cacophony of morning birdsong a welcome summer extravagance. Hannah emerged in a blue Amish dress that reached to her ankles, wearing her white kapp. She carried a wicker basket.

"Good morning," Thomas said. Hannah got in and closed the door.

"God's morning to you," Hannah said. She leaned forward and glanced through the windshield at her father's house, then placed the basket between them on the seat. She opened it.

"Wild raspberry muffins," she said. "Still warm."

"Wonderful," he said, taking one. "Thank you."

"Josiah knows I am going with you," Hannah added, quickly. "I cannot keep such a thing from my husband."

"Of course." Thomas nodded. "What did he say?"

"He said he wouldn't report me to the bishop."

"That's good news, I guess."

"My love for Gabriel comes between us sometimes. There are

things men cannot know or understand." She smiled slightly. "No offense, I hope."

"No," Thomas said. "None."

They rode a long time without speaking, Hannah sitting calmly, her hands folded in her lap. The morning was cloudy and cool, but the clouds were beginning to break. Thomas slowed to avoid a flock of wild turkeys, and then just before they reached the main highway, a doe and twin spotted fawns dashed across the road. Hannah smiled and watched them until they disappeared into the woods.

The sunlight seemed to make both of them more comfortable, and they eased into conversation. Hannah apologized for being nosy, but she asked to know more about him. Thomas talked about growing up an only child, about his early love for zoos and animals, about carrying birds' eggs home in his hat, spending dreamy hours alone in the woods. Hannah told Thomas about being raised with a sister and brothers and her love for lambs and goat kids. Eventually, they fell into a comfortable silence, exchanging smiles from time to time as they made their way south.

They arrived at the nursing home just after nine o'clock. Thomas checked in at the main desk, and then he and Hannah took the elevator up to the fifth floor and were buzzed into the memory care ward. They passed three elderly patients sitting in wheelchairs before a large-screen television with its volume on high. Two of the patients appeared to be sleeping, slumped in their chairs, folded blankets draped over their laps. The other, an elderly man wearing a U.S. Navy Veteran baseball cap, stared unseeing at the television with his mouth sagging open.

In her room, Thomas's mother sat partway up, the upper half of her bed raised forty-five degrees, arms and hands at her side, looking out the large picture window on the wall five feet beyond the metal footboard. Her tiny room overlooked the parking lot, a furniture store, and, beyond that, to the south, a series of older, brick buildings, the cream-colored bricks darkened by years of soot and worn by weather.

She got good morning sun here, at least, Thomas thought. She probably didn't know that, but she would have loved it as a younger woman.

"Good morning, Mom," Thomas said. He brushed her silver hair from her wrinkled face, kissed her on the forehead, and then sat down in a chair beside the bed.

"God's morning to you, ma'am," Hannah said. She stood at the end of the bed, directly in the line of his mother's vision. Dorothy looked up at Hannah and opened and closed her mouth like a fish. Thomas could never tell if she thought she was speaking when she did this, or if it was just her body's way of warming up for speech that might or might not come.

"Mom, this is Hannah," he said. "She's a friend."

His mother brought her lips together as if preparing to kiss someone, and then she closed her eyes and kept them closed, though Thomas could see them moving around behind the lids.

"She turns ninety-three next week," Thomas said to Hannah.

"The Lord's blessed her with long life."

Hannah glanced at the small wooden cross on the wall above the headboard and then moved around the bed to the narrow table against the wall. She smiled as she looked at an array of framed pictures, several of Thomas as a boy; two of the house where he grew up, one in summer, the other in winter; a picture of Thomas and his soon-to-be-wife, Angela, on his veterinary school graduation day. Hannah lifted each picture in turn before moving on to the next. The remaining photographs depicted his mother and father together: a wedding picture; a picture taken on their twenty-fifth anniversary; photographs of the two of them in Paris, Stratford-upon-Avon, Munich. On the end of the table was a stack of monographs his mother had written.

"She was an English professor for almost forty years," Thomas said. "She taught women's literature. I left the books here to remind her of what she could do at one time. I suppose I wanted the doctors and nurses to know, too."

Hannah picked up *A Species Stands Beyond*, pointed to the small picture of Emily Dickinson on the cover. "I know this person."

"Emily Dickinson?"

"Yes." Hannah opened the book and began to page through it. "When my mother died, I found a book of poems hidden among her things. The poems are beautiful, though some haunt me."

"You can keep that book," Thomas said. "I want you to have it."

"I couldn't."

"No, please. I have other copies at home. No one's reading it here."

Hannah held the book to her stomach. "I'll borrow it," she said. "Thank you."

"Angela?"—a whispered word from the bed. His mother's eyes opened, and she raised her small, clawed fingers, the dry, papery skin on the back of her hands blackened by spots and bruising. She reached toward Hannah.

"She thinks you're my wife," Thomas said.

Hannah turned to Dorothy and gently took her hand in both of hers. "God be with you," Hannah said. "*Wie geht es ihnen.*"

Dorothy's face warmed. Her lips twitched as she smiled. "*Hallo, schönes Mädchen.*"

Hannah laughed. "*Du bist mit einem schönen Sohn gesegnet.*"

Dorothy smiled. "*Danke,*" she said, her breathy voice just above a whisper. "*Er sammelt Schmetterlinge.*"

"Your mother speaks German!"

Thomas shrugged. "She learned as a girl. Her father was an art historian. They lived in Dresden for several years when she was young."

"*Mein Sohn ist ein Träumer,*" Dorothy said. She placed a hand on Hannah's arm to keep her attention. Hannah sat down beside her on the bed.

"What's she saying?" Thomas asked.

"She says you are a dreamer, and you collect butterflies."

"*Warum bist du wie eine Nonne gekleidet?*" Dorothy whispered.

Hannah smiled. She touched her kapp with one hand. "*Ich bin Amish,*" she said.

"*Heute besuchen wir Gemäldegalerie Alte Meister,*" Dorothy said. "*Vater hält Vorlesungen. Wir werden Eis essen.*" She closed her eyes.

"*Wundervoll!*" Hannah said, warmly. She turned to Thomas. "Today her father is taking her to the Old Masters Picture Gallery. He is giving a lecture. Then they'll get ice cream."

Thomas nodded. "The art museum in Dresden. She used to talk about going there with him. She was an only child, and he adored her. He took her everywhere."

"She was blessed to have such a father," Hannah said. "Your mother is so lovely."

Thomas stood up. "I wish you could have met who she was. I felt terrible putting her in here, but I couldn't care for her alone, being so far away and gone so many nights for my work. She'd made all the arrangements herself, even toured the place, I found out later." Thomas approached his mother across the bed from Hannah, kissed her again on the head, and motioned toward the door. "We can go," he said.

It was a little after ten in the morning. Hannah huddled over Dorothy's bed and said a prayer in German, then followed Thomas out the door.

"We'll head to Chicago, have some lunch down there," Thomas said.

"That sounds lovely."

"Have you ever been to an art museum? Do you know what they're like?"

"No," Hannah answered. "I haven't."

"Would you like to go?"

Hannah shrugged. "I don't know," she said.

"There's a magnificent art museum in Chicago, the Art Institute. We'll get some lunch, and then if you're up to it, we'll spend the afternoon at the museum. We'll have time."

"My hands are sweating all of the sudden."

"Why?"

"I'm nervous."

Thomas smiled. "You don't have to look at anything you don't want to see."

"I suppose you're right."

26

Hannah Fisher

When I attended the English school as a young girl, I enjoyed my lessons in art, though I showed no talent for it. On one occasion, we were tasked with molding small sculptures out of clay. I sculpted a small sheep, pushing wet clay through a window screen to fashion the wool, but hard as I tried, I could not form proper legs. Defeated, I stuck my ewe on top of a clay bale of straw and said she was sleeping. Mother laughed and laughed when I brought this sad, legless little sheep home, then told me to put it in a safe place, by which she meant somewhere my father could not find it.

My childhood home harbored no art of any kind. Even our blankets and the curtains on our windows were devoid of images. If a label on a can of food or boxed dry goods from the store included a picture, Father removed the label or covered it over. When my grandmother died, Mother received her beautiful ceramic tea warmer, decorated with a lovely blooming rose, in bas relief. Father allowed her to keep it, but only after he had carefully chipped off the flower with a hammer and chisel. Each month, he pinned black paper over the picture on our wall calendar, though when he was outside, Meg and I sometimes peeked beneath the paper to see the calendar's beautiful colored pictures of birds, flowers, sometimes seascapes. Mother did as well.

Father was stricter than most Amish in this regard. Because he associated religious iconography with the papists, he forbade religious art in our home as well. We owned no crosses or crucifixes, no paintings of the Lord's pierced and sacred heart. This rigorous disapproval was made fully known to us at Meg's expense, though Mother endured the most withering of his criticism. In sixth grade, Meg had been learning about Michelangelo. This was still at a time when we attended English schools. Anyway, people had begun cleaning and restoring the Sistine Chapel frescoes, and Meg's class had watched a film about the restoration. The paintings were so lovely and colorful that Meg brought home a picture book from the school library to share with Mother. When Father discovered them paging through this book, he tore it from their fingers. It flapped like a large, wounded bird as he shook it menacingly over their heads.

"Who carried this papist idolatry into my house!"

"It's Michelangelo, *Daed*," Meg said. "Aren't they beautiful?"

"No!" Father ranted. "No, they are not! Read *Martyrs Mirror* if you must bury your nose in a book. Papists pressed burning coals into the mouths of our people. They burned Amish martyrs at the stake. A few pretty paintings on the ceiling of a church cannot atone for that!"

"Absalom," Mother said. She always spoke softly, but particularly at moments such as this, when he was at his most volatile. "Absalom, please leave the girl be. I asked her to bring the book home so that I might see these paintings for myself."

Father pivoted aggressively toward Mother and roared as he rent the heavy book in two, tearing it down the cloth spine before tossing both halves onto Mother's lap.

"Burn it," he said. "Outside. I don't want any hint of the corrupting smoke in my house."

Mother met his eyes with a piercing stare. "I will not," she said. I had never seen Mother defy Father so overtly. She was a strong woman, but usually an obedient and compliant one.

Father raised his hand and pointed a finger at Mother's face. "Obey!" he said, his voice hoarse with his fury. "You forget yourself."

Mother remained quiet for some time, gathering her thoughts. This I had seen before. She often used silence as a tool during heated conversations with Father. A boiling kettle needs constant heat to continue bubbling; when you deny it flame, it cools.

"I love and obey the Lord as you know I do," she said. "And I am sorry you are offended. But I will not burn this schoolbook. I will repair it as best I can, and Margaret will return it in the morning."

Father waved a hand dismissively. "If you must go to hell, so be it," he said. "Don't take the children with you."

Mother's eyes spilled angry tears. "How dare you!" she said, her voice now loud and shrill. "How dare you!" She squeezed both halves of the book together and lifted it from her lap. "This book burned no Amish martyrs, Absalom Yoder! It has brought the Lord's word to life in your daughter's eyes, though you are too blinded by hatred and selfish prejudice to see it."

Father crossed his arms and began to pace, as if considering what more he might say. But I think he understood that he had pushed Mother into some new realm of defiance. If anger fills every bucket lowered into the well, it is cheapened by its plenty. But when it is rare, when the bucket must go deep for it, it is rendered more potent.

"Leave us, please," Mother said to him, her voice soft again. Father did as she asked. He crossed the room and left the house. Meg looked at me, and the faintest of smiles came to our lips.

I shared this story with Dr. Kennedy as we walked toward the steps of the Art Institute. I talk a lot when I'm nervous, one of my many imperfections. At the foot of the steps, we paused to admire the bronze sculpture of a lion, larger than life-sized, regal and magnificent, and weathered to a lovely green patina. Two such lions stood guard outside the museum. We started up the steps, but I hesitated. I stopped with my right foot one step above my left, like a child touched in a game of freeze tag. Dr. Kennedy turned and came back down to me.

After so many years of a rigorously plain and Godly life, I feared it might be a mistake to open my heart to the seducing beauty that surely lurked inside an English museum. My father was a hundred and fifty miles away, but I could feel his shadow over me still, the heavy weight of his certain disapproval, were he ever to discover my apostasy. And yet I did not wish to offend my kind host. I sat down to sort my thoughts amid the busy horns and rumbling of cars and buses on Michigan Avenue. With the tall buildings around us, it felt as if I were in a deep valley surrounded by mountains of glass and concrete.

"Are you tired?"

I shook my head. "No," I said. I pointed at the place where my dress ran over my knees. It quivered, the fabric aflutter like a hummingbird's wings. "My legs are shaking."

Dr. Kennedy smiled. "We don't have to go in," he said. "We can just sit by the fountain or take a walk along Navy Pier."

"No, please," I said. "Give me a minute. We came all this way. I have never been inside a museum. I would like to see one."

Dr. Kennedy reclined beside me, bracing his elbows two steps above the one he sat upon, tipped his chin up to the sky, and closed his eyes. The sun shone on our faces and warmed us. We sat quietly like this until my heart slowed.

"Let me ask you something, Dr. Kennedy."

"I wish you'd call me Thomas."

I smiled. "Do you think my venturing inside will make my heart an unfit vessel for the Lord and His word?"

Dr. Kennedy frowned and sat upright as if his answer could not be conceived otherwise. He thought about my question for a long while before he spoke.

"I wish I could answer that. I'm not a religious man. What I can tell you is that whenever I leave an art museum, I feel two things, no, three. First, astonishment. Second, I feel sad, maybe even disappointed in myself, for not having done more with my life."

"You do so much!" Hannah said. "You care for the least of the Lord's creatures. You do far more good than most men."

"You're kind to say so."

"It is simple truth, not kindness."

"Still," he said, and nodded. "Thank you."

"What's the third thing?" I asked.

"Oh, yes," he said. He laughed. "Exhaustion! All that walking around looking at things just wears me out. Some of the paintings in here, the Hoppers, for example, or the Impressionists on the second floor, are famous and revered all over the world. There's a Monet painting of stacks of wheat, just an ordinary farm scene in France, that looks as if it had been painted with sunlight and sky rather than oil paint. I could look at that Monet all day long."

Dr. Kennedy's explanation did not ease my fears. Perhaps he could read the hesitation in my face. "Hannah," he said, his voice gentle, "the Art Institute isn't going anywhere. Perhaps you'll come back another time. Let's enjoy the sunshine for an hour or two, then we'll find a nice Italian restaurant and have some Chicago-style pizza before heading over to the United Center to see Gabriel."

I rose to my feet. It struck me that I'd been like a young girl standing on the high dive for the first time, fearful of plunging into the water. The line of children behind me was getting longer; some of them were yelling at me to jump, which only enhanced my terror. And then suddenly, one by one, they descended the ladder and left the pool, and I stood alone at the end of the diving board, and the decision to stay or to jump became mine, and mine alone.

I jumped.

"I want to see those stacks of wheat painted with sunlight," I said. "I want to see everything. Come on, let's go before I change my mind."

For the next two hours, I was transported, moved beyond the limitations of my earthly body, into realms of clearer light. Of course, we stood with the crowds to admire the museum's famous works, Hopper's *Nighthawks*, Picasso's *The Old Guitarist*, those beautiful Impressionist paintings Dr. Kennedy mentioned, and yes, they were striking and distinctive, the Monet so beautiful it brought tears to my eyes. But what surprised me, what most overwhelmed me, were the many works of faith. I did not imagine an English museum would be so given over to them.

I stood enrapt by all of it: huge altarpieces and small crucifixes from the Middle Ages, so old the paint crackled like the glaze on an old porcelain cup; life-sized portraits of Adam and Eve from the Renaissance; El Greco's magnificent *Assumption of the Virgin*; a glorious white marble sculpture, *Samson and the Lion*. Almost always, as we stood before these works, Dr. Kennedy and I were alone with them. I could press my face to within inches to examine the tiny dots of pigment depicting nails in our Lord's hands and feet, or the faded golden halos about the heads of the Virgin and Child. The emotion and faith this artwork stirred in my heart so overwhelmed me that at times I stopped breathing, as if breath itself would be a distraction from the glory witnessed by my humble eyes.

Once I even fell to my knees. I did not intend to, and I certainly would not kneel before idols like a papist, but when I saw this work, my legs simply buckled. It was, compared to many, an uncomplicated work, though large, nearly ten feet high: Francisco de Zurbarán's 1627 portrait of Christ on the cross. My Lord was larger than life-sized, His humbled flesh muscular, glowing, and beautiful. Forgive my sacrilege, but the Lord's crucified body looked so familiar! How could this be? I thought. Gradually, it brightened in my mind: the body of Zurbarán's crucified Christ resembled that of my humble husband, Josiah, when he was a younger, more vigorous man, and we were newly married.

Jesus wore a simple, twisted white cloth about His waist. The heads of the spikes in His hands and feet glowed in the light, and His face rested peacefully against His shoulder. His eyes were closed; a tendril of blood spilled from the wound in His side; the crown of thorns appeared as a thin wisp of reeds across His forehead. His body was unmarked by the scourging He had endured at the hands of centurions, barbarians who tied tiny pieces of bone to the tips of their whips so they would open flesh to the ribs.

I stayed with this painting a long time, and Dr. Kennedy waited patiently. The intensity of the experience exhausted me, but it was a fatigue born of devotion and adoration. Though my body sagged, my brain burned with the energy of renewed faith.

I had believed that entering this English museum might be apostasy, that it would open my heart to the beguiling whispers of the Dark Prince, who lurked in all sensual pleasure to steal the souls of men. But it was the opposite. I could see the Hand of God in it. The Lord had secretly extended His dominion over the earth by giving artists the skills to render His word in marble and pigment, on wood and canvas.

"Well?" Dr. Kennedy asked, as we descended the steps in twilight, my legs tired, my mind and soul ablaze.

Sometimes there are no words to match the glory in our hearts. Anchorites lived alone and in silence for decades to seek communion with the Lord, and when He comes again, as we know He will, His Holy Face will render us blind and mute.

I could not answer Dr. Kennedy. Though I jabbered like an inconsiderate debutante on our way to the museum, now I could think of no words adequate to characterize my experience. Instead, without thinking, I reached over and took Dr. Kennedy's hand. I entwined his fingers in mine, squeezed his hand in gratitude and in love, the Lord's agape. We walked this way, in silence with our hands together, until we reached Dr. Kennedy's truck.

As the sun dropped behind the tall buildings, we drove to a crowded, noisy Italian pizzeria that smelled of garlic and roasting tomatoes. We ordered a pizza as thick as one of my rhubarb pies, and a young woman delivered it to our table sizzling inside a cast-iron fry pan. It was the most delicious food I'd ever tasted.

"What are these green sprinkles?" I asked Dr. Kennedy.

"That's oregano," he said.

"And these?" I pointed to tiny, fragrant chips of red and gold that fired the tongue.

"Red pepper flakes." He smiled at me. "You've never eaten oregano or red pepper flakes?"

"No," I said. "I use some spices. Cinnamon sugar, sage. Thyme on pastured pork. But never oregano or this red pepper. My father banned all spices from Mother's kitchen except humble salt from the Lord's oceans. Even our tongues, he said, must practice humility. I use a few more, but not many."

"Your dad sounds like a real piece of work. What's the harm in a little spice?"

"You mustn't think poorly of my father," I told him. "He is the most devout man in our district. Sometimes his zeal overwhelms his judgement, but who among us is without fault?" I took another bite and closed my eyes, smiling in pleasure at the sweet, savory, and spicy flavor. "This is delicious."

"Yes, it is," Dr. Kennedy answered. "Nothing like deep-dish pizza when you're in Chicago. I'm so happy you like it." He reached across the table and took my free hand. I did not pull away.

27

Thomas Kennedy

They arrived at the United Center long after the undercard matches had begun and could hear yelling and clapping coming from the heart of the arena. Each time they passed an open passage into the auditorium, the sound swelled. When they reached their section, a young usher with a flashlight, his clothes reeking of marijuana, looked at the tickets on Thomas's phone.

"We didn't miss the championship match, did we?" Thomas asked.

The man shook his head. "No, sir. Coming up next." He motioned with his flashlight. "Your seats are right down near the floor! How'd you score these?"

"We got them from a friend."

"Dude!" the usher said, pointing to Hannah's dress and kapp. "You must be a fan of the Giant. Love your costume."

"Thank you," Hannah said.

"That shit looks real! Where'd you get it?"

Hannah looked down at her dress, awkwardly rubbed a hand along the fabric. "I made it," she said.

"I'm gobsmacked, man," the man said, waving her in.

They went down the stairs and found their seats. Hannah squeezed in first next to a young man holding a plastic axe, and Thomas sat beside her, next to the aisle. Before them, on the floor of the arena, the brightly lit wrestling ring glowed, a large, canvas square surrounded by thick red, white, and blue ropes. The canvas was blue, with the words "SIZZLING SUMMER SLAM" in all caps in white in the center, around a painted globe.

A mixed doubles match already underway paired two preening, heavily tattooed blonds on one side against a short, muscular Black man and a woman dressed all in red, with her hair dyed apple red as well. The challengers were Mars and Venus, Thomas learned, glancing down at the program held by the person sitting in front of him. The blonds, Jake and Jill, called themselves Atomic Blondz, and they were the champions, defending their title. At the moment, the two women were inside the ring, the blond overtly sexual in a red, white, and blue bikini, her almost boundless hair in a ponytail on top of her head. Venus, however, was in control. She executed a series of body slams, and as the fans screamed their approval, she flipped the blond to her back and flopped down on top of her for the pin. But as the referee began to count, her blond partner leaped over the top rope, grabbed Venus by her hair, and threw her out of the ring.

Boos erupted throughout the United Center; people cupped their hands over their mouths and screamed at the referee. The match went on this way, half inside, half outside of the ring, and it ended when Atomic Blondz lost by disqualification, having body-slammed the referee onto a ringside scorer's table, which then collapsed, rendering him incapacitated, and having somehow knocked both Venus and Mars unconscious somewhere on the floor. Referees and other wrestlers came running down the aisles, lit by giant spotlights, and the bell was rung, ending the match. Though losers by disqualification, Atomic Blondz kept their sparkling championship belts. They put them on, flexed their biceps, kissed, and then walked like runway models toward the wrestlers' exit, while fans booed them and screamed obscenities. When they disappeared, loud music began to play, and people stood and talked or returned to their seats to rest.

The lights came up for a brief intermission, and some of the people left their seats to head for the bathrooms or concessions. Others ate from boxes of popcorn or bags of peanuts; some drank from plastic cups of beer purchased from vendors who went up and down the stairs between the rows of seats. Thomas went to the bathroom, returned to find Hannah seated alone, watchful and curious.

All around them, men and women began to reach under their seats into plastic grocery bags or paper sacks, backpacks, large purses. Across the arena, it looked as if round, paper moons the size of dinner plates were being taken from these bags and held aloft. Then, two rows down from Thomas and Hannah, a young man with a tattoo of a lightning bolt on his cheek bent over, and when he stood up, he wore a round Amish straw hat; the woman next to him was carefully working her black hair beneath a kapp similar to Hannah's, but dusted with sparkling, gold glitter. Across the arena, hundreds of other men and women were doing the same thing.

"What is this?" Hannah asked Thomas.

"They're fans of Gabriel, I think," Thomas said.

"They know he is Amish?"

"Yes," Thomas said. He wanted to explain that this was a common feature of sports fanaticism, like Green Bay Packers fans wearing cheese heads during football games, or Dallas Cowboys fans wearing cowboy hats, but of course he understood it was not the same.

A young man across the aisle from Thomas wore a white shirt, suspenders, and a black felted Amish hat, and then as his wife laughed and applauded, he carefully applied a false Amish beard to his chin and cheeks as well. Some of the younger women stepped into navy blue Amish-style jumpers that seemed to be made of paper.

The lights inside the arena went dark, and a loud, repeating riff of electric guitar music began. The music started quietly, and each time it repeated, it grew louder and louder. Applause and cheering swelled as a dozen spotlights darted and swirled like wasps across the crowd from high above the stadium floor.

"Ladies and gentlemen!" a bright, loud voice boomed through the speakers. "We have come to our main event! The biggest show on planet Earth! The glory of the galaxy! The maddest mayhem in the Milky Way! This is a no-holds-barred fight to the finish for the Championship of the Universe!" People were on their feet, clapping and cheering.

The spotlights merged into a single, large cone of light that fell on the far corner of the floor where tall, purple velvet curtains hung over a darkened hallway. The guitar music faded, and new music began, a loud frantic series of notes played on a sitar or an oud, like the soundtrack of an Arabian bazaar scene in a Hollywood movie. "Ladies and gentlemen!" the announcer shouted. "Please put your hands together for our world champion! He is the prince of pain! Certified insane! The master blaster of disaster!" The crowd booed. "Suckled by wolves and raised by tigers, please welcome the Killer King, your current Champion of the Universe, the Sheik of Siam!" Flash pots exploded, the purple curtains parted, and a garishly decorated palanquin was carried into the arena by six muscular young women wearing flowing pants the color of saffron and matching string bikini tops. Their hair had been arranged into beehives atop their heads, and these were circled by strings of flowers.

Seated on a bright red velvet throne was the Sheik of Siam. He was an extremely large, dark-skinned Japanese man who looked somewhat like a sumo wrestler, though his crowned head was completely shaved. Dark tattoos around each of his eyes made his face look a bit like an owl's. He entered the arena shirtless, his championship belt strapped across his belly. As wide as a frying pan, the center of the belt sparkled and shimmered, the spotlight reflected by thousands of crystals embedded in the gold and leather. Saffron tassels dangled from the tops of the Sheik's silver wrestling boots. As the women carried him into the arena high on their shoulders, he smiled and threw confetti into the booing crowd as if he were being greeted by adoring subjects.

When the six women reached the wrestling ring, they carefully set the palanquin on the floor, and two of them helped the Sheik down from his throne. He kissed each of the women in his harem on the cheek, and as they carried the palanquin back down the aisle and exited the arena, the Sheik pulled himself up into the brightly lit ring and circled the ropes, pointing to his championship belt or flexing his massive arms as hundreds of cell phone cameras flashed.

"He looks mean," Hannah said.

"He's supposed to," Thomas said, smiling.

The spotlight shifted to the opposite corner of the arena, to a set of tall, burgundy-colored velvet curtains. The music quieted and then stopped. A murmur, like a whispered, rhythmic chanting, began to ripple through the crowd. "And now, ladies and gentlemen," the announcer roared, "your young challenger!" The crowd's murmuring grew louder, a series of three syllables, chanted over and over, gaining in both speed and volume. Some of the fans around Thomas and Hannah had their hands cupped over their mouths to direct the noise down toward the ring. "Standing a hair under nine feet tall and weighing in this evening at five hundred and eighty-six pounds!" The chanting grew louder and faster; people were taking deep breaths and shouting now, and Thomas finally understood: They were repeating Gabriel's wrestling name, over and over: Anakim. Anakim. Anakim. "He hails from the beautiful rolling hills of Lancaster, Pennsylvania! He can move mountains and change the course of mighty rivers! He is the eighth, ninth, and tenth wonders of the world! Ladies and gentlemen, put your hands together for your challenger! Anakim, the Amish Giant!"

Thomas glanced over at Hannah. Tears streamed down her face.

The arena exploded in screaming and applause, the curtains parted, and Gabriel stepped into the light, wearing an Amish beard, his long hair blond, smiling broadly, taller and more beautiful than Thomas had ever seen him. He was dressed as a young Amish man again, in straw hat, white shirt, thick, black suspenders, and black pants that reached to the leather work boots on his humongous feet. Over his broad, muscular shoulders he carried a mature angora ram; its swept-back horns had been painted metallic gold, and they shone like trumpets in the spotlight. Gabriel limped slightly as he walked, his gait a bit shorter each time he extended the prosthetic leg. As he walked along the aisle toward the ring, fans rushed the ropes and reached up to him. With his right hand, Gabriel held all four of the goat's feet tightly together, just below his throat; he extended his other, giant hand down toward the wrestling fans, who shook it, slapped it, or kissed it as he passed. The goat's lustrous ivory mohair hung down over Gabriel's shoulders and upper arms like a wrinkled cape. Its nostrils flared and its eyes bulged in fear. From time to time, it opened its mouth and bleated, the sound evaporating in the pulsing arena.

When Gabriel reached his corner of the wrestling ring, he lowered the goat to its feet and put his forehead to the animal's head, kissed it. Two assistants fitted the animal with a leather harness, then quickly led it from the arena. Gabriel removed his hat, climbed up onto the ring apron, and stepped over the top rope into the ring, where the Sheik stood glaring up at him. Gabriel pulled down his suspenders, ripped the white shirt from his body, and slid the suspenders back up over his shoulders. His muscled body rippled and glistened like a colorful quilt, his arms and shoulders, chest and back covered in vibrant tattoos. Suddenly, all the other lights in the arena went black, leaving only the square ring aglow.

Gabriel stood two and a half feet taller than the Sheik and outweighed him by at least two or three hundred pounds, but in professional wrestling, Thomas knew, such advantages meant little. Gabriel dominated early in the match, with the crowd wildly cheering him on. He threw the Sheik around the ring like a rag doll, at one point launching him out of the ring and into the second row of ringside chairs as the people scattered. "Anakim! Anakim! Anakim!" the crowd roared. Thomas marveled at the dexterity of these two large men. The slaps and chops, the lifts and throws, the crescendo of action followed by moments of rest and recovery, all seemed choreographed to bring the crowd to the peak of excitement.

Gabriel's domination continued through the first ten minutes, his monumental strength repeatedly on display. Twice he lifted the Sheik completely overhead, only to step forward and let him drop behind him to the floor. Fifteen minutes into the match, Gabriel's domination ended at exactly the moment when he seemed certain to win the championship. As the crowd roared its approval, he body-slammed the Sheik twice, and then the second time the Sheik got to his feet, Gabriel lifted him completely overhead and backed into his corner of the ring. The audience began chanting "Heaven! Heaven! Heaven!" delirious in anticipation of the finishing half of Gabriel's signature move, when he would cast his opponent down into hell.

But before that moment arrived, a masked man appeared behind Gabriel, carrying what looked to be the bloody fleece of the angora goat Gabriel had carried into the arena. He threw the bloody fleece over Gabriel's head, as if he were trying to asphyxiate him, and Gabriel dropped the Sheik into the ring. The Sheik took advantage of the moment, striking Gabriel through the fleece with a series of forearm shivers to the face, knocking him to the floor.

The crowd booed and jeered as the Sheik delivered one elbow drop after another into Gabriel's head and chest. Each time Gabriel rolled to his knees to return to his feet, the Sheik kicked him in the side, and Gabriel rolled to his back again. By now, his face and body were covered in blood. Gabriel managed to get to a sitting position, and raised one leg to stand, but the Sheik suddenly lifted Gabriel's suspenders over his head, one from each side, and then tightening the suspenders around Gabriel's throat, he put a boot into his back and pulled.

"The bastard's choking him!" a young woman behind Thomas screamed.

Hannah stood. "I hate this!" she said.

"It's not real," Thomas said. "He's not really choking."

"I don't care."

Suddenly the masked man, dressed in black, leaped into the ring, and together, the two men lifted Gabriel to their shoulders and dropped him. As the crowd screamed for the referee to intervene, they lifted Gabriel again and again, each time dropping him, so it appeared as if his throat were landing on the top of the rope, while his body fell into the ring. The noise in the arena reached hysterical levels. Women screamed and cursed. Men cursed the referee, the Sheik, the masked wrestler. When the referee attempted to regain control of the match, he was thrown from the ring.

Then, with the masked man holding Gabriel by the arms, the Sheik tugged hard several times on Gabriel's prosthesis, and the leg slid from his residual limb and out from Gabriel's pants. As the crowd screamed its disapproval, the Sheik raised Gabriel's leg overhead like an axe and brought it down across Gabriel's chest. When he raised the leg a second time, Thomas felt Hannah's hands against his shoulder. She pushed past Thomas and hurried up the concrete stairs. Thomas followed. He caught her in the hallway.

"Hannah, wait," Thomas said. She slowed and Thomas caught up to her. "We have backstage passes. I told Gabriel we were coming. He's expecting us."

Hannah wiped her tears with the back of her hands. "I can't," she said. "I'm sorry. I can't."

"What do you want to do?"

"I want to leave," she said.

"Are you sure?"

"I'm leaving."

"Okay," Thomas said, checking for the exits. "Okay."

28

Hannah Fisher

I did not reach up to touch my beloved grandson's shoulders, pull his body to mine, kiss his face, feel the weight of his broad arms across my back, everything I had dreamed of just that morning as I lay awake long before sunrise. I had prayed for these things. I had asked the Lord to forgive the weakness of my human desires and to allow me to have them. But he denied me, and I myself became the instrument of that denial.

Until that moment, the whole day had been a beautiful dream. Weeks earlier, I had written to my sister to tell her my plan to visit Gabriel in Chicago; joyfully, I had told Abiah, too. They knew how much I loved Gabriel. And when the day finally came, I had been so happy, so filled with life. The newness I had tasted with my tongue, touched with my fingers, seen with my eyes, had left me feeling exalted. It brought to mind one of Miss Dickinson's most lovely poems:

Exultation is the going
Of an inland soul to sea,—
Past the houses, past the headlands,
Into deep eternity!

Bred as we, among the mountains
Can the sailor understand
The divine intoxication
Of the first league out from land?

In joy I had set down my shield. I had let the English world send its darts into my heart and foolish brain, permitted my eyes to wander its wonders; I had unstopped my ears but remained alert for the quicksilver of Satan's slippery tongue, confident I could scent foul breath from the Deceiver's throat. Dr. Kennedy had been the perfect host and escort, a kind, generous, loving man of sound moral principles. Could he be Satan's unwitting disciple? Could he have been deceived into becoming the blasphemer's guide and deliverer? I did not believe it was possible.

Once inside Dr. Kennedy's truck, heading for home, my tears flowed, a bitter flood. My body shook, and my jaw quivered as one lost in cold, teeth chattering, so far did I find myself from the warm embrace of the Lord.

"Hannah," the good doctor said. "What's wrong? Please, tell me."

In my distress, I could not speak. I could not make sense of my own confusion. I'd heard thousands of people cheering for my beloved grandson, saw them on their feet as if in worship, singing his name. I swelled with pride, of course. Who would not? All his life, Gabriel had been larger than the life he had inhabited, always eager to display the strength of the giant body he'd been given. And now it seemed that Gabriel's destiny had revealed itself at last. He had been gifted vast riches; he had sold them for useless dust.

"Gabriel is fine!" Dr. Kennedy assured me. "Those two men, that was all a show, a choreographed dance. Gabriel came back to win that match, I'm certain of it. Tonight, he became the wrestling champion of the world!"

Though Dr. Kennedy meant to comfort me, his words brought only deeper pain. Across the earth, beyond the Lord's mighty oceans, people knew Gabriel by the new name he had taken: Anakim. He had adopted the tribe of biblical giants as his own, and, to increase his English fame, he claimed the Amish heritage he had rejected. As I meditated on this, surrounded by English in Amish dress, my humble shift signaling devotion to the Lord now a vulgar, gaudy decoration, my pride in Gabriel dissolved into an all-encompassing shame. Rachel died bringing him into the world; Jasper had given his life to raise him; and this is how Gabriel had repaid their sacrifice. Yet there I was, standing with the mob, paralyzed by the spectacle, lost and alone among the multitudes. How could I begin to explain this to Dr. Kennedy, my dear friend? I could not. In vain he tried to cheer me, to calm my soul. I spilled brackish tears and silently begged the Lord for succor that would not come.

When we neared Milwaukee, Dr. Kennedy told me he would like to show me something else if I would consent to it. It was not yet midnight. A full moon shone like a bright, silver coin in the night sky. I had stopped crying. I felt the afterquakes only, the body's mending stitches. I said yes, if he desired it.

"I'm afraid I've been poor company."

"Nonsense," he said. "You've been marvelous company, beautiful company."

We traveled the interstate into Milwaukee and drove along the lakeshore for several miles, then north, stopping at last near a large, beautiful home, two stories of cream-colored brick, three cupolas across the roof, with an iron gate blocking a wide, cement driveway that glowed in the moonlight. Glass windows stretched up the full two stories in the center of the home, and I could see the moon reflected in them. Trees—a spruce, sixty feet tall, a stately sycamore, a hedge of yew or juniper, Japanese maples—had been planted in the front yard, all lit by bright lights planted somewhere in the ground.

Dr. Kennedy turned off his truck and we sat still along the curb. He opened the windows. The air smelled of fish from the nearby lake.

A whip-poor-will sang in the far distance. Somewhere nearby a dog barked; a door slammed, and the barking stopped. "This used to be my home," he said, "before I moved to Lakota."

"It's so beautiful."

"I lived here with Angela." He leaned toward me so that he could see more of the house through my window. "I didn't think I'd ever see this house again."

I did not want to pry. I knew Dr. Kennedy had once been married. Just as many English are divorced as not. I leave it to God to judge.

"The trees are bigger," he said. "The driveway's been redone. It was brick and blacktop." He paused. "In the beginning, Angela and I were happy here. It never lasts, does it? That dreamy joy of those early years?"

A wife's duty is to love and submit to her husband. He is her head. She gives her heart without condition and serves him without question. She adorns herself only with the imperishable beauty of a gentle and quiet spirit, which in God's sight is very precious. These are the Lord's commandments, and I have heeded them. I have heeded them. "It does not last," I said. "Other things follow. Sometimes sweet things. Sometimes not."

"We redid the bathrooms, remodeled the kitchen. When she finally got pregnant, we didn't know if it would be a boy or a girl, so I painted the nursery pale green. Tranquil Pasture. Crazy that I can still remember that paint color." He pointed to an upstairs window. "We had a crib in there, a changing table, a drawer full of cloth diapers, already washed and folded. And then she miscarried."

"I'm so sorry."

He shrugged. "It was difficult, but we knew we got pregnant once, we could again. And eventually we did. But that's as far as we ever got. Angela could get pregnant, but she could never carry to term. It happened five times in ten years, probably more, I really don't know. She stopped telling me."

"Oh, Dr. Kennedy," I said. This kind, gentle man took me to this house to distract me, to take my pain back on himself. I felt such warmth for his kindness in that moment. I reached for him, rested my fingers on his forearm. "A husband and wife must cleave together. He must cleave unto his wife and become one flesh. Especially at such times."

Dr. Kennedy shrugged. "We stayed together, but we weren't together, if that makes sense. Angela's sadness and resentment overwhelmed everything. I wasn't paying attention. I was running away from her." He pointed to the driveway. "She didn't want to live anymore. But she didn't want that to be easy for me."

His voice quivered. He seemed as if he might begin to cry, but through long practice, perhaps, like so many men, he was able to stop himself.

"This is the hard part," he whispered.

I squeezed his arm gently. I became aware of my own breathing, aware of a slightly cooler breeze blowing through the open window.

"It was Saturday morning, late, almost lunchtime. I'd taken the day off to catch up on some billing. My beeper went off—we didn't have cell phones in those days, we carried beepers. Someone had an animal in distress, a mare with a prolapsed uterus, I believe, a half hour's drive north, so I had to leave quickly. I tried to find Angela to tell her I was going on a call. I searched through the house, but I couldn't find her. In the open doorway, I shouted, the last words she heard me say. 'Angela!' I yelled. 'Got a call. I'm leaving.' Then I got in my truck and started it up.

"When I came home late at night, I always parked up against the house, because the porch lights would shine through the windshield and I could see what I needed to take inside, and so forth. And then when I left again in the morning, I'd back up into the turnaround over there"—he pointed to a section of driveway bounded now by a bright, green hedge of boxwood—"then pull forward, turn out onto the street and be on my way. That morning, that's what I did, same as a thousand times before.

"But this time when I backed up, my truck had no power. It

was like I'd forgotten to take off the parking brake or had backed up against a tree, or something. Maybe on another day, in another state of mind, I might have put the truck in neutral and gotten out to check. But I was in a hurry. So, I just wiggled the parking brake to make sure it was all the way down and gave her more gas. The engine roared as I lurched backward. The tires squealed a bit on the pavement and then the truck bucked and shook once, and then a second time, and I stopped. It felt like I'd driven over a log or a rock or something. And before I even thought to turn out toward the highway, I looked down over there"—he pointed to a spot on the driveway—"and I saw Angela. She'd been lying on her back under my truck on the far side, where I couldn't see her, with her ribs pressed against the tire."

"Had she fallen? I don't understand."

"No." He swallowed.

"Oh, Dr. Kennedy, how awful. How awful."

Dr. Kennedy stared, unseeing, through the window. "The police talked to me for hours. They searched the house. The newspapers reported the death as suspicious. I felt like everyone who looked at me knew I had run over my wife in our driveway. I took a leave of absence, put the house up for sale, and lived with my mother for a while." He shrugged. "Long story short, that's how I ended up in Lakota, doctoring your dairy goats. Mr. Edwards's turkeys. Mel and Birdy's Arabian horses."

"You've been a blessing to all of us," I said, and added, "me most of all."

"Thank you."

"And you mustn't blame yourself. Your wife made a terrible choice, and she made you the instrument of that choice. It was cruel, an abomination. Yet you must forgive her with your whole heart. Think of her suffering."

He nodded, put his fingers on the keys, started his truck, put up the windows. "You're right," he said.

"And you must forgive yourself."

*   *   *

The gentle rocking of Dr. Kennedy's truck on the highway lulled me to sleep, and when he woke me, we were five miles from home. It was nearly two in the morning. Moths and other insects flashed through the headlights and collided with the windshield. The buds and shrunken blue flowers of chicory leaned in over the edge of the roadway.

My house was dark when he pulled in the driveway, but I declined Dr. Kennedy's offer to walk me to the door. "My feet know the way," I said. "Thank you for today! I will never forget it."

"You're welcome," he said. He leaned across the seat to kiss my cheek, and I let him. "Neither will I."

I waited there as Dr. Kennedy backed down the driveway. His headlights sliced across my legs and the side of my house, and the truck rumbled away. I watched the red taillights shrink until they were swallowed by darkness. When I rounded the corner of my porch, I looked across the yard at my father's house, nervous that he might be awake and waiting, watching from his window. There was no sign of him, and the full moon shining on the house's chalky whitewash gave it a calming glow.

I lit a lamp and carried it up to the bedroom, removed my clothing and kapp, put on my nightdress. I put out the lamp and got into bed, but sleep would not come. My mind wandered through the day's many, vibrant rooms, the visit with Thomas's mother, the art museum, our dinner together, Gabriel's wrestling, the trip to Thomas's former home. The feel of his rough fingers intertwined in mine. The press of his lips against my cheek. Sometimes I'd begin to drift toward more tranquil waters, but soon found myself bumping back against the shore.

Then, something like the sound of strong, spring winds driven against the house woke me, a rumbling like a powerful gale or distant thunder. Though my eyes remained closed, the room glowed as bright as it might at midday through the curtains. Thunderstorm? I thought, at first.

I opened my eyes and left the bed, went to the window, and parted the curtains. My knees buckled, and a startled cry leaped from my mouth: my father's beautiful house was in flames, each window an eye blown out by roaring, crackling fire! I did not pause to light a lamp. Heart racing, I rushed from my room, down the stairs, and out the porch door. I crossed the dewy grass toward the burning house, but the heat, like that of a thousand suns, forced me back. The trees growing in a line along the southern side of the house swayed and danced in the superheated air like witches at the devil's sabbath, and the fire roared like a beast as it breathed in the air, huffing and snapping, the sparks swirling and rising to heaven.

I screamed into the night, though none but my goats and chickens heard me. I walked and ran, my feet bare and bleeding, nearly two miles to our nearest Amish neighbors, Henry and Anna Stolzfus. By then it was nearly four in the morning. I pounded their door until they answered and summoned help.

By eight o'clock, the blackened chimneys and stone hearth of the fireplace were the only parts of my father's house that remained. The putrid scent of smoke and smoldering ash polluted the air. English firefighters found my father's body in his first-floor bathroom, inside his cast-iron bathtub. They said he'd probably suffocated—the fire consumed all the oxygen, leaving none for him to breathe. He also could have succumbed to smoke inhalation. In either case, they said, he was certainly dead before the heat of the fire boiled away the water in the tub where they'd found his charred remains.

When I finally returned to my own home, my face and nightdress dirtied by smoke, my hair similarly scented, my feet black and bloodied, I discovered an envelope on the threshold, just inside the house. It had been slid under the porch door sometime in the night. I had not seen it when I arrived home from Chicago with Thomas, but it had been dark, so perhaps I'd missed it. My name had been printed on the front of the envelope, in my father's shaky script. I recognized the writing. I'd seen it often on vouchers and contracts at the mill. I sat down in the kitchen and stared at that envelope for some time.

Perhaps, I thought, I'd wait for Josiah to arrive before opening it. I needed to boil water to bathe myself. But my curiosity overcame my reluctance. I wish I would have waited. In fact, I wish I would have cast the envelope into the woodstove without opening it at all.

29

Billy Walton

Though it's poor form to speak ill of the dead, I don't think many people cried in their beer when they heard Absalom Yoder had gone to the great beyond, boiled in his bathtub like a lobster. Maybe the old crustacean had his virtues, but I know of no one who enjoyed his company. Yes, he did a good deed once in a while. But don't let that fool you. Absalom Yoder was a cantankerous son of a bitch. Some of my customers used to goad me. "Billy," they'd say, "you just hate old Yoder because he's Amish." And I'd say, "Being Amish got nothing to do with it. I hate him because he's an asshole."

There's some family history there, as I've said, but my pop wasn't the only one with no use for Yoder. That old bastard squabbled with all his neighbors, both Amish and English. He accused merchants of trying to cheat him and routinely showed up at town board meetings to protest the size of his property tax bill. For years, after the state began requiring that bright orange triangle on the back of Amish buggies on paved highways, Absalom made a point of driving his buggy down the middle of the road, sometimes for miles, while a dozen or more cars snaked behind him, unable to pass.

When Danny Albright from the county sheriff's office came in asking if I knew of anybody who might want to burn down old Absalom Yoder's place, I told him me for starters, and probably a couple hundred people in our county alone.

"Yeah." Danny chuckled. "I've been hearing a lot of that."

"Is the fire suspicious? You thinking arson?"

"No," Danny said. "They don't believe so. The fire marshal found a lamp tipped over in the bathroom where the man died, and there had been candles all over the place, too. Guessing he was just a little careless, maybe fell asleep while having a soak."

"You want a beer?"

"No, I'm good. I was just passing through so thought I'd stop to say hello, chew the fat a bit."

"Well, I appreciate that. Come back in when you're off duty and you can have a cold one on me."

"I'll do that."

I know it's uncharitable, but all day long, I couldn't stop thinking about Yoder's bubbly end. Sometimes, maybe karma has a way of balancing out the ledger. Yoder's meanness might have given him some temporary advantage in life, but in the long run, being a dick for so long and to so many came back to bite him in the ass.

30

Hannah Fisher

Through the turmoil of that night, and then throughout the next day, until Josiah came home, the Lord alone carried me. Hours moved like glaciers. If it had only been the loss of my father in the fire, I could have endured it. Death comes to us all, to loved ones as well as strangers, and we are right to see this for what it is, an earthly loss—though painful—in exchange for eternal gain. But what I carried in my heart was a far greater, far more horrifying burden.

I took the envelope my father had left for me upstairs to my bedroom. I drew back the curtains to allow the sun to shine in. I sat on the bed and tore open the envelope. Though I have read it over many times since, the letter seems to smolder in my hands each time, so close it is, so close it must be, to the perpetual flames of hell.

Dear Hannah,

Like the heretics of old who could be purified only by burning alive at the stake, I am resolved to confess my sins before submitting my body to the flames. I have tried to live righteously, to walk humbly before our God, but I have failed. Only by fire can I seek atonement for my transgressions, for yielding to the most foul of all animal lusts. You have been the one chaste, Godly woman in my life, Hannah. You never enticed me with the curls and shine of your golden hair. You did not seek to conquer my carnal weakness by temptation as your sister did. She seemed to revel in the power her Satanic tresses held over me, and in the devilish allure of her beauty. Only your mother's intervention kept me from dragging her completely into the viper's pit. When Margaret moved away, I believed I was free of the carnal disease.

But Rachel, your dear Rachel, more beautiful than Meg she was, more Godly, too, which resurrected the demon. She honored me as she honored you and Josiah, her mother and father. I fought it, but the demon crawled inside me, a vastly deeper infection than before. Out of that carnal disease sprang Jasper, a horror I could barely comprehend. Like Simon Peter, I denied him until one day, his last, he surmised the truth. And then, so many years later, Gabriel arrived, a monster born of my monstrousness, now parading around the world, the embodiment of my sin for all to see.

Colossians tells us, "Put to death therefore what is earthly in you: sexual immorality, impurity, passion, evil desire, and covetousness, which is idolatry." Only by burning will the demon be extinguished. I am sorry for everything I have done. May our Lord and Savior have mercy on my soul.

My hands shook so violently as I read this letter, I believed the paper would tear to pieces in my fingers. How could this be? How, dear Lord in heaven, could this be? Anger, wrenching sadness, bafflement, confusion grew like a tangled maze inside me, and I could see no way clear of it.

Understand, the way of our people is immediate forgiveness. Even as our Lord suffered and bled on the cross, he begged forgiveness for those who persecuted him, and we hope to do the same, always. It is an ideal, our model of righteousness. Many years ago, in Lancaster County, Pennsylvania, not far from where Meg and Samuel raised their family, a young English man, thirty-two years old, a milk truck driver, barricaded himself in West Nickel Mines Amish school with over twenty girls and young women. He carried knives, rope, several guns, zip ties, chains, and wire. He intended to do unspeakable things to those young girls. But the police arrived, and while they kept the worst from happening, they could not stop the assault. The young man killed five Amish girls, each shot in the head, and wounded five others, all between the ages of six and thirteen. The young man then killed himself.

Such tragedies occur in America, it seems, almost weekly. But the violent deaths of those girls are notable mostly for what occurred afterward. That same day, members of the Amish community comforted the young man's widow, extending forgiveness to her, her husband, and all members of his family. The young man's distraught father sobbed for nearly an hour in the arms of an Amish man who comforted him. Thirty Amish attended the man's funeral, and they established a charitable fund for his widow and the young children left behind.

I remembered this as I held my father's letter in my trembling hands. I wish I could say such forgiveness flowed into my heart.

Thus does the Lord send affliction when we have strayed from Him, so that we might know His power and His glory at last.

31

Thomas Kennedy

That night after their trip to Chicago, as he drove away from Hannah's home, Thomas put down the windows of his truck and let the cool night air flow through the cab. Drawn by the residual heat on the blacktop, leopard frogs pogoed across the road. Moths and other insects flashed across his headlights, and the moon hung overhead like a bright, welcoming lamp. He felt as he did as a boy after a stimulating day, his brain racing, thoughts running together in a beautiful kaleidoscope of sounds and images. Something long dormant in him had been coaxed from the depths. Of course, nothing could come of it. Falling in love with a married woman, Amish at that, was the deadest of dead ends. It was absurd to contemplate anything more than friendship. Still, he kept seeing the gentle curve of Hannah's jawline backlit by sunlight, the elegant wisps of hair that had escaped her kapp and fell loosely down her neck, the deep mahogany brown of her eyes as she listened or spoke, her voice gentle, her words earnest and thoughtful. He felt her thin, muscular fingers entwined in his own, the palms of their hands pressed together.

At home, he showered and opened the windows to better hear the chorus of peeping crickets, katydids, and tree frogs as he drifted off to sleep. In the morning, he was startled awake by pounding on his door.

Nine o'clock. His eyelids felt thick and heavy. A police cruiser idled in the driveway. He pulled on pants, hurried to the door. The interview was brief, confirmation he'd been in Hannah Fisher's company the previous day and night. It was then he learned from the young officer that Hannah's father had died in a house fire earlier that morning. An accident, they believed. Hannah, thankfully, had not been harmed.

On the evening news, over footage of the smoldering remains of Absalom Yoder's home, the newscaster noted that the Amish man was the great-grandfather of Anakim, the Amish Giant, the professional wrestler. When the news ended, Thomas typed out a short email message to Gabriel and sent it. Within minutes, his phone rang. Gabriel was in a chartered jet on the tarmac at O'Hare, awaiting departure for Philadelphia, where he was scheduled to wrestle in a twenty-five-man battle royal for a purse of a quarter of a million dollars that coming Saturday. He'd defeated the Sheik for the world championship belt in Chicago, as Thomas had predicted.

"What happened to Grandpa Yoder?" Gabriel asked.

Thomas told him what he knew, which was only that he'd died when his house burned down.

"I can't believe it. That's awful. Are Grandma and Grandpa okay?"

"Your grandfather is away working. Your grandma was at home, but she wasn't hurt."

"Should I come home? Can I help?"

"I don't think there's anything you can do right now, Gabriel," Thomas said. "I'll let you know when the funeral will take place."

"Okay, thanks. I miss everybody. Tell Grandma I love her and I'm so sorry."

"We saw you wrestle last night in Chicago. Gabriel, you really look amazing."

"Thanks. I didn't know if you guys came. Why didn't you stay to see me afterward? I waited for you."

Thomas sighed. "It got pretty late."

Gabriel paused. "It was the Amish deal, right? My costume? I probably should have refused, but the marketing people said fans would love it, and they do. Every time someone buys one of those hats or fake beards, I make fifty cents. It's kind of ridiculous, but it adds up."

"Hannah loved seeing you, Gabriel. I know she did."

Gabriel spoke to someone on the plane.

"We're about to take off here," he said. "I have to ask you something. I think I maybe have something wrong with my eyes. Sometimes it feels like I'm looking through a tube. For a while it was just the one side. But now it's both sides. I think I took a boot to the head, or something."

"Gabriel, that's not normal. Have you seen a doctor?"

"No," he said. "Not yet. Things are going so well. I want to stay in the ring right now. I get headaches at night sometimes, but I can take meds for those, and I smoke a little weed. Just a little. It helps me sleep. Please tell Coach Beathard I loved hearing from him, and that everything is under control, okay? Tell him I really appreciated his letter. It meant a lot to me that he wrote."

"Sure thing, but Gabriel, I insist you see a doctor."

"All right, got to run, Doc. Great talking to you. Give Grandma and Grandpa my love. I'll be in touch."

"See a doctor, Gabriel," Thomas said. "Please." But Gabriel had already gone.

Absalom Yoder's funeral took place in Josiah and Hannah's barn, his covered, simple pine casket resting on three worn wooden sawhorses on the floor. Church benches from the local district had been delivered and arranged in rows to accommodate the mourners. Thomas had spoken only briefly with Hannah after stopping to offer his condolences. Hannah's brothers and their families had arrived the night before. Her sister, Meg, arrived by train the morning of the funeral.

Amish buggies already filled the roadside for a quarter mile in front of Hannah and Josiah's home when Thomas arrived. He walked into the cavernous barn and sat near the back with his right shoulder along the wall. Though the floor had been swept, bits of straw, animal

hair, and a few hardened goat pellets remained. The interior carried
the sweet scent of hay and the pungent odor of diesel fuel. Most of
the Amish mourners had already arrived and were seated on other
benches. Some of the children turned back to look at Thomas. He
smiled and wiggled his fingers at them, and a few shyly returned his
smile before their parents nudged them to face forward.

Hannah, Josiah, and their relations sat near the front, Hannah and
her sister beside her dressed completely in black, including the kapps
on their heads. Thomas had never met Meg but recognized her immediately. She and Hannah had the same narrow face and pointed chin,
the same, thick, arching eyebrows, and they whispered to each other
like two people with much to share who had not seen each other in
some time.

Several hymns were sung, a cappella, in Old German, comforting,
droning melodies. After the hymns, two different men spoke, each
of them standing beside Absalom's coffin and occasionally resting a
hand on it in a gesture of love or respect. Though Thomas enjoyed the
cadences of the language, he could not understand anything they said,
and the Amish listening betrayed little emotion. Thomas's mind wandered. He watched motes of dust drifting across the shafts of sunlight
that bore through spaces between the weathered barn boards. He saw
several children near the front looking up and followed their eyes to
find two orange kittens peering down from the haymow. Sometimes
he looked at the back of Hannah's kapp, hoping she'd turn so that he
might see the profile of her face, but her attention remained fixed on
the funeral.

The interment took place six miles away in the Amish cemetery,
a sloping field of twenty acres along Cottonwood Road, surrounded
by simple three-board fencing, painted white. Though he would have
liked to have met Hannah's sister, whom she'd spoken of many times,
Thomas decided not to return to the Fishers' barn after the interment
for a meal the women had prepared. He hoped to see Hannah soon
but did not know when that might be possible.

Only once, during the service, did he and Hannah lock eyes. As the bearers loaded Absalom's casket onto the carriage for transport to the cemetery, Hannah looked over at him. He met her eyes and nodded once. Her face did not change expression, but she watched him, as he watched her, for close to a minute, before she turned to Josiah, who reached for her hand to help her into their buggy for the journey.

32

Hannah Fisher

All my life, autumn has been my favorite time of year. By mid-September, jars of fruits and vegetables filled our pantry shelves to sagging; hundreds of carrots and potatoes nestled in the sand of our root cellar; hay to last the winter had been cut, baled, and stacked in the barn. The mornings were cold and still. I would rise long before Josiah and dress in the dark. As early light washed the night gray, I would pull on my boots and slip out the door. I'd tread the road away from my father's house, out of sight of my still-sleeping goats, walking the half mile to a pasture we'd left fallow for years, bounded by the river in back and overgrown hedgerow on two sides, five acres gone to wild beauty. It is one of my favorite places.

I would enter the field just as sunlight began to color the earth, my boots following deer trails through the tall grass. I'd smile at the impressions of their delicate feet in the earth, like a string of small, broken hearts. At that time of year, goldenrod is in bloom. Lacy stands of staghorn sumac have gone red, the seed horns a beacon for cardinals and chickadees. Along the far hedgerow, a flock of cedar waxwings might weave through the hawthorns, gorging on the tiny, red fruit. My dress would grow heavy and wet along the bottom where it was mottled with cockleburs and brambles, and I would marvel at the

Lord's genius in making me, like the wind and birds, a sower of the seeds of His bounty.

Alone with my thoughts, I often reproached myself for shameful jealousies, bewildering moments of vanity, inexplicable impatience, wrenching anger with Josiah. It troubled me that age and experience had not ameliorated my imperfections. If anything, when I examined the arc of my life, I found that thoughts or actions I at one time would have avoided for fear of damnation, I now engaged in with only minimal worry. Or none at all.

In the days after my father died in the hellish flames, hideous dreams haunted my sleep. In one, Rachel was crossing a treacherous river with Gabriel in her arms, and the roiling waters knocked her off her feet, sending them tumbling downstream. I ran along the shore calling to them, thickets of wild raspberry canes tearing at my dress. The water went black and burst into flames, and I awoke with Rachel's screams still in my ears. In another, I was rocking Rachel as she suckled at my breast, when a howling blizzard blew open the front door. Driven snow drifted around my chair, piling up my legs and over my lap. It crept up my face, covering me and Rachel in an icy, suffocating tomb.

I awoke gasping for air, my heart fluttering, a fawn cornered by wolves. I rolled from bed, slid my panicked hands along the wall until I found the doorway, and descended the stairs to the kitchen, where I lit a candle and prayed to calm myself. I had told no one about my father's letter, not even Josiah. I am not certain why I kept something so monstrous to myself; perhaps because I believed it was the only way to contain the evil, to force it to curl on the vine. But I intended to talk with Meg about it when the right time arrived.

Meg seemed to take Father's death especially hard. She did not join the procession passing his coffin before it was taken on its journey to the cemetery. And as Father's body was lowered into the earth, and we mourners sang "The City of Light," she bowed her head and stood off alone. Obviously, she had not enjoyed the relationship a daughter hopes to have with a father. I used to think that he raised us capably

in the Word, at least, but now, of course, I knew he was not what I'd believed him to be. In any event, his gifts did not allow him those gestures a child often yearns for: a hug in sad times, a sunny afternoon unexpectedly granted away from chores for a cool swim, a forgiving wink following some small transgression. But he passed on strength, stoicism, an unceasing trust in the Lord that carried us through hard times. If he wasn't one for laughter or play, it was because, I believed, his vigilance would not relax, even for a moment. Satan, he told us, lurks beside every blade of grass, in every drop of rain. Forget that for one second, he said, and the Prince of Darkness will have his talons in you. I now understood he knew the sting of those claws, and had inflicted them on Rachel.

On the day of her scheduled departure for the train to Pennsylvania, Meg was in the kitchen when I descended the stairs. She'd already dressed, and she sat at the table, a short candle burning inches from her Bible. It was five in the morning. I carried Father's letter, folded in the pocket of my dress.

"I'm going for a walk," I said. "Join me?"

"I'll just slow you down."

"Please, Meg. I'm in no hurry."

The stifling morning air was humid, like breathing steam from a boiling pot. A putrid, pungent odor rose from the charred rubble of Father's house. The grass remained singed in a wide, black circle all around it.

Meg and I walked side by side, and I took her left arm at the elbow. Grasshoppers sprang from their perches in the tall grass along the roadside and flew on ahead. When we reached the fallow pasture, we went one before the other. The deer trail took us through the field to a narrow woodlot on a ridge above the river. Below us, we could hear the water bubbling where it flowed over rocks in the shallow riffles.

We talked of pleasant things, and for a time it felt as if we were young girls again, giggling in bed, covering one another's mouths to keep Father from hearing us. When our talk turned to our dear mother,

she asked me if I believed Mother and Father were together in Paradise, without sorrow or care.

"I don't rightly know," I said. "But I believe so. What do you think?"

"They're not together if Mother had any say in it. Father was rough as a rasp. I never could understand what she saw in him."

When I was a young woman, I sometimes allowed myself to wonder the same thing. Often, even now, I look at other couples, too, and ponder. It is hard to know a man well, even one well-loved, and each marriage journey takes its own, winding path. Sometimes the path becomes a maze, and a wife is lost forever.

"When Josiah and I began courting," I said, "he was so shy he would barely speak to me. Sunday afternoons, we'd sit together and smile at each other for hours. Finally, I said, Josiah, perhaps you should write down what you'd like to talk about, and when Sunday comes, we can have a conversation. The first Sunday, he asked me which I liked better, tomatoes or tomatillos. Tomatoes, I said. Then he moved on: Carrots or potatoes? Leeks or onions? This happened again the next week, and the next. Quizzes, not conversation. I got so frustrated I was prepared to end our courtship. Then one Sunday Josiah asked permission to touch my hand. I said, Josiah, I wish you would. He took mine in both of his, and that seemed to break the spell. He opened his heart to me in his hesitant, halting way. We married three months later. As we rode to his parents' home, where we stayed until we'd built our own, he asked if he might hold my hand along the way. I told him, Josiah, you're my husband now. You need not ask. My hand, and all else I have, is yours."

Meg laughed. "He was so sweet. Nothing like Father. You chose the opposite."

"Maybe so," I said.

"I did, too," Meg said.

I took Father's letter from my pocket. "I have something I need you to read." I handed her the envelope, told her when and where I'd discovered it. As she read, her eyes flooded with tears. She folded the letter and returned it to me, put one quivering hand over her mouth, too overcome to speak.

"Meg, I didn't know," I said.

She nodded.

"Mother cried every day for weeks when you and Samuel went away. I was angry at you for leaving her. For leaving me."

Meg wiped her eyes with her fingertips. "Now you know. Mother arranged everything. Samuel's been a good husband. I have no regrets about that. But—Father. I hate him. I have hated him since the day he sheared off my hair. What did I do? Nothing! I was his *daughter*. Rachel was his *granddaughter*!"

"We must not hate," I said. "We must forgive."

"Have you forgiven him?"

"No."

"I can't. It is unforgivable, what he's done. At first, when I learned Rachel was with child, pregnant with Jasper, I suspected. I did. I cannot deny it. I even talked to Samuel about it. He said no, it couldn't be. A granddaughter? Leave it alone." She shook her head and sighed. "He said maybe he'd mention something to Josiah, but I don't know if he ever did. I'm so sorry, Hannah."

My dear sister leaned forward on her cane and stood up.

I reached for her arm. "Did Samuel tell Josiah? Did he know about you and Father? Please, it's important."

"I don't know," she said. "I don't want to talk about this anymore." Leaning on her cane, she went into the sunshine of the field. She struggled through Indian grass and thistle, skirted clumps of red osier dogwood, the shortest, but pathless, route back to the road. Deer flies swirled about her head like reckless planets out of orbit, and honeybees dislodged from purple thistle flowers fled in agitation. I followed behind her, walking where she'd divided the weeds and grasses with her footsteps as a girl's hair is parted by a comb.

Before she reached the road, Meg paused to rest, and she turned to me, her breathing labored. "I'm so sorry," she whispered.

"Change your ticket," I said. "Stay another day or two. Please."

But she would not be moved. After lunch, one of Josiah's English friends took her to the train station in Milwaukee for her overnight trip back to Lancaster.

After she left, I dropped so deeply into the pit of despair, I could see no light. Night after night I wandered our home, moving from window to window like a panicked bird fluttering against the glass.

The vile truth of my father's predations resisted comprehension. How, Lord, I asked, can this be? Was it Your will? If so, to what purpose? How can I forgive this? My childhood rested on a bedrock of lies. My faith on a foundation of deception. My sister and mother had also failed me. One fled; the other, in weakness, honored her marriage covenant and kept silent, thereby securing the suffering of my dear, beautiful daughter. Each time I imagined Rachel's defilement, my mind went black with rage.

Josiah skulked about the house like a dog with a rotting hen tied about his neck. Did he know of my father's attempts at Meg's defilement? Did Samuel warn him of it? Did he suggest we protect Rachel from her own grandfather, as monstrous as that is to even contemplate? And yet, I was afraid to ask. If Josiah lied to me, I would know it. How could we cleave together with a lie so monstrous between us? But if he told the truth, if he knew and did nothing, how could we go on as we were?

Finally, one night, as I tossed, unable to sleep, I spoke into the darkness. Josiah had tried to take my hand beneath the covers, as he often does, but I tore it away. He sighed heavily, perturbed, but said nothing. And so I gathered my courage, and I asked, simply, "Did you know my father lusted after my sister when she was a girl?"

I waited. I waited many minutes, my heart racing. But Josiah said nothing. "Josiah?" I said, and waited. Still nothing. He remained mute as the wall.

My anger boiled over. All night, as I tossed and turned, I gradually resolved to take action. Who now remained for me? Who could be trusted? I determined two men, alone: my grandson, Gabriel, who was off in the English world, foolishly seeking riches and fame, and my English friend, Dr. Kennedy. In the morning, with Josiah's telephone, I called Dr. Kennedy. If you care for me, I said, come and take me to your home. Please.

Josiah watched as I folded dresses and underclothes, kapps, stockings, sweaters and shawls, into my mother's trunk. I added my comb and barrettes, hair bands. My Bible, a yellowed envelope of Rachel's baby teeth.

"Hannah," Josiah said. "Please. What will people say?"

This moved me so quickly from sadness to fury I did not recognize myself.

"'What will people say?' Really, Josiah? That's what concerns you?"

"Marriage is a covenant that cannot be broken," he said.

"Do not preach to me, Josiah Fisher!" I hissed. "I am going to stay with the only person on this earth who has never lied to me."

"I've never lied to you."

"A lie of omission is a lie, Josiah. Willful ignorance is cowardice. I can't even look at you right now."

When Dr. Kennedy's truck pulled up, he and Josiah eyed each other without speaking. Dr. Kennedy slid my trunk into the bed of his truck, and he gently tucked the loose fabric of my dress behind my legs before closing the door. I put down my window.

Dr. Kennedy accelerated, and as we surged around a curve in the road, the wind rushing through the cab blew off my kapp. It fell on the seat between us, and I left it there. The breeze felt lovely against my head, and I reached back and pulled the pins from my hair, letting it fall against my neck and shoulders. It blew in the wind like the tail of a horse at full gallop.

When Dr. Kennedy lifted his right hand from the steering wheel and let it rest on the seat beside him, I took his hand in both of mine, not as a lover or even a friend, but rather as someone drowning might cling to the only thing nearby that could keep her afloat.

Dr. Kennedy made a private space for me, converting his office into a room with a bed (formerly Gabriel's), a soft, comfortable chair, and a desk with a mirror mounted to the wall before it, where I might sit to pin up my hair or read by a small lamp in the evenings. He selflessly cooked and cared for me. Like a ransomed queen, I slept ten hours that first night in Gabriel's bed, awakened after nine o'clock only by the loud braying of a neighbor's donkey. My exhaustion embarrassed me, and yet the next night I slept eleven hours.

On Saturday, Josiah came to inquire if I intended to accompany him to Sunday meeting the following morning. I did not. As we spoke, Josiah's eyes wandered to my hair, which cascaded to my shoulders unpinned and uncovered by my kapp, a small rebellion that grew more comfortable to me each day. To his credit, Josiah did not chastise me for it or urge me to modestly cover my head.

When I went back inside, Dr. Kennedy did not ask about Josiah's visit or my intentions. In fact, in five days, though he could see my distress, he'd never inquired why I needed to stay with him. And when I asked if he might drive me to town when we'd finished eating, he agreed.

The thrift store smelled of mothballs. Two long racks of women's clothing stretched along one wall: shirts and sweaters, slacks, shorts, and skirts, all sorted by color. I felt paralyzed by so many choices. Where to begin? I stood staring at the racks with my arms crossed.

One of the shop's workers, a young woman wearing blue jeans pocked with holes and a baggy, multicolored T-shirt with the word "NAMASTE" across the front, came to me. She had a tiny, red stone on her nose, powder on her eyelids the pink of a sunrise. "I'm Olive, maybe I can help you out. What size you looking for?" she asked. She blew a bubble with her gum and popped it.

"I don't know," I said.

"We look about the same size. I'm an eight, give or take. So that would be medium, most of this rack right here. Fitting room is back there. Green tags are half off all week. Any other questions, just hunt me down."

"Thank you."

I tried on nine blouses, several sweaters, more dresses and skirts than I counted, and several pairs of blue jeans. The clothes were beautiful on the hangers, but once on my body, everything looked so bright and garish! Perhaps it was the lighting, or the quality of my reflection in the mirror. I had a pile of clothing on the bench, and I couldn't decide.

Then came a knock on the door.

"How's it going in there?" Dr. Kennedy's voice.

"I have no idea what I'm doing!" I said. "How does anyone decide?"

"Sounds like we need a woman's perspective back here!" Olive's voice. She knocked on the door. "Can I help?" Before I could answer she had squeezed into the room beside me and closed the door. "That blouse is really cute. I wish my arms were ripped like yours. But those jeans . . ." She shook her head. "Those are ultra-low rise, dude, totally out of style. Besides, they show your crack every time you bend over. Guys like it, but it's uncomfortable as shit. Take those off and try these." She handed me a dark pair of jeans. As I pulled on the new pants, she went through the dresses, blouses, and skirts. "You like flowers."

"I do."

"Those jeans feel better?"

"They do."

She nodded. "What about shorts? I can bring a few you could try on."

"I'm not ready for shorts, but thank you all the same."

"Okay, pull off those jeans, and I'll take all these up to the register. Don't worry about the rest of this stuff, just toss it in the basket. Someone will get it back out on the rack."

"Thank you." I felt a surge of courage. "May I keep these on? The pants and the blouse, I mean."

Olive shrugged. "Sure. Let me pop those tags off for you." She unpinned the price tags, holding the first between her lips while she undid the second. I pulled the pins from my hair and shook it down. Olive smiled.

Dr. Kennedy nodded politely when Olive and I finally emerged from the fitting room. I felt like a moth crawling from a cocoon, my wings wet and untested. I trembled, but Dr. Kennedy gently put a hand on my elbow, and whispered one word, "Beautiful." Olive loaded my purchases and my Amish dress and slip into two large, white plastic bags.

"Anything else I can help you with?" Olive asked. She passed the bags to me.

"No," I said, my heart no longer racing. "You've been so wonderful. God bless you, Olive."

"I didn't sneeze, but okay, God bless me."

Outside, the sidewalks were crowded with English, families with young children, noisy groups of teenaged girls and boys, elderly couples arm in arm. None of them stared. No one pointed. We left my purchases in Dr. Kennedy's truck and walked two blocks to get ice cream. It was warm, midafternoon. The sun felt hot on my hair and uncovered shoulders.

I was thankful we had to wait in line at the ice-cream shop. It gave me time to decide which of the thirty-three available flavors I might want to try. I knew chocolate and vanilla, but I vowed to try something new. When my turn came, I asked for North Atlantic Storm, sea salt and caramel in dark chocolate ice cream, with small chunks of chocolate fudge. It was so delicious I finished long before Dr. Kennedy and sat wishing I'd ordered the larger size.

When we got back to Dr. Kennedy's house, we sat outside in the shade, and I told him in confidence of Absalom's predations and my struggles, my weakness, my inability to forgive. I was a boiling teapot, the steam whistling out of me. By the time I'd finished, the sun was setting, and crickets had begun chirping. For a long time, we just sat watching the sun disappear, listening to the insects and frogs.

I confess the comforts of English life entranced me. Steaming water came forth at the turn of a handle, cold water at the turn of another. Many mornings, I let the hot water run over my back and shoulders for so long the room filled with dancing fog. The shelves held soaps and shampoos that smelled of mint, rosemary, and lavender. In the kitchen, small, noisy machines crowded the counters. One made coffee; another churned vegetables into a slurry; a third—thankfully silent—toasted four slices of bread at once. The microwave oven warmed food in mere seconds, humming like a small generator. At night, any room could be made bright with the flick of a switch on the wall or the turn of a knob on a lamp. Sometimes the noise and brightness overwhelmed me, and I retreated to the darker silence of my room. Dr. Kennedy had kindly purchased soy candles poured into large jars, one scented with pine, the other apple, and I enjoyed the peace of reading in silence, by candlelight.

Dr. Kennedy also kept a computer on a small table in the living room, and he used a large, plastic beetle to move the arrow on the screen, clicking one of the beetle's wings when the arrow fell upon something he wanted to see. (He said this control was called a mouse and laughed when I told him that made little sense since it had no tail, no head, and no fur.)

Most appealing to me were two tall, sun-drenched shelves on one wall of the living room, filled with books. For several days I looked at them as if they existed in a single dimension, like a large, colorful painting on the wall. But one day I pulled a book from the shelf, and then others. I told myself I would read each one just long enough to satisfy my curiosity. Novels cast a spell, carrying me off to far worlds or into the minds of characters that seemed fully flesh and bone. In a daze, bewitched, I would look up from my reading to discover an hour, or even two, had passed in an instant. At one time, I feared this alchemy to be the work of Satan; now, having looked into the face of my father so many times, I was no longer confident that good or evil were recognizable to me.

Josiah continued to come by weekly. He frowned the first time he saw my English clothes but held his tongue. Sometimes we sat together outside in the sun and conversed a bit, though haltingly, Josiah never one to spill words by the bucketful.

"Your goats are well," he said. "Hens are laying good."

"That's nice to hear. Thank you."

"The Hochstetlers lost a calf to coyotes," he said.

"How terrible for them."

Eventually he ran out of things to tell me, and he'd take a deep breath, stand up, and announce it was time he headed for home.

Each time Josiah left, reining Gideon to a canter as the buggy rattled down the road, I felt neither victorious nor defeated.

33

Billy Walton

Sometimes when a little thing happens, it opens a space for bigger things, and before you know it, all hell breaks loose. Truth is, I didn't figure life would ever change for me, and I was okay with that. I'd burned through a couple wives early on, messed up with my kids to the point I barely know them, have seen my grandchildren only in pictures. Water under the bridge. Dwell too long on your fuckups and you'll find yourself in a bathtub with a straight razor bleeding out from both wrists. I had a decent business going, some good friends, lived in a place that was peaceful, safe, and friendly enough. Other than my prostate problem, which is a slow boat to China, not first-class airfare to the great beyond, my health is decent. The eggs in my head remain unscrambled.

Where am I going with this? Couple months ago, I was driving home from town. I'd met a couple buddies for brunch, half-pound burgers and fried cheese curds, delicious stuff, though they tell me it turns your blood to glue. A mile from my place, I came upon Estelle Smithson pulled over on County Y, her car's rear left tire flat as a bar coaster. She had the trunk open. She was dressed in her Sunday best—a flowered blouse, long black skirt, faux-pearl necklace and earrings. I drove past at first, but then I turned around and came back. I hadn't changed a tire in thirty years, but I figured Estelle could use the help, what with Duke long gone and all. Every time I drive by that tree where they found him, I still think of Duke frozen to it like a tuxedoed Popsicle.

"Stella!" I said. "You're holding up all the traffic out here. Need some help?"

"Oh, Billy," she said. "Thank you." She'd been to St. Anthony's and was on her way to Madison to have an early dinner at her daughter's house. It was her son-in-law's birthday. He was a civil engineer. Her daughter was a teacher. She explained all this as I searched her trunk for a jack and tire iron.

I started in on the lug nuts, which must have been tightened by King Kong. I couldn't budge them, but my manhood would not accept defeat. I discovered by placing the tire iron on each nut with the bar parallel to the ground, and then jumping on it, I could break them loose. A bit undignified, but it got the job done, and in twenty minutes I had her ready to go.

"What day are you closed, Billy?"

"Mondays."

She pointed at me. "Monday night, six o'clock, you come to my house, and I'll cook you dinner. You like roast beef?"

"That's not necessary, Stella," I said.

"Oh, Billy, just come for dinner." She started the car. "See you tomorrow."

To my surprise, I had a good time. Her small home was tidy, every chair and sofa covered by something beautiful that she had knit or crocheted. Yarn heaven, you could say. Framed pictures dotted the walls, her two daughters, her grandchildren, a black-and-white photograph of Stella and Duke on their wedding day. Stella had a little white poodle named Snowball who took a liking to me, wanted me to carry her around like a baby. I'd put on an old sport coat before I left. I didn't own an iron, but I heated a saucepan and ran it down my dress slacks to give them a crease, splashed a little Old Spice on my face. Stella wore a midnight blue dress and pearls, but while cooking she covered the dress with a long apron that said, "I'm cooking two things for dinner: take it or leave it." Dinner was delicious—beef roast, carrots, and potatoes with gravy, and cherry pie for dessert. Afterward, she made coffee, and we played cribbage, a tournament, best of three, while Snowball slept on my lap. Stella beat me two games to one, but I suspect she threw the game I won because she put a good number of fives and tens in my cribs.

The evening ended around ten o'clock. Stella walked me to the door and stood on tiptoe to give me a hug. She smelled lovely, like a ripening fruit basket with a couple roses nearby. As the night progressed, I'd found her more and more attractive. Funny how that is. I guess I never really looked at her before. I don't know what got into me, but after she hugged me, I bent down and gently lifted her chin with my fingers, and I kissed her, once, right on the lips.

"Next week, same time?" she said. I could feel her breath against my mouth.

"Yeah." I smiled at her. "I'll bring dessert."

I went back to Stella's the following Monday. I returned the Monday after that one, too, and this time I didn't go home until Tuesday. I will spare you the particulars. Suffice to say, decommissioned parts remain in working order. Stella knew her way around those parts, and she wasn't shy about it. She produced a bottle of massage oil, too, to grease the wheels. Smelled like strawberries.

Next thing you know, we're going out to dinner and to the movies, and Monday mornings we're driving to state parks to see the fall colors, or we're off to a local orchard to pick apples, and later in her kitchen I'm peeling while she's slicing to make a pie. After we sample the pie warm from the oven with a big dollop of vanilla ice cream melting off the top, she puts on a record, and we slow dance in the living room a little bit. Snowball lies on the sofa, watching. When the music ends, Stella takes my hand and leads me down the hallway and, well, you know the rest.

All because I stopped to change a tire.

Something must have been in the air that fall, because folks started seeing Doc Kennedy in town with a new woman, too, and a week or so later Charlie told me that woman was Hannah Fisher.

"Can't be," I told him. "Can't be Hannah Fisher. That's impossible."

"They were in line at the ice-cream shop, Billy," Charlie said. "I was standing right there, three people behind them. She was wearing blue jeans and her hair was down, but I know Hannah's pretty face. It was her."

Not long after that, on a Friday night, the door opened at my place, and who should wander in but Josiah Fisher. He looked a little chunkier than I'd remembered. I think every man's front porch gets a little bigger with age. His beard was streaked with gray, with bits of sawdust clinging to it near the bottom and dusting the hair on his arms. He sat slumped over, elbows on the bar, staring down at his hands. Broken, was how he looked, though maybe I'm reading it by what I learned later.

I brought him a glass of ice water and he ordered a perch fry.

"Sorry about Absalom," I told him. "Quite a shock."

"Yes, it was."

He wasn't a talker, as I knew well enough. "Hannah doing okay?" Josiah nodded.

"That's good," I said. "Must be hard on Hannah, losing her father that way." He nodded once. Sometimes a man comes into a place like mine because he wants to be surrounded by other people but left alone, a comfort-in-the-herd kind of deal. "Big batch of fish will be out of the fryer in a couple minutes," I said, and then I let him be.

Josiah picked at his fish and chips, ate a bite of coleslaw, and left the rye bread on his plate. He put on his hat, paid his bill, and left.

Josiah was barely out the door when Charlie rushed over. We're no better than a couple of old gossips, Charlie and me. "He didn't say one way or another," I told him, before he even asked.

"He wouldn't have been here alone, otherwise," Charlie said.

I had to acknowledge he might be right. It turned out that he was, at least in part. I know for a fact what you see with your eyes does not give you the whole story, as many men and women who have married for beauty alone have found out the hard way.

34

Thomas Kennedy

December snows came, followed by January cold. The sun rose late and set early, and the long darkness and winter silence seemed to bleed into the house's walls. Hannah ate little, rarely smiled or spoke, never laughed. Josiah visited her weekly, but she refused all others. She seemed hollowed out, so distracted by pain that she could barely function. At her request, Josiah delivered a large oil lamp, and she asked Thomas if they might light the lamp and candles in the evenings instead of the electric lights, which, she said, burned her eyes with their brightness. She also asked if he'd be willing to set aside the noisiest of his kitchen machines, the food processor and the microwave oven. They sounded, she said, like chainsaws in Eden. Though he mourned the loss of his microwave, Thomas assented.

In time, Hannah emerged, though a different woman. She became almost obsessed with reading, devouring books with a hunger that reminded Thomas of his mother's love for them. Most evenings, Hannah spent hours with a book, her body still, her face knit in concentration. Thomas went into the basement and brought up the remaining books from his mother's library—every work by Jane Austen, the Brontës, Edith Wharton, Virginia Woolf, Willa Cather, Zora Neale Hurston, and Kate Chopin; Anaïs Nin's *Diary* in six volumes; the collected short stories of Flannery O'Connor and Eudora Welty; poetry from Elizabeth Barrett Browning, Sylvia Plath, Anne Sexton, and Sappho; essay collections by Susan Sontag, Annie Dillard, Simone de Beauvoir, and others.

"All of these were my mother's," Thomas said, as he arranged the books on the shelves. "You might enjoy them."

In January, Hannah read all of Austen; in February she started Nin's *Diary*. She caught Thomas watching her, dog-eared a page, and lowered the book to her lap.

"This is true?" she asked Thomas. "This woman did these things, with men and with women, sometimes both together, and then did not hide it?" Hannah shook her head and sighed. "She lived so far from God."

"Well," Thomas said. "She was in Paris, after all."

Hannah recognized this as a joke and smiled. "Gabriel's been to Paris."

Thomas nodded. "He has. Several times. His apartment's in London, which is just across the Channel."

"I hope he doesn't meet her," Hannah said. "She is no doubt beautiful and beguiling in person. He's stopped writing to me. Do you hear from him?"

Thomas shook his head. "He has his life. I'm sure he's busy. I don't want to pester him."

"I wish he'd never left," Hannah said, opening her book again. "He is my grandson and my half brother." She shook her head. "So strange. I haven't told him. I don't know if I will."

"Someday you'll decide. Waiting does no harm."

Hannah abandoned Nin for Zora Neale Hurston. She read *Their Eyes Were Watching God* in a single night, finishing after Thomas had fallen asleep in his recliner. When he awoke, she was still in tears.

"This was so beautiful. Tea Cake took Janie fishing!" She smiled. "Josiah once took me fishing, but I didn't want to hurt the fish. I insisted on fishing without a hook, so he tied a paper clip to my line instead and bent it such a way that a worm might stay on for a while.

He said, Hannah you're not fishing, you're feeding fish. I said, that's fine by me."

Thomas chuckled. "I can take you trout fishing in the spring when the ice goes out."

Hannah nodded. "Maybe," she said.

During a February thaw, Thomas and Hannah went for long walks in the early afternoons, and Hannah would hold his arm at the elbow for balance if the footing became slippery. They spoke again as old friends, their revelations and suppositions growing more intimate and uncensored.

"They have not excommunicated me," Hannah said, one afternoon, as they ambled along the roadside, "nor sent the bishop to have words with me. I don't know why. Josiah says it is the patience of compassion, the grace of true fellowship."

"Perhaps it is," Thomas said.

"I want to believe it."

"Do you miss it?"

She nodded. "Yes," she said. "Very much."

"What most?"

"The certainties," she said. "At times, as a young woman, when I struggled, I would allow myself to peek behind the curtain. But I'd quickly turn away, believing Satan's hand covered my own, tempting me beyond my cloistered life. Now that I have ventured there—here— much is as I'd imagined. So much convenience, so much space, the mind can fill with sky. But I miss waking in the morning and never having to wonder what clothes to wear. I miss hearing my language spoken, and my language in song. My animals. The slow pace of life. These are small, simple things, habits really."

Thomas felt pangs of jealousy, but he guarded them closely. "Why not go back?"

She smiled. "Sometimes, in that other life, I would wonder what it might be like to have other things. Television, maybe. Beautiful things. Books. The seed was already planted in me, I think, and waiting, but then reading my mother's book of Miss Dickinson's poems caused it to sprout." Hannah shrugged. "My dear mother would have said you can't put a pumpkin back into its seed. But I may have to try." She forced a smile. "Someday."

Thomas took her gloved hand in his, and she let him. "And what does Josiah think of all this?" he asked.

Hannah sighed. "My Godly husband has the patience of Job! If he had resisted, or chastised me, or belittled me with anger, I could no longer see him. But he has listened, as you have, and trusted, and cleaved to the wife of his youth, but with long arms. He says this is my second *Rumspringa*, my senior *Rumspringa*, and he will wait as long as necessary."

"Is that what it is?"

"We are not allowed it," she said softly.

Thomas tried not to show his disappointment. He still held some small hope that Hannah would stay, that their friendship would grow into something more intimate and permanent.

"What if we'd met as teenagers?" Hannah said, suddenly. "Would you have asked Absalom for permission to court me?"

"Of course," Thomas said.

"He would have denied you," she said. "An English agnostic with a feminist atheist for a mother? He would have shunned you as a son of the devil."

"True," Thomas said. "But I can be persistent. I would have asked again and again. I would have come every day for months until he tired of answering the door."

Hannah laughed and took his arm in both of her hands. "And after he denied you a hundred times, I would have snuck out to meet you," she said. She kissed the shoulder of his heavy wool coat. "I would have made a ladder out of my bedsheets and come to you after dark."

"You can make a ladder out of bedsheets?"

"I can make anything out of a bedsheet!" Hannah said. "A dress, a tablecloth, pajamas, a ladder." She paused. "I snuck out to meet Josiah once."

"On a ladder sewn from bedsheets?"

"No." She laughed. "Before I went to bed, I put tiny pieces of dry oats on the stairs where they didn't squeak. Then I drank a quart of water. The pressure to void urine woke me just after midnight. I snuck down in my stocking feet, pulled my shoes from where I'd hidden them under the porch. Josiah met me down the road."

"Did he make it worth your while?"

"He did," she said, nodding. "He put down a blanket hidden in the trees, and we kissed and kissed until my face felt so flushed, I thought I'd caught fever. I snuck back into the house after three, but when I got to the stairs, my trail of oats was gone."

"No way."

"Yes, it was gone! I thought maybe mice had eaten them. I tried to remember where to put my feet, but three of the stair treads screeched like a rabbit in the jaws of a fox. And when I got to my room, Mother was sitting on my bed, waiting.

"She'd gone downstairs and discovered the front door wide open. I'd closed it so softly it didn't latch, and the wind blew it in. With one sweep of her arm, she threw me into bed, still in my clothes, and covered me. It was then I heard the floor creaking out in the hall, and my father staggered into my room."

"'Miriam, what are you doing?' he asked, his voice gruff.

"Mother whispered, 'Hannah may be feverish. I came to comfort her.'

"Father sighed heavily. 'Let the Lord comfort her,' he said. 'Come back to bed.'"

"Wow," Thomas said. "Your mother saved you."

"She did," Hannah answered. "If Father had discovered me out, he would have striped me with his belt, and I would have deserved it. I had to wake for chores at five in the morning, and I was so tired I could barely keep my eyes open. Mother guessed where I'd been. After lunch, as I helped her with the dishes, she winked and told me I must be allergic to something I ate, because my lips were as swollen as dumplings."

* * *

In late March, as the cranes returned and the geese began passing overhead on their journey north again, Thomas was in Oxford at Mel and Birdy's ranch examining a newborn foal when his phone buzzed in his pocket. He ignored the call as he finished his work, checking for a message only after he'd returned to his truck. The caller had left no voicemail. Thomas didn't recognize the number, but he returned the call. On the other end, the phone rang a long time before someone answered.

"Yes?" A woman's voice. When she learned who was speaking, she passed the phone to another. Gabriel.

Thomas's mouth went dry. Gabriel had awakened in a hotel room in Spain, and when he opened his eyes, he could no longer see.

"What?" Thomas asked.

Gabriel repeated the news: he was blind. Taken first to a hospital in Barcelona, where crowds of paparazzi pushed against one another to get his photograph, and then airlifted to London, he had a series of tests over several days. Doctors found a large tumor in his brain. It had grown beyond the pituitary gland, its branches extending across the optic nerves. The tumor had spread to other parts of his body as well, to the vertebrae along his spine, his lungs, his liver.

Thomas's voice quivered with emotion.

"Gabriel, I'm so sorry. When are they operating?" Thomas asked. He'd need to apply for a passport. "I'll come to London as soon as I can."

"There's no operation," Gabriel said.

"No operation? What do you mean?"

"They can't remove it," Gabriel said. "Nothing can be done."

"Something can be done," Thomas said.

"No. Please listen. I'm on a flight to Chicago that leaves tomorrow. It's a lot to ask, I know. But can you pick me up at O'Hare? And can I stay with you?"

Thomas swallowed back tears. "Of course," Thomas said, again and again. "Of course. I will come for you. Just tell me when."

Part Four

35

Hannah Fisher

Gabriel's bed stretched parallel to the south-facing picture window that opened onto Dr. Kennedy's sunny yard, and every morning I raised the shades to admit the warmth of the rising sun. It poured golden through the glass and spread across Gabriel's body, and the colorful tattoos along his arms and chest glowed like blooming flowers. If the night had been cool and Gabriel had wrapped himself in the down feather bed, the scent of him would rise in the stirred air as I passed. It was not the sweet, burnished odor of a young boy, nor the pungent, ammoniac bite of an elderly body breaking down, the diminishing life leaking out by drops. With Gabriel it was as if one could smell the disease itself, a scent like rich humus decaying beneath a mottled skin of fallen leaves.

On each side of the main glass was a tall casement window that could be cranked open to admit air, and I opened these windows every morning, rain or shine, to let the cool, spring-scented wind blow through, and to amplify the beautiful arias of birdsong. Sometimes I would discover the windows already open, and Gabriel would acknowledge that he'd wanted to better hear an owl or the barking of a fox in the night when he was unable to sleep. Lying on his back, he could reach the handle. Soon he'd be too weak to do even that.

Beneath his colorful skin, death's corruption ate at his flesh and bones from the inside.

For many days in the beginning, Gabriel rarely spoke and refused to leave the house. He refused all visitors. A deep sadness had overtaken him, a wellspring of tears that seemed bottomless. I yearned to comfort him, but could not. Give him time, Josiah said. With his manly matter-of-factness, he added that Gabriel was feeling sorry for himself, as anyone would, under the circumstances, but it would pass in time. No matter how long the storm or drought, water eventually returned to its own level, and Gabriel would as well. But if I could have taken on Gabriel's pain, if I could have traded places with him, I gladly would have done so.

Josiah's words proved true. One morning, Gabriel agreed to leave the house to go for a short walk with me, and these walks became a regular part of our day, and a treasured gift to me. For some weeks, Gabriel could walk without assistance, but eventually he needed the use of a sturdy ash staff Josiah had fashioned for him. Because the corruption had spread to the bones in his spine, he wasn't able to bend over without pain, so I'd help him put on his leg and then kneel on the floor to tie his shoes. Once on his feet, he'd gently reach down to take my hand. I'd place my palm against his fingers, and it would disappear like a mouse into a sack of grain.

We'd wander country roads together, listening to birds, luxuriating in the warmth of the spring sun on our faces. Gabriel could identify every bird we encountered by its song, and sometimes he would stop walking and cock his head to the side to listen more closely. If I saw something beautiful, Gabriel would ask me to describe it for him. He'd smile and squeeze my hand as I tried to explain what I was seeing. I often struggled to find the words. The Lord, I told him, has given us imperfect language to describe His wonders.

Whenever we passed a livestock pasture, Gabriel could smell the animals long before we reached them. English farmers a quarter mile from Dr. Kennedy raised Suffolk sheep with a guard donkey loose among them, and each morning, several hundred sheep and the donkey would surge toward Gabriel with a noise like a quilt flapping in the wind as we made our way to the fence line. Gabriel would kneel and reach through the wire, rubbing his hands along their heads and necks until his palms were dark with lanolin. A mile in the other direction, a young English couple raised alpacas. These strange, skinny animals, with necks like giraffes, and large, gentle eyes, initially feared Gabriel. They had never seen a man of his size, wide as a bale of hay is long at the shoulders. But in minutes he'd won them over, and they now leaped over one another's backs to be closer to him each time we approached.

Eventually, I decided to tell Gabriel about Absalom's depredations. I could not keep it from him. That conversation spanned the better part of a misty afternoon. Though surprised to learn Absalom was our shared father, Gabriel did not complain. He was far more concerned for my own well-being. The only time he seemed close to tears was when he confronted the brutal effect Absalom's terror must have had on his mother.

After discovering the truth of his birth, and perhaps because he did not know how much longer he would be with us, something shifted in Gabriel. He began to speak with greater enthusiasm, greater candor. He wanted, he said, to teach me something of the world he'd seen on his travels. He was like an explorer who had discovered wonders but struggled to fully explain their grandeur to those who hadn't seen them.

Gabriel regaled me with stories from the many countries he'd visited, the food he'd eaten, the magnificent things he'd seen: the windmills of Amsterdam, the Alhambra in Spain, the Duomo in Milan, the Great Wall of China, the Eiffel Tower, the Roman Colosseum, the beaches of Rio de Janeiro. Everywhere he went, people swarmed him, asked for his autograph, posed with him for photographs. Parents asked him to lift their young children in his arms. Chefs came from their kitchens to watch him eat the prodigious quantities of food they'd prepared for him.

He swam in nearly every one of Earth's oceans and heard more different languages spoken than he could remember. And he told me about the art museums he'd visited: the Uffizi in Florence, the Prado in Madrid, the Louvre and Musée d'Orsay in Paris.

"I've been to an art museum!" I told him. "In Chicago. Thomas took me there the day we came to see you wrestle."

"Then you know what it's like. My favorite was this little museum in Paris that no one visits, the Cluny. It's full of medieval art, mostly religious stuff. You would love it. There's never a line to get in, and I often found myself alone, which is also maybe why I liked it so much. In one room, they have these huge tapestries, six of them, I think, hanging from the ceiling, called *The Lady and the Unicorn*. They were woven by someone a long time ago, and every one depicts a lady, kind of like a princess, in a beautiful garden surrounded by fruit trees and all these animals—an amazing unicorn, of course, but also a lion, a leopard, rabbits, dogs, a goat, lots of birds. The room where they're hanging is kept dark to keep the colors from fading, and sometimes I would just sit there for hours. It made me miss being home but also made me feel closer to home, if that makes sense. I missed the darkness here at night. The quiet. The animals. The solitude. Sometimes when I had a headache coming on, I would lie down and close my eyes and imagine I was back home in the pasture, surrounded by our goats and the sound of chirping crickets. I would pretend if I blinked my eyes three times before I fell asleep, I would wake up in my own bed, here in Lakota. My body wouldn't be sore. My headaches would be gone. People wouldn't be trying to touch me everywhere I went." He took a deep breath and let it out. I squeezed his hand.

"I'm so sorry, Gabriel."

When Gabriel grew too weak to take more than a few steps at a time, our daily walks ended, and instead I would lead him through French doors to Dr. Kennedy's sunny flagstone patio, where we'd sit listening to the birds, smelling the flowers, with one or both of Dr. Kennedy's cats asleep on his lap. He said he could tell the time of day by the quality of the sun's heat, and he knew darkness had come when the temperature cooled and the frogs began to call from the ponds and ditches.

I told myself to treasure every minute I had with him. It is a lesson we should heed every day we spend with those we love, but we squander so many of our earthly hours. I vowed to be more attentive to love in the time we had left.

36

Trey Beathard

When Thomas called to tell me doctors had discovered an inoperable tumor the size of a grapefruit in Gabe Fisher's brain, and that he'd gone blind and was coming home to Lakota, my guts felt like they'd turned into a tangled knot of rattlesnakes. Messed me up for days. I couldn't eat. I couldn't sleep.

Nothing says life has to be fair. My daddy said that to me so many times he should have had it tattooed on his forehead. But damned if life wouldn't make a whole lot more sense if evil were punished and kindness rewarded.

After giving Gabe some time to settle in—and after discovering that Hannah Fisher was now living at Thomas's place, too, though I'm no one to judge, obviously—I went to see the boy. It got emotional, seeing him like that, blind, for the first time. I wouldn't have blamed his grandparents if they held it against me for pulling the boy away from them and into football, but Hannah Fisher offered me nothing but kindness and care. After that first visit, I made an effort to swing by as often as I could. In the beginning, Gabe seemed subdued, frightened, wondering out loud what would happen to him, how it would be. Thomas drove him to Madison a couple times to see some specialists in oncology, but their tests confirmed what Gabe had been told in

London. The primary tumor could not be removed, and there were so many secondary tumors, the side effects of any effort to control their growth with chemicals would themselves prove fatal. Barring a miracle, Gabe Fisher, not yet twenty-three years old, was going to die.

Looking at him, that was hard to believe. He was a massive skyscraper of a man. He'd grown into his body, as young athletes do. I didn't ask about steroids—my mama always used to say, "Don't ask if you don't want to know"—but I can't imagine any human being building biceps the size of basketballs without a bit of help. But as time passed and he became bedridden, weakened by his disease, Gabe seemed to shrink a bit every day. It killed me to see him that way, and for a while I stopped going by. I just couldn't take it. But Thomas called and said Gabe had been asking for me, and so I went back. This time, at Merryn's urging, I volunteered to take an overnight shift once a week, keeping vigil at his bedside, Sunday nights into Monday mornings, to give Thomas, Hannah, and Josiah a bit of a break.

On the scale of human misery, for most people, feeling helpless is probably not going to crack their top five. Far worse things can happen to you. Physical pain, despair, crippling anxiety, emotional devastation, abject shame—like everybody, I've endured all of those, but for some reason, helplessness makes me so desperate I can barely stand it. Unlike physical pain or anxiety, for which medication is available, there's no pill you can take, no beverage, no herb to ingest to alleviate the symptoms. The less I can do for someone, the worse it is. I get so agitated I want to crawl out of my skin.

I was okay if I could read to him for a while, or if he woke up and wanted to talk for a bit, or he needed a drink of cold water. Anything, really, was better than sitting in a chair in the quiet, watching him suffer, unable to help. And then early one morning, must have been almost three, everything black and still, the pain woke him. He moaned softly, he winced, then he started blowing air out between his teeth, moaning some more. I put a hand on his arm and said, "Hang on, son. Breathe through it, be strong, let it pass," words I often said on the field when a player was down injured.

"Coach," he whispered. "That you?"

"I'm right here," I said.

"Can I have some water?" I grabbed the pitcher of ice water and moved the straw to his lips so he could drink. He took several long draws and swallowed each time, then pushed the straw from his mouth with his tongue.

"You in pain, Gabe? You need more medicine?"

"No, I was dreaming," he said. "About Bella, my old girlfriend."

"Yeah? A good dream?"

"We were fighting. I've been thinking about her a lot, maybe that's why I dreamed about her." He put his hand on my arm, as if to hold me there. He told me about her, about when they met, about their days and nights together in Madison, about the agonizing days of conversations that led to their breakup before he left for London. She would have dropped everything to make a life with him. She wanted them to go to London together. She said it would be an adventure. But he broke up with her. He wanted, he said, he *needed* to devote himself solely to succeeding in his new career.

"I was so stupid," Gabe said.

"Don't be so hard on yourself," I told him. "Ambition is a jealous lover. She wants you all to herself. Believe me, I know."

"But it was a mistake."

"So call her and tell her. I'm sure you can find her."

"What's the point?"

"Son, listen. You've heard me say this a million times. You can't change the past, but the present and the future are under your control."

"Not true. I'm dying."

"So am I. And so is she."

"Not the same."

"All the more reason not to waste any more time thinking about it. When the sun comes up, get her on the phone. For God's sake, Gabe, call the girl."

"No," he said. "I can't."

* * *

About eight the next morning, as I passed through the kitchen to head for home, I asked Thomas if he remembered the last name of Gabriel's old college girlfriend. He knew her first name, Isabella, but he had to think awhile to remember what I needed. Alvarez. Isabella Alvarez. Thomas said the last he'd heard, after graduating from college, Bella had moved back to California. That's all he knew.

Merryn rolled her eyes when I brought it up, told me to mind my own business, that I was too old and too ugly to play Cupid. She had a point on both counts. What I didn't tell Merryn was that I'd already googled "Isabella Alvarez, California," and discovered that Alvarez is a popular name in California, and so is Isabella. Besides, Merryn added, again rightly, how do you know she hasn't married and taken a new last name? Without hiring a private detective—and don't even think about it, she added—the odds of finding her are slim and none.

"Sleep on it, Trey," Merryn said. "In the morning, you'll realize it's a dumb idea. Let it be."

I tried to sleep on it, but halfway through the night I woke up and had zero chance of falling back asleep anyway, so I went downstairs and turned on the computer. Starting from major cities in southern California, I began googling Isabella's name and, say, San Diego, or Los Angeles, Bakersfield, Salinas, working my way north, then scrolling through the possibilities. I'd been at it over an hour, my eyes were dry, and I was about to hang it up, and suddenly there she was: Isabella Alvarez, age twenty-five, graduate of the University of Wisconsin, a major in elementary education.

"Found you," I said, aloud.

There was more to her story than I expected, but I'll leave it at that. At nine o'clock California time, I reached out. That afternoon, Bella reached back.

37

Billy Walton

It broke my heart to see the boy wasting away, cancer chewing on him like a dog on a bone. I mean, here's a kid who brought only joy to people, just a few months shy of twenty-three years old, strong as an ox and big as a goddamn redwood tree. Son of a bitch, but life can be a kick in the balls. The world is full of assholes who live forever, and a big, beautiful kid like Gabriel gets snuffed out young. It ain't right.

If that wasn't bad enough, we had to deal with all the online bull-shit, too: Gabriel's dying of AIDS, or syphilis, or he's the product of an Amish woman bred to a horse, or he's not dying at all but in hiding, that it's all a plot by the wrestling federation to build drama for his comeback. Or my favorite idiocy: Gabriel was not a giant at all, just a normal-sized guy photoshopped to look huge. I mean, Judas Priest, the internet is a sewage dump, a toilet where anonymous ass-holes compete to out-ignorant each other.

Worst of all, once it got around that Gabriel was staying at Doc Kennedy's place, you had the gawkers driving by, rubbernecking and tangling up traffic, trying to get a peek at him, and then the out-of-state paparazzi, camping out with their cameras, with lenses the size of megaphones, trying to get pictures of Gabriel to sell to the trashy checkout line magazines. It had everyone in town aggravated and edgy.

Then one Friday, Coach Beathard and his wife, Merryn, were in for a fish fry, along with Mel and Birdy—Trey's aunt and her partner, the horse breeders—who were taking turns holding baby Caroline on their lap. Trey mentioned he'd been to visit Gabriel and he could hardly get to the house with all the traffic, and we got to talking about that. Somebody said, why don't we just run a roadblock, lock up the whole damn road a half mile in both directions, drive those bloodsuckers back to whatever swamp they came from. Mel and Birdy about hopped out of their chairs agreeing to join in on that, said they could hook a horse trailer to their truck and leave it parked as long as necessary; Coach Beathard volunteered as well. Before you knew it, we had commitments from fifteen or twenty people willing to join the blockade or invite others to do the same, including Stella's brother, Rick Dalkey, who offered to bring along a couple guys with guns, just for show. Being from Texas, something they usually kept to themselves, Mel and Birdy both knew their way around a six-shooter and said they could holster peacemakers as well, if need be.

Rick's a good man, but he's had some involvement with the local militia, what Stella calls the camo-and-face-paint crowd. I didn't want any violence, so I pulled Danny Albright into the loop. He said maybe the sheriff's office could erect some No Parking signs a mile in each direction of Doc Kennedy's place. It might take a week or two, he'd have to talk to some people first, you know, politicians and so forth. I said if you put up No Parking signs, what's to keep people from just walking in? It's a public highway, Billy, he said. What do you want me to say?

I told him we had a crew and a plan and we'd be fine but that Dalkey was lining up a couple antigovernment guys and that made me nervous, though Stella said she could handle her own brother. Danny said, Billy, Jesus Christ, I don't want any shooting out there. Nah, we'll be fine, I told him. We're just going to lock up the road for a few days. Locals will know how to get where they need to go. No one wants them assholes hanging around.

Danny didn't like it, but he said he'd tell the folks in dispatch not to get too excited if any calls came in about traffic congestion out that way. But if the shit hits the fan out there, he said, arrests will be made. Yeah, yeah, I said. Don't worry.

We coordinated the timing at my place, and that morning by five A.M. we had so many cars and trucks and tractors and trailers blocking the road in both directions that you couldn't get within a mile of Doc Kennedy's place. Most of the paparazzi got the message in the first couple of hours and decided the hell with it. One guy walked in and climbed with his camera thirty or forty feet up a box elder tree in the woods behind Thomas's house. Oliver Edwards said he'd been shaking turkeys down out of trees for twenty-five years, he'd take care of it, and he did. Couple other photographers were stubborn sons of bitches, drove their tan Jeep around the roadblock and out along the grass ten feet off the road, parking in a field across from Doc Kennedy's driveway. When Dalkey and his men confronted them, one of the paparazzi, wearing bright blue mirrored sunglasses, opened his sports jacket to reveal a pistol in a shoulder holster. He said the highway and median were open to the public, and he was the public, so fuck off. They set up cameras on tall tripods that reached well over the top of their Jeep and aimed them over both rows of parked vehicles toward Thomas's house.

Dalkey's about six foot four, broad shouldered, vulgar as a drunken sailor. He used to be a game warden before he retired. He walked around behind those guys and pulled an old-fashioned can opener from his pocket, the kind with a sharp point on one end, and holding it down by his side, he jammed the pointed end into their Jeep's rear quarter panel and dragged it slowly against the painted finish from the back end all the way to the hood, leaving a deep, wavering gouge in the metal.

"What the fuck!" Mr. Sunglasses said. He pulled out his cell phone. "I'm calling the police, asshat." Dalkey's patriot friend, Brian Klanderman, who for some reason had covered his face in blue and white grease paint that morning, as if he were a Scottish highlander preparing to battle the English, knocked the phone out of the guy's hand and stomped on it so hard the screen shattered. Then he stomped on it three or four more times for good measure.

"What the fuck!" Mr. Sunglasses said, again. He was a man of limited vocabulary.

His buddy looked like he'd pissed his pants, and he took a step back from his camera. "We don't want any trouble. We're just trying to earn a living like everybody else."

"Earn it someplace else," Dalkey told him.

Mr. Sunglasses reached inside his jacket and pulled out his pistol. First, he pointed it at Dalkey, but then he turned and aimed at Brian's nose. Brian stared at the little pistol, which was so close to his face he appeared cross-eyed.

"What you got there?" Brian said.

The tiny revolver was nearly concealed by the man's hand. The barrel was an inch and a half long. "It's a Ruger, asshole."

"A twenty-two?" Brian looked over at Dalkey and grinned. Dalkey sidled over behind the guy and leaned in.

"Yup, looks like a Ruger LCR," Dalkey said. "Nice little piece if you're shooting rats at the dump."

Dalkey unsnapped his holster and withdrew his weapon, holding it up so the photographers could see it. "This is a Desert Eagle forty-four. A forty-four-caliber bullet makes a hole the diameter of a dime going in. Coming out, though, sometimes that hole's the size of a cannon ball."

Mr. Sunglasses squinted at Dalkey's pistol, but his buddy was already unscrewing his camera from the tripod. "Come on, man," his buddy said. "Let's just get out of here."

"Listen to your friend," Dalkey said. "Or maybe you'd rather have a duel. Let's say, twenty paces? I'll even give you the first shot."

"You assholes are crazy," Mr. Sunglasses said. He shook his head and returned the pistol to his holster. In five minutes, they were gone.

Frankly, I felt guilty about the scratched Jeep and the busted cell phone, but in the end, we ran those leeches out of town. We kept that blockade going for about three days, just to be sure, and then we took turns driving by, checking on things, to ensure Gabriel's privacy was being respected.

38

Hannah Fisher

As the blast furnace of summer heat arrived, Gabriel grew too sick to leave his bed. His pain grew more pronounced as well, and Dr. Kennedy arranged for an English nurse to begin visiting. She provided a prescription to dull the pain, pills that Gabriel was to swallow several times a day with water. These pills often put him to sleep. She recommended an electric bed so that Gabriel could be lifted to a sitting position with the push of a button, but Gabriel declined it. He was content to be propped on pillows during the daylight hours, so he could feel the breeze on his face. When the nurse offered to intervene on his behalf if the expense of such a bed was what he feared, Gabriel told her he had enough money to buy a thousand such beds, but that he'd prefer to lie on a bed of straw if given the choice of the two. It was one of the rare times I heard Gabriel speak in a tone of unkindness, and he apologized immediately. The nurse put a hand on his shoulder and said no apology was necessary.

Though he'd lost weight, Gabriel's size still made meeting his needs difficult. The visiting nurse taught us the proper placement of a bedpan, but the ones she left proved too small for Gabriel to use. Josiah drew up plans and took them to Henry Stolzfus, who did some welding, and using an old tractor seat and the bed from a gardener's wheelbarrow, Mr. Stolzfus forged a bedpan thirty inches across by two feet long. We used these as long as Gabriel could help us position them. Because of the occasional spill, and not infrequent accidents, we needed to change the sheets on Gabriel's bed more frequently, too. The nurse taught us to do this as well, though it required Dr. Kennedy, Josiah, and me all working together, and took the better part of a half hour to complete. Josiah added six old lawn mower wheels to the bottom of Gabriel's bed, and this made it possible for any one of us to move the bed as needed.

When Gabriel became bedridden, the Hochstetlers delivered a thick wool mattress pad made from their beautiful flock of Rambouillet sheep. The Hochstetlers cleaned, matted, and sewed this wool into pads that allowed air to circulate and helped to prevent bedsores. Comforted by these fleeces, many elderly Amish spent their final days and hours awash in the honeyed scent of the Hochstetlers' Rambouillets.

Friends and loved ones continued to visit, though often Gabriel felt too weak to do more than smile at them. Coach Beathard continued to come regularly with his wife and daughter; so did Mr. Walton and his lady friend, Stella, and Charlie Mayfield, who once coached Gabriel in Little League. Muscular young men who had once played college football with Gabriel arrived by the carload; Oliver Edwards stopped by and left us a beautiful turkey, freshly slaughtered and cleaned. Two elderly English women, friends of Dr. Kennedy named Mel and Birdy, visited every week with an elegant dessert: one week a soufflé, another an elegant cheesecake. Sometimes Gabriel would awaken and visit for a few minutes. Usually, he did not.

When it became clear we would not be able to provide the care Gabriel needed, I felt terrible distress. Moving him often required more strength than Dr. Kennedy, Josiah, and I could muster together. Despite Gabriel's desire to remain in Dr. Kennedy's home, I could not fathom how that might be done. At some point soon we would have to send Gabriel to a hospital or a hospice care center. It would be a strange place, where he would be tended by strangers, in an electric

bed he would despise, likely far too small for him, and where photographers would no doubt discover him and sell the images of his
distress to the highest bidder. I cried each night I contemplated this,
yet was so weary from the long days that I struggled to remove my
clothes to step into my nightgown. Defeated, exhausted, filled with
shame, I tearfully told Josiah I could no longer continue. He nodded
calmly, said he would help to make the proper arrangements.

Around noon the next day, an Amish buggy arrived, and four women
carrying buckets and washcloths, a large basket of fried chicken and
fresh rolls, and freshly laundered sheets custom-sewn to fit over a ten-
foot mattress and thick merino pad knocked on Dr. Kennedy's front
door. When I opened the door, I could not stop my grateful tears. There
stood Abiah, Maddie, Rose, and Evelyn, the dearest of my friends, each
bearing her small burden, and collectively come to bear mine. I hugged
each of them as they entered, sobbing at last in Abiah's arms, while the
others went directly to where Gabriel lay, removed their kapps, and set
to work.

They stayed until six P.M., when a group of four more Amish
women arrived to relieve them. At midnight, a third group came, then
at six A.M., another. Day after day, night after night, these women
arrived, a procession of gentle, industrious angels, all carefully scheduled and organized by Abiah. Dozens of women, old and young, most
from our district, many from more distant places, took their turns min-
istering to Gabriel. They whispered among themselves and sang
Amish hymns. They set out warm meals and did the dishes and the
cleaning afterward. They gently washed Gabriel's body with warm,
clean water; positioned and emptied his bedpans; carried his soiled
clothing and sheets away to be washed and dried. Someone sat with him
at all times, offering sips of cool water and small morsels of food.
They massaged his cramping limbs with oil of lavender and chamomile.
While he was awake, they read aloud to him from books he had chosen,
animal stories he'd loved as a boy about dogs and horses and pet deer.

When Gabriel's pain grew so severe that even with the balm of
pills he still thrashed and moaned through the day and night, the English

nurse arrived to administer morphine, which dripped down a long, clear tube through a needle into Gabriel's colorful arm. As the morphine flowed, Gabriel's thrashing stopped; his breathing slowed, and he slept soundly, his eyelids quivering with bright dreams of some distant corner of the world none but he could see.

It was at this dark time, when Gabriel's suffering was at its greatest and his end so near, that unexpected visitors arrived, as if to restore our faith in a just and merciful God at the moment we needed reminding of His wisdom and glory.

The knock on the door came on a bright late-July afternoon. Abiah and I had finished the lunch dishes. Gabriel was napping. Thomas had gone out on errands. I wiped my hands on my apron and answered the door, and there, silhouetted by the bright sunlight, was a beautiful young woman, her ebony hair in a thick braid. From one arm dangled a small suitcase. In her other hand she held the smaller hand of a young toddler, a boy of about two years old.

Of course, I recognized her immediately, but words left me.

"I'm sorry for coming without calling," she said. "I'm Bella Alvarez. And this little guy"—she wiggled his hand in hers—"is Raphael. He's Gabriel's son."

Few women are less deserving of the comparison than I, but in that moment, I believe I felt as Mary might have when the angel Gabriel came to her, saying, "Hail, thou that art highly favored, the Lord is with thee: blessed art thou among women." It took all of my strength not to fall to my knees. I gathered Bella into my arms in a warm embrace.

39

Thomas Kennedy

The arrival of Bella Alvarez and Raphael sent waves of joy throughout the household. Anyone wondering whether she might be a con artist after Gabriel's money only needed to see Raphael's face to put that suspicion to rest. Though sons often favor their mothers, Raphael was a miniature version of Gabriel. Hannah could not believe the resemblance and noted that she saw something of Rachel in the little boy as well.

Seeing Bella and meeting their son brought Gabriel out of the fog into which he'd descended, and for several days it reduced his need for morphine, which allowed him to stay awake for longer periods. A new exuberance, and joy tinged with sorrow, poured out of him. He ran his hands over Raphael's little body, hugged and kissed him on the head again and again. For several days after Bella's arrival, someone would take Raphael out to play so that Bella and Gabriel could be alone and converse in peace, as they did, often, for hours at a time, with Bella lying beside him. Whatever passed between them they kept to themselves. Each night, as darkness fell, Bella and Raphael would drive to Josiah and Hannah's house to spend the night. There were extra beds there, Hannah told her, and Josiah would make sure they had breakfast in the morning before they returned to be with Gabriel during the day. Bella had rented a car at O'Hare and did not need to return to California immediately. She was an elementary school teacher and did not teach classes in the summer.

Some afternoons, Raphael napped in bed beside his father, the boy's tiny body nestled in the crook of Gabriel's giant arm.

When Gabriel's need for morphine increased, he returned to sleeping most of the time, and Bella joined the others in helping to care for him. Thomas marveled at the efficient, industrious care provided by the women moving through his home. They seemed to have access to some mystery he could not understand. Their bodies formed new life and pushed it painfully into the world, and their knowing hands expertly comforted the dying as they prepared to leave it. He remembered with some shame how quickly and unquestioningly he'd ceded the care of his elderly mother to strangers.

Abiah often summoned him to help in the kitchen—to dry dishes, to whip a bowl of boiled potatoes with cream and butter, or to taste the level of salt in a large pot of soup or bouillon she simmered nearly every day. She'd glance over his shoulder to judge the quality of his work, and more than once she playfully slapped the back of his hand with a wooden spoon for sampling one of her fragrant dishes with his fingertips.

Josiah visited every day, and one afternoon, in a private moment outdoors as he prepared to leave, he confided to Thomas that he could not bring himself to build the boy's coffin. He'd kiln-dried two hundred board feet of quartersawn oak and planed it smooth, but each time he tried to begin construction, he could not will himself to do so. Abram Glick had made the boy's shoes all his life, and after some discussion, he told Josiah he'd make Gabriel's box, too. Josiah hauled the wood to Abram's shop and told him the necessary dimensions: ten feet long, four feet wide, two feet high. Abram ran his hands along the planed oak and complained the wood seemed too ornate, too beautiful, for a box. "We bury in pine," he said. But Josiah would not be moved. "No," he insisted. "I want Gabriel in oak, quartersawn and an inch thick." Abram looked him in the eye and stroked his beard a long time before responding. He put one hand on Josiah's shoulder. "Ten foot's a long span," he said, finally. "We'll need the extra strength oak will give us."

Josiah also confided that Hannah had so far refused to discuss details of a funeral and interment. She had grown so English in her habits, he said, that she'd been denying the fact of death, as so many English do. Amish ministers had offered to visit the house every week to instruct Gabriel in the articles of the Dordrecht Confession so that he might be baptized into the faith prior to his passing. In response, Hannah had said only that it would be up to Gabriel, and Gabriel had not been interested. Yes, she said, she understood what that meant.

Josiah arranged for Gabriel to be interred with Rachel and Jasper in the small English cemetery just south of Richford, the Cemetery of Peace. Surrounded by cornfields, and shaded by a few towering white oaks, remnants of the oak savannahs that had once dominated the region, the cemetery had been created by Presbyterian Welsh who had settled in the area in the mid-nineteenth century. It held several dozen Welsh graves, most of them farmers, their wives, and children, dating back to the 1850s, though by the twentieth century the cemetery had become secularized, and anyone who could afford the fees could be interred there. Rachel and Jasper had been laid to rest along the northern border near a tangled hedgerow of honeysuckle and wild plum, and every spring the white petals of the sweet, fragrant blossoms fell like snow on their modest footstones.

At least, Josiah said, somberly, the three of them will be together.

40

Hannah Fisher

Gabriel's immortal soul ascended to heaven on a glorious summer morning, the second of August, just as the earth turned toward the heat of the rising sun. Morphine dripped like a slowly melting icicle into Gabriel's colorful arm. Each hour, I dipped a finger in mint-scented balm and ran it gently along his cracked lips, and every thirty minutes I immersed a muslin cloth in ice water, wrung it dry, and placed it across his forehead. The bones of his face and hands, his shoulders, clavicles, and ribs, rose against his skin from the inside like stones in a stream shallowed by drought.

Thomas—I had finally agreed to call Dr. Kennedy by his Christian name, abandoning my stubborn resistance to this final intimacy—and Abiah joined me in a vigil at Gabriel's bedside. Though he left during the day to tend to our farm and to make other necessary arrangements, Josiah returned each evening after Bella and Raphael had settled in at our home for the night. On his own, he'd been tending to details of Gabriel's funeral service, and only once did he humbly seek my approval, though my patience failed me. He wondered aloud whether we might hold Gabriel's service outdoors. At the furthest reach of our land was an unfenced field too low to pasture animals as it flooded every spring and remained underwater into June. This location offered acres of space, and it was hidden from the road by a long, undulating hill. In the northeast corner, a small lean-to still stood on higher ground, pitched from years of buffeting by northwest winds. Josiah said he could straighten the structure with the horses and reinforce the posts, but as he went into more detail, I stopped him. I said, please, Josiah. Flesh of my flesh, bone of my bone, I trust you. I don't need to hear more.

As a younger woman, I often found myself bewildered by Josiah's ability to carry on with practical concerns while rocked by affliction. I had come to see this as a gift from the Lord, perhaps a gift He gives to all men in greater abundance. For so long I'd misread Josiah's steady calm, his ability to build things, to eat with a robust appetite, even to sleep soundly most nights, as indifference. But it is his own way of shouldering into hardship, like a sailor on deck in a gale, refusing, on principle, to turn his back to the howling wind.

Just after three thirty in the morning, nearly an hour before the gray-light singing of birds announced the arrival of a new morning, Gabriel spoke in his sleep, his voice at first a hoarse whisper. The sound woke me, and I lifted my head from the edge of his bed. "Gabriel?" I whispered. I looked into his face and could see he remained sleeping even as his lips moved. It was not English or German, perhaps no human language at all, yet the mysterious sounds carried a bright, joyful tone. Then his voice grew more animated, and Abiah awoke, too.

"What's he saying?" Abiah whispered.

A warm wind blew through the open windows behind her and stirred the sweaty wisps of hair stuck along her face. Outside, heat lightning forked like branching rivers across a purple sky.

Gabriel's voice changed in timbre, and from his throat emerged a lovely falsetto humming, no recognizable melody, but musical, nonetheless.

"He's singing," I whispered.

And then the most beautiful thing began to happen. Outside the window, I heard the fluttering of a bird's wings. A few more. Then a dozen. Hundreds, then thousands, more. They arrived like a thunderstorm, first a distant rumbling, a few drops of rain, then the deluge. I'd heard something similar only once before in my life, in the early fall, when what must have been a thousand red-winged blackbirds roosted in the highest branches of our silver maple tree. I was hanging laundry at the time, and the noise of their approach, the beating of so many pairs of wings, startled me. Those birds alighted and began singing and squawking, and I sat down on the lawn to watch and listen. For nearly fifteen minutes, they rested and continued their garbled singing. If a dog barked or something else alarmed them, they went silent in an instant; when the danger passed, their singing commenced again. Finally, they rose together and departed.

But that August morning, it was not a flock of a single species, but hundreds of varieties arriving at once. I heard the wingbeats of smaller birds, then larger ones, even the heavy flapping of waterfowl, as it happened, ducks and geese, cranes and tundra swans, turkeys too. I put one hand on Gabriel's arm and leaned forward to listen, strained my eyes to see through the sheen of glass into the darkness. Thomas's yard looked to be covered in large, moving stumps. Nearer to the house, the branches of a magnolia tree sagged with feathered ornaments. In the distance, against the lighter sky, tall trees—box elders, red oaks, black cherries, maples—sagged with the weight of this avian visitation. Then, for a moment, all went still.

"My dear Lord, what is happening?" Abiah whispered.

From somewhere on the ground just beneath the window, a single whip-poor-will began its dusk song, a lovely refrain I'd heard so many times, "PUR-ple RIB! PUR-ple RIB! PUR-ple RIB!" A second whip-poor-will started singing, and a third. Other night-singing birds joined in, wood thrushes, hermit thrushes, screech owls, great horned owls, followed by the deep honking of Canadian geese and the gravelly cackling of ducks, the shrill bugling of cranes, the soprano whooping of tundra swans.

"Are we dreaming?" Abiah asked.

The cacophony of singing birds soon woke the men. Thomas sat up in his chair, his brow furrowed in surprise and confusion. Josiah, who'd been on the floor, rose to his feet and went to the window, pulling his suspenders up over his shoulders.

A male cardinal began calling, followed by other daytime birds: grosbeaks and red-winged blackbirds, bluebirds and sparrows, warblers and finches. The singing rose in a rolling symphony that lasted many minutes, every species of fowl seemingly taking a turn, and despite the volume and the number, each note found its own place, each song nestled into every other song, seamlessly and beautifully. And then as abruptly as it began, the singing slowly faded and stopped. By twos and threes, tens and twenties, in a flurry of beating wings, the birds departed. All went silent again, except for Gabriel. A melodic humming continued to vibrate from deep in his throat each time he exhaled.

Outdoors, the silence did not last long. From faraway farms, we heard the bleating of goats and sheep, the neighing of horses and donkeys, the lowing of cattle. Roosters crowed, dogs barked, and domestic geese joined in with their nasal honking. Then, from just across the river, came the excited yipping of coyotes.

Josiah smiled. "We need to take the boy outside." He nodded toward the window. "This is for him. Hannah?"

"Yes," I said. "Of course."

"We can roll the bed out to the patio," Thomas said. On his knees, he unstopped the wheels under Gabriel's bed. Gabriel was still singing. I pressed the clear plastic line from the morphine drip under the edge of his pillow, then gently tucked the sheet around his body, leaving his arms above the covers. The four of us wheeled Gabriel's bed through the living room and out through the doors. The stars had begun to fade, but the air was humid and warm; even the breeze felt heated. The flagstones were rippled and cool beneath my bare feet. I stood at Gabriel's bedside with both hands on his arm. All around us, the sound of calling animals echoed.

Coyotes yipped and howled; foxes barked. Gray squirrels chattered in the trees, and chipmunks chipped and clamored through the underbrush. Tree frogs began their wet ga-lurping in the woods, and soon crickets and katydids joined in, a sweet, metallic buzzing that echoed off the house. Above us swirled a glorious tornado of bats, the peeping of their echolocations a soft, mezzo-soprano refrain.

I put my mouth to Gabriel's ear. "My dear Gabriel," I said. "Please wake up."

Gabriel's eyes, though unseeing, opened, and I propped a pillow beneath his head to raise his ears, that he might better hear this visitation. I told him what was happening, what I saw, and for once my language did not fail me. He closed his eyes again. His lips widened in a broad smile.

"Well, look at that," Thomas said. From the edge of his grassy yard, where the earth sloped into thick woods that led to the river, five white-tailed deer stepped clear of the tree line, two bucks with antlers of chocolate velvet and three does. Beside them wandered a chattering family of raccoons, six in all. Two skunks emerged from behind the deer, the bright stripes along their tails glowing, and a large opossum waddled beside them. Two adult otters and four small ones walked clear of the woods farther down, and along the grass I could see the shining shells of turtles. These animals approached slowly, without fear, stopping perhaps twenty or thirty feet away. The deer stomped their front feet and tossed their heads the way horses do when annoyed by flies.

Then came flying insects, thousands of them, beetles, crane flies, damselflies, dragonflies, butterflies, moths of every variety, some with brightly decorated wings three inches across. The sound they made was like rushing water in a fast-moving stream, and I could feel the wind of their beating wings against my face. They hovered so thickly around Thomas's faded porch light that the backyard went black; it didn't stay dark for long. Up from the grass and out of the woods came a bright green glow, as tens of thousands of flashing fireflies moved into the yard and coalesced into a single, vibrant cloud above us, a swirling column of light growing brighter, blindingly bright. Tears filled my eyes as I whispered a description into Gabriel's ear.

Soon those fireflies descended, hovering like an insect hurricane over and around Gabriel's bed. They alighted on his body and across his mattress and the frame of his bed, filled every available space on the sheet and pillows, his arms, his face and head, even the rubber tube and clear plastic sack of morphine, until everything glowed and the light became so bright we had to close our eyes, and so much brighter still that our eyelids failed us and we had to turn away.

In a clamor of buzzing wings, the fireflies rose in unison. The sound was like a strong wind in the pines. They ascended like winged cherubim, and though my own eyes remained closed, I knew Gabriel's earthly life rose with them, up off the bed, above the house, and then over the trees. Unmoored from Earth, from sickness and pain, from hardship and affliction, arrayed in heavenly light, Gabriel's soul departed.

When we finally opened our eyes again, the animals and insects were gone. Abiah, Thomas, Josiah, and I stood mute around Gabriel's body. A single porch light cast our shadows far into the yard.

We could not immediately speak of what we'd just seen. I looked at Josiah, and tears flooded our eyes. Her face beaded with sweat, Abiah bowed her head and clasped her hands in prayer. Thomas left us. Slowly, he walked deeper into his yard, looking intently at his feet, brushing his shoes from side to side along the grass. From time to time, he bent over to pick something up, then moved farther on.

To the east, a sword of glowing orange opened a thin cut along the horizon. Early morning birds began to sing. Somewhere far off, the rumble of a tractor, the horn of an approaching train.

When Thomas came back to us, in one hand he clutched a bouquet of feathers: pheasant, turkey, tundra swan, cardinal, crane, horned owl, goldfinch, many more. He solemnly handed some to each of us, then laid the most beautiful—an iridescent blue feather from a mallard's wing, tipped in ivory, the brown-and-black-striped tail feather of a turkey, a pure white wing feather of a whooping crane—across Gabriel's still chest.

In reverent silence, we watched the daylight come in.

41

Billy Walton

Word of Gabriel's passing traveled from mouth to mouth, a chain of love and mourning from Lakota upriver to Richford and Coloma, then down through Grand Marsh, Brooks, and Oxford, across to Westfield, Harrisville, Budsin, and Neshkoro. With the sad news came a whispered reminder, an urgent refrain: no social media. No email, no Facebook, no goddamn Twitter. Though he might have belonged to the world at one time, Gabriel was ours first and last, and we intended to send him home without bringing the circus to town.

At my place, the mood was somber. I put a framed ten-by-thirteen picture up over the bar, an action shot from Gabriel's freshman year at Wisconsin. He looks invincible in his XXXXL red home jersey, reaching down to sack Michigan's quarterback. He's got three offensive linemen in maize and blue hanging on to him like swollen dog ticks on a grizzly bear, and one big paw the size of a serving platter full of jersey, preparing to introduce that QB to the Camp Randall turf. I look at that picture and I can feel the sunshine on my face. I can hear the crowd and smell the autumn air. That kid gave me so much in his short life, but now it feels like I took it all for granted, like I wasted time doing things that didn't really need doing when I could have been living bigger. Here's a kid nine feet tall and almost six hundred pounds doing things that will never again be done on earth, and sometimes I was just too busy to notice. I was like a hound dog chasing his own tail while a hundred rabbits cavorted in the yard.

I never saw Gabriel wrestle in person, not one time. I intended to. But you get older, and huge crowds start to annoy you, and you can think of a dozen reasons to just stay home and sit on your ass instead of putting yourself out there. After Gabriel's first wrestling match against the Sheik in Chicago, I figured there'd be another match nearby, hell, another dozen, or more, just like every night you go to sleep figuring you'll wake up to another morning. But then one day you don't wake up, and everything you didn't do piles up in a heap like boxcars in a train wreck a mile long.

When Doc Kennedy called that morning to share the news of Gabriel's passing, I grabbed my keys and drove straight to Stella's place. I'd stopped in her driveway and had the door open before I realized I was still in my pajamas and bedroom slippers. It was only eight in the morning. Snowball started yipping when I rang the bell. Stella came to the door in her robe, just out of bed, no makeup on, face wrinkled, her hair like cotton candy caught in a strong wind. I told her she'd never looked more beautiful, and I meant it. I walked into her open arms like a boy who needed comforting and told her the news. And then I dropped to one knee right there on her living room floor, took her hands in mine, and asked her to marry me. I said if she'd have me, I'd marry her in a church, at the county courthouse, a county park, or right there in her living room, it didn't matter. We could host a reception of ten people or a hundred or a thousand, whatever she wanted. Estelle Smithson, I said, it's taken me most of my life, but I'm ready to be the kind of husband a woman won't regret marrying. I've been the other kind twice, I said. So I know the difference.

Stella took my face in her hands and pressed her forehead to mine. "Billy Walton," she said, her beautiful eyes shining with tears, "you are the good wine saved for last. Of course I'll marry you."

Three days later, Gabriel Fisher's funeral took place on one of the most beautiful August afternoons Wisconsin can give you. The morning dawned bright and dry, the skies blue, maybe eighty-two degrees, with just enough of a breeze to keep your forehead dry and the insects grounded. Stella and I arrived a half hour early, and by then the Amish buggies were lined up down the road on one side for miles, and there were about twenty cars parked in a little, whopper-jawed line in the hayfield across the way. We joined them, then left the truck and tugged the wrinkles out of our nice clothes.

On the river side was empty acreage fenced along the length of the roadway except for a single opening, through which passed an overgrown tractor path that from the scent of it had recently been mown. It ran down the ditch, through the fence, then up a small rise, where it disappeared as the land dropped down toward the river. On both sides of the path waved acres of goldenrod six feet high, Queen Anne's lace, Canada thistle, some wild raspberry canes, and a lot of tall grasses. The field looked to be ten acres or so, land I didn't even know Josiah and Hannah owned, being about a half mile from their home. To throw any lurking Hollywood dogs off the scent, a large painted sign had been posted at the entrance to the tractor path: "Fisher Barn Raising, August 5th." Rick Dalkey, Stella's brother, had also nailed bright orange "No Trespassing" signs on every third fence post the full length of the property.

Stella and I made our way up the hill, sweating in the bright sunlight, and when we reached the top, we stopped to catch our breath. Barn swallows swooped and darted overhead, chasing invisible insects, and from far-off woods we could hear the buzzing of cicadas. Down below, in a mown clearing around an old lean-to, the roof shining silver and streaked with rust, a large crowd had gathered. Hundreds of people, many of them Amish, dressed in black and white, but not all Amish, were seated on backless wooden benches that had been arranged in an uneven circle around the old lean-to. Beneath the roof, shaded from the sun, Gabriel's rough wooden casket sat on a platform of four sawhorses, with the cover removed and leaning against the side. Even from a distance, the casket looked twice as long as the usual, and double-wide. Behind us on the road, more cars and Amish buggies continued to arrive.

Stella and I continued, wandering down to the clearing to join the others. We took seats facing north and felt the warm sun on our backs. I made eye contact with Josiah and nodded at him, and he nodded once and touched the brim of his straw hat. He and Hannah stood together, shoulder to shoulder. Hannah was wearing a black Amish dress and kapp. Gabriel's lady, Bella, stood next to Hannah, their little boy, Raphael, beside her. I could not bring myself to approach Gabriel's casket, not then. From my chair, I could just make out his forehead and hair, his head propped up slightly on what looked like a thick flake of alfalfa hay.

Once we got settled, I took a look around. Charlie had come, of course, and was seated with Coach Beathard and his wife and young daughter; Oliver Edwards sat alone a couple rows back in a dark suit and string tie, taller seated than some of the women who stood nearby, whispering to one another. Doc Kennedy sat with the lady horse ranchers from out near Oxford, both of whom wore broad-brimmed hats to shade their faces from the sun. Stella waved to her brother, who sat with his wife and children, with the families of a few of his militia buddies in the rows behind them. It was not difficult to find Gabriel's former teammates from the University of Wisconsin. They sat together wearing their red home uniforms, many of them shading their eyes with dark sunglasses. A large group of young women sat near these men as well, many of them swaying from side to side to comfort babies or toddlers seated on their laps. "There are no flowers," Stella whispered.

I shrugged.

"No pictures, either."

"Amish," I said. I had never been to an Amish funeral, so I didn't know if that had anything to do with it or not, but I was guessing that it did.

When the time came, the Amish bishop or minister, an older, stern-looking man with a white beard and a thick, red scar across one cheek, rose and spoke a few words in German. All the Amish picked up the old books that had been scattered among the benches, opened them, and, following the lead of the minister, began to sing. It was the first of three songs, sung consecutively over the first twenty minutes of the service. Though each song was pleasant to the ear in a droning kind of way, like the sound of steady rain on a metal roof, we could not understand the lyrics. When these songs were finished, the minister spoke in English. He apologized to the non-Amish at the service who did not speak the language and said he hoped we would now join in another hymn, instructing everyone to turn to the back of the hymnals, where a thin pamphlet of English hymns had been glued inside.

Once again, he began singing a hymn, entitled "Take My Hand and Lead Me." For the first time, I heard my Stella sing, and she had a lovely voice. I listened quietly. I'm no singer. My voice can best be described as a hoarse croaking, really, but Stella kept looking up at me as she sang, holding the book over my way, so I figured, what the hell, and I joined her on the final verse:

> *Hold my hand in Thine, O Father,*
> *Till I reach the pearly gates;*
> *There I'll leave my cross and burden,*
> *For my star-gemmed crown awaits.*
> *Then I'll sing in strains of rapture,*
> *In the light of perfect day;*
> *Thou didst deign to guide me, Father,*
> *And hast led me all the way.*

The chorus repeated itself far too much for my liking, but I added my croaking to the final time through on that as well:

> *Take my hand, take my hand,*
> *For I cannot see the way;*
> *Take my hand, take my hand,*
> *For I cannot see the way.*
> *Guide me, guide me*

There to live through endless day;
Guide me, guide me
There to live through endless day.

After all the singing, the Amish minister spoke for about ten minutes, alternating between German and English. He didn't say all that much about Gabriel, which I found a little odd, choosing instead to praise God for pretty much everything and to urge the community to remain steadfast in their love of God, who gives and takes life, and so on and so forth. My attention wandered a bit, truth be told, so I might have missed the highlights. When he finished, in English, he said that following the final procession to view the body, the burial would take place at the Cemetery of Peace, but before that, he thanked the many English friends who had come and noted that while it was not proper for Amish to do so, given the circumstances of Gabriel's life and death in two worlds, if any English wished to speak, they could do so.

There was a bit of awkward looking around at one another, and I thought that would be the end of it, but then Charlie got up from his chair. We turned toward him as he pulled a piece of paper from his pocket and unfolded it. In a quivering voice, the paper shaking in his hand, he read a poem. I only know it because he later pinned it to the wall beside the picture of Gabriel sacking Michigan's quarterback, where it remains still. It was called "To an Athlete Dying Young." I don't know where he found it. The first two verses are all you need to hear to start the waterworks:

The time you won your town the race
We chaired you through the market-place;
Man and boy stood cheering by,
And home we brought you shoulder-high.

Today, the road all runners come,
Shoulder-high we bring you home,

And set you at your threshold down,
Townsman of a stiller town.

Though the Amish listened politely without any discernible reaction, I don't think there was a dry eye among the rest of us. When Charlie sat down, Coach Beathard stood up and said a few words, talked about the first time he saw Gabriel throwing bales of hay up on a wagon, and the joy with which Gabriel did everything in life, even after he lost his leg. Doc Kennedy broke down when he talked about his love for Gabriel, and he thanked everyone present for the way they welcomed him into the community at a difficult time in his life. He praised Gabriel's love for people and animals, the uncanny way he seemed to understand what they needed. He thanked Hannah and Josiah for their kindness and friendship.

One by one, we said what needed saying. I'm a talker, but when I finally stood up, I really had no idea what to say. I made one false start. I pointed at Gabriel and said, "I loved that kid," but I couldn't get anything else out. Sadness seized me by the throat, and I would have cried like a baby if I kept on going. I pulled myself together, and I changed tacks. I don't know how appropriate it was, but I did what I usually do, I guess. I told a joke.

"You know," I said, "the other day, me and Charlie and Doc Kennedy were chewing the fat and we got to talking about what we'd like to hear people say about us while we're lying in our caskets on a day like today. Doc Kennedy, he says, 'Well, that's easy,' he says. 'I'd like people to say I healed thousands of animals and cared for the people who owned them the best that I could, you know, all of that.' Charlie, he went next. He said, 'I'd like people to say I was a good husband to Carol, a loyal friend to you, Billy, and a guy who could really hold his liquor.'" I looked over at Charlie to see him nodding and smiling at me.

"And then Charlie said, 'What about you, Billy? What do you want to hear people say about you when you're lying dead in your coffin?' I want to hear three words, and three words only: Look! He's moving!"

Laughter rippled through the crowd, and even a few of the Amish smiled. Josiah shook his head, but I could see he was smiling, too. I sat down, and Stella reached over and squeezed my leg. At the very least, I guess, I hadn't made an ass of myself.

Finally, one last person stood up, rising like a big old tree in the field, the turkey farmer, Oliver Edwards. He stood and slowly made his way to where Gabriel's casket rested. He bowed his head for a few seconds while we all waited, then he raised his chin and closed his eyes, and from his mouth came the most beautiful sound I ever heard, a voice as sweet and clear as a church bell. He sang "Amazing Grace," and while he sang, the swallows who nested beneath the roof of the lean-to returned to feed their young and then swirled out over the crowd into the sky again, their wings flashing blue in the sun. I felt the warm wind on my face, and Stella's hand in mine, and I looked at Hannah Fisher, her expression neutral and unchanged, but tears streaming down her cheeks and dripping from her jaw, making small, darkened spots on her dress.

Following that, all the Amish stood, and the rest of us stood with them, and like a slow-moving river, in single file, we passed Gabriel Fisher for the last time while the Amish sang an English hymn: "The City of Light":

There's a city of light 'mid the stars, we are told,
Where they know not a sorrow or care;
And the gates are of pearl, and the streets are of gold,
And the building exceedingly fair.

When my turn came to look at Gabriel one last time, he was just a shell of the beautiful man he was in life, and I thought about how ironic it was that after all those years of looking up into the beautiful face of the tallest human being ever to walk the earth, we were now looking down at him. He was dressed simply in a Wisconsin T-shirt, short sleeved, the tattoos on his arms and throat glowing in the sun like fields of blooming flowers. He had about a three-day growth of beard on his face, no makeup to speak of, and with one hand, I gently brushed back his hair and kissed him on the forehead.

Gabriel's casket was loaded onto a hay wagon and drawn down the road several miles, where he was buried next to his mother, Rachel, in the small, overgrown Presbyterian cemetery, and opposite his brother, Jasper. No headstone or footstone was placed on the grave, just an unadorned piece of limestone from a farmer's field, etched only by a small fossil, a plant of some kind, in the shape of a cross.

42

Hannah Fisher

Even when we have strayed far from the path, when our hearts burn with the fire of anger, or ache with the numbing cold of despair, when we are wallowing in the swamp of doubt, even when we feel forsaken, and none more deserving of it, we may discover the Lord has been with us all along.

I am an old woman. My hair is silvered, my face wrinkled, my arms weak. I look back and wonder where the years have gone. I say this now without complaint: life has been hard. I have buried an infant son, a grown daughter, and two grandsons. Once I believed with the certainty of the holy Amish martyrs that filled my childhood dreams. As a young woman, I yearned for affliction to test my faith, which I wore like a warm, protective blanket. Yet time and again, throughout my life, when those tests came, I failed them. What troubles me still is that these failures yielded pain, yes, but also compensation, even riches of a kind: an intimate empathy, for a time, with my dead mother; a loving, gifted friendship—words imperfect to name it—with Thomas; a mind opened to the wondrous stories and thoughts of others, particularly women unknown to me, near and far, ancient and modern, who wrote beautiful books my father once would have burned, and me with them.

If only we could instruct the selves we have left behind in time! What would I say to that young girl now? She would no doubt rail against these thoughts as blasphemy, but I would tell her this: all zealous belief, secular and spiritual, relies upon some blindness in the believers. Only in the brokenness of true humility can we see beyond the false borders we ourselves, saints and sinners alike, erect. Thomas, an agnostic who has done more for God's creatures than perhaps any random hundred believers together, puts it more simply. Life, he says, is complicated.

It is never easy navigating the hours and days following the loss of a loved one, let alone a beloved child or grandchild. Absence is everywhere. You move around it as you might skirt a large boulder dropped into your kitchen; it insists upon your attention. At night, when the dark silence magnifies your thoughts, the sorrow overwhelms.

And yet when heaven calls, earth must answer. We attended to the few physical things Gabriel had left behind. Josiah disassembled the extravagantly large bed he'd built so many years ago, loading the pieces of wooden frame on the wagon to repurpose at some future time. He built wooden crates to cradle Gabriel's false legs (they were not buried with him), and we shipped them to University Hospital in Madison, hoping the components might be used to fashion prostheses for others in need. I folded and boxed Gabriel's clothes, the shoulders of his shirts as wide as my outstretched arms, the pants reaching from the floor to my chin. For a young man with so many riches, Gabriel owned so little, and my heart beat with some pride at this, thinking it was the Amish in him.

The day after Gabriel's funeral, a local alderman came to Thomas's house to ask if we'd be willing to sell Gabriel's shoes. He'd been authorized to offer us $1,000 for the pair. They would be bronzed and put on display, and in time, people would come from all over the world to see them. They would spend money in local shops, stay in local hotels, eat in local restaurants. The county had already contacted the University of Wisconsin to inquire about purchasing Gabriel's football helmet, and they hoped to procure the costume he wore when he wrestled as Anakim, the Amish Giant, including the golden fleece of the angora goat he always carried with him to the ring.

We sent the man on his way and returned Gabriel's shoes to Abram Glick, who'd made them. I believe the last pair were size 36 or 37. There was enough good cowhide on them to make shoes for four or five normal-sized men, or a dozen or more children.

Word of Gabriel's passing could not be held close for long. It spread like a virus through the wires of the English, on their televisions, telephones, and computers. There were news clips and tributes, and a few aggressive people stopped by in person seeking interviews, but interest faded quickly. In the English world, there is always a new ghost to chase.

Thomas mourned with the intensity of a father or grandfather, and my heart ached for him. His shoulders slumped with the weight of his sorrow, and he grew quiet and pensive. In the days after Gabriel's burial, he continued with his work, sometimes spending whole days away. Livestock still got sick; mares still went into labor to deliver their foals. He knew, of course, before I even told him that I would be returning to Josiah, that I had a new calling. I now had a great-grandchild, Gabriel's lovely son, Raphael. And even though Bella did not hold the legal standing of Gabriel's wife, I counted her as a granddaughter in spirit.

In the early evening, Josiah came for me in the buggy but waited outside, patiently, while Thomas and I said our goodbyes. In over fifty years of marriage to Josiah, I had never pressed my body in love to the body of another man, but that night, standing in his kitchen, I took Thomas to me, pressed my face into his chest, and wet his shirt with my warm tears.

"My sweet man," I said. "In another time . . ." But I could not finish my thoughts.

Thomas placed his lips against the top of my head. His body shook as he cried into my hair. His strong arms encircled my back.

"Josiah is my husband," I said. "I have wronged him, over and over, turned my back to him in anger and spite, and yet he has cleaved to me. And I must cleave to him now. I must put the pumpkin back into the seed."

In our shared life, Josiah and I have grown together, lichen on stone; in marriage, man and woman become one flesh, one body. And yet I held Thomas so tightly my arms quivered. I held him fast until Thomas himself pushed me gently away. I shook my head no but took a step back. I pinned my hair up against my head and pulled on my kapp. I shook my head no even as my feet carried me from the bright light of Thomas's house out the door to where my husband waited, his face half lit by the soft orange glow of the lamp hanging from our buggy.

Gideon's powerful muscles tugged us toward home, his shod feet clopping a steady rhythm on the warm blacktop. A thin crescent moon hung from the firmament like a fishhook. Insects droned in the ditches, and out over the fields, fireflies flashed sporadically in the humid August air. I took one of Josiah's hands in mine, and he held the reins with the other. I had never appreciated his silence more. What is forgiveness but an undeserved gift given, light as air, beautiful as a moonlit ride home?

As we approached the house, I could see the warm glow of lamplight in the windows. In back, I saw dozens of tomato bushes in the garden, laden with fruit. Gideon stopped with the buggy at the porch. Stepping down, I heard the soft, gentle bleating of goats at rest in the pasture.

"You go on in," Josiah said. "They're waiting for you."

Bella and Raphael sat at the table in the lamplight. Bella's silver crucifix glowed in the light where it rested on the placket of her dress. I thought of my father's rage at popish adornments. No doubt I myself, at one time, would have ridiculed this crucifix as well. No longer.

Raphael was in pajamas, eating a bedtime snack. He swung his tiny feet as they dangled beneath the chair, and he smiled at me.

"Hello," I said. Bella whispered to him in Spanish.

"Hola!" he said, his voice bright.

"And what are we eating?" I asked. Raphael looked at his mother. She whispered to him again.

"Graham cracker," he said.

"Delicious!" I said. "Your father loved those, too. Listen, it's a warm night. If it's okay with your mother, I think we can catch some fireflies in a jar before you go to bed. They can keep you company as you fall asleep."

Bella smiled and nodded.

When Raphael finished his cracker, she slipped on his little shoes. I took a mason jar from the cabinet, and the three of us went outside. The night air smelled lovely, scented by drying alfalfa hay and contented pastured livestock. The grass was already wet with dew. "You have to sneak up behind them as they rise to heaven," I said, "and then you hold the jar over them, and they fly right in."

43

Thomas Kennedy

Thomas moved mechanically through summer's dog days, distracted, preoccupied, in mourning. He'd fill the coffee maker but forget to turn it on. He'd put bread in the toaster, then go outside for the mail, putter for a couple hours, and find cold toasted bread waiting when he came in for lunch. Often, he stood outside the bedroom Hannah had occupied. On the dressing table, she'd left behind a beautiful comb, white teeth set into a faux-mother-of-pearl handle, which rested across a small, gold-rimmed saucer. Perhaps, Thomas thought, she found the comb too ornately decorated. When he held it to the light, he could see five or six strands of Hannah's hair still clinging to it, filaments as fine as spider's silk. He handled the comb carefully each time so her hair would not be lost to him.

Beside the comb, wrapped in an Amish kapp, she'd left him something else, a coverless book, the crumbling glue of its binding yellowed, the pages held together with soiled string neatly tied like a bow on a package: *Poems of Emily Dickinson*. Thomas smiled and untied the string. Hannah had pressed a white trillium flower between its pages, and the book fell open to the flower. At first, he didn't believe it had been placed intentionally, but then he saw a simple inscription in Hannah's tiny script, in pencil, in the top corner of the page: "For Thomas." He read the poem through twice, and though he didn't really know what it meant, the final lines were clear and poured like starlight into his heart:

> *So We must meet apart—*
> *You there—I—here—*
> *With just the Door ajar*
> *That Oceans are—and Prayer—*
> *And that White Sustenance—*
> *Despair—*

* * *

As summer tipped toward fall, and the need for his services diminished, Thomas fished several evenings each week, wading the Mecan River for brown trout. Sometimes Trey Beathard would join him on the water, and Thomas welcomed the company. After Gabriel died, Trey had given up coaching to spend more time with his wife and daughter, and to have more time to himself, as well. He'd fished some of the big rivers of Montana—the Gallatin, the Yellowstone, the Bitterroot—a few times when he coached at Montana State. He said he'd found that standing waist-deep in running water was about the most peaceful thing he'd ever done. "I've been to every state in the union recruiting football players, but none of them can hold a candle to Montana for beauty," he told Thomas. "Course, I was drunk a lot of the time I was there, so maybe I was hallucinating."

Thomas laughed, and they continued fishing, working their way upstream, taking turns casting grasshoppers Thomas had tied the previous winter to undercut banks and rocky structures. As night fell, and tiny brown bats began to dart over the water, chasing insects, Thomas and Trey would hear barred owls hooting in the woods and coyotes yipping in the distance. They'd light little cigars—the smoke kept the mosquitoes at bay—and when it got too dark to see at all, they'd climb up out of the water and head for home.

Sometimes, where the river snaked near the county roads, Thomas could hear cars passing, the sound of Amish buggies rumbling behind trotting horses, occasionally the steady, mechanical hum of a tractor. The sounds made him remember the first time he'd been to Lakota, trout fishing, as it happened. Since then, he'd grown to love the sandy barrens of scrub oak and jack pine and had long ago come to appreciate the humble simplicity of his Amish neighbors, the proud independence of the area's farmers, even the boisterous celebrations of beer-drinking hell-raisers whose roaring cars and trucks dragged sparking mufflers across the county at all hours of the day and night.

Now, every day, leaving Lakota consumed his thoughts. When Trey told Thomas he'd recruited athletes in every state of the union, Thomas was too embarrassed to share that he'd never been out of the Midwest. In fact, he'd spent his whole life in just two states, Wisconsin and Minnesota. His years in veterinary school in Minneapolis constituted the one time he'd been west of the Mississippi River. He felt even more isolated when he thought about Gabriel, who'd lived just a third of Thomas's lifetime and yet had been around the world. But Thomas also felt the weight of his commitments. Farmers and ranchers in the area relied on his services. He had a mother living in a nursing home in Milwaukee. He could not, he told himself, simply dismiss those obligations.

Then, late in August, his mother passed away. She'd previously requested that her remains be cremated, and she wanted no memorial service. She'd even designated the mortuary to retrieve her body. Though it felt more like relief than true loss, Thomas felt a deeper sadness than he'd expected. All her life, his mother had made things easy for him, and she'd done so even after death.

Thomas drove to the nursing home to gather up his mother's few remaining belongings: slippers, dressing gowns, barrettes and hairbrushes, a small wooden cross. We come into the world with nothing, he thought, and we leave with it, too. He retrieved his mother's ashes from the funeral home, delivered to him in a waxed cardboard box lined with a clear plastic bag. The funeral director offered to show him decorative urns available for purchase, but Thomas declined. He put his mother's ashes on the passenger seat of his truck and drove to Lake Michigan. He crossed the green toward the rocky shoreline, hoping to find a secluded place where he might surreptitiously deposit the ashes in the water. His mother had loved Lake Michigan. When Thomas reached the rocks, he peered down, disappointed to discover a young couple picnicking on the narrow strip of sand, two bright kayaks, one red, one yellow, pulled up beside them. They wore swimsuits and sunglasses, and they sat on beach towels, drinking beer.

Thomas offered them twenty dollars if they would allow him to borrow one of their kayaks for ten or fifteen minutes. He couldn't see their eyes behind the sunglasses, so when they didn't respond immediately, he went ahead and told them why.

"These are my mother's ashes," he said. "She used to sail out here."

They stared a moment longer, and then the young man nodded vigorously. "Yeah, of course. Absolutely. Take mine."

"Thank you. I appreciate it." Thomas gingerly made his way down the rocks. When he reached the sand, the young man moved his yellow kayak to the water's edge. He declined Thomas's offer of money, held the kayak steady as Thomas got in, then handed him the paddle. Thomas rested the box of ashes on the bow just ahead of the cockpit, then gently eased the kayak out into deeper water.

Though the winds were calm, Thomas felt unsteady, like a fly bobbing on a cork in the ocean. He paddled cautiously for five minutes until well out from shore, then opened the box. His mother's remains were a creamy gray, sprinkled with tiny, white dots of bone. Thomas poured them downwind into the water, where they floated for a time in a clump before gradually swirling through the surface tension and drifting into the depths.

Thomas used the occasion of his mother's passing as a reason to visit Hannah a final time. After some initial awkwardness, she agreed to take a short walk with him. She wished him God's peace on the loss of his mother, saying she treasured the hour she'd spent in her company.

He thanked her for the gift of the book of Dickinson poems. He asked about Bella and Raphael. Gabriel had left his money to Bella, and the joy in Hannah's voice was evident when she shared that Bella had accepted a teaching job in the area. Bella wanted Raphael to grow up knowing his great-grandparents and all the people who had loved his father.

As their walk turned back toward Hannah's home, Thomas told her he'd be leaving Lakota. He wasn't yet certain where he'd be going, but he couldn't stay. He hoped she'd understand.

Hannah nodded and squeezed his arm. "Of course I understand."

As they stood together in the shade of the porch, he decided to ask Hannah one final thing. It had been on his mind. He'd done some research, but he could find no satisfactory answers or explanations. The night Gabriel passed away, all those birds, animals, and insects. What did she suppose had happened? What did she make of all that?

Hannah smiled warmly. "It was a miracle."

"Inexplicable by natural or scientific laws, possibly," Thomas said. "A miracle? Not so sure."

"Oh, Thomas!" she said. "You've seen the miracle of birth so many times. How can you not see that death is also a miracle? Unburdened by the shell of his body, Gabriel's soul ascended to heaven. You saw it as I did."

"What I saw was the biggest hatch of fireflies I've ever seen in my life. Family Lampyridae, according to my field guide. An amazing volume of insects. Maybe the birds came to eat the insects. And the other animals, well, mammals can be curious creatures. I think a lot of them might have come out just to see what all the fuss was about. I don't know. It's a hypothesis, a conjecture."

She nodded. "Well, I like my conjecture, as you would say, better than yours."

Thomas laughed. "I'm not surprised."

As he drove away, he felt sick with longing, but also more firm in his conviction to leave. Seeing Hannah, walking and talking with her, had brought on the same terrible yearning. If he stayed in Lakota, he would continue to ache for her intimate company, and he could never have it. His speculation hadn't been wrong: the time had come for him to go. This clarity arrived with the finality and grief of permanent loss, but contained, around its edges, a glimmer of something else. Rather than prolonging his natural tendency toward indecision and equivocation, the pain gave him the resolve he needed.

He put his house on the market with a local Realtor and began to make his way through the clutter of a lifetime of belongings, boxing up his professional instruments, his computer, clothing, other items he wanted to keep, and trucking the remainder on daily donation trips to the thrift store. Then he called Trey Beathard and asked him to meet him on the one-lane bridge over County Road JJ for a bit of fishing. When Trey arrived, they didn't do any fishing. Instead, they sat on the bridge and talked about where Thomas might buy or rent a place on a decent trout river in Montana.

Trey contacted people he still knew in the football program out in Bozeman, and a real estate agent sent Thomas a file of a half dozen river homes for sale, all of them well over $2 million, far too expensive. But then someone Trey had worked with knew someone who knew the family of a fishing guide who'd recently passed away. He'd lived in a single-room cabin surrounded by public land on the Missouri River. Woodstove for heat. Shallow well point. Rustic, in need of some TLC, but weathertight. The family sent pictures and video of the place. The view out the front door was of a river, and across the river, a wide, green meadow, and beyond the meadow, mountains. They faxed a contract. Thomas wired a down payment. The cabin belonged to him.

The first advertised open house scheduled by Thomas's Realtor attracted over a hundred visitors to his home, most of them, unfortunately, only gawkers who wanted to look around inside the house where Anakim the Amish Giant had died. But, the agent told him later by telephone, one serious buyer had made an offer.

"It was a lovely young woman with a little boy, an elementary school teacher who just started teaching in the district. She's looking for a place to live. She made a cash offer. It's ten thousand dollars below your asking price, but if we counter with the full price, I'm sure she'll take it. It's a seller's market. There aren't a lot of livable places for sale out here."

Thomas smiled. "No," he said. "Let's just accept her offer as it is."

"Why? You're leaving money on the table. I know we can get more."

"That's okay," Thomas said. "I've got enough."

Thomas spent the rest of September visiting, for a final time, the good people who'd befriended him in the years he'd spent in Lakota. He'd grown to love many of these people, and the goodbyes were sometimes difficult. On an early Saturday afternoon in October, he drove to his real estate agent's office to receive the cashier's check and sign the contract ceding ownership of his home to Isabella Alvarez. Bella was already waiting, and she got up and walked into his arms when he arrived. Thomas had hoped he'd get to see Raphael one last time, but Bella said the boy was napping at Hannah and Josiah's house.

He wished Bella and Raphael well, told her he hoped that she would enjoy living in Lakota as much as he had.

The following morning, just before first light, Thomas finished loading the rental trailer with the remainder of his belongings, got into his truck, and pulled out of his driveway for the last time. He remembered the long-ago afternoon when Jasper drove up that same driveway and Thomas pulled the bloodied infant Gabriel from the body of his dying mother, a woman of such extraordinary beauty and moral character the thought of her sacrifice still brought tears to his eyes. And he thought about the strange, winding paths that human lives take, and how the short life of a really, really tall young man had touched nearly every corner of the earth, especially this one.

In the satchel on the seat beside him, he could see *Poems of Emily Dickinson* protruding from an unzipped pocket, and he thought about his love for Hannah Fisher. The last night they'd spoken, she told him everyone takes two journeys alone, the one that brings us to Earth and the one that takes us to heaven, and it is the path we have trod in between that gives the measure of a life. It is the good we leave behind us, she said, that makes a life worth living.

Though Thomas had his headlights on, he could already see the wash of pink and red in his rearview mirror as the sun rose in the east. He felt a quiver of anticipation as he thought about the drive to come, twelve hundred miles across rivers and mountains and prairies he'd never seen. He was seventy-one years old, yet he had the exhilarating sense that his life was just about to begin.

Acknowledgments

I must begin by recognizing the short, remarkable life of Robert Pershing Wadlow (February 22, 1918–July 15, 1940), the tallest person who ever lived. Just eight pounds five ounces at birth, Wadlow stood eight feet 11.1 inches tall, weighed 439 pounds, and had size 37 feet at the time of his death, at age twenty-two, his extraordinary growth driven by hypertrophy of the pituitary gland. For a time, Wadlow toured with the Ringling Brothers Circus and promoted shoes for the International Shoe Company, but he seems to have sought a normal life, resisting efforts to define him exclusively as a circus attraction. He died of an infection in Manistee, Michigan, and is buried in Oakwood Cemetery in Alton, Illinois. My musings about how the twenty-first-century world might react to a giant in its midst provided the initial inspiration for this novel. Though Gabriel Fisher is an entirely fictional creation, I based Gabriel's growth on Wadlow's reported size at various stages of his life, and I think of Gabriel as Wadlow's spiritual twin, a fellow traveler in the rarefied, preternatural realm of giantism.

My research into Anabaptist history and the nuances and complexities of Amish life included consultation with several fine books, most notably *The Amish* by Donald Kraybill, Karen Johnson-Weiner, and Steven Nolt (Johns Hopkins University Press, 2012), and Kraybill's *Concise Encyclopedia of Amish, Brethren, Hutterites, and Mennonites* (Johns Hopkins University Press, 2010). While the largest populations of Amish people in the United States live in Pennsylvania, Ohio, and Indiana, some twenty-five thousand Amish live in Wisconsin in over sixty different communities, including a small group of about six hundred members in Marquette and Waushara Counties, the setting for this novel. In giving voice to Hannah Fisher, I hope I have respectfully captured the depth and breadth of Amish faith and honored without sentimentalizing their difficult but beautiful way of life.

Like all writers, I've spent years sitting alone at a desk while the world outside turned without me. Though it has given much richness to my life, writing has also kept me from doing other things, most importantly, spending more time with the people I love, none more cherished than my wife, Jenna, my beautiful children and grandchildren, and my family and friends, near and far. By some magical algorithm, I hope that even though I've left behind the best of me in these pages, sentence by sentence, year after year, I've also given you my best as well. My life would be empty without you.

I also want to acknowledge the many colleagues and friends who have inspired and supported me over the years, particularly my fellow creative writers at the University of Wisconsin–Oshkosh: Douglas Haynes, Laura Jean Baker, Abayomi Animashaun, Stewart Cole, Pam Gemin, Paul Niesen, Doug Flaherty, Stephen McCabe, and Bill Gillard, but also Karl Boehler, Jordan Landry, Alphonso Simpson, Margaret Hostetler, Sam Looker-Koenigs, Roberta Maguire, Paul Klemp, Jen and Steve Szydlik, Sabrina Mueller-Spitz, Tish Crawford, Jim Feldman, John Koker, Colleen Byron, Gary Rodman, and David Graham.

The university has provided me with a valuable intellectual home, sabbatical support to work on longer projects like this one, and the opportunity to spend semester after semester talking about books and writing with students I treasure. I cannot imagine a more joyful or meaningful way to earn a living.

Thank you to all of the teachers and professors I've had over the years who inspired with their passion for books and writing. There are far too many to name, so I'll permit one to stand in for all—my kind, soft-spoken third- and fourth-grade teacher at St. Joseph's Catholic School in Big Bend, Wisconsin, Mrs. Pritchett, who read to us every day after lunch recess for twenty minutes (*Charlotte's Web*, *Little House in the Big Woods*, *Little House on the Prairie*), which lit the fire for storytelling inside of me.

Thanks to Heike Alberts for proofreading and correcting my German, and for fun companionship during the hours we spent avoiding downward dog in yoga class.

Thank you to the editorial team at St. Martin's Press, most of all George Witte, who took a chance on this manuscript and then provided the wise, gentle editorial assistance needed to make it better. This book would not be what it is without your skillful judgement. Thanks also to Brigitte Dale, Lesley Allen, and Susannah Noel. I have been dazzled by your editorial skill and grateful for your kindness, and I cannot thank you enough for the care you've taken with this book.

Finally, special thanks go to my extraordinary, indefatigable agent, Julia Livshin, who helped me discover the heart of this manuscript and then guided the book through unfamiliar waters, always with hope, determination, and expertise.

About the Author

Ron Rindo taught English and creative writing for many years at the University of Wisconsin–Oshkosh. He has previously published one novel, *Breathing Lake Superior*, and three short story collections. He lives in Pickett, Wisconsin.